The Merrimack Event

The Merrimack Event

David A. Tatum

Fennec Fox Press

The Merrimack Event

Printed in the United States of America
First Trade Edition, 2017

ISBN-13 978-1-943830-01-5

Fennec Fox Press
Ashburn, Va 20147
http://www.FennecFoxPress.com

Cover art by Joel C. Payne
http://wishpictures.com/

Acknowledgments

This book was an absolute nightmare to put together. For those of you who have not been visiting my blog or any of my social media accounts, you probably haven't heard, but this book has been in the self-publishing equivalent of "development hell" for over two years. Editors vanishing on me, non-responsive cover artists followed by a cover artist I had to fire (and finally the one who produced the magnificent cover art you now see), the loss of one fully-edited version of the manuscript while attempting to make a back-up (resulting in my having to completely re-edit it from a much older version), and more.

However, even if you had been following my blog and social media, you probably were unaware that the original version of this manuscript was completed thirteen years ago – even before my debut novel, "In Treachery Forged." And it was a horrible manuscript. After becoming a self-publisher, when going through my "older" work to decide what to try and publish and what to ultimately reject, this manuscript was the most borderline of the bunch. But I saw a diamond in the (really, really) rough, here, and I've been working to polish it ever since. If I were writing this book today there might be a few stylistic choices I might have made differently, but after all of the work that's been done on it I think it came out pretty good. Of course, that's for you readers to decide.

By the time I decided to be a self-publisher (even before the "development hell" situation), the manuscript had been checked over by several people, all of whom added touches to it. There were problems with this (I think, ultimately, people were trying to selectively edit certain sections to conform to six different style guides, but no-one in the process applied the same style guide to the whole text. Sorting that out was just one of the things that caused that development hell pain), but they all helped make it better in the end.

As usual, I would like to thank my family for all their help with this book. My late father inspired my love of books and, in a sense, taught me how to write. My mother and brother have both done everything they could to help, including acting as beta readers for a time.

I also want to thank Joel Christopher Payne for finally resolving the whole cover art mess. After having had to fire my previous cover artist, I was about to give up entirely on this book, but then he stepped up to the plate.

I also want to express my appreciation to the Society for Creative Anachronisms, for the use of their name, and Boosey & Hawkes, who let me know in e-mail that Sir Henry Newbolt's "Old Superb" would be falling into the public domain before this book was to be published. (That was years ago, back when this thirteen-year-old book was still fairly new). Also, I would like to thank the anonymous person who provided OpenClipArt.com the free-for-commercial-use chess graphic I included.

Finally, as mentioned above, this book has been touched by numerous hands over its thirteen years of pre-publication existence. Some of these people may not even remember working on it, it's been so long ago (a few I lost touch with before I'd even settled on a title for this book), but I would like to thank everyone who helped: Andrew "MageOhki" Norris, Ed "Kickaha" Beccera, June "KaraOhki" Geraci, all those people in chat whose real names I never learned (including the programmer of Akane "the Magic 8-Ball" Bot, who I'm not sure I ever met but whose chat bot provided a lot of laughs and even a bit of inspiration), Sarah Myers (if you ever see this, and remember designing that uniform, PLEASE contact me! I'd like to hire you again, but my old e-mail for you doesn't seem to work any more), certain fellow members of the Washington Capitals message boards that I can no longer get in touch with, and anyone else who I've forgotten from across that thirteen year gap.

Oh, and a big "thank you" to everyone reading this book. Enjoy!

Table of Contents

Prolog

Dr. Whitlow Foley wiped the sweat from his forehead. The power was out again, and all of his equipment, environmental control systems, and recreational facilities were offline. This was one part of being a xenoanthropologist and archaeologist that he hated – the complete lack of protection from the elements. He had once been the top field archaeologist in Pleiades, but had been trapped in academia for years before he found a sponsor for this multi-dig expedition. This was his return to the field, and he was not as fit as he used to be. Worse, the heat of Pleiades Alpha's multiple suns didn't exactly agree with him.

This time of year, three stars lit the sky every hour of the Earth-traditional day. If it weren't for the very advanced terraforming techniques humans had been using for centuries, Pleiades Alpha would have been uninhabitable... but nothing could completely fix the brutal weather. For that reason alone, he thought it was a lousy place to have built the capital of the Pleiades Republic... but Pleiades Alpha did have its rewards for a xenoanthropologist like him.

Foley wanted to start work at the excavation area, a new zone about a kilometer east of their initial site, where he had found evidence of a city from some long dead alien civilization. He had not found any fossil evidence, nor any apparent writing, but that was no surprise. From studying other ruins on the planet, however, he was convinced that there should be an 'art gallery' of sorts, somewhere on the eastern outskirts of the ruined city. Several such 'galleries' discovered in the past were quite spectacular, and he needed to find something big. So far he had found nothing of any significance since his return to the field. He was wondering if he would have anything at all to show his patrons when it was all over.

That was another issue he disliked about being an archaeologist: The politics required to solicit funding. At the start, Foley had been confident that the Pleiades Republic's Government Science Directorate would finance the dig, given his credentials, his well researched proposal, and the directorate's current budget levels. To his astonishment, they refused. It was the only time he had ever been refused funding for a dig of this type in his career. He had withdrawn to academia for several years, still trying to find a way to fund this project. Foley eventually found a handful of reputable private sources of funding, however, and managed to gather enough private funds to proceed. It was only after he'd done so much work begging for the money he needed that the Government changed his mind and decided to sponsor him anyway. Since then, Dr. Ian Karlsson, the Pleiades Director of Science, had sent him more money and personnel – mostly in the form of university interns – than Foley had ever seen in an archaeological expedition.

Unfortunately, Foley was having severe problems with this dig despite those resources. Some initial excavations around the buried city had been completed quickly and efficiently, but still they yielded little of interest. It was after moving to a new dig site closer to the heart of the city that his troubles began in earnest, though. The expedition seemed to be encountering new problems every hour, each one resulting in work stoppages and slow downs. The disruptions often were relatively minor, like the current power outage or a misplaced tool cart, but some were more serious: Chemical leaks from the equipment, the theft of a portable generator, even a wrecked transport vehicle. One of his students had jokingly suggested that someone was trying to sabotage the dig, but Foley had waved him away dismissively. Regardless, they weren't making any progress or discoveries worth reporting, much less coming close to anything worth inspiring sabotage.

"Dr. Foley!" called one of his graduate students, apparently in a panic. The student belonged to his class at the local university and not one of the fifty or so supplied at various times by the Pleiades government. At first Foley was surprised by how much harder and better his own students were working than anyone else in the dig. Later, after observing more of the interns' efforts, he concluded that the science directorate was simply using his expedition to dump its most embarrassingly incompetent students. He wondered if that had been the government's true motive for funding his dig: Providing a jobs program for underachieving youth.

"Dr. Foley, come quick!"

Foley sighed. "What's gone wrong, now? Did the dirt catch fire or something?"

The student looked at his professor, gaping. "What? Is that even possible?"

The doctor shook his head disgustedly. "If it were, I'm sure it would have happened to us by now. What is it?"

"Well, sir, a few of us were talking, and we kinda decided to go ahead and start the dig by hand, since we don't have any power to run the electronic tools," the student explained. "We remembered your lecture on excavations prior to the introduction of all of the fancy equipment we have now, so we got started using spades, brushes, sticks and twine to mark out spots, dirt—"

"Yes, yes," Foley interrupted impatiently. "I get it. You decided to dig with archaic tools and methods. Admirable, perhaps, but you should have come to ask me about it first, you know."

"Well, yeah, maybe," the student admitted, abashed. "But that's not the important thing. We found something. Something... uh, interesting."

Foley cocked his head. "Interesting how?"

"Bones, Dr. Foley. Fossils. And this is the funny thing, professor: They looked like human bones. *Prehistoric* human bones – Neanderthals unless I miss my guess."

"Neanderthals?" Foley exclaimed. "But... how?"

"I don't know how, Professor, but you've got to come check it out. It's... I want you to be there, just to document that we aren't trying to pull a hoax."

"Right, right," Foley said, picking up the pace as they hiked to the site. Still, he had to wonder. No-one had ever found a skeleton of the aliens who inhabited the stars of the Pleiades Republic, even in fossil records. In any human-explored star systems, in fact, even if there were ruins of now dead civilization on many worlds. It was as if each planet had been deliberately scrubbed of all non-human intelligent life long before humanity reached for the stars... but if this really was an alien skeleton, then that would mean... what? That humans were planted on Earth in the form of Neanderthals? That Neanderthals were somehow taken off of Earth millennia ago, to populate planets like this one?

Assuming, of course, the student was right, and these were, indeed, Neanderthals. *If this checks out, I'm going to need some help working this. Real, professional help.*

Part I

Opening Gambits

Chapter 1

Earth Alliance Naval Academy, Earth Campus

"Come on, Chris. Wake up! Rachel just commed me – she's on her way here, now! You can't afford to get any more demerits," Cadet Lieutenant Wolfgang Schubert admonished, shaking his bunkmate. "There's no more time – wake up!"

Christopher Desaix, also a Cadet Lieutenant at the Earth Alliance Naval Academy (formerly the Earth Alliance Treaty Organization Naval Academy, but it was shortened several centuries before. Even the bureaucrats felt that was too wordy), opened bloodshot eyes to peer up at his room mate. He had a few other acquaintances, people he played games with or studied with and the like, but Chris suspected he'd lose touch with them once the semester ended. Schubert, however, he would probably know for the rest of his life. A rare, true friend.

Schubert had languished his entire first year as a Midshipman, only being promoted to Cadet Ensign in the summer. His Lieutenant's bars were a recent award, received for academic performance at the semester break... largely thanks to Chris' study help.

On paper, it would be difficult to see what the two had in common, at least career-wise. Chris, as a freshman, would not have normally ranked above Ensign, but he had been given an 'out-of-sequence' grade jump by a patron who was impressed with Chris' work on a major tactical exercise.

Despite his achievement, Chris refused to major in tactics – the short path to command – in favor of engineering, his true passion. At the personal insistence of Admiral Michael McCaffrey, who had sponsored the exercise that won him his promotion, Chris was taking the introductory courses required for a minor in tactics.

Chris was hardly a model of naval discipline, and cared little for his rank. He joined the Navy primarily to get an advanced education in starship engineering, and his obvious lack of ambition did nothing to win him any friends. Professional jealousy over his promotion didn't exactly help in that area, either.

Schubert cared about none of these things. He did, however, think Chris seemed unusually cranky.

"I feel like hell. Can't whatever it is wait for another hour or so?" Chris squinted at a nearby clock – an antique dial-face clock with laminated gold numbers. "I just got to sleep an hour ago."

"Didn't you hear what I said? Rachel's already on her way, and she sounded royally pissed off. You've got to get up and get into uniform, pronto!"

"She's always pissed off with me, so that's no big surprise," Chris snorted, making a haphazard grab at the same pair of socks he'd been wearing the previous evening. "What's it about this time?"

"Something about Morrison's class, I think," Schubert replied.

Chris buttoned up his heavily wrinkled uniform shirt and scratched the back of his head in puzzlement. Captain Morrison, his professor for strategy and tactics, came down on her students hard enough for their frailties without his fellow classmates berating him as well. Even Cadet Lt. Commander Rachel Katz, his barracks CO and resident hard ass (at least where Christopher Desaix was concerned), knew that. So what was she bugging him for now?

"Oh, yeah," he remembered, looking around for his pants. "Open the desk and grab my hand comp for me, will you?"

Shaking his head as his fellow bunkmate stumbling around, Schubert stepped to the small workspace they shared and waved a spare key wand at the wall. A matte black drawer labeled "Desaix" slid silently out from its brushed aluminum frame. Shoving aside a jumble of antique electronics, Schubert fished out the one piece of modern equipment Chris owned that he seemed to care for. "Why's she so steamed at you, anyway?"

"She's my partner in a tactical sim," Chris explained. "It's due today."

Schubert nodded slowly in understanding. "She said she was going to rip your head off if you weren't awake when she got here."

Chris frowned and shook his head. "I've heard that one before. Either she's starting to go soft on me, or she's run out of threats to use. What's the weather like – do I need my jacket?"

"Probably," Schubert replied dryly. "It *is* the dead of winter around here, you know, and we had a pretty nasty ice storm not two days ago. Not that you would have noticed, as you haven't left the compound since Friday."

"Hey, I've been busy!"

Schubert rolled his eyes. "Yeah, fixing those antiques of yours again. You spend so much time on those things it's a wonder you're passing any of your classes. Why don't you ever go out and do something? This may be a military academy, but it's still got all the social scene of your average college. Parties, a pool hall, parties, a theater, parties, game rooms, and did I mention parties?"

"Hey, it's just a hobby," Chris replied, fastening the magnetic clasps on his jacket. "I'm not much of one for the party scene. Besides, I've been too busy with class work to even touch one of my restoration projects, lately. Do you see my glasses anywhere?"

Schubert shook his head, and handed him the wire frame lenses. "More antiques. You really prefer these fragile things to one-time laser surgery you could be done with in ten minutes?"

"Well, for one thing, these aren't antiques. They were made to my specifications." Chris replied. "As far as the laser surgery is concerned, I had it once already. It wasn't able to fully correct my vision, however, so...." He shrugged.

"You're stuck with them," Schubert finished for him. "How did you get into the Academy, then, if your eyes were that bad?"

"I'm ineligible to try out for helmsman or small craft military pilot," Chris clarified, "but there are areas where having perfect vision isn't a requirement – tactical studies, engineering, environmental controls, that sort of thing. I'm not the only one with glasses in the Navy – or the Academy, for that matter. We're just something of a rarity."

"Who else in the Academy wears glasses?"

Chris smirked. "Well, I'd tell you, but then I'd have to kill you. The person who I saw usually wears contact lenses, and doesn't want the secret to get out." He frowned. "The instructors all know, of course."

"And just how did a recluse like you find out, then?" Schubert laughed.

The door chimed for their visitor's arrival. Chris put on his much-maligned glasses, grabbed his hand comp, donned the uniform deerstalker cap, and glanced in a mirror to ensure he hadn't forgot anything. "Oh, entirely by accident, I assure you," he said, nodding to himself. "Now, if you'll excuse me, I have an irate classmate to attend to."

Schubert snickered. He knew that one Cadet Lieutenant Commander Rachel Katz would be plenty "irate" with his roommate's rather disheveled appearance, regardless. And, just like one Christopher Desaix, Schubert loved to see their barracks CO in a snit... at least when she wasn't in a position to administer discipline to him personally. "Good luck."

Chris waved in acknowledgment before opening the door and stepping out. "Hi, Rache. What's up?" he drawled casually.

He stood about a head taller than the small, lithe young woman in front of him, and was built with an athletic, if slender, frame. That, however, didn't prevent her from glaring up at him and slamming him up against the wall with one hand. "'Hi, Rache?' You, Mr. Desaix, are to address me as 'Ma'am' when on duty, and 'Ms. Katz' when off. You are *never* to address me as 'Rache!'"

Chris rolled his eyes. "When we're off duty, I'll call you whatever I want to call you, Ms. Cadet Lieutenant Commander Rachel Katz, ma'am. So what's got you so steamed this time, Rache?"

Rachel growled, baring her teeth in frustration and wrinkling her nose up. "Where the blazes were you yesterday? I had to cover your thrice-damned ass to both Commander Shirokauer and Captain Morrison! That's the fourth time this month I've had to save your miserable career, Mr. Desaix. And *this* time, I had to tell them that you were running the computer evaluations of our tactics project on the base macro simulator. I doubt they would have believed anything else, considering how many times you've called in 'sick' to work on your stupid antiques. You are aware that this is a military academy, and that you can actually be arrested by the MPs if your teachers think you're going AWOL?"

"Of course I know that." Chris said, shaking his head. "And your cover story was the truth. Sanchez commed me right before Shirokauer's class to let me know our request for macrosim time had been approved, but only if I was able to use it right away. You know how he is with freshmen...."

That put Rachel in a quandary. She wanted to berate him for not keeping her informed, but Chris was right. Lt. Commander Sanchez governed the macro simulator schedule zealously, especially with freshmen. If Chris had been even slightly late, he would have lost out on a rare opportunity to test the results of their project.

"Oh," she said hesitantly. "How did it go?"

"Ran smoothly. I've got the results here, if you want to see them," he said, handing her his hand comp. "Under the filename 'project3.'"

Rachel nodded absently, perusing the file. After few moments, she handed the tiny computer back to Chris, studying him with one raised eyebrow. "I guess your plan worked, Chris. Good job."

That was a surprise to Chris. In the six months he'd known Rachel Katz, he had never heard her compliment anyone, or refer to them by their first name. "Uh, thank you."

She looked at him again, and her smile quickly disappeared. "Your uniform is an absolute mess, however. Get it cleaned up and pressed before class."

Chris sighed. Of course it couldn't last. "Look, Rache, I've been busy working on that thing for the past two days. I've had less than an hour's worth of sleep in the past three days. If I look a little wilted, I'm sorry, but it's your fault for waking me up just as I'd finally gotten to sleep!"

Rachel's eyes narrowed. She knew he had a point, but to put the responsibility of his poor appearance on *her* head was very aggravating. He had to know that – he had to be goading her into replying.

"Mr. Desaix, you should know better than that. You are an officer, after all. As an officer, you are expected to present a spotless appearance at all times, regardless of your personal condition!"

Chris sighed, closing his eyes in frustration. Normally, he liked a nice, spirited argument with this girl. He usually encouraged them, in fact, just for the fun of it. Right at that moment, however, he was much too tired to fight with her. "Why do you care, Rache?" he groaned out, exhaustion filling his voice. "It's not like you'll suffer if I get in trouble, after all. You've got the grades and the ability to make it through the academy with no problems, regardless of what I do."

If his eyes had been opened, he would have seen Rachel blink in surprise. He'd never sounded so... defeated, before, in their association. He obviously was worn out, but he'd been tired before and not sounded like this. For a brief moment, she was worried for him. For a very brief moment, that was.

"I *don't* care!" Rachel snapped, making Chris open his eyes. "But, by some odd chance, you are my executive officer *and* my teammate for this project. In *either* role, your appearance reflects on me. With that in mind, you better believe that if I see you in another shirt as wrinkled as that one,

I will take action."

I should have known not to expect any sympathy from her, Chris thought, wincing. "I'm terribly sorry to annoy you so, Ms. Cadet Lieutenant Commander Rachel Katz, ma'am. Forgive my impertinence in being woken up unexpectedly after hardly any sleep and with less than three minutes to get dressed. I'll be sure to have a clean uniform pressed and ready to go next time. Now, if you'll excuse me, I'd like to get some sleep before Commander Shirokauer's class. I've only got two hours before I have to get up to get into my uniform *properly*."

"Fine," Rachel replied, storming off. "But don't expect me to cover for you if you're late to class."

Watching her go, Chris just shook his head. *I never expect you to cover for me, anyway, so why should today be any different?*

Rachel sighed as she looked around the small, auditorium-style classroom. It was less than a minute until Commander Francine Shirokauer (retired), started the Spatial Theory and Philosophy class. As she watched, the walls blackened and then re-colored to form a wraparound image of the night sky – Commander Shirokauer's favorite "wallpaper." A faint whirring of fans signified that the central HoloPoint projector and Classnote recording drones were already starting their warm-up sequence. *Of course Chris isn't here on time. I wonder what kind of excuse he'll have? He's probably still sleeping, he looked so exhausted....*

Lt. Desaix, hand on his hat to keep it from blowing away, burst in through the rear door just as the chime sounded announcing the time. "It is now 0900," an electronic voice intoned, in the Navy-standard synthetic accent Chris had once jokingly dubbed 'British female announcer number three.'

"Atten-HUT!" called Cadet Commander Robert Orff, the senior cadet in the room. Everyone immediately stood at attention, obeying the order.

"Sit down, sit down," their instructor said, hands waving dismissively. "I'm not in uniform, anymore. No need to stand on ceremony for me."

Chris darted to a seat between Rachel and Cadet Ensign Jeff Cohen, one of his closer acquaintances. Cohen was his first choice on most classroom activities, but had been assigned Rachel for a partner in their tactics class – a point of friction for the both of them.

"I see you made it, Lt. Desaix," Rachel whispered to him dryly. "I was beginning to wonder."

When he didn't shoot back one of his typical biting replies, she frowned. Something was wrong with him – maybe something more serious than just a lack of sleep. He wasn't acting like himself at all.

"Okay, class," Shirokauer began. "Let's go back to what we were talking about yesterday. I believe you and Ensign Drake were having a bit of a debate, weren't you, Mr. Evans?"

"Yes, Ma'am," replied Cadet Ensign Wayne Evans, a hopeful science officer for one of the future colony expeditions.

She snorted. "Please. After having been called nothing but 'ma'am' for the past sixteen years I've worked here at the academy, it's nice to finally be rid of that moniker. Call me 'Francine,' or if you can't manage that, 'Mrs. Shirokauer.'"

"Uh, yes, Mrs. Shirokauer," Evans replied bashfully. He was a sophomore, and had just spent a year and a half getting used to the idea of always referring to his professors as 'sir' or 'ma'am.' The sudden switch disturbed him. "At any rate, if I recall correctly, Mr. Drake and I were debating the boundaries of the universe. I believe that there are no boundaries, and that the universe is infinite. No matter how far you push out, you'll continue to encounter the void of the universe. As far as he was concerned—"

"As far as he is concerned, he can speak for himself. So, Mr. Drake, what was your side of this argument again?"

"Well, I'm not necessarily against the concept of an infinite universe," replied Eric Drake, also a Cadet Ensign. "But I definitely believe the existence of hyperspace, the very method by which we travel to the stars, is proof that there are other universes outside of our own. So the only way I see for the universe to be 'infinite,' as Mr. Evans calls it, is if it is shaped in a sphere. There are several well-reputed articles which state that the universe may be shaped as a sphere, a cylinder, a moebius strip, a... well, you get the idea. Mr. Evans' claims only work if the universe is shaped as an infinite plane, and an infinite plane only works if there is only one universe. To be blunt, I feel uncomfortable with the concept of an infinite plane as the shape of the universe..."

Chris tuned them out. Spatial Philosophy never interested him. Instead, he flipped on his hand comp and started fiddling with some figures, trying to see what refinements he could make on his and Rachel's project now that they had seen the sim results. Shirokauer wouldn't notice that he wasn't paying attention – she was entirely focused on the debate unfolding in front of her. If he fell asleep trying to listen to something as boring as a theoretical discussion of the construction of the universe, however, she would certainly slam him for not paying attention. He could give an opinion on the topic if asked, anyway. Chris figured that Evans had the right idea, and decided that Drake was something of a... a macro-agoraphobe, for lack of a better word. The man couldn't accept the possibility that the universe was infinite, and never seemed comfortable on spacewalks, either.

If I just adjusted the formation so that all the ships were just three hundred meters further apart, that would significantly increase its flexibility and allow the ships to make those tight turns about fifteen percent faster. The drawbacks would be negligible with that minor a change, as well. Hmm.... Chris thought as he looked over his figures. Both he and Rachel were required to critique their own battle plan with "recommendations for improvement" now that they'd seen the sims. He wouldn't be able to get any more macrosim time to test his recommendations, but that wasn't required. Few students would be able to test even their initial plans on the system before handing them in, but those who had such opportunities were expected to make them count. Rachel probably already had written her improvements, since she'd had two hours of time to work on it while he was sleeping, but he only had one free hour remaining until the project was due. Thankfully, he had this class to work on it, too.

It seemed like he had barely started when he felt someone tapping on his shoulder. Startled out of his thoughts, he glanced over to see Cohen standing beside him, smiling. "Hey, Chris. You seem out of it – didn't you notice class is over?"

Chris saved his work and smiled up at him. "Sorry, Jeff. No, I didn't – what's up?"

"I was just wondering if you'd care for a quick game of chess?"

Chris hesitated. He loved playing chess, and his only regular chess partner was Jeff Cohen. However, Cohen was so much better than he was that their matches were usually quite lopsided. Still, Chris enjoyed the game enough that he was more than willing to undergo the multiple drubbings handed to him in order to keep playing it.

"Sure, even though you'll probably beat the living hell out of me. When?"

Cohen chuckled. "Heh. You know, it's funny. You're probably the best tactician I've ever seen – even better than Captain Morrison – but you can't play chess worth a damn. Ever try to figure that one out?"

Chris shrugged. "I dunno. Chess is too... one dimensional. Or maybe I should say two dimensional. I don't like not being able to move multiple pieces, not being able to take advantage of terrain, not being able to use camouflage, things like that. It's... too simple for me, I guess."

"Yeah, that sounds like your kind of problem," Cohen snorted. "So, what do you say to a game now?"

"He can't play, now," Rachel Katz said disapprovingly from over his other shoulder. "Cadet Lieutenant Desaix and I still have to finish up a few things on our project for Morrison's class next period."

Chris shot a questioning look at her. "We do? What do we have to do?"

"We need to compare notes on what recommendations we're making on the sims. It'd be a bad idea to go in there without coordinating those things."

With an instinctive snort of disgust, Chris realized she was right. "I guess there's your answer, Jeff. I don't seem to have any say in my own life any more, thanks to this project."

Cohen smiled sympathetically. "Well, good luck, then. I'll see you in an hour."

"Yeah, see you."

Picking up his hand comp, Chris stood up and glared at Rachel. "So, where do we go to work on this thing? We don't really have time to go back to either of our quarters."

Rachel matched his stare with her own, and for the first time saw how bloodshot his eyes were. "Well, I'm betting you overslept. You probably haven't eaten anything at all, today, have you?"

"No, I guess I haven't," Chris replied sheepishly.

Rachel smirked. "Didn't think so. Come on – let's go to the cafeteria. I'll even buy you some breakfast, and we can go over our project."

Uh oh. I wonder why she's trying to be so nice? Chris shrugged, nevertheless. Breakfast definitely sounded like a good idea. "Okay, Rache. Now, I've had a few ideas already – I spent some of this class period working on it all. I think the biggest thing was that the formation was too tight; our ships weren't able to maneuver properly, so I was thinking...."

Breakfast had been a good idea. Now that Chris had gotten a couple of cups of coffee and a cinnamon bun into him, he was looking infinitely more refreshed, and they'd still been able to figure out most of the problems from their sim. She would never admit it, at least not to him, but he had really come through for her this time. This whole project had finally made her realize how he'd earned that Lieutenant's bar on his lapel:

His tactical genius was higher than she'd ever seen.

The tactical situation they'd been given was nearly impossible by design. The assignment was to "get the best possible solution," not to win. In fact, Captain Morrison had stated that she wasn't expecting anyone to succeed. Even Admiral Ken Pratchet, the highest ranking officer in the Navy, had failed to succeed in his time at the Academy.

That hadn't stopped Rachel from trying, though. And she thought she'd done well. She knew she couldn't win against the odds presented to her, so she had instead tried to find a way not to lose. In doing so, she had found a perfectly acceptable way to reach an 80% probability of stalemate, which she had been certain would be better than anyone else in the room could have boasted.

Except, perhaps, for Cadet Lieutenant Desaix. He had looked over her work, nodded approvingly, and said, "Nice try. Mind if I have a go at it? Then we'll work on the one we both agree is the best." His answer infuriated her. In fact, his attitude had made her wonder how anyone could ever have promoted him to Lieutenant as a freshman.

She learned why, quickly, once he put his mind on that project. Rachael didn't believe his results when she first saw his figures, so she'd double checked them. And then triple checked them. It was a highly unorthodox strategy, but that didn't matter – he had the better strategy, hands down. She didn't have much to say after that beyond making a few minor suggestions to his plan that, she hoped, improved it a little. And she no longer cared that he'd dismissed her own plans so off-handedly.

Ever since she'd seen that, she started doing whatever she could to push his career forward, including covering for him when he was absent and yelling at him when he needed a good kick in the pants. But now she had a funny feeling this would be the wrong approach – he hadn't been acting like himself all day, and thinking back she wondered if she'd been pushing him a little too hard, lately.

Something else was bothering him, though, and she couldn't tell what it was. It was more than just his present exhaustion, for she'd seen him worn out before, many times, and in all those times he'd never acted like this. Nor had he had those bloodshot eyes. Nor had he ever refused to banter back at her when she delivered her sermons.

She hated knowing that she cared about him. Not that she didn't care about people – far from it. Rather, there was just something about *him*, in particular, that rubbed her the wrong way. This was despite the fact that she had lately been spending most of her free time with him. In return, he constantly tried to present her with those weird antiques he kept tinkering with in his dorm. And it wasn't like she didn't appreciate that – against her better judgment, she found herself accepting a few of them, and they always proved useful..

But, at that particular moment, she was more worried about him than she'd ever been for any of her other friends or colleagues. *He's been working too hard,* she thought suddenly. *Come to think of it, I've only seen him get a regular night's sleep once in the past three weeks we've been working on this project. Outside of that, he's been catnapping or catching one or two hours sleep between classes. Maybe he really is just tired, but if so it's because of undue stress. Maybe I've been riding him too hard.*

"How's the coffee?" she asked, hoping he would open up. Until that moment, Rachel hadn't realized quite how hard she had been riding him over their project. She'd also been gradually squeezing out all of his stress relievers, she realized, like those chess games with Ensign Cohen or his usual hobby of restoring and adapting antique electronics. Their arguments were all he had left... and she'd been gradually wearing him down with those for weeks. She wasn't sure what she could do for him to make amends, but she had to try something.

"Weak, like it always is here in the cafeteria. Modern coffeemakers just don't cut it. You all laugh at my antique restoration, but often what I work on most is the more practical stuff. Like coffeemakers – my antique coffeemaker will brew a better, stronger cup of coffee than anything built in the past hundred years."

Rachel winced. "I've drunk coffee from that thing. It's just too strong. I think I'll stick to the modern brew, thank you very much."

Chris shrugged. "That's not the coffeemaker's fault, Rache. That's me having poor-quality beans and you not taking cream or sugar with your coffee. If I had better beans or you diluted your coffee with some cream, I suspect you'd like it."

Rachel raised a dubious eyebrow. "Maybe," she said. "I haven't left you much time to tinker with your toys these past few weeks, have I?"

"Not much, no," Chris said. "But I've been able to do a little despite the extra workload."

"Yeah," Rachel agreed dryly. "At the cost of your chess games, your meals, your attendance, your sleep...."

Chris chuckled. "Yeah, I guess."

"Well, I'm laying off, tonight. Get some sleep, that's an order. Then, since we don't have class tomorrow, I'll see if I can borrow Jeff's chess set."

She grinned ruefully at him. "I'm not nearly as good at the game as he is, since I haven't played much, so maybe you'll stand a chance against me."

Chris raised an eyebrow suspiciously. "I didn't think anyone else around here knew how to play chess. I'd love a game or two, Rache."

Rachel smirked. "Good. Because after tomorrow, I'll be going back to riding you hard. You're a good tactician, but you still have a lot to learn about being an officer."

He smiled back tiredly. "You're giving me a temporary truce, aren't you? Letting me recover before we lock horns again?"

"Something like that, yeah," Rachel replied. "To put it bluntly, you don't look too healthy at the moment. I figured you need the rest."

"I'm fine!" Chris snapped back. "I just haven't slept much, lately."

Rachel was a little surprised at his heated reply, and in the awkward silence that followed she made a mental note to add it to her discussion with Schubert. She bit her lip to keep from arguing back, having resolved to let him recover from his problem, whatever it was, without adding to his stress by shouting at him.

Chris bit his lip and sighed. "Sorry. I guess I'm a bit edgy, too. Using several gallons of coffee to keep you awake will do that to you."

Rachel was about to reply to him when a chime sounded. "Well, let's get to class. Time to see what Captain Morrison has to say about your solution to our little sim."

Chris sighed and nodded, downing the last of his coffee. "Yeah. Let's get this over with. I'm looking forward to that nap," he said, smiling at her good-naturedly.

Rachel frowned as she led him off. Something was off about that smile... but she didn't have time to think about it just then. It was just another thing to file away for her talk with Schubert.

She had to schedule that talk, and soon.

Chapter II

"Despite your so-called 'best efforts,' your Dr. Foley has managed to unearth the *only* thing that we actually didn't want him to find." The hooded, heavyset figure stood behind the desk of Pleiades Science Director, Ian Karlsson, looking distantly out a tinted window at the fountain area below, the center of Gov-Tech Hexagon Park. Turning around, he looked accusingly down at the man seated across the desk from him "There were probably a multitude of artifacts in that area which would have been perfectly fine for him to discover. Your bumbling, however, has now allowed him to find the graveyard! What are you planning on doing now?"

"It's too late to do much," Director Karlsson admitted, squirming a little in his seat. When that brought no immediate reply he started tapping his fingers on the surface of the polished mahogany desk, trying to think of something to say. "I had hoped that by planting some of our people in his group, we could direct the dig away from that area or stop them when they got too close. Unfortunately, his students decided to try and show some 'initiative' without informing Dr. Foley or any of our own staff."

"In other words, you relied too much on trickery, when competent exercise of your authority as Science Director should have been enough."

Karlsson shook his head. "Our system doesn't work quite like that. Foley is a scientist, but that doesn't mean he works for me or responds to my direction. He's independent. Another month and we could have pulled his funding. With his reputation staked on this dig, the failure would have discredited him so that no one would back another attempt, and no one would ever ask to return to site thirty-nine. He would have been forced to abandon the hunt, and your burial ground would be safe from future digs. I didn't count on a bunch of overly enthusiastic college students who shouldn't have even been digging in the first place making the discovery themselves."

"So hire him. The discovery he made is as good a pretext as any for offering him a position. Then he *would* be working for you, and you could keep him sidelined."

Karlsson closed his eyes thoughtfully. "That might work. I'll try it, but it may not be sufficient. I think our best option now is to try and contain the news, take over the dig, and in a few months 'conclude' that what they've found is merely a hoax. No-one will ever be interested in digging at site thirty-nine again after it's been associated with such a hoax, and your burial ground will once again be hidden."

"And if word has already spread too fast to be contained?"

"Well, we'll have to set up some kind of distraction to keep people from pursuing the find until we can discredit it. Something big."

"War." The man stepped quickly out from behind the desk. His uniform, the hooded black wrappings of World Internal Security, Pleiades Republic, fluttered slightly in the breeze from the antique overhead fan. WISPR agents typically styled themselves after ancient Japanese ninjas. This one, however, looked bulkier and more menacing than average.

The Science Director flinched slightly. "That would definitely be distracting, but a full scale war wasn't quite what I had in mind."

"You're concerned you might lose." It wasn't a question.

"Not seriously. I'm not disputing the benefit of the technology you've given us, and at this point we've had enough time to prepare and integrate your designs into almost a third of our Navy's warships. It's just that I don't like the thought of starting a war before we're ready *just* to be a distraction from one man's findings in an archaeological dig. I'll alert the Admiralty to start making contingency plans, but hopefully it won't come to that. No, I'm actually more concerned about the possibility that your secrets might be discovered."

"You had better hope not. If we are discovered, we'll be forced to act openly." The man paused. "In that case, I'm not sure your species would survive."

Earth Alliance Naval Academy, Earth Campus

Captain Anne Morrison surveyed her students with a critical eye. It was time for the presentation of everyone's projects, and she had a twinkle in her eye as she noticed how many of them looked nervous. As always, no-one had believed her that the situation was virtually a no-win scenario, and all of them were expecting to be berated for having failed. Well, most everyone. Cadet Lieutenant Commander Katz and her partner seemed at ease, although said partner seemed decidedly under the weather. Morrison wasn't surprised. In the cafeteria that morning, Lt. Commander Sanchez had drawn her aside, commenting on Cadet Desaix's diligence in staying at the macrosim center until almost four in the morning. Presumably he had completed the computer evaluation of their initial tactical solution, but Morrison wondered if the pair had been able to make any serious revisions to their plan in the intervening hours.

Knowing the answer already, she asked, "Did anyone here manage to get to the macrosim and run trial evaluations on their project? I'm not expecting that you did, necessarily – I know how tough it can be to get by Lt. Commander Sanchez to run sims for a mere sophomore level tactics class." Katz and Desaix raised their hands, of course. So did a rather reluctant Cadet Ensign Cohen and his partner. She nodded. "Okay, we'll allow your two teams to go last. You're likely to have more complex results, and if necessary we'll postpone them to the next class, which will give you more time to evaluate things. Let's hear everyone else's first, then."

As she suspected, the teams all had pretty similar results. For this particular assignment, Captain Morrison was not looking for success, but rather to see how they handled themselves. These scenarios were designed to encourage thinking outside of the box, so those who stuck too closely to the 'book' would be marked down, while those who showed creativity would be graded higher. She didn't really care whether her students had succeeded in cutting down their enemy by half or not at all, though she did take note when someone was particularly successful.

As everyone's projects were being presented, she watched the faces of her other students. Most of them looked decidedly relieved, knowing finally that she had been telling them the truth about how difficult the sims were. Ms. Katz had been relaxed the whole time, and her face never changed – but she had something of a stoic personality. Mr. Cohen and his partner, however, seemed downright elated – perhaps they'd achieved something the others hadn't.

It was Lt. Desaix, Rachel Katz's partner, who puzzled her the most. The more he heard of the other students' efforts, the more perplexed he seemed. Even though they were tainted by exhaustion, his eyes were bright with interest. Morrison had no idea what that meant, but she figured she'd find out later.

Finally, the students who hadn't had macrosim time were finished. The next pair of results would likely be more interesting – the macrosim allowed students to prevent more refined strategies and better post-simulation analysis.

"Well, Ma'am," Cohen began. "We seem to have had a bit more success than the others in the class. Thanks to the results we received from the macrosim analysis of our tactical simulation, we were able to refine our plans to offer a good 50% chance of stalemate."

That's right up there with the best I've seen. Morrison made a mental note to start shepherding these two along better. She watched as the cadet laid out his team's plans carefully. As he did, she could have sworn she heard Lt. Cmdr. Katz whisper something along the lines of, "...like my first response plan," but shrugged it off. The odds that two people would devise such a particularly ingenious solution in the same class were slim.

Cohen finished up, and Morrison nodded, already planning in her head some syllabus revisions to start pushing his talents. It would be tricky to do without damaging the overall integrity of the class for those less gifted, but she was most impressed.

She felt a little sorry for Lt. Cmdr. Katz, having to follow a performance like that. It would be hard on the girl – especially since the cadet was a pretty good tactician herself – but those were the breaks. Maybe a humorous note to ease her in?

"So, Lt. Commander Katz. What do you have to show us to top that performance? A victory, perhaps?..." Morrison's voice trailed off as she caught a smug look on Rachel's face.

"Actually, ma'am," Rachel said, her voice confident and cheerful. "Thanks in large part to Lt. Desaix's fine work, we achieved something close to an 88% chance of victory." Morrison's eyes widened; the best possibility of a victory any student had *ever* achieved on their particular assignment was only rated at about 70% probability.

"That was, though, before we ran the solution through the macrosim, and compensated for our errors. We now have a virtual certainty... ma'am?"

Captain Morrison sat down in her chair, hard. As an instructor, she had her work cut out for her. "Please continue your briefing," she said somewhat faintly.

Wolfgang Schubert looked up in surprise as the door chimed. He glanced over to make sure his bunkmate was still asleep before going over to answer it. He wondered who it was – he wasn't expecting anyone and, as far as he knew, Chris wasn't, either.

He stepped out of the room and saw, to his surprise, Rachel Katz standing there. Usually, she commed before coming over. "Hey, Rache. What's up? I hear you and Chris practically knocked Old Lady Morrison out with your project!"

Rachel flushed slightly. "Well, we did do rather well."

Schubert laughed. "Well, I've heard her nerves were the reason Morrison was grounded to a desk. The brass was worried she'd freeze up in the middle of a stressful action, but she was worth too much as a tactician to put her completely out to pasture. So what's up? You aren't here to ask me out on a date, are you?"

Rachel rolled her eyes. "Don't be ridiculous. Is Lt. Desaix awake, Mr. Schubert?"

Schubert's eyes hardened. "No. But I'm not waking him up this time."

Rachel laughed bitterly. "I've woken him up a lot lately, haven't I? Well, I don't want you to this time – he needs his sleep. In fact, I ordered him to go straight to bed tonight, and not to tinker with his antiques or anything. I just wanted to talk with you about him privately."

Schubert's brow furled at that. "Oh? Well, then, let's go somewhere else to talk. Like you said, Chris needs his sleep."

"I don't want to be overheard. My quarters are nearby, and I don't have a roommate," she said. She marched at a fairly rapid pace down the corridor, Schubert following swiftly at her heels. She keyed in the code to open the door and gestured for him to follow her inside.

Schubert was somewhat surprised by the room. As intensely military as she was, he somehow expected her dorm to be either very Spartan in appearance or (as he'd seen some of the more 'dedicated' officers he met) to be decorated in a manner that was the exact opposite of her outward appearance. Rather, it was neither. It was fairly well organized, although there were a few signs of impending clutter. A few tasteful decorations were scattered here and there, including a small collection of antique, replica, and miniature weapons from eras past. Schubert recognized one of those, a "radio controlled" (whatever that meant) model tank Chris restored. He'd had his eye on that one, himself – he wondered why Chris had given it to Rachel, instead.

There was a utilitarian desk and a perfectly made bunk bed, just like in every other dorm room. A few additional pieces of small, non-regulation furniture made a comfortable setting. A portable range which had recently been used to make some soup (another restoration project by Chris, Schubert realized), a rolled up futon in a corner, a nice leather desk chair, and a mini-fridge completed the picture. Schubert had a mini-fridge, too, but his was a restored antique, courtesy of Chris; Rachael's was a modern masterpiece complete with all of the latest devices to regulate the temperature of everything in it precisely. Not something Schubert would have expected Rachel to own, but not something he could say went against his read of her character.

Much to his surprise, he saw a poorly hidden case Schubert recognized as a storage unit for eyeglasses. *So,* Rachel *is the person whose secret Chris was protecting. And with all those other things he's built for her....*

Rachel turned to Schubert and frowned, chewing on her lower lip. "Is there something wrong with Lt. Desaix? He hasn't been acting like himself the past few days."

Schubert smothered a laugh – and the thought which inspired it – before answering. "I'm not sure. What, in particular, have you noticed?"

"Well, little things. First, it's his exhaustion. Now, I know I've been riding him a little harder than usual these past few weeks – probably harder than I should have – but he seems even more tired than that should account for."

Schubert scratched the stubble on his chin absentmindedly. "Well, now that you mention it, he does seem a bit more tuckered than usual."

"If it was just that, though, I wouldn't be so... concerned," she winced. Schubert couldn't help the snicker this time. He shut up quickly when she glared at him, but his suspicions were growing every moment. "You know how we always fight with each other? Well, he's not fighting back like he normally does. At first I thought it was just the lack of sleep, but something's telling me it's more than that."

Schubert shrugged. "Maybe he just doesn't want to fight any more?"

"No, it's not that," Rachel said, frowning. "There's more to it. His eyes are bloodshot all of the time, even after he's had a chance to sleep for a bit and recover. And when I recently suggested that he looked like he needed a little shut-eye, he snapped at me. It was... disturbing. He got real defensive, claiming nothing was wrong, but that was blatantly untrue."

"Now, that is strange," Schubert said, frowning. "He argues tooth and nail if he thinks he should, but he's never lost his temper like that."

Rachel sighed. "But there was one more thing that has me worried. When we were headed for Captain Morrison's class, we were talking about his desperate need for some rest. There was something odd in his voice – it almost sounded like he, well, resented having to sleep. Have you got any clue why that might be, if he really is as exhausted as we figure he has to be?"

Now, Schubert was genuinely alarmed. "No. But now that you mention it, he's not had a pleasant time of it when he has had the chance to sleep, lately. He's always tossing and turning, moving around almost violently. Frankly, the noise keeps *me* awake, sometimes."

Rachel sighed. "So you really don't know what it is that's disturbing him, either?" Schubert shook his head. "Well, then, I don't know what to do. But keep a close eye on him, would you? And be sure you let me know if you find out anything – even if you can't tell me what it is."

Schubert had never really liked Rachel. She'd always seemed too stuck up for his tastes, but now it appeared as if he needed to re-evaluate his opinion of her.

"Trust me, Rache – you'll be the first to know."

———————————

Morrison shifted nervously. It wasn't often she was called in to talk to Pierre Mumford, the lone five star Admiral in the fleet. By some twist of fate (the fifth star being honorary), he was only the *second* highest ranking Admiral in the Navy, but that knowledge did little to sooth her frayed nerves.

She didn't know for sure why she was here. Perhaps word had reached the Admiral that someone actually managed a flawless victory in one of the "mission improbable" scenarios, as they'd come to be called. If that was it, she knew she was going into the meeting under-prepared. Her little dizzy spell had made it impossible for her to look over the strategy that Rachel Katz and Christopher Desaix had used and she had yet to talk to either one of them about the incident. She just hoped it wouldn't hurt her career.

A middle-aged person emerged from the office, and to Morrison's surprise she was a civilian. Dr. Kimiko Beccera, a top archaeologist and xenoanthropologist, was a very striking woman. By marriage, she held dual citizenship in both the Earth Alliance and the Pleiades Republic – the largest and the second largest nations in the known universe, respectively. The story, as Morrison heard it, was that she had fallen in love with an Army officer at the Alliance's Consulate, and spent the better part of three years hunting him down. Then she spent several more trying to get him to marry her.

That man, Colonel Andrew Beccera, had finally given in when he turned forty. She was only twenty-three at the time, and while he worried she was a too young for him he figured he had better give in to the inevitable while they both could still enjoy themselves. Years of legal wrangling surrounded their marriage – they struggled to keep both their respective careers while remaining citizens of their respective countries. In the end, it actually required an interstellar treaty for their marriage to be made official. Their love story was almost legendary.

While the Army never sanctioned their marriage, the Earth Alliance benefitted greatly from Kimiko's dual allegiance. By comparing analyses of ruins discovered by the Earth Alliance and ruins discovered by the Pleiades Republic, she had been able to predict where additional ruins might be found. Using her methods, ruins decorated with the first ever example of a non-human written language had been discovered. This language had yet to be translated, but the discovery had nevertheless won her numerous accolades.

None of which made her presence in Admiral Mumford's office easier to explain. Morrison had no time to think about that, however, as Sally Hannah, the Admiral's civilian secretary, gestured to her.

"The Admiral will see you now, Anne."

"Thanks, Sally," Morrison said, walking past the doorway into the Admiral's office. Her nerves, which had momentarily disappeared while she puzzled over Mrs. Beccera's presence, were back in full force. She could hardly imagine why Admiral Mumford would be so keen on her class results, but she couldn't think of any other reason why he might have called her. She had actually anticipated a call from Admiral McCaffrey, who would periodically take an interest in one or two of her students, but Mumford was too high in the command structure for such minor pursuits.

"Ah, Captain Morrison. Please, come in, come in," Mumford said, gesturing fervently for her to enter. "I'm having a bit of a problem, and my granddaughter said you might be able to help. She says you're her favorite tactics instructor and that I should trust your judgment. I'm sure you won't let either of us down."

That sent her mind whirling. *Crap. What's his granddaughter's first name again? Oh, right – Emily. Cadet Lt. Commander Emily Mumford. Bright kid, but so tactically inept I've always thought she owed her rank to a small degree of nepotism.* "I'll be sure to thank Emily for her kind words. Now, what can I help you with, sir?"

Admiral Mumford tapped a few keys on his desk comp. Gesturing to the screen, he said, "The Wargame is coming up soon."

Morrison nodded. The Academy periodically held a number of war games, but there was only one event which could be called *the* Wargame. Descended from a centuries-old need to demonstrate the Alliance's military might and intimidate hostile powers, the Wargame was held once every three or four years so that no Academy student graduated without participating in it at least once. It was the largest military exercise in the known universe, and occupied much of the Navy's attention whenever it ran. Every student at the Academy, both officer candidates and those in training for enlisted duties, would be required to participate. So would almost thirty thousand regular Naval personnel and their ships. Naval stations on every Earth Alliance world outside Sol would be stripped to provide the manpower and warships for it... and even that wouldn't be enough. Several shipyards full of 'retired' warships, mothballed due to age, would be raided in order to provide more.

By tradition, the scenario was simple. Take three Alliance systems, preferably lightly defended start-up colonies in need of military reinforcement. To one system, deploy a fleet composed of veteran crews and modern warships. Academy crews (supported, and often commanded, by reservists) would operate an equivalent force of warships refitted from the decommissioned stores in another. The third planet was the so-called 'disputed territory.' For three weeks, the two sides were to wage a simulated 'war.' Frequently, the 'Fleet' side of the Wargame was victorious, but more often then not it wound up as a stalemate. It was rare that the Academy side actually won, but it *had* happened on occasion. The record was Fleet 14, Academy 6, and Stalemate 27.

The dates for the Wargame, even the exact year in which it would occur, were kept secret until the last possible moment. Mumford letting her know that it was "coming soon" was big – just what role did he intend for her to play?

"Sir?"

Mumford smiled at her. "I'm talking to several Academy instructors, assigning each of them to act as personnel officers and recommend a crew for each ship. I figure, as their teachers, you know the students best. You don't need to worry about the Marines – the Marine Corps Academy will take care of them – but this will still be a difficult assignment. Your assignment will be easier than most – all you have to be concern yourself with is the crew for a corvette."

Morrison nodded. While some of her senior co-workers might have considered such a small role an insult, she normally wouldn't have been given any role at all. "Thank you, sir. Can I ask for some specifics?"

"She's about a hundred and twenty years old, and the last survivor of her class even in mothballs. Regularly crewed by about two hundred and fifteen men, twenty of whom are Marines, she was armed with fourteen single-barrel broadside-mount rail guns, two turreted particle cannons, and a bow chaser armament of two missile tubes and three particle cannons." That caught Morrison by surprise – particle cannons were incredibly powerful (if only usable for a very limited duration before they needed to be recharged), and that kind of chase armament sounded like it belonged on a frigate, not a corvette. Her disbelief must of showed, because the Admiral gave her a rueful grin. "She was a converted gunboat."

The naval philosophy of building "gunboats," or small warships with powerful chase armaments and no broadsides, had been prevalent for a brief period. The theory was that, when attacking en masse, small, relatively inexpensive gunboats could be more powerful than frigates on a per-ship basis. What it actually proved to be was a quantity-over-quality plan of construction on the cheap.

In their first major war, most of the gunboats had been demolished in a single horrific battle. Even so, post-combat analysis showed that the philosophy had proven relatively sound... up to a point. When the action had started, Alliance gunboats and their enemy's frigates had matching losses. Once a few of the small ships were gone, though, and the initial charges for the particle cannon capacitor were drained, the philosophy failed. Every gunboat lost had exponentially weakened the one hundred and twenty gunboat squadron, and the tide turned quickly. As the action continued they scattered, many of them destroyed. The surviving gunboats were recalled, refitted with light broadside armaments, and re-commissioned as corvettes.

Morrison had thought the last of them had been destroyed in the years that followed, but apparently she was mistaken. "Who is she, sir? And what is her crew manifest breakdown?"

Mumford chuckled. "She was named the *Chihuahua* when she was first commissioned as a gunboat – they gave those converted gunboats some pretty silly names – and my staff found no record of that having been changed after her conversion. As far as a crew breakdown, it's a bit unusual. You'll need weapons techs, engineers, environmental engineers, navigation specialists, and roughly thirty officers for command and control. You don't need to worry about a captain – the Wargame administrators will assign you a commanding officer, a chief engineer with the appropriate background to refit this ship, and possibly one or two other officers if you need them. Due to the *Chihuahua's* size, however, you'll be on your own for most of the bridge crew, execs, and tactical officers. You'll need to identify an equal number of alternates for each officer's position – if someone responsible for a bigger ship wants an officer you've listed, you'll likely lose out unless you can come up with a damned good justification for why that person belongs on a corvette instead of one of the battleships."

Morrison hesitated. "I'm not sure I'm very well placed for this, sir. I don't teach any classes open to enlisted personnel or non-command line officers, so I'll likely be even worse off than a regular personnel officer."

"I doubt it. After all, Captain, there's a reason we decided to have our officer candidates share their dormitories, specialized classes, and common rooms with enlisted during training." He grinned. "I'm sure some of your students will be able to recommend the other officers and enlisted you'll need. And you're better off than any of the twenty teachers I assigned to find crews for the Sirius class battleships we intend to use. They have to find eleven hundred men each!"

"Sirius class? Those are even older than you say the *Chihuahua* is supposed to be!" Morrison gasped. "They'll hardly be a match for our newer heavy cruisers, much less any modern battleships. I take it you aren't exactly planning on an Academy victory this year?"

Mumford shrugged apologetically. "I hate to admit it, but the Wargame scenario is driven more by politics and computer recommendations than common sense. And it's even worse than you think – we'll probably wind up using several of the new Argus-class battleships on the Fleet side."

Morrison shook her head. "I understand the political realities, I'm just not sure what the students are going to learn from an exercise that's so completely stacked against them." She stopped as another thought struck her. "I hope you're putting someone good in overall command of the Academy fleet."

Mumford smirked sourly. "Well, you're in luck – all bad. As usual, the Academy force is being placed in the charge of a captain up for flag rank. Captain John Green is an arrogant asshole, and truthfully is a poor officer. But he's lucky, and luck is frequently valued as being more important than skill."

"The Academy would be better off under Cadet Katz's command," Morrison muttered almost to herself.

"Cadet Katz?" Mumford says. "I don't believe I've heard of him."

"Her," Morrison corrected, and then realized she'd have to explain. Mentioning her had been a mistake. She prayed he wouldn't ask too many questions. "She and Cadet Desaix, Admiral McCaffrey's newest protégé, presented me with a winning plan to one of the Mission Improbable scenarios today."

Mumford looked intrigued. "What probability?"

"Virtual certainty, according to their sims. I haven't had a chance to look through it as well as I would have liked, myself." She paused, then thought of something that might keep him from asking for details. "I was planning on talking to Sanchez about using the macrosim to see how it ran."

Mumford frowned. "So who was the brainstormer? Katz or Desaix?"

"I... don't know yet, sir. Cadet Desaix is just a freshman, but he did win a grade jump in the tactical scenario contest Admiral McCaffrey sponsored last semester. They both have an extremely high aptitude for tactics, though, and while they may have an adversarial relationship they work well together. Mr. Desaix, however, is only minoring in tactics, so I'd guess Cadet Katz. But that's just a guess."

Mumford stroked his chin. "What is Cadet Desaix's major?"

"Engineering."

"Then, may I make a suggestion, Captain?"

"Of course!" Morrison replied.

"Don't bother with running the sim – you'll need the time for this new assignment. Instead, go along on the *Chihuahua* as an observer. You aren't a command line officer, so it won't disrupt the chain of command, but it will give you an excellent opportunity to evaluate both of those cadets – we'll be sure to assign Katz to be your senior tactical officer and Desaix your Executive Engineering officer. Gather the best command crew you can find – you've made me curious enough to back up your personnel decisions, so you'll have a free hand to see what sort of force you can make out of this little corvette. And see if these cadets are as good in action as they are in sims. If we can build a team of superior officers using your little corvette, perhaps the big political farce governing the Wargame won't render it completely worthless to the Navy."

Morrison saluted. "Yes, sir."

Chapter III

Earth Alliance Naval Academy, Earth Campus

A roguish young man with short, dark hair shut off the connection from his end of the comm line and sat down on his Academy bunk. His name was Joel Farmburg... or Brent Fornello, depending on where he was at the time. A girl dressed in nothing but a terrycloth robe came out of his bathroom and walked over to him. Seeing his distress, she walked over and started massaging his naked shoulders.

"What's wrong, baby?" she cooed.

"Take a hike, love. I need to deal with this one alone."

"Are you sure?" she whispered, rubbing her body up against his back. "I could help you relax, you know."

"Yeah," he said, grabbing her grasping hands and pulling them away. "I'm sure. I don't particularly feel up to... relaxing... right now, Suze."

"Humph!" the girl puffed, retrieving her arms and stepping away. "Well, in that case, I guess I'd better go. Call me?"

"Yeah, whatever," he said, waving her off impatiently. "Go, I need to think."

Sighing, she said, "I'll just get dressed, then."

He waited until she had gone before he pulled his hand comp out of its hiding place. Calling up a special decryption program, he started reading the message again.

It had been his job to identify the best and the brightest in the Academy, finding those people that were worth watching. His first deep cover assignment, he didn't yet know how his superiors planned to extract him without arousing suspicion. However, he'd entered the Academy as planned, trusting his superiors to help him find a way out.

Then, a year into the task, his mission had suddenly changed. In addition to identifying and reporting on the best and the brightest, he was supposed to disrupt their education and careers as best as he could. So far, his biggest coup had been forcing one of the Academy's better teachers to retire by maneuvering him into an affair with a student. His superiors now wanted reports on anything significant the Earth Alliance might know regarding Pleiades, and they wanted it yesterday.

Frustrated with his orders, his thoughts turned to the girl who had just left his room. That was another case of where his mission had expanded after he had arrived. Suze had been an excellent find, a marvelous body attached to a passionate woman. His superiors had targeted her for elimination based on his reports, and gave him the job of doing it. He figured the best way to 'eliminate' her was to ruin her career... by getting her into bed so often she couldn't study any more, sabotaging any chance of hers to study, and possibly altering her grades somewhere down the line so that she flunked out. He figured at least this way he wouldn't have to kill her.

Farmburg stewed awhile, wondering what was driving the urgency of his latest orders. Arriving at no conclusions, he decided to clear his mind of any questions. He would need his wits to step up his pace without giving himself away.

Schubert frowned, watching his roommate toss and turn. Just as Rachel had suggested, it was fairly obvious that something was bothering him enough to interfere with his sleep. He vaguely wondered if sleeping like this should be considered rest at all, but what could he do to help?

The comm beeped. Schubert answered it automatically. "Cadet Schubert speaking."

"This is Katz. I'm afraid you'll have to wake Chris again."

"What?" Schubert exclaimed, feeling betrayed.

"Not my choice. Captain Morrison is calling for us to see her, right away. And any officers I feel might be good in other areas – including navigation and piloting. I want you to be there, too."

Schubert blinked. "What's this all about?"

"Don't know. Just wake him up, get him dressed, and get him down here."

"Yes, Ma'am," Schubert snapped, then cut the comm. Glancing over at Chris, he sighed. Well, it would at least stop him from tossing and turning.

―――――――――――

"Hello, ladies and gentlemen," Captain Morrison greeted. "You're undoubtedly wondering why I called you all here. This meeting is classified Top Secret. There will be no discussions about this briefing beyond this room. Now that the formalities are out of the way, let's start by introducing ourselves. Just provide your name, rank, year, and specialty, please."

It wasn't a very large gathering, but all of the seats in the small office had been filled by the time Chris, Schubert, and Rachel had arrived. They recognized some of the other cadets, but not all of them.

"Hi," the first of them said. "My name is Emily Mumford – junior year. You may know my grandfather, Admiral Pierre Mumford. I'm a Cadet Lieutenant Commander. One Admiral in the family is enough, though, so I'm majoring in communications and diplomatic studies instead of any of the command tracks."

"Robert Orff. Junior. Cadet Commander. Tactics."

"Lauren Weber. Navigator, friend to Emily, and Cadet Lieutenant. Oh, and I'm a junior."

"Cadet Midshipman Yannis Langer. I'm kinda undecided about my major so far. Freshman, of course."

"Cadet Lieutenant Commander Rachel Katz. Sophomore, majoring in tactics."

"Jeff Cohen, sophomore, majoring in tactics. Cadet Ensign."

"Christopher Desaix. Majoring in Engineering, though I'm reluctantly considering a second major in tactics. Freshman."

"And your rank?" Mumford asked, curious.

"Cadet Lieutenant."

Mumford squinted at him, as if trying to see something she'd missed. "And you're a freshman?"

Chris sighed. He'd figured everyone knew by now. "Yes Ma'am."

"Chris got special patronage from Admiral McCaffrey after winning a contest," Schubert said, saving him from having to explain yet again. "I, by the way, am Cadet Lieutenant Wolfgang Schubert, navigation. This is my sophomore year."

"And I, of course, am Captain Anne Morrison. I am assembling a list of people to crew a corvette in an upcoming war game, and I was hoping you cadets could help me. I have a captain and a chief engineer promised to me, and I'm told I don't have to worry about the Marines, but all of the rest of the personnel responsibilities have fallen to me." She smiled. "Mr. Orff, I intend on making you the ship's Exec. Ms. Katz, you'll be Chief Tactical Officer, with Mr. Cohen and Mr. Langer as your assistants. Mr. Desaix, you will be the Assistant Chief Engineer. Mr. Schubert, Ms. Weber, you'll be in navigation. Ms. Mumford, Communications. I've selected you to be the command staff, but I will need your help in filling out the crew. Any recommendations would be helpful."

Robert Orff sniffed. "Would I be wrong to assume that this is *the* Wargame, then, ma'am?"

"I can't answer that as yet," Morrison said, smiling. "But I think just saying that gives you your answer."

Chris looked thoughtful. "We're staffing a corvette, you say? Can I ask what the breakdown is for our crew, and any other information you can give us about the scenario, so far?"

Morrison nodded at him. "Good questions. I'll give you each an encrypted file with all of the information I'm allowed to provide, but here's the situation in a nutshell: The ship you'll be assigned to a converted gunboat, perhaps the last of her kind to come from the failed policies of a century ago. Her name's the *Chihuahua*." This produced some chuckles in the room." It'll be your job to get her ready for action in just three weeks. And Admiral Mumford," she nodded to Emily, "Has assured me that he'll support any requests for personnel I make. He wants to see what we can do."

"Ma'am," Rachel began. "How long do we have to give you our lists?"

Morrison considered the question for a moment. "I need to give Admiral Mumford my list in ten days if I want to get my choices guaranteed. I want a little time to evaluate your proposals, too, so... get them to me as soon as possible, but no later than Thursday." She paused. "If you want to work in groups of two or three, that would be all right, but I want enough independent lists to provide me with real alternatives."

"Yes, ma'am," the cadets all chorused.

"Okay, then, people. Get to work."

Rachel followed Chris and Schubert into their quarters. By some unspoken agreement, they had decided to work together for this latest project. Schubert sat on a chair, Rachel took up position against a wall, and Chris collapsed into his bunk, pillowing his hands on his crossed forearms.

"I don't know if I can do this," Chris sighed. "I barely know fifteen people in the Academy by name, much less two hundred and fifteen. And I wouldn't even recommend everyone I know for shipboard duty! Take Wayne Evans and Eric Drake, for example. I imagine they'll make great scientists, one day, but they're too interested in theory to concern themselves with what'll be needed to restore an antique corvette!"

Rachel turned. "An antique corvette? I hadn't thought of it, that way... I suppose this'll be right up your alley, won't it, Mr. Desaix?"

"Well, maybe once we start working on the ship, itself," Chris replied, grinning reluctantly.

"Actually," Schubert interjected, thumbing through the files Captain Morrison had given them on his hand comp. "I think they both would be good choices. Wayne's scientific interest is not particularly useful once the Wargame starts, but he'd probably be a pretty good choice to head the environmental engineering section. It's only got nine people, and none of them are battle-critical – their main job will be working on environmental systems for the refit, which they're ideal for. Plus, if we're going to add in features to modernize the safety systems, it might be good to have a theorist aboard. I mean, *Chihuahua* doesn't even have an antigrav system installed yet – just magnetic boot lockers and suspension chairs. Someone who understands the theory and specializes in environmental systems would be able to rig one up more efficiently than an engineering generalist like yourself."

Antigrav, while sought after for centuries, was a relatively recent invention, having come into service roughly seventy years beforehand. It allowed people to remain standing on the deck, and compensated automatically for any amount of g-force strain a ship's acceleration might cause. Prior to its invention, when magnetic boots were used to simulate 'real' gravity, any significant acceleration (and consequently, any combat action) had to be done after the crew had strapped themselves into the suspension chairs at their duty stations. These chairs were very good at deflecting the force of gravity away from the person seated in them, but had the very nasty habit of giving out at around one hundred and fifty times normal gravity, thereby limiting acceleration. Thanks to the invention of antigrav, however, ships were now able to accelerate to their top speed as fast as their engines would allow – which was extremely fast indeed in the case of the fusion drive, like *Chihuahua* had. The newer quantum wheels took longer to accelerate from a dead stop to full speed, but even their acceleration was significantly higher than what a shock chair could withstand.

"True, I suppose," Chris agreed reluctantly. "And I guess it might be good to have someone like Eric in the Engineering room to help integrate the newer systems I might not be entirely familiar with. But I'll probably need to actually use those Lieutenant's bars of mine – someone will need to keep him from trying one of the engineering 'experiments' he's devised based on the crackpot theories he follows."

"Uh, do you know any enlisted people, by the way?" Schubert asked.

Chris gave him a wry grin. "Oh, well, I guess I know one. Petty Officer Trainee Jonathan Rosebaugh, working to be a weapons tech. But I don't think he's exactly the sort of person the Old Lady wants."

"Well, we'll list him, anyway. I don't know many qualified weapons techs, and I doubt Rache does, either."

Chris turned his eyes back on her, as if suddenly noticing that she'd gone quiet. "I suppose this means my off day is going to have to be spent hammering out a crew manifest with you rather than playing chess, right?"

Rachel frowned. *Well, that's what we should be doing… but I don't like the look in his eyes, still. I've got to find out what's been bothering him. And we* do *have a week.*

"If you believe a little thing like this is going to keep me from beating the pants off of you at chess tomorrow, Mr. Cadet Lieutenant Christopher Desaix, you've got another thing coming!" she snapped, her face a comic parody of her usual stern expression as she sputtered out a little modification of his moniker for her. "I've got to get some sleep before we play, but at 0900 tomorrow you *will* report to me in my quarters for a best-of-five set of chess games, and that's an order. Then, and only then, will we worry about scheduling times for us to get together and work on this project."

Struggling to keep from laughing, Chris gave her a sloppy salute. "Aye, aye, Cadet Lieutenant Commander *Rache*, ma'am."

Smiling at the officious use of her hated nickname, Rachel nodded. Some of his playful spirit was back, at least when it came to teasing her.

Schubert waited for Rachel to leave before turning to his bunkmate. This wasn't exactly a conversation he wanted to keep secret from her, but he didn't figure Chris would open up to him while she was around. He had to find out just what was wrong with the man.

The problem was, Schubert had no idea how to broach the subject.

"Seemed as if you and Rache weren't fighting as much as usual, today," he said.

Chris yawned, rolling slowly off his bed. "We've got a bit of a 'truce' in place. Just until we recover from the long hours we spent working on that last project... and, I suppose, from the hours we'll spend working on this coming project, too."

"Really?" Schubert answered, grinning. "And how long will it take you to recover, huh?"

Chris grabbed a pair of pajamas and headed into the bathroom. "I'll let you know when I have. It depends on how many hours I have to put into repairing the *Chihuahua*," he said over his shoulder.

"And how long do you think Rache will give you to recover?" Schubert said through the door.

"Until she gets bored of beating me at chess," Chris replied, yawning audibly. "Which shouldn't take too long, unless she's even more vindictive than I give her credit for."

"I have yet to understand why you like the game so much, considering how poorly you play it."

Chris emerged from the bathroom, buttoning up his pajama shirt. "It's a fun game, and it's thousands of years old. Need I say more?"

Schubert rolled his eyes. "No, I suppose not."

"Well, I gotta go to bed," he said hesitantly. "I want to stand a chance tomorrow."

Schubert noted the hesitation, and didn't like it. Whatever was bothering Chris was making him reluctant to go to sleep, and it didn't seem like he'd get a chance to talk with him about it.

Well, maybe Rachel will have a chance, tomorrow. I'll have to let her know.

Rachel blinked, not quite believing what she just saw. "You're opening with the Paris Defense? Are you trying to lose this game?"

The Paris Defense, sometimes known as the Paris Gambit, the Paris Opening, the Drunken Knight Opening, the Ammonia Opening, or even the AMAR (Absolutely Mad And Ridiculous) Opening, was a rather unique chess maneuver. Instead of pushing forward a pawn or moving a knight to a central position, the knights (starting with the King-side knight) were pushed to the edges of the board in the first two moves. It was rarely seen in chess play, however, as it seemed to have one extremely serious flaw: It was almost impossible to win using it.

"Well, Rache," Chris replied. "This is our first game against each other, and you don't know how I play. I certainly don't know how you play, either, but in this case the advantage is more mine than yours, since I have a very hard time 'reading' what my opponent is going to do. I have to figure my best shot is putting forward something you haven't seen before... and I doubt you've matched up against a Paris Defense very often, have you?"

"Well, no, never, but the move is suicide!" she answered, recovering enough to consider her moves carefully.

"I'm hardly likely to present much of a challenge to you unless I try the unexpected from time to time. I annihilated Jeff the first time we played using this opening. I figure I've got at least a shot of winning, this time."

Rachel narrowed her eyes suspiciously. "I thought you weren't any good at chess," she accused, moving a pawn.

"I'm not," he shot back, moving one of his rooks a step towards his king. "Or, to put a qualifier on it, I'm not when I've only got two dimensions to consider. What Jeff doesn't know is that, if you add in a chess clock and include the losing condition of 'out of time,' I actually have a pretty decent record. But Jeff doesn't have a chess clock, so he's never had to deal with that factor. Since I usually win by stalling until my opponent runs out of time, my best chance without one is to take other players by surprise. Like I told him, though, my biggest problem with the game is that there are only two dimensions. The clock, however, adds a third."

"I'm surprised you haven't spent some of your time working on a chess clock, just for that reason." Another chess piece, this a bishop, came into play.

"I will," Chris noted. "But parts are hard to come by, and I only got the last of them a couple weeks ago. I haven't been able to get started yet." His own movement was swift and sure as his pawns started to come into play.

They traded their next few moves in silence, but Rachel wasn't keeping her mind on the game. Schubert had secretly called her that morning, letting her know that Chris was still sleeping fitfully. He'd said he hadn't been able to talk to Chris about it, though he'd tried. Rachel thanked him for the report, and immediately decided to confront Mr. Desaix that day.

After a brief flurry of moves in which both sides lost a number of pawns, Rachel finally came up with something to say. "How long would it take you to fix that chess clock of yours, now that you've got the parts?"

Chris considered things for a moment, quickly took her queen with the knight he had moved his first turn of the game, and shrugged. "Well, that's very delicate work. The better part of a day, at least."

Rachel couldn't believe she'd made such a stupid mistake, but then he'd been right. She didn't know how to deal with the tactics he was throwing at her and the game needed her full attention if she was going to win. Which, she realized now, she wasn't – she'd been too absorbed in other things to realize what Chris was doing to her, and now it was too late to get out of his trap. She might escape this particular strike he'd set up, but she wouldn't have the pieces left she needed to win. It was time to start looking for the draw.

"Uh, well," she said, trying to remember what she had been about to say. "How about you and I meet up with Schubert and work out those rosters for Captain Morrison after lunch? Then I'll let you have tomorrow off to build that clock." She started trying to punch a hole out for her king to escape through. "I've played chess against Jeff, myself, and he's a monster. If you think you stand a real chance against him in a timed game, I'm all for the opportunity to humiliate him a little."

"Good plan. And thanks – I've wanted to get that clock built since my second game with Jeff." He studied the board and shook his head. "You know, tactically, you and Jeff have a lot in common. I saw that plan of his for the sim. It was a lot cruder than the proposal you'd put together, but it was similar. Very similar." He made another move. "And you made the exact same mistake against my version of the Paris Defense that he did. Checkmate."

Rachel gawked at the board. She'd just lost to the Paris Defense! She must have been even more out of it than she'd realized. Well, she couldn't let that happen again. She had to try that one more time. "Another game. Now."

Chris laughed. "Hmm, somehow I expected you to say that."

He started to set up the board, and Rachel returned to thinking about how to make him open up about his problem. She started the game, but as much as she wanted to get revenge for her first defeat, her heart wasn't in it.

"What's on your mind?" Chris asked softly.

"Huh?" Rachel said, blinking up at him.

"Well," he said, taking one of her bishops with a pawn. "It seems pretty obvious you've got something on your mind, and it sure isn't chess. You were playing better last game – as good as you are, if you were paying any attention you should be wiping the floor with me. Are you worried about something? Is it the Wargame?"

Rachel paused. Well, this was as good an opportunity as any. "Yeah, I'm worried about something... but it isn't the Wargame."

Chris grinned. "Well, what is it? Maybe I can help."

"Other way around," she said, catching his eye. "What I'm worried about is you."

"Me?" he squawked with restrained laughter. "What am I doing to worry you?" He looked down and inspected his clothes – in honor of the occasion, he'd shown up in his uniform khakis. "Is my gig line crooked or something?"

"I wish it was that simple," she answered, smiling weakly. "Look, Chris, it's painfully obvious to those of us who know you reasonably well that something's bothering you. You look more exhausted than our work on the sim can account for. Schubert tells me you're moving around violently in your sleep... and you seem reluctant to even take a nap to rest yourself. Something's obviously bothering you, Chris, and I feel like it's my fault."

Chris waited patiently and sighed. "Are you finished?" he asked steadily. Rachel reluctantly nodded, so he continued. "Okay, I know I don't look well. I know my eyes are bloodshot, my comebacks aren't as fierce, and my speech is a little slurred." Rachel blinked – that was one symptom she hadn't noticed. "I'm honestly not even surprised to hear how I'm thrashing about in my sleep. But it's nothing – really! I've just been under a lot of stress lately, and now that I do have some time to rest I'm having a few nightmares. It's not a big deal, so don't worry about it."

Rachel nodded, but refused to drop it. "Okay, I can understand that. But don't tell me not to worry about it – I can decide what I should worry about and what I shouldn't. And you aren't getting away with saying you're having nightmares that violent without telling more about that."

Chris snorted. "And just how are you going to make me tell you about them? You don't have the right to order me to, that's for sure."

"You're right, I can't order you." She smirked, but it didn't reach her eyes. "But I can still ask you, and trust you respect me enough to give me an honest answer."

The battle of wills turned into a staring contest as Chris tried to glare Rachel into backing down. She refused to yield, though, and he finally relented.

"I'm not sure if I can explain it very well," he said.

"Just try. That's all I ask."

Chris chewed his lip hesitantly. "Well, I suppose the first step is to show you something. Hold on."

He started unbuttoning his shirt, and Rachel looked at him questioningly as she realized what he was doing.

Chris shot her a wicked glance. "Don't worry – I'm not planning on showing you anything you haven't seen before. I'm just taking off my shirt – I'm wearing something underneath."

Rachel flushed slightly. "Well, warn me next time!"

He just shook his head in amusement as he continued to remove the khaki shirt and pulled up the t-shirt underneath about chest-level. The revealed skin showed a rather nasty-looking bruise and various other minor abrasions. Rachel was astonished – what could have done this to him, and what did this have to do with his nightmares?

"I have very... realistic nightmares," Chris said. "Sometimes I even get a bruise or some other minor injury tossing around while I'm asleep." He tucked his undershirt back in and started replacing his khaki top. "I talked to a doctor about it, and he sent me to a psychiatrist. The psychiatrist sent me back to another doctor – a sleep specialist. I got them all together and they finally agreed that it's a psychosomatic condition related to the nocebo effect. I'm not the only person this has happened to, though it's rarely affects people as much as it does me, and even the Navy medical department says it's nothing serious to worry about. That is, unless you consider minor bumps and scrapes a serious medical condition."

"That looks like it's a lot worse than *minor* to me," Rachel noted.

"Well, it wasn't that bad, at first. At first, it really was just a little sore spot, not even a bruise." He grinned wryly. "The problem is, like when you take repeated punches to the same spot, it tends to bruise up... and when I have the same nightmare several times in a row, well, I think you get the picture."

Rachel closed her eyes and leaned back in contemplation. "So you've not just been having nightmares, you've been having the same nightmare over and over again, is that it?"

"Pretty much," Chris said. "Oh, there are always minor differences, but... the end results are always the same."

"Chris," Rachel said slowly. "What is this nightmare about?"

There was a pause, where Chris seemed to be having a debate with himself. Resolved, he pulled out his hand comp and started keying in a few commands. Nodding, he handed it to her. "That is what I keep dreaming."

Rachel looked at the display on the hand comp briefly. "These are eval results from the macrosim. And for our project, too... why didn't you show them to me?"

Chris closed his eyes tiredly. "I did, just not in that much detail. They're the worst-case sims. I go to sleep at night and see myself in command of a fleet of ships just like we were given to work with in the scenario. I see myself following my plans. And then something goes wrong, and I can't think clearly enough to fix it... and suddenly, my fleet has been wiped out, and the enemy force combines their fire on my flagship. And then I see a piece of debris headed for my chest, slamming into it... and then either I wake up, or... well, or I dream about it again." He shrugged. "There are times sleep just isn't very appealing to me, however much I need it."

Rachel swallowed nervously. It really was all her fault – she had been putting too much pressure on him. True, the Academy was supposed to put its students through as strenuous a life as possible to try and wash out as many officers that couldn't hack it as it could, but as a freshman he hadn't been trained to deal with that level of stress, yet. He was being pressured for bigger and better things from a full Admiral for crying out loud, and *she* had the gall to add to it by nitpicking his uniform's appearance after waking him up at four in the morning.

"I'm sorry," she whispered.

He laughed. "This is why I didn't want to tell you. Please, don't feel responsible for any of this – it's all on my head. And now that I don't have to worry about this project any more, I'm pretty sure I'll get back to normal soon. But I hope you see why I don't want a career in tactics, now. Something I doubt Admiral McCaffrey and his friends will ever understand."

Rachel smiled up at him softly. Obviously, he was trying to say he didn't want her to let up on him too much. For him, apparently, changing that about her would be worse than the pressure she was already putting on him. *Well, if that's what he wants...*

"Oh, I'm not sure that I don't still agree with them, even after learning about this," she said, grinning. She would keep pressuring him... but she'd start by helping him learn to cope with stress better, first. "Things could change. Wait until you're through your sophomore year before ruling it out, okay?" Her eyes twinkled. "And I'll be keeping you on your toes until then, so you'd better listen to me!"

He smiled back. "I'll think about it. In the meantime, I think it's your move. So, just how are you going to deal with the loss of that bishop, anyway?"

Chapter IV

Staff Sergeant Roland Murphy, acting as a messenger, rapped on the oak door to Colonel Andrew Beccera's office three times and waited. He'd never met the Colonel before, but he knew him by reputation. Beccera had been a Captain some thirty years before, the last time that the Earth Alliance Army was deployed in anger, and was in some respects still recovering from that war. He'd won a battlefield promotion to Major early on, but later was severely wounded in action. He was promoted to Colonel, and the Army had tried to give him a desk job. Beccera refused to accept it, however, even though the surgeons who had repaired his wounds spent almost a full year (unsuccessfully) trying to remove all of the shrapnel. Thanks to the recent peace, the Army was able to keep him from a major duty station, but not for his lack of trying. He had repeatedly avoided assignments he saw as a permanent desk jobs, going so far as refusing several promotions in order to retain field duty eligibility.

That Murphy was the secretary and Aide-de-Camp for Brigadier General James Austin didn't make him feel any less uneasy. After all, General Austin was the officer in charge of personnel, and that automatically made him the natural enemy of officers who loved to refuse desk assignments. He was just there to coordinate a time for the General and the Colonel to meet, however, so maybe he would escape unscathed this time.

"Come in," a gruff voice said from the other side of the door. Sergeant Murphy winced – that did not sound like a man in a good mood.

"Sir!" he said, saluting as he entered the office. His eyes traveled over the room. In Murphy's opinion, it looked more like a museum than an office. On top of a set of file cabinets lay a number of historic trinkets, including an antique Japanese katana, various classical styles of firearms, and a number of hats and caps representing numerous era's different military forces. Pinned to the walls were more uniforms from antiquity, old-style photographs, a few tattered cloth flags. Add in the dozens of other little trinkets from various eras of military history, and the place had the sense of being a shrine to the armies of the ancients.

Colonel Beccera returned the salute. "I'm afraid I wasn't told of your coming, Sergeant..."

"Murphy, sir."

"Sergeant Murphy. May I ask why you're here?" He seemed somewhat amused, although a little wary.

"I'm here from General Austin's office. He wishes to schedule a face-to-face meeting with you as soon as possible."

The Colonel's eyes hardened. "Ah. I see. You should have just commed my staff to do that."

"I did, sir," Murphy said, carefully keeping all emotion out of his face. He knew when he was being given the run-around. "But for some reason, once I told them where I was from, I never could find anyone who would allow me to talk to you directly. So I took a shuttle from Earth, transferred onto the next cutter delivering your supplies, and came here in person. I figured that was the only way we'd ever talk."

Beccera continued to glare at him for a few seconds before a smile cracked his lips. "Well, I can't imagine why my staff is having so many problems. Since you've gone to all this trouble, I suppose I can at least hear you out. What's this meeting about?"

"Well, sir, your time in this post is up. In fact, you're overdue for a rotation elsewhere," Murphy began, watching the Colonel closely. Beccera just nodded impatiently, so he continued, "Essentially, we have more than one assignment open to you, and General Austin wishes to discuss your options. I am told at least one of these options may expire if you fail to meet with him within the next few days."

The Colonel grimly nodded, leaning forward. "I see. And if I refuse to attend any of these meetings?"

Murphy smiled devilishly. "I believe in that case the General will be making your decision for you."

Beccera stood up and offered his hand. Somewhat hesitantly, the Sergeant took it, and they shook. "Good day, Sergeant. Please, see Corporal Deborah Culp on your way out. She'll be in a better position to give you an answer than I."

Murphy walked out. *Did I just get him to agree?*

Earth Alliance Army Headquarters. CAC Building

Sally Hannah gave a pleasant smile as she entered the room. "Vice Admiral Craig sends her apologies, gentlemen, but she will be a few minutes late. An unexpected storm is forcing her to shuttle in from further out than she would have liked."

Admiral Pratchet, the Navy's senior most officer, nodded. "Well, we can start without her. Why don't you stick around, Sally, and take some notes to help bring Lee up to speed when she arrives."

Hannah looked at Admiral Mumford, who nodded. "Very well, sir. Just give me a moment to get my hand comp."

"Most of us know each other, but not everyone, I think." Pratchet grinned. "So everyone, please let us know who you are before you speak. Pierre, would you care to get the ball rolling?"

Mumford nodded. "Pierre Mumford. I am in overall command of assembling the personnel we need for this thing, though I have to admit I've delegated much of that to the two people sitting next to me." He nodded to the man on his right.

The only person in the room not in a Naval uniform stiffened, all eyes on him. "General Alexander Preble. I'm the new Commandant of the Marine Corps. This will be my first encounter with the War Game – I've always been on the outside looking in. I'm officially in charge of picking which Marines participate and which get to stay on station like I always have."

"Mike?" Pratchet prompted, gesturing to his left.

"Admiral Michael McCaffrey. Pierre's being modest – he's done a lot of work. Really, it's taken a lot of co-ordination between us to get this far. This exercise is so manpower-intensive, one of us needs to be in charge of picking people to assign to the Wargame and the other has to figure out how to cover for the absence of those same people."

"The drain on manpower is scary," Mumford agreed. "But that is a topic for another meeting. This is about the Wargame itself. Ken?"

"At this time, I'd like to introduce the command structure for the Fleet side of the Wargame," Pratchet said ruefully. "But Lee hasn't gotten here yet. Most of her fleet commanders are, however – and I'm guessing they'd rather introduce themselves than have me do it for them. Arnold?"

"Rear Admiral Arnold Honeycutt," a plump, somewhat jolly-looking man laughed. "And I'm not sure I want to know what you'd tell people about me, Ken. I'm told I will be commanding the First Division for the Wargame's 'Fleet' side." He grinned, pointing to his lapel. "The second star's new, and it's the first time I'll command such a large force – even in a simulated environment. Looking forward to it."

Pratchet snorted. "You'll do fine – you've been good commanding smaller forces. Leanne?"

"Commodore Leanne Chapelle. I'll be taking the Second Division. This will be my last hurrah before assuming command of the Pleiades Embassy Station."

Pratchet snorted. Pleiades Embassy Station was one of the cushiest duty assignments in the Navy – practically no responsibilities outside of having to schmooze at a few parties, and the Embassy always had the best of food and entertainment as part of the "putting a good face forward" part of Earth Alliance propaganda. "Enjoy your vacation. Amanda?"

"Commodore Amanda Klingler. But why call on me? I thought I was supposed to be the chief liaison to the local civilian authorities."

"Sorry, Commodore, that's my fault," McCaffrey said apologetically. "I told Ken before I told you. You may wind up commanding the Third Division, instead," McCaffrey noted. "But only if there is a Third Division – we're still working on that."

"But that brings up a point," Pratchet said. "There is a civilian authority during these exercises, and we'll all have to be especially careful not to step on their toes. I don't suppose you know who any of them are, yet, do you?"

Amanda shrugged. "I recently met with Dennis Lindquist, Deputy Governor of Colony Station Alpha-32 in the 94 Ceti Beta System. All three systems are in the infancy of their development, and currently they're the most developed – they've actually terraformed some habitable sections of their planet, which the other two systems have yet to do. At the moment, one of the other two systems is occupied by little more than claimant buoys, and the other is still an early stages of their terraforming operation. I have yet to meet the Governor himself, however – someone named Geraci. I have no idea how involved either will be in the exercise."

"Also," Pratchet continued as Sally returned. "Vice Admiral Lee Craig will be the Commander-in-Chief for Fleet. Now that the introductions are over, Pierre? You're up again."

Admiral Mumford nodded. "Well, I'll be in overall command of the exercise, but in practice that means very little. I'll be an observer and will adjudicate any disputes that the computers can't resolve automatically. But most of my job will be over once the Wargame starts. Until then, though, I'm also the person who's responsible for the whole mess."

"The Wargame is always a logistical nightmare," Commodore Klingler snorted. "Earth Fleet must contain at least forty percent of all commissioned military ships, by law. More ships than we could possibly need, all in one place, and we can't touch them at all for this exercise."

"The law's the law," Pratchet shrugged.

"What I don't see is why you put an idiot like Captain Green in command of the Academy Forces," Rear Admiral Honeycutt complained. "The sides are already so unevenly matched that Fleet is going to make mincemeat of the Academy. Can't we make it a better challenge by at least posting someone competent in command?"

"Captain Green is hardly an incompetent," Admiral Pratchet said with a warning look. "He's been on the fast-track for promotion ever since he joined the Navy."

"He's more lucky than good," Honeycutt argued doggedly. "And his skills are not as a tactician, but as a diplomat. In the context of fighting the Wargame, he *is* an incompetent."

General Preble of the Marines shifted his weight uncomfortably. "This worries me. Was his appointment a result of our request?"

Admiral McCaffrey's lips quivered. "The Marines want a say in the Academy's CO? Now, why haven't I heard anything about this?"

"Sorry, Mike," Admiral Pratchet apologized. "Alex approached Admiral Mumford and I asking that the person we picked as a CO be a Captain with less than thirty years seniority." He grinned. "Considering we always choose a Captain looking for promotion up to flag rank, and we don't have any captains with nearly that many years seniority in the Navy, we figured it wouldn't be enough of a problem to concern you."

McCaffrey considered, then turned to the Marine general. "Just why did you make that request, if I may ask?"

Preble smiled slightly. "It's a long story. It has to do with a handshake deal I made with General Austin of the Army, and that's all I'm going to say about that."

"But why would the Army—" McCaffrey began.

"Mike, drop it," Pratchet intervened. "Suffice to say, it had no impact on our decision, as it eliminated no-one from consideration."

"Then why was Captain Green made the CO of the Academy?" Honeycutt asked.

Pratchet grimaced. "Green was not selected by us, but by the civilian authorities. The Senate Defense Committee wanted him for the job."

Silence met that pronouncement. "Forgive me for my ignorance," Preble finally said. "But I'm afraid I don't quite understand. Why is the senate able to affect the minutiae of such things as who gets what command in a simple war game? That oversteps anything that has happened to me in my tenure as the Marine Corps commandant."

The Wargame veterans looked at one another knowingly. "I suppose I should explain," Pratchet began softly. "Most war games are small affairs, involving only a few ships in a very isolated part of space. *The* Wargame is a little different – it is the largest military exercise we run outside of an actual war. Hell, it's larger than some wars. We need a significant amount of support from the civilian government, just to obtain the physical resources needed to try it. We don't just need the permission of a local government, but the support of the entire Congress and the President in order to use three star systems and a large percentage of the Fleet. We're fortunate that Captain Green's appointment is the only thing the Senate insisted upon, as it stands."

Preble grimaced. "Fortunately, Commandant of the Marine Corps is a less prominent position to politicians eyes – while my job has involved a lot of political schmoozing, I haven't had to deal with that kind of interference. At least not yet – I'm less than a year into my term."

Pratchet grinned ruefully. "You've been lucky. But enough about that. We still need to discuss how we'll come up with the necessary ships for the 'Fleet' side of the Wargame. Our Navy currently maintains eighty commissioned battleships, forty of which are in Home Fleet. Twelve of the eighty are deployed on various foreign assignments, and simply aren't available. That leaves us with a pool of twenty-eight battleships to draw from. Now, the Academy will have twenty admittedly old battleships, which will be re-commissioned for the exercise, so I would like to give the Fleet side at least fifteen of its own." He sighed. "Vice Admiral Breslau's Division would be able to supply more than half of those needs, but our Ambassador in 16 Cygni thinks we need his ships cruising near her post for political reasons. We're going to have to strip planetary defenses to the bone, it looks like. We've been directed to avoid removing ships from dispatch or convoy duties."

McCaffrey sighed. "I always hate this part of the Wargame. It makes our border planets so vulnerable."

"They're always vulnerable," Admiral Mumford complained. "As things stand, we can only cover home fleet and a handful of our major systems with the ships we have, and some of those systems are barely covered at all. Border worlds are generally forced to use Orbital Guard ships for protection. We need more ships."

"That is precisely why we haven't retired the Cleopatra class battleships yet," Pratchet sighed. "And won't, even after the next fifteen in the Argus class are complete. In fact, I'm tempted to leave the twenty Sirius-class battleships we're restoring in service after the Wargame, and maybe some of the other re-commissioned ships, too. We're finally getting the financial backing to start upgrading our support fleet the way we need to, but if we ever go to war we'll need more ships. We can only fully defend three worlds outside of Earth, and barely maintain a token presence in a dozen other systems. If we end up at war any time in the next twenty years or so, under projected construction rates, we'll lose almost thirty systems without even being able to fire a shot." Pratchet shook his head. "Let's hope we can convince the money counters to buy in the Academy's refit ships. The only reason the vulture states like the 16 Cygni Confederation haven't attacked us is that we've developed a somewhat unwarranted reputation for never losing a war. Sure, on paper we've got the largest military of anyone, but we're spread too thin."

"I wouldn't be too worried," General Preble said. "We might be stretched a little, but the only nation which has shown us any hostility in the past thirty years is 16 Cygni itself, and while they may be tempted to raid us we could easily annihilate their entire nation in response. Who else would risk starting a war against us?"

The Navy personnel present all had grim looks at that, but no-one said anything.

"Well," Pratchet said, changing the topic. "We need to get back down to the business of selecting the ships for this assignment. Admiral Honeycutt, your recommendations?"

Cygni Confederation, 16 Cygni, Earth Alliance Embassy

"Rear Admiral Fulton is here to see you, Ambassador," the intercom echoed through Noriko Goldsmith's office.   Goldsmith was the Ambassador for the Earth Alliance to its strongest historical enemy, the Cygni Confederation. It was a thankless job, and a difficult one, but the very existence of an embassy on Cygni was something of a feat.

Around the star 16 Cygni orbited one of the more bizarre inhabited planets in the known universe. It was the capital of a major interstellar power literally founded on piracy some four hundred years before. Eight pirates, looking to retire, used their plunder to purchase four whole planetary systems and established a 'constitution' based on their articles of piracy. The government had slowly evolved from its pirate origins into a more legitimate institution, but it was still known for launching quite a few wars over some rather creative 'grievances.' Most of those wars were very short, ending as soon as they'd been able to raid and plunder a planet or three. Their longest war had been against the Earth Alliance, with Cygni supported by the Federal Republic of Iota Draconis and a small cluster of independent systems. In the end, Iota Draconis turned against Cygni when they learned that their allies had misled them about the Earth Alliance's culpability in the action that started the war. Despite Iota Draconis changing sides, Cygni had somehow escaped the war with more planets than it had started with, having annexed many of the independent planets which had been its "allies" in the war.

That had been over thirty years ago, and Cygni no longer had any special hatred for the Alliance, but that had never stopped them from starting a war last time. That was what made Goldsmith's job so difficult – she had to keep Cygni from finding some justification to start a war.   She knew just how vulnerable the Earth Alliance really was, and was very concerned that information would leak out to Cygni.

In truth, the Alliance had never recovered from the last war. It still had a plethora of battleships, but not enough for a new conflict with Cygni. Thanks largely to Cygni's massive strikes against Alliance shipping (and hence, the warships that had been assigned to escort major convoys), most of the Navy's smaller ships had been destroyed or crippled in the last war. The peace treaty which ended it put a serious limit on how much new construction each naval base was permitted, but thankfully that only applied to bases built at the time the war had ended. It took decades to establish the support necessary for a new shipyard of sufficient size, but recently a massive Navy Yard was completed at Epsilon Eridani. It was beginning to look as if they might finally be able to build up enough force to defend their borders within the next few years, but every Ambassador the Alliance had was given a special briefing on just how important it was to avoid conflict at *this* time, in particular.

Goldsmith shook her head. There wasn't time to worry about that now. She had to find out what brought one of her Navy's Admirals out for an unscheduled meeting. "Send him in," she said.

A middle-aged Navy man wearing a rather battered-looking white dress uniform stepped into the room, holding a hand comp and a stylus. "Hello, Ambassador Goldsmith," he said.

"Admiral," she nodded, acknowledging him with the minimum of formality. "Please, have a seat. Are your ships being recalled or something?"

Hawkeye Fulton, one of the more experienced Rear Admirals thanks to his years on the Cygni Patrol, grinned at her. "Hardly. No, someone upstairs is actually listening to you, for once. It's a bit of an open secret in the Navy that we're amassing a fleet for the Wargame. Instead of doing what we've often done in the past and pulling ships from the two undersized squadrons patrolling our most dangerous border – this one – they're stripping some planetary systems down to the bare bones to provide the necessary forces." He cleared his throat. "However, *your* ship is being recalled."

"Eh?" Goldsmith blinked. "You're taking the *Terrapin* from me? Why?"

"Vice-Admiral Breslau's orders. Since you've requested a 'show of force,' he thought the Ambassador's Yacht should be something a bit more powerful than a thirty year old corvette. He's replacing her with one of our Valkyrie class heavy cruisers." He paused, then smiled sourly. "At least that's the official reason. Her hyperspace drive was acting up a little, so he's making the switch. He figures she should stay here until they figure out what's causing the problems with her engines. The transfer is as permanent as it gets, though."

"Well, that's interesting," the Ambassador said. "But that doesn't really explain why *you* are here. I'd have expected the captain of the incoming heavy cruiser to report to me himself."

"Normally he would," Hawkeye replied. "But I was down here anyway, so I figured I could deliver the news, myself." He set his hand comp in front of her. "Here. Latest reports from Military Intelligence."

As she read through the report, Noriko paled. "Are these numbers correct?"

"As near as I can tell," he replied. "Within the next two months, the Cygni Confederation fleet will have another twenty battleships commissioned. With sixty-three warships of that size at their disposal, they'll be a match for us again."

"Which means that within the next two months, they'll be ready for another war," Noriko sighed. "Great. Looks like I'll be even busier than usual for a while. Well, at least you're able to keep your squadron nearby. With your ships in the neighborhood, we can at least try to bluff that we're still a match."

"Maybe," Hawkeye replied doubtfully. "But I'm guessing not. Their intelligence on us is probably as good as ours, if not better. They have to know we're in deep shit when it comes to our tactical position. Sorry, Noriko, but my squadron being here is next to useless. Be on your guard while we're gone – if they're going to start a war, it'll be now." He paused. "And we won't be ready for them."

Chapter V

"You *were* aware that scientists in this directorate are supposed to submit findings to my office for review before sending them out for publication, weren't you, Dr. Foley?" Director Karlsson demanded. Flanking the Director stood a WISPR agent in full black armorwrap, complete with hood and mask. Foley wasn't sure of the reason for his presence, but wasn't about to ask.

He swallowed nervously. Director Karlsson was a very important man, and a very powerful one. He was also one of the strictest authoritarians ever assigned to his position. He could ruin the career of any scientist if he desired. In Foley's case, he could do even more: Foley had signed a confidentiality agreement when he accepted funding from the Directorate. Violating that agreement was punishable with severe fines or even imprisonment.

Foley coughed. "I was, Director Karlsson."

"And yet you went ahead and published this report to the interstellar nets without even sending it through the peer review process. It took a replay of your findings in a *foreign* news report for us to discover that you had done it. That caused the Earth Alliance to ask if they could send an expedition to join the dig next month." Karlsson chided. "If you had submitted your paper for review, you would have learned that we had some concerns about announcing this before we had investigated it ourselves."

"I thought it was for the best," Foley protested. "We need some of the best experts from other star systems in order to properly investigate the finding. We don't have the right linguists to help decipher their language, for example. Several of our top scientists have left Pleiades over the last few years for a variety of reasons. I viewed this as a necessity – there are no peers to properly review my findings in Pleiades any more." Suddenly remembering who he was talking to, he paused and collected himself before continuing. "At the very least, we needed to get the services of Dr. Kimiko Beccera. Although she is not a linguist, she's the best when it comes to investigating alien artifacts. We would have had to tell her at least some of what we found to get her interested. She would have brought in some of her associates in the Earth Alliance anyway, despite her Pleiades citizenship."

"No outside participation was authorized," the WISPR officer growled. He had an unusually gravelly voice, as if with age, but instead of making him sound elderly it conveyed a great sense of power. That tone startled Dr. Foley, causing him to flinch back.

Director Karlsson raised a hand, turning to the security man in annoyance. "Skorrjh, please. What's done is done."

Skorrjh? Foley pondered nervously. *What sort of name is that?*

Karlsson turned his attention back to the archeologist, lips twisted into a false smile that looked more menacing than reassuring. "Dr. Foley... Whit. It's too late to recall your reports. I understand that. Now, we have to do some damage control, so I've got a job for you. If you do it, then you can continue on with your assignment and we won't levy any fines or additional charges against you."

"What is it?" Foley asked, anything but reassured.

"It's simple. I want you to hide the fossilized Neanderthal-like skeleton and claim it was destroyed accidentally. We don't want anyone else to study it," Karlsson explained.

"The skeleton?" Foley said, startled. "Why the skeleton? I thought... well, out of all the things I discovered I thought that would have the least security implications. That's one of the reasons I focused on it in my report and gave only a brief mention of the writing and other things we found later. A simple fossilized skeleton is never going to give anyone a technological advantage or anything like that."

Skorrjh slammed a palm down on Karlsson's desk, bouncing a small collection of trinkets and gizmos. "You ask too many questions, Dr. Foley," he growled evenly. "Consider this. How many of your foreign colleagues would have dropped their own work to travel here without your publishing that skeleton report? The linguists would have been interested in the writing, certainly, but they could have studied that from the pictures without leaving home. There are various political reasons why we would prefer to minimize foreign visitors at the moment, and there are too many Earth Alliance 'researchers' poking around here already. You've made that situation worse. Do you understand?"

Foley frowned. "But this is a tremendous scientific discovery. We don't have the proper people here in Pleiades to investigate a find like this! We need all of the help we can get, just to confirm how close it really is to a Neanderthal skeleton. One of the people we invited, Dr. Frank Orwell, is the closest thing in modern times to an expert on Neanderthals. We need his expertise if we want to know what we're looking at!"

"Whit," Karlsson sighed. "I appreciate that you were trying to do what you thought was the right thing. But this is not optional. And it's not like I'm asking you to cover up much... as you pointed out, it's just a simple, fossilized skeleton."

"But—"

"And, Dr. Foley," he continued, reverting to a more formal tone of voice. "If you feel uncomfortable lying, we could make sure the skeleton really is destroyed. Unfortunately, if we have to do that, we might accidentally catch some of the other items you particularly prize in the process."

Foley's jaw dropped. Why would Karlsson and this 'Skorrjh' fellow take such drastic measures just to hide a skeleton? The only reason Foley could think of to go to such extremes would be if he already knew about the fossils before he'd found them. But what could a fossilized skeleton hide? He had to know, but worried about what these people might do to him for investigating. Or what they might do to him if he refused. Recollection of another archaeologist from a dig similar to his, later found dead after an 'accidental' moment of explosive decompression, came to mind.

For the moment, Foley had to do everything these men wanted. Even co-operating wouldn't save him for long, he suspected, but it might buy him some time. Nodding briskly, he answered, "Very well, sir. If you want to hide that skeleton, we'll hide it." Deciding to make himself even more useful, he continued, "I even know of a convincing explanation for why it was accidentally destroyed, should anyone come by asking about it."

Karlsson nodded. "Good. See to it that you keep the story straight in your head, though. It wouldn't do for someone to get the 'wrong' idea."

Foley nodded hastily. "Yes, of course, Director."

"Now, get out of my office," Karlsson snapped, losing all pretence of collegiality.

"Yes, sir," Foley replied, making a hasty retreat. Foley would do everything in his power to determine what was going on, but he would have to do it quietly. And, in the meantime, he would make sure he followed the Director's orders. It wouldn't do to make the man suspicious.

Skorrjh addressed the Director once he was sure Foley had departed.

"I don't like it," he growled. The officer removed his mask, sweeping back his sandy blond hair, revealing an inhumanly heavy brow ridge.

"Neither do I," Karlsson replied. "But I don't think we've got a choice. The damage has already been done – we have to contain it as much as possible. If he does as instructed and tells the other scientists that the skeleton was destroyed, we might be okay."

"That's not sufficient" the WISPR officer growled. "Those scientists cannot be allowed entry to the ruins."

"What do you expect us to do? These are the top scientists in their field. Denying them entry would look suspicious at this point, and their reputation would make it difficult to arrange for some 'accident' to happen to all of them without serious repercussions."

That clearly didn't satisfy the WISPR agent. "I need to speak with your President. If we can't deny them entry one way, then perhaps we can find another."

Earth Alliance Naval Headquarters, Admiralty Building

Admiral Mumford frowned as he looked down the list that Captain Morrison had handed him. "You seem to be one person short," he said coolly. "Would you care to explain the omission?"

Morrison nodded. "Yes, sir. I needed a specialist and knew no-one who qualified. I'm requesting that you find me a reservist for the position. As the head of his department, I would have expected him to be assigned to me, anyway."

Mumford nodded slowly. He had given her wide latitude because she seemed competent when he'd talked to her, and because his granddaughter had recommended her, but now he was having some doubts. "What position is it?"

"I need a chief surgeon. I don't want a nurse or an intern in a position like that, should an emergency situation arise," Morrison replied. "Let's face it – with this many rookies on board a ship, there are bound to be a few serious accidents."

He realized she had a point, but the Academy had one of the better medical schools under its care. She was right about the dangers inherent in this exercise, but there wouldn't likely be too many of them for a Naval surgeon's first experience. "I suppose we can arrange for a reservist with a medical background to join your crew. I would prefer we use an internist from the medical college, however."

"I considered them, sir, but I had to reject the idea of using an internist," she interrupted without hesitation, surprising Mumford with her boldness.

"Oh? None of the other instructors complain about using internists, Why is it so different for your crew?" he asked, finally letting his frustration show in his voice.

Morrison hesitated. She hadn't expected the Admiral to be this annoyed at her request. She quickly found her resolve, however. Her fainting spells might prevent her from ever commanding a ship, but she didn't get to the rank of Captain by being completely unable to stand her ground in stressful situations.

"Simple, sir," she replied, looking him dead in the eye. "Most of your other instructors were looking for crews for ships that have more than one doctor. Thanks to her status as a former gunboat, the *Chihuahua* has a smaller medical complement than any other warship in the exercise, modern or restored. Even the other corvettes have billets for two people who can hold the watch as a doctor. In my case, I had only one... and, if there's a chance of a medical emergency, I wanted the crew to have a seasoned professional who we know can handle it rather than an inexperienced first-time surgeon who has no-one to cover for him if he freaks out." She paused. "And I did obtain the nurse and both orderlies from the medical college."

Mumford checked the crew requirements again. She was right – they did call for a lone doctor to handle the medical care of all two hundred and fifteen personnel. Some smaller ships, such as light transports (when not transporting passengers) could get away with it, but the requirements usually called for multiple doctors – usually one for every one hundred and twenty personnel on board. When the *Chihuahua* was a gunboat, she only had a crew of ninety. Her expansion into a corvette more than doubled the crew size, and that didn't even account for the added Marine complement.   Apparently, a new doctor was not added to the staffing requirements after the refit... and he hadn't checked it before handing her the assignment.

He was tempted to tell her to go ahead and double the requirements for medical staff, giving two more opportunities for the Academy Medical College's doctors. That wasn't advisable, however – most of the extra space for crew quarters had been carved out of the missile storage lockers the *Chihuahua* used when she was a gunboat, and still the crew and even some officers had to hot bunk in order to fit everyone. Adding more medical staff would only exacerbate a different problem. No, a veteran doctor was a significantly more practical solution than increasing the crew size.

"Yes, I see that now." Mumford said. His tone surprised Morrison; he wasn't known as the most forgiving of people. "I'm sorry to say that in the rush to select the ships for this year's Wargame, we didn't pay attention to your crew requirements – we just took the old list from when she was last commissioned. I'll get you that doctor, Captain Morrison. And, as I promised, I will support these other crew selections." He checked the list she had provided and almost laughed. "Four of the most requested tactical officers are in your crew, and one of them *isn't* in your tactical staff. Although I understand why he isn't – he's also one of the top ten most requested Engineering officers."

"Are you speaking of Cadet Desaix, sir?" she inquired.

Mumford nodded. "He, along with Cadets Katz, Cohen, and Langer were the four most requested Tac Officers. Ms. Katz was requested personally by every single one of her instructors, and Mr. Cohen and Mr. Desaix by several as well. Langer was too junior for anyone to seriously consider him as their senior tactician, but there were a fairly sizable number of calls for him to be an assistant tactical officer.

"Dare I ask if any other of my requests will ruin my fellow instructors' plans?" she joked.

Mumford laughed. "A few. Mr. Wolfgang Schubert was one of the top ten requested helmsmen and Eric Drake was asked for by quite a few people. Lauren Weber and my own granddaughter, Emily were both requested by other instructors, as well." His eyes twinkled. "I think your students just might surprise a few people on the Fleet side. Not enough to change the result – the Argus-class battleships just make it too lopsided – but enough to get their names noticed if they do well."

"It should be interesting, sir."

The Admiral grinned. "Yes, it should be *very* interesting."

Earth Alliance Naval Academy, Earth Campus

The door chime for the quarters shared by Christopher Desaix and Wolfgang Schubert rang softly, but no-one answered it. Rachel Katz, the sounder of that alarm, was starting to get rather frustrated at the lack of response. She, Schubert, and Chris were supposed to be meeting before the party Robert Orff was throwing. A sort of last hurrah before the 'big event.'

They would soon be boarding the *EAS Gnat*, their transport to the Wargame. Orff, in his capacity as their corvette's executive officer, had decided that the crew needed to "bond" before they had the stress of refitting a warship on their hands, and this would be the final opportunity to do so. If Chris and Schubert left for that party without her, Rachel would be 'bonding' with them using her fists.

The three of them had started working together with more of a sense of camaraderie since the Morrison project ended. Chris's nightmares had settled down to more irregular occurrences, according to Schubert, but Rachel was still keeping an eye on him to ensure his stress levels didn't get too high. Chris was slowly growing on her, though they still bickered from time to time. And she found an increasing level of respect for him rising in herself, as well — she was learning that her initial impression of him as a lazy idiot who got lucky with Admiral McCaffrey's was very mistaken. He still lacked a proper military attitude, and he still spent an amazing amount of time working on his antiques to the detriment of his class work, but he got away with it because he was *very* good at the subjects he took. As far as she could tell, he was as good at engineering as he was at tactics, if not better. Besides, he'd shown on their joint projects as partners that he was willing to pull heavy hours for class work when the pressure was on.

He was definitely going to be a very valuable resource in the upcoming Wargame. The *Chihuahua* restoration project would be difficult even for experienced engineers, but Chris was quite possibly the best man for it. He had the technical expertise for the modern engineering, but his hobby of restoring antiques would help him understand even the most archaic piece of equipment better than most active duty engineers. He would be wasted on the routine maintenance work he would be expected to handle once the *Chihuahua* was commissioned, though, which made her really wish there was some way of combining the engineering and tactical positions for him. Then again, considering how much pressure that would add (and how many nightmares that, in turn, would likely give him), perhaps it was just as well to leave it alone. Maybe, though, she could convince whoever was assigned as Captain of the *Chihuahua* to include Chris in the ship's tactical briefings.

She had also established a better rapport with Schubert. Her only real complaint with him in the past had been that he'd always sided with Chris in the 'epic battles of wit and wisdom' they had. While the man was much too brash – and occasionally foul-mouthed – for her taste, she had learned to respect the navigator-in-training's steady resolve. And his loyalty to his friends.

She had been disappointed some four days beforehand when Schubert had been suspended from the Academy for three days after a bar fight. She later was astonished to learn that someone she didn't even know named Joel Farmburg was badmouthing her, and Schubert only got into the fight because he spoke up for her. She didn't know what rumor Farmburg tried to spread, but from the scuttlebutt flying around the dorm it was, "something *she* would have kicked the bastard's ass for," as Jeff Cohen had put it. Schubert sent the man to the hospital, but had only been suspended for three days – whatever was said must have been bad enough that the Academy's disciplinarian had even sympathized with him.

When she'd asked Schubert about the matter directly, he'd answered with a rather cryptic, "It wasn't exactly the gist of what he was saying that I objected to, Ma'am. Rather, it was the tone of his voice and the crudity of the words he chose to express himself with." She didn't quite understand how that explanation would match with what she'd heard, but she intended to find out. Especially considering how formal and stilted the obviously prepared line he had used, with "Ma'am" instead of the usual "Rache" he had adopted from his roommate. Chris seemed to be just as perplexed by his answer as she was; apparently he'd been treated to the same speech, word for word (he'd even accidentally started to say "Ma'am," according to Chris).

Regardless of what was said, Schubert had leapt to her defense against the one who said it. She had briefly feared he had a crush on her or something – she definitely didn't want to deal with something like that – but apparently not. Oh, he had flirted with her on occasion, but in ways that made it obvious he was joking around rather than in any serious way. Rather, he seemed to have decided that "any friend of Chris' is a friend of mine," as he once said. She would *definitely* have objected to the term of "friend" to describe *that* relationship, but Schubert apparently thought she was close enough.

And perhaps he was right, at least in a sense – Chris seem to have very many people whom he could even consider long-term acquaintances. Jeff Cohen was a "chess partner" who Chris hardly met outside of class. Lots of Rachel's fellow classmates were jealous of Chris's accelerated promotion or were intimidated by it. Worse, she'd been given (with some censoring, as she *was* only his superior in cadet rating) a copy of his personal information file when he arrived in the dorm hall. She was the Commanding Officer of Dorm House Seven (a position similar to the RA in civilian college dorms) and received files on all of its residents, but she almost never looked at them. In recent days, she'd pulled that file out and taken a look. A lot of the file had been redacted, especially when it came to "personal history," but she noticed a conspicuous absence in the field labeled "Next of Kin." He had once mentioned a sister, but it was the wistful reminiscence of someone who hadn't spoken to his family in years.

It was unfortunate. He was a nice guy who deserved friends and family in his life. It was also unfortunate because he might need a next of kin if he didn't open that damned door pretty soon – she was starting to get frustrated enough to kill someone and he was one of the two most likely targets.

Rachel sighed. She had the skeleton key for all of the rooms in her section, and it wasn't as if it would be the first time she'd barge in on the privacy of the occupants of this particular room. She pulled it out and typed in the code for entry to the dorm room, slid the card into the optical reader, and waited impatiently for the overrides to take effect. She always felt it was counterproductive for the skeleton key to give a ten second warning chime. She had yet to figure out why that particular part of the procedure was included, but it didn't usually matter in the performance of her surprise inspection duties.

The door finally opened and she stormed inside, intent on tearing a hole into both of her fellow cadets for taking so long. She finally realized the reason for that ten second alarm when she caught Chris hastily wrapping a towel around his waist. His hair was dripping wet and a formal set of clothing that unexpectedly complimented her own choice of civilian attire was laid out on the bed. He looked somewhat embarrassed.

"Hey, Rache," he said a touch too quickly. "Sorry I'm running late – Wolf was supposed to let you know. Where is he, by the way?"

She blinked. He didn't know where Schubert was, either? "Good question. I thought you two had forgotten about me, you were taking so long... I wonder what happened to him?"

Chris grabbed his clothes and headed to the bathroom, closing the door only part-way so they could still talk. "He told me he was going to let you know I was going to be late. I thought he was going to comm you, but apparently he forgot. When did you get here?"

"I've been waiting at your door almost ten minutes. Why are you so late, anyway?"

"Got held up talking to Admiral McCaffrey," Chris answered. His voice was so casual Rachel wondered if he didn't have "chats" with the Admiral every day.

"Uh, what about?" she asked hesitantly.

"Technically it's classified, but I suppose your clearance is as valid as mine," he said, emerging from the bathroom as he buttoned up his shirt. Rachel was watching, and noticed him accidentally skip a button. She was going to say something, but decided to wait to see how long it took him to notice. "I was under the impression it was only classified because he doesn't want certain people to know he thinks they're absolute imbeciles. He warned me that I would quickly learn the man who has been put in command of our Fleet in the Wargame is an effective desk officer but tactically incompetent. He cautioned me that it would probably be unwise to criticize him."

"I'll say it would be," Rachel squawked. "Criticizing any superior officer is contrary to discipline, and can ruin the career of anyone foolish enough to say something where the person in question can hear it!"

"I know that much, I'm not a complete idiot," Chris muttered, tucking in his shirt without ever noticing the missed button. "But apparently our ship's CO doesn't. The Admiral was asking me to quietly relay that 'suggestion' to him. He even gave it to me in writing."

"Any word, yet, on who the regular Navy people are?" Rachel asked, trying to distract herself from his shirt, again.

"For the Academy side or the regular Fleet?"

"Both."

"Well, our captain is going to be one Lieutenant Commander Conrad Burkhard, a veteran XO from a frigate. He's up for promotion, and I'm told he's very good, but he has a habit of arguing with his senior officers if he thinks they've made a mistake." Chris grinned. "Mike said he's usually right."

Rachel shuddered at the use of "Mike" as a nickname for someone as exalted as Admiral McCaffrey. As a four star Admiral, only the Navy's senior-most flag officer (Admiral Pratchet) and the Acting-Chief of Naval Operations (who, by quirk of fate and the premature retirement of the former CNO, was also Admiral Pratchet) officially outranked him. Admiral McCaffrey was treating Chris as his newest protégé, so possibly they really were familiar with each other enough to address each other so informally, but even so the thought of a mere cadet like Chris (or herself) talking about a four star Admiral that way gave her the chills.

"Well it sounds as if we've got a good captain, at least," she said, trying to recover. "We'll need a good veteran officer, given what we're going to be flying. Any others?"

"The man Mike warned me about is a Captain John Green. He'll be the Commander-in-Chief for our fleet. He's known as a poor leader and a terrible tactician, but he's an excellent diplomat. The Senate loves him, and they requested him personally."

Rachel winced – this time for more than Chris' casual use of the Admiral's name. "I can see why Admiral McCaffrey gave you that order."

"I've heard the Army is lending us an officer to be our ship's Marine CO, but there's no word yet on who," Chris said, sitting down and slipping on his shoes. "Other than that, the only person I know who's going to be involved on our side is Lieutenant Raymond Sharpe, the captain of the *Gnat*. He and his ship are going to be acting as 'civilians' that will need to be protected."

"Do you know anything else?"

"Well, fortunately for us, Admiral Mumford will only be observing us from a 'designated-neutral' ship and will not be leading the regular Navy forces, as I feared. Unfortunately for us, the person he picked was Vice Admiral Lee Craig."

Rachel's eyes widened. "*She's* going to be in charge? Wasn't she supposed to be the brains behind that operation in Castor Sector a few years ago?"

"The same. I'm not entirely sure she won that battle because of her tactical ability, but she showed great courage. And, if our own fleet's CO is as poor as McCaffrey was hinting, then she's probably more than a match for him. I'm not looking forward to our chances." He finished tying his shoelaces and stood up. "Ready to go?"

Rachel paused for a moment, then laughed. "I am, but you aren't," she said, moving over to him. "Can't you even dress yourself properly, Mr. Desaix?"

"Huh?" he asked intelligently. Shaking her head and smiling, she casually reached out and grabbed the bottom of his shirt. "Hey, what are you—"

Ignoring his protests, she pulled his shirt out from around his waist and unbuttoned the bottom three buttons, then buttoned them back up correctly. "There. Now, tuck your shirt back in – we're late as it is, already."

Chris just blinked, and did as she said. *What's gotten into her? The Rache I know would never be so... presumptuous.*

Schubert frowned as he looked from side to side. He had intended to comm Rachel about Chris running late for the party, but now he himself was running late. Chris had just stepped into the shower when Schubert had been commed and ordered to report to Captain Morrison's office ASAP. He figured he could comm them from Morrison's office, but it was locked up tight and the Captain was nowhere to be seen. Now he wasn't sure what was going on.

On his way back to his quarters he noticed he was being followed. He couldn't see by whom, but it didn't matter. Someone didn't impersonate an instructor at the Naval Academy just to be all nice and friendly. Schubert wasn't sure what they wanted, but he didn't think he should go back to his quarters; not until he knew their intentions. Instead, he slowly started making his way towards the places where there were usually crowds of fellow students.

Unfortunately, most of the places he went were shut down. The senior cadet for each ship in the Wargame had followed the tradition of organizing a 'meet and greet' party for all of the cadets they'd be working with, and to encourage attendance at these parties all of the usual Academy hangouts had been closed. The MPs had also been called off their usual stations to make sure these parties didn't get out of hand.

Damn, Schubert thought. *Not many more places to try. Rachel's probably mad as hell at me right now – we should be at the party already and I never commed. Now there's an idea – maybe I'll be able to lose this idiot at the party.*

He picked up the pace, making his way in the direction of Orff's party. He'd just about reached it when his pursuer – or, rather, pursuers – caught him.

"Well, hello," Schubert said casually, his mind racing as he tried to identify them. "I don't believe we've met... but you all seem so anxious to talk to me. May I ask your names?"

It wasn't looking good. There were six of them, and they all looked big, tough, and dumb. Schubert figured he could handle two, maybe three of them, but against all six he was in serious trouble, and none of them looked like they could be talked down.

The largest of them laughed. "You don't need to know our names. You won't be able to do anything with them when we're through with you."

"Is that so?" he shot back with more confidence than he felt. "May I ask, then, just why you seem so upset with me?"

"Does the name Joel Farmburg mean anything to you?" the thug asked.

Schubert's eyes narrowed. "Yeah. He's the jackass who was mouthing off about a couple of my friends."

"You put him in the hospital!" one of the other musclemen snapped.

"And we're here to return the favor," the first one finished, smirking.

Schubert grinned back, cracking his knuckles. "Is that so? Well, if you are, then how about I take a few of you with me?"

He waited for the first punch – not only would that give him a hole through which to counterattack, but he didn't want anyone to call him the instigator of this fight. He'd gotten into enough trouble after the bar fight, despite the fact he'd been outnumbered there, too.

Schubert leaned to the side avoiding the massive fist heading for his jaw. He felt the breeze of its passing, but didn't have any time to worry about it. Instead, he concentrated on his own attack, grabbing the shoulder attached to that fist. He pulled on it for leverage as he leapt forward, sending a flying knee into the brute's gut and following up by dropping an elbow onto the back of the man's head.

The first man went down quickly, but there were still five others. Schubert briefly considered making a break for it – he was only a couple hundred yards away from the clearing where the party tents had been set up – but he knew he'd never make it. Just to try, he'd have to give up the initiative and allow them into his blind spot, so his best chance was still to stand and fight. Taking a couple of steps back in order to keep all six of his attackers in his line of sight, he crouched down in preparation for a charge.

"Hey, is this a private beating or can anyone join in?" a female voice interrupted. Schubert turned his head slightly to see two young women watching them. Schubert vaguely recognized the one in front. Her name was Lauren Weber, and – at least for the next few weeks – she would be his crewmate on the *Chihuahua*.

"Get the hell out of here," one of the thugs growled. "This is our affair."

Weber smiled menacingly. "No."

The two women moved in, taking flanking positions around Schubert. The thugs opposing them stood somewhat confused for a moment, before the big man Schubert had dropped earlier gasped, "Get them, you idiots!"

They ran in, and Schubert met them head-on. Weber and her friend were right beside him. *They don't stand a chance – I'd better finish this fast,* Schubert thought as he tackled one and started pounding on him. Once he was sure the man he was facing was out, he leapt up to deal with the other thugs... to see them running away from the two girls as if their lives depended on it. He stopped, and looked at them.

Weber smirked at him and held out her hand to help him up. "Hi. Your name is Wolfgang Schubert, right?"

Wow, Schubert thought. *She's something else!*

If Chris couldn't believe Rachel's behavior in his dorm room, then Rachel had an even harder time with it. Why had she just grabbed at him like that? She couldn't puzzle it out. She should have just told him to button the shirt up properly, and left him to handle that job on his own. Maybe hanging around with him was getting to her.

She distracted herself by wondering where Schubert had gone off to. If he had said he would comm her about the delay, she felt certain he would have. She knew him well enough to believe he was a reliable sort of person, and his absence was definitely out of character for him.

She had suggested to Chris that the two of them look around for their missing friend before heading to the party, and so far they'd checked most of the routes they figured he might have taken to her dorm room. Failing to find him anywhere, Rachel suggested they go back to his quarters and check to see if Schubert had returned while they were out looking.

"Damn it," Chris cursed, still seeing no Schubert and no note. "Just what the hell is going *on* around here?"

Rachel shook her head, obviously just as concerned. "Your guess is as good as mine. Do you want to keep up the search or what?"

Chris sighed. "The only place left I can think to check is the party itself. This isn't like him at all, though, and it worries me."

Rachel put a comforting hand on his arm and squeezed. She had only known Schubert for a few weeks, but she'd found his absence strange as well. Chris' strong reaction to his disappearance only served to confirm her own feelings that something was wrong. It was possible they were just blowing it out of proportion, however.

"He'll be all right," she said with a confidence she didn't feel. "Hey, for all we know he found a girl and has forgotten all about us."

Schubert frowned. "I dunno... I guess they already left for the party," he said. "I just keep getting the automated messenger service when I call."

"Did you really expect them to be waiting for you three hours after you said you'd meet them?" Lauren Weber asked, rolling her eyes. "They're probably at the party, themselves, already. Where I'd like to be. By the way, I want a dance for saving your ass back there, you know."

Schubert rolled his eyes, even though he didn't really object to dancing with the rather attractive girl who had, as she put it, saved his ass. However, there were more important things at the moment. "You don't understand. I haven't shown up, so they're going to be out looking for me. If they happen to follow my steps, they might instead find... oh, never mind – here they are."

"Hey!" an outraged cry rose from behind the two girls. There stood a rather angry Christopher Desaix and one somewhat amused Rachel Katz – exactly the opposite of how Schubert was expecting them to be at any given moment. They both had a palpable sense of relief on their faces, as well, however.

"Chris! Rache! I was just trying to comm you."

"Is that so?" Rachel said doubtfully. "And why didn't you earlier? Did you forget all about us thanks to your new friends, here?"

Schubert, gesturing with his hands, started to lead the small group to Orff's party. "First, let me introduce Lauren Weber and... Linda Flint, was it? They just saved my ass from being pummeled."

"Hi," Weber waved, smiling crookedly. "Cadet Lieutenant Lauren Weber, at your service. Always happy to help out a friend, and given we're both going to be helmsmen on the *Chihuahua*, I'm pretty sure Wolfie and I will become *great* friends. This is a buddy of mine from my civilian life, and now our fellow crewman, Chief Petty Officer Trainee Linda Flint."

"Yo," Flint chimed in.

Chris blinked. "You were attacked?"

"Yeah. I didn't recognize any of them, but they claimed they were friends of that jackass, Joel Farmburg. Big brutes, all of them."

"I recognized one of them," Flint replied hesitantly. "At least, I think I did. Seaman Trainee Jefferson Flay, from my Environmental Engineering class. I believe both he and Mr. Farmburg are designated for Academy service aboard the Heavy Cruiser *Natsugumo*. At least, if he really was Flay – I didn't get a good look at him."

"Hmm," Rachel said, no longer quite so amused about Schubert having been 'distracted' by not one, but *two* young women. "So what really happened?"

"Basically, it was an ambush. I got a message to meet at Captain Anne Morrison's office ASAP, and it seemed to be authentic. She wasn't there, though – Lauren tells me she's already aboard her transport bound for the Wargame sector, so it must have been a forgery. When I got to Morrison's office and realized I'd been set up, I started to try and comm you, but I couldn't get through. It was then that I noticed I was being followed."

"And you led them here," Rachel concluded.

"Well, I was running around in search of a group of people I could get lost in, first. I would have commed you at the first chance, I promise," Schubert apologized.

Chris smiled. "You're off the hook, this time. Next time you're going to go out unexpectedly, though, leave a note for God's sake!"

"Yes, sir!" Schubert replied, laughing as he parodied a salute. "I'll be certain you know where I am at all times."

"Good," Chris said, nodding. "Now, you might want to tell the MPs about the forged orders. Maybe they can track them back to those bozos."

"We can't prove they started the fight," Linda pointed out. "What's the point? Let's just enjoy the party. By the time we get back from the Wargame, all of this will have blown over."

"Are you kidding me?" Rachel snapped. "A crime has been committed here. We have a possible identification of one attacker. It's also very likely there'll be some DNA evidence as to who the others are, if we get the MPs here in time."

"Rache," Chris said calmly, placing a hand on her shoulder. "You aren't thinking clearly. Schubert had his fight in a public thoroughfare, so there's bound to be an extensive amount of DNA contamination. Worse, he was recently in a bar fight, and was labeled its instigator."

"But that's my point!" Rachel exclaimed. "They could claim they were the attacked party, if they get to the MPs first. And, from what I've seen, it looks like Wolf did most of the beating – if he makes the accusation first, it'll be his word against theirs."

"They won't say anything," Flint remarked. "There were six of them vs. one of him. And Lauren and I will testify to that fact. They know better than to assume they'll get the benefit of the doubt in this case. It's a case where it could go either way no matter who reports it, so it's best just to drop it."

Rachel looked around her stubbornly, hoping for support from someone. She had none. "I don't like it. They can still find out who was pretending to be Captain Morrison, and if Joel or his friends were willing to go to those lengths already, who knows what they'll do now."

"There, I definitely agree with you. Not that you'll ever hear me say those words again, mind," Chris said playfully. "But I don't think the MPs will be of any help at this point. The only thing they might try is backtracking that forged comm signal, but with everything else going on right now they're not likely to consider it a high priority. They won't even try until the Wargame is over, and by then any evidence will be gone. I also doubt Farmburg, Flay, or any of their cronies will try anything else any time soon. There's just not enough time for them to set something up between now and when we leave."

Rachel glared at him, wrinkling her nose. "And so we should just ignore it in the meantime?"

"No," Chris answered. "But I don't see contacting the MPs as helping more than they'll hurt. We keep our eyes and ears open, though, and if there's any chance one of us might encounter Farmburg's goons, we make sure we never do it alone. I'll try to come up with a plan, but please don't do something so counterproductive in the meantime."

Schubert grimaced. "There you two go again. I guess the truce is over, huh?"

Chris and Rachel looked at each other, and suddenly Chris chuckled. "Well," he replied. "I'd hardly say that. If the truce was over, we'd be fighting tooth and nail. This is just a friendly disagreement."

Weber raised an eyebrow. "I can tell being on a ship with you three will be an interesting experience indeed."

Part II

Zwischenzug

Chapter VI

Sol System, Earth, Nicolai Tesla Conference Center

Kimiko Beccera smiled as she stepped into the room. Finally, after months of petitioning, she was being allowed into the inner sanctum where the members of the Pleiades Expedition were meeting. Now she was going to be part of that expedition, herself.

"Ah, I see we have a newcomer in our midst," someone said upon seeing her. "Dr. Beccera, I understand?"

Beccera reached out and shook the other woman's hand in greeting. "Yes, but please, call me Kim. And you are?"

"Dr. Angel Carter. I suppose if I call you Kim, I'd better let you call me Angie." She grinned. "I'm the project coordinator for this little expedition, as well as the chief linguist. Please, come in. Since this is only the second time the whole expedition has gathered, we figured we'd start by simply reviewing the complete preliminary report of the Pleiades Dig. Most of us have only received censored copies, to date."

Beccera frowned. "Censored?"

"Surely you don't think that the only reason we're launching this massive expedition is to study some math symbols we've already seen?" Angel asked. "That may have been the biggest discovery, but it wasn't the only one."

"Biggest discovery my ass!" a male voice from behind her said.

Angel rolled her eyes and sighed. Stepping aside to make room, she gestured behind her, where a trio of other scientists were gathered.

"Dr. Beccera," Angel said formally. "I'd like to introduce you to three of our fellow researchers on this project. You'll probably find them more interesting than me, since I'm just a simple linguist, and they're all xenoanthropologists like yourself. This is Dr. Phillip Heinlein, who will be heading your department." Kimiko shook hands with the man. "Next to him is Dr. Mara Sommers."

Kimiko froze. She knew that name. "The same Dr. Mara Sommers who discovered that alien starship some years back?"

Mara nodded, and sighed. "Yes, I'm the one. I just wish there had been at least one alien body with it, though, so we would at least know what the people who flew it looked like."

"We can cut it down, easily," the third, as yet un-introduced person said. Kimiko recognized his voice as the same one which had interrupted Dr. Carter earlier. "From the configuration of various instruments, seating arrangements, and even bathroom facilities we know they were a bipedal species. One which had opposable thumbs... in other words, very similar to humanoids."

"That doesn't really limit it down much, though," Dr. Heinlein complained. "We've found remains that indicate there were bipedal species similar to humanoids in many ruins of once-space-faring societies. We aren't saying that all intelligent species were humanoids, mind, but it appears humanoids intermingled with pretty much every space-faring society. Of course any ship built would contain facilities for them."

"Makes sense," Kimiko agreed. "But it's good to know that the ship is consistent with that theory. While humanoids may not be 'surprising,' it does cut down some possibilities as Doctor... I'm sorry, I didn't get your name?"

Dr. Carter gave a long-suffering sigh. "Well, I suppose we should introduce him, too. Dr. Kimiko Beccera, meet Dr. Frank Orwell. He's been on his part of the project longer than anyone else, and he's come to believe his studies are more important then any of the other scientific teams' concerns."

"That's only because they are," Dr. Orwell grumbled. "We've made the biggest discovery in the history of xenoanthropology, no question. Possibly the biggest discovery in the history of any form of anthropology."

Kimiko looked startled. "There's a xenoanthropological element to all of this? I was under the impression that most of the anthropological paths from the initial dig had already been explored, outside of the actual translation work. I thought I was being called upon for the upcoming dig of the surrounding area – was I mistaken?"

"Not exactly," Dr. Carter said. "Just misled. Even I haven't been told what most of these 'great xenoanthropological discoveries' are, yet. That's partly what this series of pre-expedition briefings was supposed to do – give us all a chance to hear the whole story."

Kimiko refocused on the anthropologists. "Can you give me a sneak preview, Dr. Orwell? Or is it too complicated to summarize in two minutes or less?"

"Oh, I can summarize it in one rather short sentence," he answered cockily. "Simply put, we discovered skeletons in the Pleiades system that strongly resemble those of Neanderthal man. In fact, they may be identical to them – we still need to make a few more complex measurements to be certain, though."

Apparently, even though she was the project director, this was news to Dr. Carter. "Excuse me, did you say Neanderthals? You mean the stereotyped hunched backs, thick eyebrows, and funny bow-legged walks?"

Kimiko almost laughed. That image of the Neanderthals had persisted for hundreds of years even though it had been conclusively proven to be false. She noticed the other anthropologists in their little group were holding back their amusement as well. Well, except for the one who brought Neanderthals up – he looked rather disgusted.

"It's true that some of them may have had funny walks and hunched backs," Dr. Orwell said, taking on a tone of superiority as he took over the conversation. "But it's hardly likely that was common. That troublesome model of the Neanderthals came from the skeleton of a very elderly and possibly arthritic Neanderthal. Later skeletons disproved the bowlegs and the hunched backs. In fact, they were quite advanced. Possibly more advanced, biologically, than modern humans."

"Oh?" Dr. Carter inquired, intrigued. She didn't know much about pre-modern humans.

"Well," Orwell continued. "With the exception of the pronounced brow ridges, they may have looked identical to early modern humans, but their skeletal structures tell us much more. They had a very dense bone structure, which probably indicates they were significantly stronger than modern humans. Their brain pans were also larger, which could mean that they were more intelligent than their contemporaries."

"The size of someone's brain has very little relationship to their intelligence, you know," Sommers snorted.

"Perhaps," Orwell replied dismissively. "However, the stone tools they produced were more advanced than the tools of their contemporaries."

Carter was intrigued. "If Neanderthals were so advanced, why did they die out while modern humans achieved supremacy?"

"Well, they did have a few natural disadvantages, as well," Orwell admitted. "Perhaps the greatest was that, from the skeletal remains of female Neanderthal pelvises, we can estimate that their average gestation period took longer – likely was a full year – while modern humans could reproduce within nine months. Essentially, Neanderthals were out-bred." He grinned fiercely. "There is plenty of evidence that Neanderthals cross-bred themselves with Homo Sapiens, and that they didn't die out so much as were absorbed by modern humans."

This was far from Kimiko's field of anthropological expertise. The news that a fossilized Neanderthal-like skeleton had been found on another planet, however, fascinated her.

A chime sounded. Carter reluctantly stopped the discussion there. "Ladies, gentlemen. As fascinating as this all is, I'm afraid that we don't have the time to discuss the origins of humanity any more. Let's take our seats – the Navy is about to begin briefing us on our travel procedures."

Orwell sniffed in annoyance at being interrupted, but Dr. Beccera didn't even notice. She was looking up at the dozen or so uniformed Naval officers approaching the platform in front of the briefing room. Being the bride of an Army officer, she was well familiar with how a properly worn dress uniform should appear, and the person holding the highest rank in the assemblage was, to her critical eye, demonstrating how *not* to wear one. His tie was crooked, his shirt and pants were wrinkled, and his shoes were non-uniform.

I wonder how a slob like him is able to hold a Captain's commission, she thought.

"Hello," the ill-attired officer began, speaking into a microphone. "My name is Captain Theodore Bradford. I command the light cruiser *Camel,* and it will be my job to make sure your butts don't get fried on the way to Pleiades. My ship will be more than adequate to fend off any pirates we may encounter, but just in case Commander Iskovich will be accompanying me in the corvette *Yellowjacket.* Safety is still an issue, however, as your Newton class science vessels are completely unarmed and ridiculously undefended. If someone manages to get a shot past us before we can kill them, there's a pretty strong chance you could be killed." He paused, sucking air into his lungs and showing a sizable gut through his clothing. "For that reason, I'm going to tell you exactly what you need to know in case we ever come under attack. And if you forget these things and live through the battle, realize that it'll just be a short reprieve, because I'll kill you myself for risking the lives of everyone else in this convoy." He paused, and grinned toothily. "So, should we get down to business?"

Sol System, Earth Orbit, En Route to Dockyard Waystation 3

The collection of ships loomed large on Academy Transport Shuttle 85's monitors. The bridge crew of the *Chihuahua* watched their approach to the dockyards with varying degrees of curiosity and excitement. The ride had been rather quiet – no-one wanted to talk and spoil the moment. The silence didn't last, however, when a voice crackled over the passenger compartment's comm unit.

"I don't normally give these tour-guide type speeches when I fly people out, but I figure you Academy types might want to take in a few sights on the way," the pilot said. "For example, those of you who wash out may want to consider a career at the station I'm now displaying on your monitors. This is the headquarters of the Orbital Guard. If you've never been off planet before, you might not have heard of them. They fill the same role as the Coast Guard does on Earth – primarily search and rescue, but they've got a few lightly armed ships to deal with smugglers and the like."

Rachel smiled softly, though no-one could see it. "My parents used to work there," she said offhandedly.

Chris turned his head to try and look at her, but could just barely catch her face out of his peripheral vision. "I didn't know that."

"Dad captained one of the armed cutters," she said. "They're about as big as a small corvette because of their engine and power systems, but they don't have any jump drives or particle cannons. Rail guns only, if they're armed at all. And they only have very small crews – smaller than anything in the Navy... except perhaps some transports or science ships, and then only if you don't count passengers."

"And your mother?"

"She had an administrative position," she replied. "Which is why I was able to live in the station with her from time to time. I remember flying in my dad's cutter more than sitting in her office, though."

"Now on your screen," the pilot's voice broke in. "You can see one of the most powerful starships in the Fleet: the *Skjoldebrand*, an Argus class battleship commanded by Captain Duncan Black. We currently have forty of these built or under construction. Each one needs a crew of one thousand four hundred and twenty sailors and one hundred forty five Marines, so most of you who manage to get past your senior year will wind up serving the bulk of your career in one of these babies."

Chris grimaced. "Battleships have their place in the Navy, but I'd hate to ever serve aboard one. Anyway, you were saying about your father?"

"I was just reminiscing – it wasn't anything important," Rachel said, realizing suddenly how personal the conversation had become. It was time to change the subject, and quickly. "Why wouldn't you want to serve on a battleship?"

"Like I said, they have a big role in the Navy, but that role is not particularly interesting," he answered. "Their job is to get into the middle of things and blast away until either they or the enemy are dead. In a sense, they're just there to keep the enemy battleships busy while the smaller, faster, more maneuverable support vessels do the important tactical work."

Rachel raised an eyebrow. "So you think the size of a battleship is unimportant?"

"Not entirely, no," Chris replied. "Every extra bit of firepower, every additional inch of armor, any added power to the targeting computer – all those things count. But historically, battleships are rarely outclassed even by stronger battleships. They just match up against each other, and the side which has superior numbers wins. True, in one-on-one fights a more advanced battleship will crush a weaker battleship. That's not very likely to happen, though – battleships are always grouped together for fleet actions. Even a good commander with a more advanced fleet will have trouble winning when outnumbered in a battleship fight."

"But in our tactics sim for class, you were able to win when outnumbered in a battleship sim!" Rachel protested.

"Only by never letting any of my battleships get outnumbered," Chris pointed out. "I had them maneuvering so that we always had a two-to-one advantage over the enemy force in localized areas. And I could only do that because the frigates, corvettes, and heavy cruisers under our command were able to make themselves enough of a nuisance to keep the simulated enemy fleet from altering its formation. And those smaller ships could only survive those tactics because they were smaller, faster, and more maneuverable. They were the important part of our tactical simulation – not the battleships."

"And now, on your screen," the pilots voice once more intervened. "Is the *Roanoke*, a Venture class frigate commanded by Captain Nigel Hickox. A few of you lucky people may wind up serving aboard her one day."

"Damn straight we'd be lucky," Chris said. "They should never have halted construction on the Venture class. They were the best damn ships in the fleet with a perfect balance between firepower, speed, and armor. No quantum wheel, but I look at that as a plus. Until they can make the quantum wheel maneuver a ship as fast as a fusion drive, I won't care for them."

"There are advantages to quantum wheels, you know," Rachel said. "Lots of advantages."

"But so many things about the design haven't been perfected yet," Chris sighed. "And they've been in production for, what, seventy years now? The designers of the Venture class frigates realized that they hadn't ironed out all of the kinks, and weren't likely to any time soon. When practical cold fusion came out – finally surpassing the standard fusion reactor after centuries of development – they decided to see how a fusion drive would react to having a power source that provided more energy while consuming less mass and less volume. What they got was the fastest frigate ever built – only a few corvettes have ever been able to get more functional speed."

"Speed was never why the quantum wheel was accepted," Rachel argued. "It was the way the magnetic fields produced by a quantum wheel would remove the undefendable sensor blind spot all ships have on their stern."

"Yeah, but fusion drives don't leave that much of an unprotected blind spot, either," Chris replied. "There's only a small place on the stern of a fusion-drive starship vulnerable to anything but a particle cannon. The heat produced would melt any missiles or rail gun ammo before it hit. I think the loss of acceleration, top speed, and maneuverability you get with a quantum wheel is more of a hazard than the tiny window a fusion-drive ship presents." He shrugged even though no-one could see it. "Quantum wheels might be practical on a very large warship where speed is less of a factor, like a battleship or a heavy cruiser, but until they iron out the bugs I won't care for them on anything smaller."

Rachel sighed. "Well, the *Chihuahua* has a fusion drive. You won't have to deal with a quantum wheel this time."

"Yeah," Chris said. "But I have to wonder... will I ever have a chance to be on the crew of a Venture class? Will there be any left when I graduate?" He sighed. "Oh, what am I saying. The only place they'll have room for us is aboard one of those Arguses."

Rachel hesitated. Once more, she felt as if she was placed in the awkward position of comforting her sometime rival. His concerns were much like her own, however – while she wasn't sure of his assessment of the quantum wheel, she didn't want to be assigned to a battleship, either. She wanted something which might allow for an independent cruise, and a Venture class frigate would fit the bill nicely.

"Well, Chris," she said softly. "Who knows? They rarely crew a new ship entirely with recruits, and they have to draw those veterans from somewhere. That means they'll probably put some graduates from our class in something other than battleships. Maybe even in Venture class frigates – you could still get your wish." *And maybe I'll get mine, too.*

EAS Gnat

"This is the pilot speaking. End of the line – we have now completed docking with the *EAS Gnat*. Please disembark in an orderly fashion. Your baggage will be handled by the *Gnat's* crew. Good day, and good luck."

The cadets from the Academy had only met the Fleet officers they would be crewing the ship with as they waited to board the shuttle taking them off Earth. They had so far only been told the name of one of them – their captain, Conrad Burkhard. He was the first person to extract themselves from the straps of their grav-safe chairs, and he made his way to the airlock before anyone else could join him. "Ladies and gentlemen," he said. "I've already been in contact with the *Gnat's* captain, and I've made a reservation for meeting room Epsilon in..." he checked his watch. "...two hours. You lot are going to be my bridge crew, and I'd like to find out more about you before we have to depend on each other in battle. That goes for your two staff members as well, Colonel Beccera."

The entire gathering turned to look at the Army officer. His was a famous name, and it was a big surprise to know he would be on their crew. "Thank you, sir," the Colonel said courteously.

"Bah. Don't call me sir – you outrank me by two whole grades," Burkhard snorted. "You'll be my subordinate until we've familiarized you with your shipboard duties, but as a Marine colonel there may be times you may will also be my superior for parts of the Wargame. But please, this is just a simulation. When we aren't in that simulated environment, let's not keep up these awkward formalities, okay? Call me Conrad, and I'll call you Andrew."

Beccera slowly grinned and nodded. "Makes sense, but I prefer Drew. Thank you, Conrad."

"Any time. Now, I want everyone to get squared away and report to meeting room Epsilon, pronto. I'll see you there." With that, he disappeared.

Silence followed that for a moment, but then people started to line up to transfer to the new ship. Routine decontamination procedures slowed the progress through the airlock to a crawl, leaving those still in line waiting impatiently. Fidgeting a little, Schubert finally decided to break the silence. "So, Colonel Beccera, sir," he said. "What are you doing on our ship? I mean, if I was given a list of people who might be considered to command the Marine detachment on the *Chihuahua* and your name was on it, I'd have figured you'd be the last person to be given the job." He stopped, realizing that his statement might be a faux pas. "Not because you're a bad CO, mind, but because you're, well..."

"An Army officer?" Beccera said sardonically . "A Colonel? A man who's got decades more experience than any commanding officer of twenty men should have?"

"All of the above," Schubert answered, now wishing he hadn't opened his mouth.

"Well, I'm not too happy with the assignment, let me assure you of that! In fact, when the Army first gave me the option of this gig, I damn near retired rather than take it." Beccera paused and grinned slightly, taking the sting out of his rant. "They talked me out of it, but I doubt I'll really have much opportunity to enjoy myself on this assignment. What kind of job does a Marine do during a Naval simulation, anyway?"

Chris, who – along with Rachel – was lined up right behind Schubert, shrugged. "More than you'd think, I suspect. Marines are much more than just Army soldiers in. Unskilled labor, mostly – often, they get placed in the purser's staff moving crates around the cargo bays – but it isn't uncommon for a Marine to be detailed to for a gun crew or to help work on the computers."

"And it's not like Marine combat is forbidden in this Wargame, sir," Rachel noted. "The rules are a little more restrictive than normal combat, I'm told, but we still might have a mission or two to send your people out on."

Beccera sighed. "In that case, I'm going to need to familiarize myself with the differences between Marine and Army tactics. How much time will I have before the fighting starts?"

"Well," Rachel answered, "We still don't know how long it will take to get on station. When we do, we have three weeks to re-commission our ship. Then, of course, there's however much time we'll have before our first simulated combat exercise...."

"But if I want enough time to shakedown my Marines before the start of the exercise, I'll have to get *myself* ready well before then. I might be able to spend a week getting myself up to speed, at best," Beccera snorted. "Cute. I wonder if Austin knew that before he sent me out here."

Silence once more fell down on the group as they continued to wait in line. Schubert was, again, the one to break the ice. "Man, this waiting is boring."

"War is ninety percent boredom, nine percent fear, and one percent adrenaline," Beccera said. "Also known as the principle of 'hurry up and wait.'"

"This isn't a war," Lauren snorted, trying to get in on the conversation. "This is a game."

"I thought it was both," Chris quipped.

"But this is neither war nor a game," Schubert pointed out, chuckling. "This is waiting in line to get off the shuttle."

"Excuse me, sir?" A seaman addressed the Colonel from the hatch a few moments later. "You're next. Follow me, please, sir."

Things seemed to go much quicker after that.. Beccera had his own job to take care of, but the others waited around to compare notes before heading off.

"So," Chris said. "Where did they place you?"

"Deck 7, Cabin 4, Bunk 5," Rachel said. "I hear the rooms on this transport house eight people each."

"That would make sense," Schubert sighed. "Deck 7, Cabin 4, Bunk 8."

Chris chuckled. "Deck 7, Cabin 4, Bunk 6. Looks like we'll all be roomies until the *Chihuahua's* far enough along in her renovations to house us."

"Heaven help me," Rachel said, rolling her eyes.

Chris grinned. "You won't have to worry about me. I'll be too busy conducting those renovations to get into too many arguments with you. You're safe."

"I wonder if we'll know anyone else in our cabin," Schubert mused.

"Well, they're trying to keep the ships' companies together as much as possible," Rachel said. "So we'll probably know at least a few of them."

"Why don't we go down to our cabin and find out?" Chris suggested, gesturing to a nearby bank of elevators.

The elevator came, and the trio got on. As they left, a chime sounded, and a businesslike voice followed. "Shuttle Flight 970 arriving in Port 3. Commander Barbara Meier, Captain of the *Natsugumo*, is aboard. Honor guard, please report to Port 3."

There were several people in the meeting that the Academy officers had yet to meet when they arrived. They started to introduce themselves when Burkhard entered with one more guest. "Hello, ladies and gentlemen," he said. "Let's get started, shall we?" There were nods of agreement around the table, and he smiled grimly. "First, let me introduce Cadet Ensign Hector Karajan. He's the liaison officer Acting-Commodore Green assigned to us for the refit of the *Chihuahua*. Normally, he'll be stationed aboard the flagship, but I asked him to come here today to explain the specific limitations we have had placed on us."

Karajan coughed uncomfortably. "Yes... Captain Green has set a variety of priorities to the refit. He has noted that we will only have three tenders for the duration of the refit period, and just one tender once the Wargame begins. For this reason, no vessels smaller than a heavy cruiser will be permitted time in one of the tenders."

The officer who had introduced himself as the Chief Engineer, Lieutenant Jacques Rappaport, didn't react verbally. Instead, he pulled out his hand comp and started typing something furiously. Rachel, sitting next to him, glanced at the screen curiously. He was doing some math, but she couldn't determine its significance.

"What!" exclaimed Robert Orff. "But without access to a tender or to a properly equipped Navy yard, how are we supposed to make repairs?"

"That's your problem, I'm afraid," Karajan said apologetically. "Commodore Green feels that it is more important to restore the battleships and heavy cruisers to their utmost, maximizing our firepower as best as he can."

Burkhard raised a hand, forestalling further protests. "Please, ladies and gentlemen, let's not shoot the messenger. Mr. Karajan is just relaying our orders."

"Thank you, sir," Karajan sighed, wiping his brow nervously. "There is more, I'm afraid. The Commodore also is going to requisition all but one of your ship's work shuttles for the same reason. He may return them to you one week prior to the commencement of the Wargame, but until then he feels he needs to use them if he wishes to get his battleships sufficiently operable. I am aware that this cuts your capability for working on external repairs in half during that two week period, but anything I or my fellow liaisons said was ignored."

Rappaport seemed unconcerned, still typing furiously, but Orff was reddening in anger. The first officer snapped, "And has the 'Commodore' made any other rules to sabotage our attempts to restore the *Chihuahua?*"

Karajan swallowed. "Well, uh... he has said that any equipment issued in the initial supply dispersal will have to be requisitioned directly from him."

Murmurs broke out around the table. Burkhard nodded. "Thank you, Mr. Karajan. You may go now."

Karajan breathed a sigh of relief. "Thank you, sir. And I'm really sorry about all this." he apologized, rushing out of the room.

"Well," Burkhard began. "It seems to me we're being screwed over by our own Commodore. From what I understand, so are all of the other Academy corvettes and frigates. Nevertheless, we must get the *Chihuahua* fully operational in three weeks, and all we'll have to do it with is whatever spare parts our Commodore decides to grace us with."

"Actually," Rappaport said, studying the numbers on his hand comp. "As long as we have at least one shuttle, we should be fine. In fact, I think we can be done with most of the work by the time we get back our second work shuttle."

Burkhard merely looked at him, intrigued. "How do you propose to do that, Mr. Rappaport?"

"There's quite a bit of work engineers normally do that don't necessarily require trained engineers," Rappaport explained. "Demolition, swapping malfunctioning plug-in components, simple computer work, things like that. We've got plenty of unskilled labor to deal with things like that. We'll have to renovate things from the inside wherever possible..." He paused, typing in a few more calculations. "We'll be gutting much of the internal workings – if we can restore the environmental systems quickly enough, getting the rest of the crew to do that will really speed things along."

"If we're going that far with the refit, it might give us an opportunity to make some improvements I've been considering," Chris interjected.

Rappaport turned to look at him questioningly.

"Sorry, I don't think we've had a chance to be introduced yet. I'm Cadet Lt. Desaix, your deputy." Rachel had to hold back a sigh – Chris was forgetting to call his superiors 'sir' again.

"What did you have in mind, Mr. Desaix?" Burkhard asked.

Chris pulled out his own hand-comp. Rachel saw him pull up several schematics. "Well, if we eliminate the primary missile storage space entirely, we could fit in a second, more advanced power plant like a cold fusion reactor. That would give us a serious boost of engine power, with little sacrificed – missiles are never used in ship-to-ship combat, so we won't miss them. Even if you want to use them, we should still be able to keep a round or two stored in the expense magazine."

"And how do you plan to add the hydrogen collector?" Rappaport asked. Even Rachel knew that the hydrogen collectors required for any cold-fusion plant had to be mounted externally to work.

Chris shrugged. "Well, there we'd probably have to use the work shuttles, which might affect your schedule, but all we need to do is mount it to the backbone of the tower for the Hyperspatial Sensor Array – we can use the existing conduits."

Lieutenant Rappaport frowned. "Do you mind if I see your figures?" Chris gestured to the Chief Engineer's hand comp, and Rappaport nodded as Chris brought up a file from the network. "Hmm... this could work. Maybe. In fact, with the added power a cold fusion system is likely to be able to produce, I may be able to add a few other power-heavy things to improve our speed and maneuverability. Let's get together after we finish the initial survey of the ship and work out some blueprints."

Burkhard looked subtly relieved. "Well, looks like our refit's in good hands."

"One problem is we may require parts that Commodore Green doesn't see fit to give us," Rappaport warned.

Burkhard nodded. "Just give me a requisition list. We'll hold off on that part of the refit until I'm able to push our special requests through, if possible."

"Will do," Rappaport said.

"Good," Burkhard said. "Okay, next order of business: Interim assignments." He turned to Robert Orff. "Cadet Commander Orff, I'm going to ask you to supervise the engineers. I know how people like Lieutenant Rappaport and Mr. Desaix can get when they aren't given a reality check for practicality from a non-engineer."

"Aye aye, sir," Orff said.

"Cadet Lieutenant Commander Katz," he said, making Rachel sit at attention. She couldn't afford to peak at her two neighboring engineers hand-comps while the Captain was addressing her. "I'm going to give you an assignment that normally would be the job of our logistics officer. Unfortunately, I'm going to need the services of our assigned logistics officer, Cadet Ensign Polk, to try and get the equipment we'll need to get the ship operable, so you will be handling his duties until he is able to return to his regular post."

"I have no problem with that, sir," Rachel said.

"I didn't think you would. Once our engineers have provided you with definitive statistics for the number and size of our post-refit crew cabins, your first priority will be to assign the housing. You get to decide where we all sleep and who we sleep with. Don't abuse that authority." There was a twinkle in Burkhard's eye as he made that last admonition.

"Simple enough to do, sir," Rachel said, suppressing a laugh.

"Good. Drew, I'm going to arrange for you to meet with some of the other ships' Marine officers to get a crash course in the differences between Marine service and Army service. I suspect you'll find these meetings useful."

"I wouldn't be surprised. Thank you, sir," Beccera replied.

"That's Conrad to you, Drew. Next, Ms. Weber and Mr. Schubert. You two will trade off as the pilots for our work shuttle. Decide between the both of you how you will split the shifts."

"Aye aye, sir," Schubert said. "We'll decide by coin toss."

"I'll need a coin, sir," Weber said, grinning at her fellow pilot.

"I'll get you one," Burkhard said, carefully not letting any amusement show on his face. "Now... the rest of you are going to be working with the engineers until we get the *Chihuahua* more or less squared away. Does anyone have any questions?" No-one said anything. "Good. Meeting's adjourned. I don't plan to have another one until the Engineering team can release some of the rest of the crew for other projects. Dismissed."

The assembly quickly scattered, and Schubert, Rachel, and Chris started making their way up to their room. A thought occurred to Rachel that must have left a puzzled expression on her face even as they boarded the elevator.

"What's wrong, Rache?" Chris asked, concerned.

"Nothing," she said, shaking her head. "I'm fine. I'm just wondering... how in the world did Captain Burkhard know who we were?"

"What are you talking about?" Schubert asked.

"How did he know who we were? He knew who I was without even asking. He knew who you were. Hell, he even knew who Yannis was..."

but none of us, as far as I know, have ever met him before," she pointed out.

"He probably just looked at our personnel records," Chris suggested.

"Maybe, but I don't think that's it. I've seen personnel records before, in my job as the Senior Officer of our dorm room. If the records he has are anything like the records I had to deal with, he doesn't have images of us. They aren't supposed to use image files of Academy students until their graduation."

Schubert frowned. "Hmm... that's true. At least, that's what I was told in my EOD briefing when I entered the Academy."

Chris shrugged. "They probably have our images stored somewhere, even if they aren't included with our personnel records."

"Anyone who uses the Macrosim Center must create an ID Profile that includes imaging verification," Rachel recalled. "But I didn't authorize the release of my picture, and that would only work for Chris and I."

"Actually," Schubert said. "I've got an idea."

"Oh?" Chris and Rachel chorused.

"Yeah. What if came to the party last night?"

Rachel frowned. "But Robert—"

"Was *told* that he couldn't make it. But who's to say that's the truth?" Schubert smirked. "There were a lot of people at that party I didn't recognize. After all, it wasn't just open to us – our friends and family were also welcome to attend. What if he disguised himself as one of them, just to observe us all?"

"That... might be true," Chris mused. "The only way to know for certain is to ask him."

"How will we do that?" Rachel asked. "He disappeared from that meeting pretty quickly, and he just told us he's not going to call any more meetings any time soon."

Chris shrugged. "So? We can comm him."

Rachel rolled her eyes. "I know you're still pretty weak on proper protocol, but I thought you knew better than to just comm your Captain with something this trivial!"

Chris laughed. "Yeah, even I know better than that. But I'm also under orders to give our Captain a message from Admiral McCaffrey... and I haven't had a chance to do that yet."

Chris was the first one into the room, and noticed nothing out of the ordinary. Nothing, that is, except the presence of his other roommates.

There were still two empty bunks, but he, Schubert, and Rachel had discovered that those two bunks were to be filled with their friends from the party the night before, Weber and Flint. He didn't recognize the newcomers, though.

"Hello," he said, holding out his hand. "I'm Lt. Cadet Chris Desaix, and you are?"

The three men looked at each other uncomfortably, then the nearest one looked back at the hand and took it gingerly. "Hi. I'm..." his voice trailed off.

"Do I know you three from somewhere?" Schubert said as he came into the room, followed by Rachel. "I could swear I've seen you before."

Then Weber and Flint came into the room. The trio's eyes immediately went from discomfort to raw, passionate hatred.

"Hey!" Flint snarled. "What are you doing here?"

"Who are they?" Rachel asked, confused. Chris, who had since retrieved his hand, was looking just as confused.

"They're the guys from yesterday! The ones who tried to mug Wolfie!" Weber snarled.

"Damn straight, we are," the lead man growled back. "The asshole deserves it, too, for putting Farmburg in the hospital."

Chris sighed, pinching the bridge of his nose tiredly. "Well, this is going to be awkward."

Chapter VII

Acting-Commodore John Green walked into the Admiralty office's reception. His shuttle and transport were being delayed for this meeting. He wasn't exactly happy about it – most of the transports for the Wargame had already left, but his had to remain behind just for an interview with the Records and Logistics people. Why Admiral Mumford had *insisted* he attend this meeting Green would never know. Already handicapped by the poor quality of the ships he was being given, Green felt he really didn't need the added problem of arriving to his command late.

"Ah, Commodore Green," a lieutenant greeted him, holding out her hand.

Green took it. He'd been hesitating, but hearing this woman refer to him by his brevet rank dispelled any reluctance. As annoyed as he was at having to be at this meeting, he found that he liked this woman. "You have me at a disadvantage, Lieutenant."

"Maia Rehnquist, sir. Please, have a seat. Commodore Haas will see you in a moment."

Wasn't he supposed to be waiting for me? *Why do I have to wait for* him? *And why am I here, anyway?* Green wondered, sighing. With as much politeness as he could muster, he gave the aide a "Thank you" and sat down on a plushy couch.

Green found the office rather drab. The only thing of real interest was a display showing the latest Navy list – which was about to be replaced, if he remembered correctly. He checked it out and shook his head. He knew, as most of the higher-ranked Naval officers did, that the Navy was pathetically undersized for the amount of territory they had to defend, even though it was the largest Navy in the known universe.

It was hoped that, with the completion of the Epsilon Eridani Naval Station, they would be able to change that. Soon, entire new squadrons would be built in a matter of months. If the new construction yard was able to build ships as fast as the builders had claimed, it wouldn't be too long before the fleet could double its strength. Which meant twice as many flag officers would be needed, and Green was determined to be one of them. He had the political support, and this command would give him the command experience required for a Commodore's commission. If he really embarrassed himself on this command, though, he might blow his chance for fleet duty.

Green knew some of the higher ups didn't particularly respect his abilities. They would latch onto any excuse to prevent his promotion. He knew his own weaknesses all too well: He was aware that he was not the best of tacticians, and he didn't relate well with others – many felt he was too arrogant for his own good. He didn't care about being thought of as arrogant – many famous military officers from the past were known as arrogant.

Tactics, however, were a problem. He understood the politics and diplomacy needed for a naval officer in a way few others did, but he was not the best of captains. The tactical situation of the Wargame didn't lend itself to politics or diplomacy, however. Still, Green doubted even the best tactician in the fleet could do much with the Academy's overwhelming technical disadvantage. The fleet that his outmoded Sirius class battleships were going up against was powerful enough to match any current concentration of warships in the Earth Alliance, save Home Fleet. His fleet, on the other hand, would struggle to deal with *any* modern navy's fleets. Knowing he was not a brilliant tactician, Green intended to use strategies straight out of the textbooks from his days in the Academy. He'd be crushed, but using those tactics he could not be blamed when he lost the 'war.' To follow through on that plan, though, he would desperately need to get his battleships commissioned before hostilities commenced.

Which was why the delay caused by this meeting was so frustrating.

He'd scheduled things out to the minute so as to get most of his fleet ready on time – except for the light cruisers and corvettes, which might not be ready until half-way through the Wargame would – and he needed to be there to ensure that schedule was met. Besides, as hopeless as the mission was, he was looking forward to the command.

"Commodore Green, sir?" Lieutenant Rehnquist said. "Commodore Haas will see you, now."

"Thank you, Lieutenant," Green said, smiling at her as he walked out of the reception area and into the office proper.

Commodore Bernhard Haas was waiting for him at the door. He was fairly young for his rank – younger, even, than Green was. He also knew exactly what Green was going through. He'd been through it, himself, in fact – Haas had been the Acting-Commodore during the last Wargame. He'd distinguished himself well enough to have the 'acting' part of that title removed the moment the Wargames ended. Unfortunately, he hadn't held a fleet command since then. Instead, he'd been granted the position he now held... and then was promptly forgotten about. He seemed happy to be out of the spotlight, at least, but Green always felt Haas' career should have gone better.

"Mr. Green, welcome," Haas said, clasping the younger man's hand in both of his own. "I know how frustrating this likely is, so let's get started. Please, sit down."

Green took his seat and looked across at Commodore Haas. This meeting couldn't be of that great importance, considering how all of the logistical details for his fleet had already been worked out. Green, for that matter, knew of no reason he might have been summoned to this office.

"Thank you, sir. Now, may I ask just why I've been called here?"

"Just a small bureaucratic matter," Haas explained. "It's not something I wanted to be bothered with when I set off for my command of the Academy forces in my own Wargame. However, it's tradition – apparently, a part of the Wargame itself is to give the Academy's officers a taste of command's bureaucratic nonsense. In that capacity, we need to talk about some of the details that will be going into pertinent Navy pubs. In other words, I need your help for the Navy List."

Green flinched. This was why his schedule was losing time in setting up his refit schedule? Really? "Excuse me, sir, but why would I have any part in setting up the Navy List?"

Haas smiled sympathetically. "Frustrating that you're being held here for something as minor as this, isn't it?" He turned to the computer at his desk and sighed. "Sorry, this isn't my fault – I'm under orders, too. I do need to know a few things, though, so this shouldn't take us much more than ten minutes or so. Assuming you've done your homework, that is."

"Sir?" Green replied, confused.

"I need to know three things. The first is which of your ships will you be renaming?"

"Renaming?" Green repeated. "Why would I rename any of these ships?"

"As you know, about a hundred years ago someone in the higher ups decided to 'improve' the naming standards of our fleets. What you might not be aware of, however, is that each class of warship must include one namesake at all times because of those 'improved' standards. Which means each time the lead ship of a class is destroyed or decommissioned, another in that class must be renamed to replace it... and several of your re-commissioned ships no longer have those namesakes. So, one Sirius class battleship, one Asagiri class heavy cruiser, and one Phoebe class corvette that I can re-commission as the Sirius, Asagiri, and Phoebe respectively." He chuckled, checking the list. "I'd say the *Chihuahua* would need to be renamed, as well, but apparently that's been so heavily modified it no longer fits into the Lightning Bug class of gunboats, so I guess I can consider it an original class."

This was why Green had to be delayed? To discuss what he was going to name his ships? "I suppose I'll rename my own flagship, the *Gettysburg*, as the *Sirius*. To be honest, though, I haven't had more than a day or two to familiarize myself with the names of the rest of the Academy's ships. I don't suppose you have a list of them I could look at?"

As if anticipating this question, Haas flipped a switch, projecting the requested list on a large screen behind him. "Will that do?"

Green scanned the list and sighed. "I wish I could have had a chance to inspect these ships before I began renaming them like this. All right, I guess the *Ishikawa* could be renamed *Asagiri*. I had a professor named Ishikawa, once, and would feel... uncomfortable... giving orders to a ship of that name. And I don't really like the name of *Ruby* as a warship, so she can be renamed the *Phoebe*. I suppose. This is all a bloody nuisance!"

"Tell me about it," Haas snorted. "I nearly throttled the man who did this to me back when I commanded the Academy fleet. Okay, next order of business: I need to know who your command staff will be. In other words, who'll be your flag officers, and which of them will be your second in command?"

Green growled softly. "How am I supposed to make that kind of decision? I haven't met any of my captains, yet! And none of them have any significant command experience, as far as I know, so how would I be able to make a judgment on that?" He sighed. "Just designate whoever the senior-most command-line officer in the fleet as my second in command. I shouldn't need any more flag officers than that – if I do, it will be on an ad hoc basis. I may appoint others, later, as I get to know my fellow captains."

Haas nodded agreeably and typed a few keys on his computer. Then he frowned. "Wait a moment, I'm afraid the senior-most command-line officer won't be acceptable for your second."

"Why not?"

Haas shook his head. "He's Army. Colonel Andrew Beccera, on loan from the Army to fill a Marine officer's position. Apparently, the Marines were short an officer or two. It surprises me that we have a Colonel, especially one of his seniority, but he's not qualified for the position of a Navy flag officer, even if he is acting as a Marine."

An incident in the last war the Alliance had fought left a Marine as the only surviving officer aboard a frigate, and the crew had drafted him to be their captain. Unfortunately he had no idea what he'd been doing, and the end results had been nearly disastrous. Since then, Marine officers were given supplementary courses in basic starship command as part of their training, and were now given a place in the 'command structure' of a starship. As command line officers, they could even be called upon to act as fleet commanders, should the need arose. An Army officer, however, would have had no such training.

As a technicality, any Army officers would be considered Marines for the purposes of the exercise... which, in theory, gave him the right to be considered for the position of Green's second in command. However, as an Army officer, he lacked the necessary training.

"One of his seniority?" Green questioned. "How senior is he?"

"Well... he's listed as an O-6 step 6. O-6 in the Navy is the shared pay-grade designation for Captains and Commodores, which both you and I are. In the Navy, a step one is a recently promoted Captain who has less than a year's command experience. A step two, such as yourself, is a senior Captain who is eligible for promotion to the rank of Commodore. A step 3 is a Commodore of less than one year's experience, and a step 4 is a Commodore who has the time in grade needed to be considered for promotion." Haas grimaced. "I'm a step 4. A step 5 is practically nonexistent in the active Navy, however. You'd have to be trapped in the position of Commodore for over twenty years to gain it, though it is sometimes given as a courtesy step in pay for retirees. No-one has ever reached step 6."

Green sighed impatiently. He knew all of that, of course. "So what would a step 6 be equivalent to?"

"The Army does things a little differently. You come into the rank as a step 1, of course. Every five years in grade, your step increases. In Andrew Beccera's case, he's been in the position of Colonel for over thirty years. In fact, he's due for another step increase within the year."

Green nodded slowly. "Which means?"

Haas frowned in consideration. "Like I said, there's no such thing as an O-6 step 6 in the Navy. He'd outrank everyone short of a Rear Admiral. He'd probably be paid more than most Rear Admirals, in fact."

"So, he's actually senior to me," Green mused.

"Yes, but he's not able to command Naval forces. So, let's see if I can't find the next senior most officer in your—"

"Belay that," Green said with a grin. "Hell, the Navy's given me an impossible situation to begin with. It won't really matter, in the long run, who I name as my second-in-command. So, why shouldn't I just name this Army officer to the job? At the very least, his seniority should give him a shot."

Haas smiled back, and shrugged. It was unprecedented, and strategically he didn't think it was a great idea, but putting an Army officer on the Navy list might just put both of them in the footnotes of history. That was as good a justification as any, he supposed. "Very well. Now, for the real reason you had to come in person instead of just sending all of this information electronically. We've got about a hundred forms, here, for you to fill out – one, in triplicate, for each ship in your fleet."

Green sat back and sighed. "Oh, joy. Well, let's get this over with."

Cygni Confederation, 16 Cygni, Earth Alliance Embassy

"Captain Tager is here to see you, Ambassador," Noriko Goldsmith's secretary announced, accompanied by a tall bearded man she had never seen before.

The Ambassador stood up and held out her hand to the new arrival. "Nice to finally see you in person, George."

"And you, too, ma'am," he said. "I'm sorry that repairing our FTL drive has had to take priority."

"How is the *Athena*, anyway?" Goldsmith asked pleasantly.

"She's not doing very well, I'm afraid," George Tager, the captain of the aforementioned ship, sighed. "I don't know how well versed you are on quantum wheels...."

"I understand the rudiments of it," Goldsmith noted. "I may not know why a quantum wheel works, for example, but I know what it does and why it is preferred over the old fusion drive."

"I would hardly say the quantum wheel is preferred over the old fusion drives," George corrected. "It's more cost-efficient, perhaps, and has a few advantages other propulsion systems don't have, but many in the Navy dislike it." He paused. "And it is the quantum wheel that is giving me the most problems."

"Oh?" Goldsmith said. "And why is that?"

"Well... hmm. How do I explain this?" Captain Tager hesitated. "The principal advantages of a quantum wheel are supposedly twofold. Quantum wheels produce huge magnetic fields -- they can play havoc with targeting sensors. The magnetic fields produced by larger ships are so strong they can sometimes protect a ships blind spots from kinetic weapons, or even distort light."

"Yes, I knew that," Goldsmith said. "Most of what I've heard says that this defensive ability is the primary reason the Navy has become such a proponent of quantum wheels."

Tager shrugged. "Perhaps. The truth is more likely that quantum wheels are more fuel efficient. A warship with a fusion drive can rarely go for more than six months without needing to resupply -- and if the engine is subjected to heavy use, it runs closer to three. The same ship with quantum wheels would last as much as a year, with care."

"I hadn't realized there was that much difference," Goldsmith mused.

"Yes, but quantum wheels are quite problematic," Tager said. "To start with, fusion drive ships use an electromagnetic 'rudder,' of sorts, to maneuver. All ship classes in the fleet are given a top speed, but the number you see only applies to the maximum speed at which a ship can effectively maneuver. The smaller a ship, the more effective these rudders are, hence the faster a ship's top speed. At least, with fusion drive ships. The quantum wheel is completely different."

"In what way?" Goldsmith asked, intrigued.

"With a fusion drive ship, you're directing the thrust in one direction by deflecting it with a magnetic rudder. With a quantum wheel ship, however, there is nothing a magnetic rudder can deflect. Instead of using a rudder to redirect the flow of the engine, quantum wheel ships instead simply change which way they are thrusting. Doing *that*, however, presents something of a problem."

"And I take it this problem is causing the *Athena* difficulties," the Ambassador prompted, recognizing the frustration in Tager's voice.

"You've hit the nail on the head, ma'am," Tager admitted. "*Athena* is a good ship, but she's also getting old. The last Valkyrie class heavy cruiser finished construction just five years ago, but they've been around for thirty years. Of quantum wheel warships, only the Alligator class corvettes started construction earlier among active warship classes.

"*Athena* was only the second Valkyrie ever built. She was immediately sent out for long range patrols. Since she left port some thirty years ago, she has never had a chance to return home long enough to receive a refit."

"That sounds somewhat dangerous -- how is she maintained?" Goldsmith asked, alarmed.

"She's had regular visits at tenders, and she has been able to exchange crews and officers when transports come out. About twenty years ago, however, the design for quantum wheels changed to correct a problem with the steerage systems... but *Athena* has never had the dry-dock time to receive the upgrade."

"In over twenty years? But why?"

"Part of it is the nature of *Athena's* design" Tager explained. "*Athena* was built with a much larger fuel storage capacity than most ships of her class, and so is away from home for much longer periods than any other Valkyrie was designed to be. She was modified for a particular long-term assignment, but even after that assignment ended she was still in high demand. She is so unique that she couldn't be spared for the extended period of time it would take to replace the old system with a new one."

"How difficult is the repair?" Goldsmith asked.

"Essentially, the quantum wheel is disassembled, reassembled on a different frame, and a new set of electromagnetic plates is placed on the stern. The old plates -- or emitters, in this case -- were originally shaped as domes. The mechanisms inside rotated 360 degrees, allowing them to 'point' in the direction the thrust was to go. That particular design, though, had a major problem: In order for a quantum wheel to be effective, it takes thousands of semi-conductor powered magnets spinning in sequence at high speeds. In this configuration, any time the ship makes a turn those magnets are vibrated by the motion of changing thruster direction. After a while, they fall out of 'tune,' which is essentially what has happened with my ship -- it still works, but the maximum speed at which my ship can provide enough thrust to turn is getting lower and lower."

"And the new system?"

"It's a pyramid instead of a dome. Four separate emitter plates... to turn, one of the plates is shut off while the other three remain on full power. The ship is somewhat less maneuverable, but it causes less stress on the system, and therefore creates fewer situations where the magnets are thrown out of tune."

Goldsmith shook her head. "I'm afraid we're getting a little out of my depth. Let's put it this way. What can you do to get your ship running properly?"

"Well, that's what I came to see you about. I was wondering if it would be possible to request the use of one of Cygni's dry-docks or tenders. It's a simple procedure, recalibrating the magnets, but it requires a confined workspace. We would only need a few days, at most, and we already have the equipment we need. We just need a space to work."

The Ambassador hesitated. "Just how badly out of tune are your engines?"

Tager grimaced. "Pretty bad. In tune, we can maneuver at 0.21 c. At the moment, however, we can barely reach 0.12c."

Goldsmith frowned. "I suppose we can rent a private slip from one of the locals. But it will be costly, and I'm not sure the Embassy has the funds for it."

"The *Athena* has an expense account. It should be sufficient."

"There is another problem," she sighed. "Cygni is... not exactly the friendliest of nations. We needed you to present a show of strength. For you to immediately have to go into dry-dock..." Goldsmith shook her head and thought for a moment. "If you could hold out until the Wargame ends, it would be better for us all. Cygni is among the nations invited as foreign observers. and any news from its conclusion will occupy enough of their attention that your ship going to dry-dock won't be in the news."

Tager frowned. "I suppose it is possible. Let's just hope we aren't called upon to act, because as it is we would be useless in a battle."

"The last time one of the Navy ships assigned to act as an Ambassador's yacht was called into battle was several hundred years ago," Goldsmith reminded him cheerfully.

"I know," Tager smiled wryly. "That's exactly why I'm worried. We're overdue... and when something bad is going to happen, it usually happens at the worst possible time. Could the timing possibly be worse than now?"

Chapter VIII

EAS Gnat

Farmburg's trio of friends had remained mostly quiet since boarding the *Gnat*, but their mere presence made the others uncomfortable. It became especially tense during those periods when one of the five Chihuahua cadets had to leave the room for one reason or another. When Chris had to go to a private room to comm Burkhard, he was feeling especially uneasy.

The talk with his captain had gone fairly well, as far as Chris was concerned. While he doubted Burkhard would take Admiral McCaffrey's words to heart, the commander wasn't offended by the advice.

The *Gnat* was about to arrive at the primary site for the Wargame, and everyone was getting ready for their set-up duties. After drawing straws with the other pilot assigned to the *Chihuahua* (Lauren), Schubert had won the honor of taking the first set of engineers over. Chris was on that engineering team, along with Environmental Tech Linda Flint, Engineering Assistant Eric Drake, Environmental Engineer Wayne Evans, Damage Control Officer Carol Verne, and Chief Engineer Jacques Rappaport. Several other enlisted engineering trainees were being selected at random, but there still was no final word on who the remaining personnel would be.

The three friends of Farmburg would not report to their own ship until its overhaul had been completed. With Schubert, Chris, and Flint scheduled to leave in about an hour, Rachel and Weber were looking for any means by which they could escape their cabin.

"I wish I could join you guys on the shuttle," Rachel sighed.

"Hell, I wish I could fly the shuttle," Weber snorted. "Are you sure you don't need a copilot on this trip, Wolfie?"

Schubert shook his head. "Sorry, Lauren. No room for two pilots in the shuttle this time. But you'll have the next trip out."

Flint snickered behind the two pilots' backs. "Of course, by then we'll probably need two pilots, anyway. Assuming the hull's still airtight, I'm gonna make sure we get the life support systems up and running our first trip out. There'll still be the issue of the artificial gravity system, but with magnetic boots we should be able to start the heavy repair work that'll require most of the crew's participation. Oh, Rache, please have our cabin assignments ready by the time we get back. We'll probably need them."

Rachel shook her head. Flint wasn't even an officer, and technically shouldn't be making demands like that to her. She would also have to speak to her about that nickname – she already have to put up with it from the two clowns from her home dorm in the Academy. However, she wasn't in any mood to argue, now.

"Will do," she said tiredly. It was going to take an extra effort to be done by the time the engineering survey was complete, but she could do it. "I'd better get started right now, though. I think I'll go to the lounge and get to work. Someone give me my hand comp, will you?"

Chris grabbed it and shoved it into her hands. "Here. Have fun."

Rachel smiled halfheartedly at him. "Yeah, right. Well, at least I won't be stuck here... and I'll be on official ship's business, so they won't be able to kick me out after an hour."

With the passenger cabins filled to capacity, time in the *Gnat's* lounges had to be rationed. For most, it was limited to just one hour a day. If, however, a Cadet was using the room in order to work on official business, and had to maintain confidentiality from their bunkmates, he or she could gain an exception to the rule. Thanks to a word put in by Chris during their conversation, Burkhard had informed the staff at one of the lounges of her logistics assignment. When Chris had told her that he'd done that, Rachel had almost hugged him.

"I guess that means the lot of you are going to be leaving little old me all alone, aren't you?" Weber complained good-naturedly as Rachel left.

"Attention. Arriving in system HD 19994. Will the engineering survey crews please report to the Shuttle Docking Facility. Thank you," the loudspeakers announced.

Schubert glanced up at the offending speaker and sighed. "Guess so. Sorry, Lauren – we're on call."

Weber grinned. "Go on, get out of here! I'll find something to occupy me, I'm sure."

Chris stood up and tapped Schubert on the shoulder. "Come on, let's get going. The sooner we get started, the sooner we can get everyone off this tub."

Weber watched as her remaining shipmates left the room, then glanced across at the silent trio still in her room. Smiling slightly, she cracked her knuckles. "So, boys... am I going to have to deal with any problems from you while my friends are gone?" she asked.

The largest of them hesitated, remembering how she had rescued Schubert from them. "I don't know what you're talking about, ma'am. We never cause any trouble."

Weber's grin widened. "That's good. If you were in the mood to cause some, though, I think I should warn you some Marine buddies of mine will be meeting me here shortly for dinner, and they'd be mighty upset if I wasn't able to join them."

The three men looked at each. "Well," their spokesman answered. "We were just going out."

Weber sighed dramatically. "What a shame. My friends were so looking forward to meeting you. Oh, well... I guess I'll see you later."

When she left, the trio huddled in a circle to discuss this turn of events. "Well, now what are we going to do?" one of them asked. "Joel said to wait until one of them was alone and see if we could arrange for them to have an 'accident.' But we can't get them alone, so how are we going to do that?"

"Well, if we can't do that, Franco, let's try something else," the man who had been their spokesman suggested.

"Like what, Nathan?"

"How about we get one of them in trouble like we did with Mr. Schubert?" Nathan suggested. "We got him into a bar fight, and he got into trouble. If it worked with him, why wouldn't it work with the others?"

"I think we should call Joel, first," the third member of their trio suggested.

Nathan rolled his eyes. "You always want to talk to Joel, first, before doing anything. Don't you have your own mind?"

"Of course I do! But he was the one who lured Schubert into that fight in the first place, not us. Do you know what buttons to push to start bar fights with these people? And that's a lot of bar fight to start, if we want to get rid of all of them. Don't you think we need another plan?"

"Fine," Nathan sighed. Pressing a button on a nearby comm unit, he said, "Nathan Priest, Franco Kobe, and Sergio Ramsey calling for Cadet Lieutenant Joel Farmburg, please."

There was a moment before a synthesized voice replied, "I'm sorry, Lieutenant Farmburg is not available at this time. Would you like to leave a message?"

"No," Nathan said, snapping the comm off. "Well, shit. And we don't have time to wait for him, either. I've got a target in mind, but if we don't act now we won't be able to get her. Well, Sergio?"

Sergio gave a rather disgusted snort. "I won't stop you, but it's on your head if Joel gets pissed at us."

"Yeah, yeah, whatever."

EAS Chihuahua

Chris grimaced as he inspected the *Chihuahua*. "Sorry, Linda... we're going to have to hold off on starting up the environmental systems for a while," he said into his biosuit's radio.

"What's the problem?" her voice asked.

"I'm seeing a bunch of cracks in the hull," he said. "It looks like the ship was hit by a storm of micro-meteors some time ago. Until we've ascertained the extent of the damage, I don't think it would be a good idea to pressurize the hull."

"Understood," Flint said.

"I'll keep you updated."

Chris continued superficial examinations, noting areas where more intense examinations would probably be required, until he got to the computers. He switched his suit radio's channel. "Desaix to Rappaport."

"Rappaport here," the Chief Engineer answered.

"I'm at the main computer core now. Do I have your authorization to install the portable power unit and activate?"

"Install, but don't activate until I've confirmed that everyone has been told that the wiring should be going live. Let's hope this works – we may be replacing these computers later, this will go a lot faster if we can get these old systems to give us diagnostics in the meantime. Don't be afraid to cut corners as long as you can maintain a decent safety factor – if a computer blows, we can just hold off until we have a new one."

Chris frowned. He didn't like the casual disregard for any antiques, even something as clunky as these elderly computers. "We might have trouble getting replacements, sir, so unless that's a direct order I'll go ahead and take the necessary precautions to keep the computer safe."

"Whatever," Rappaport said. Chris could almost hear the shrug in his voice. "I'll contact you shortly."

Chris removed the fuel cell system strapped on his back and set it down by the computer, activating the magnetic stand to secure it to the deck. Shaking his head, Chris wondered if he'd have been able to carry the thing throughout his inspection had it not been for the lack of gravity on board. He began setting up the safety features while waiting for the word.

"Everyone's checked out, so you have the go ahead to get that computer up and running," Rappaport announced. "I'll join you shortly. I'm really interested in what that computer has to say."

"Yes, sir," Chris answered, starting to make the connections needed. He inspected some of the wiring critically. Taking out a spool of wire from one of his bio-suit's storage packs, he measured what he felt was an appropriate length and cut, replacing a grounding wire in the computer with the new piece.

Rappaport came to witness the tail end of his repair work, and nodded to himself, grinning. Unknown to most of the cadets, the regular Navy officers weren't just there to help crew the ships – they were also supposed to provide evaluations of the talent under them. His suggestion that Chris not worry too hard about keeping the old computers intact was one of his ways of testing the kid. The obvious care that the cadet was taking in repairing the archaic mainframe was proof enough that he had a proper respect for his craft. Rappaport made a mental note to include that in his daily report.

"How's it going?" he asked.

Chris started slightly. "Some of the mainframe's wiring was inadequate. It's a quick fix. I'll boot it up once I finish soldering this line."

"Take your time but hurry up," Rappaport said with a grin. It was an old joke, but all-too-often those were the expectations of an engineer. "I really need to check the automated damage control reports and see if I can find a blueprint."

"A blueprint?" Chris asked, finishing his repairs. "I thought we had one."

"My inspection shows me that the schematics we've got don't quite match up to the *Chihuahua's* configuration," Rappaport explained. "It makes sense, since she was completely overhauled several times in her career. I'm hoping her old Chief Engineer kept the blueprints on the computer updated."

"If he was any good, he would have," Chris said, powering up the fuel cell. "But he didn't necessarily store them on this computer."

"No, but this is the most likely place," Rappaport said, sitting down at one of the computer consoles. "Boot her up, Mr. Desaix."

"Sure thing," Chris said, flipping a few switches.

Rappaport sighed, and added to that report in his head that the cadet wasn't very good about using the word "sir." Oh, well – the boy was just a freshman, after all. By the time he graduated, he was bound to have the necessary formalities drilled into his head.

"Trainee Weapons Tech Jonathan Rosebaugh to whoever it is who just turned on the power," a nervous voice said on the general attention channel.

Rappaport and Chris glanced at each other in surprise. "This is Rappaport. Mr. Desaix activated a temporary power unit under my direction just a minute ago. What do you want?"

"If wouldn't be too much trouble, could you turn the power back off?" Rosebaugh asked. "I, uh, dropped a tool into an area with live wires."

Rappaport rolled his eyes and glanced at Chris, who shook his head. "Sorry, Rosebaugh. It's a fuel cell, and it's fully cycled up. There's no way of deactivating the power at the moment. You'll just have to make do until we're done." He frowned. "Where are you? I might just be able to isolate your area once the computers have fully booted."

"I'm in the ammunition storage room," Rosebaugh replied.

"How many live wires could there be in that storage room?" Chris muttered to himself, disgusted.

"I'm not sure how to isolate that portion of the ship," Rappaport sighed, not even sure why there were exposed live wires in the ammo storage room to begin with. "Just leave it for now. We'll be sure to recover it after we deactivate the fuel cell."

"Yes, sir," Rosebaugh acknowledged. "I'll make do, sir."

"Damn," Rappaport sighed as he changed his suit radio back to private chat. "How did we get probably the most crack crew in the entire Academy fleet, yet wind up with that guy?"

Chris winced. "That was probably my fault, sir. We were short one weapons tech, and he was the only one any of us knew. I figured getting someone qualified but accident prone was better than getting someone unknown and finding out they were completely incompetent. Jonathan's good, I think, but he tends to lack focus from time to time. It makes him clumsy."

Rappaport shook his head. "Well, what's done is done. Help me out with this piece of crap computer, would you?"

"Hey, the computer isn't a piece of crap," Chris protested, taking a seat next to the Chief Engineer. "It's in perfect condition, from what I can tell."

"It's a hundred years old!" Rappaport retorted.

"I never said it wasn't," Chris chuckled. "I just said it wasn't a piece of crap. It's an antique, true, but then so is the whole ship." He glanced over the mainframes. "The operating systems they had in this ship's day weren't very efficient, so to run these complex systems the designers went for superior hardware and lots of it. It's got enough computing power that we would be well within modern standards just by upgrading the software."

Rappaport shook his head. "Not with the secondary propulsion system I was planning on installing. To manage both quantum wheels and a fusion drive effectively, we're going to need more than 'standard' computing power."

Chris' eyes goggled. "Quantum wheels? In a corvette? Sir, why would you want to put a monstrosity like that in a ship like the *Chihuahua?*"

"I take it you are one of those people who isn't overly fond of present design principles in propulsion," Rappaport said, amused. "Well, normally I would agree with you. However, since we'll have the extra power to burn once you put in your cold fusion plant, we might as well use it."

"I had planned some upgrades to the weapons system, but I suppose that would work, too," Chris frowned. "We'll need magnetic plating, though. That's going to be tricky to get at this stage."

"So are most of the other things we're going to need," Rappaport sighed. "It'll just be one more impossible obstacle we're going to have to overcome."

Chris smirked confidently. "Right. And, sir? I've got the blueprints, now. They're already downloaded to my hand-comp."

Rappaport nodded. "Good job. Now, let's see what else we can find here before we have to head back, shall we?"

EAS Gnat

Rachel rubbed her eyes. They were starting to hurt from staring at her hand comp for so long. She needed her glasses, but she didn't dare risk wearing them in such a public place. She normally wore contact lenses, but until she was able to unpack in her cabin on the *Chihuahua* they were stuck in storage. She had her glasses with her – she always took that precaution – but she wouldn't wear them if she could help it. She was always afraid other officers, especially her teachers, would see her glasses as proof she couldn't do everything a Naval officer should be capable of doing.

And, the truth was she couldn't. She could never pilot a military vessel on her own, for example, even though she was probably as competent in flight sims as an ace like Schubert. She didn't understand how Chris could stand displaying this evidence of physical incompetence as much as he did.

Well, intellectually she did. After all, she knew that there were only a few things that really interested him in the Navy, and piloting was not one of them. Really, that was the only thing their eye problems prevented them from becoming.

Pondering such things wouldn't help her headache any, though. Maybe she should go to the medical bay and see if she could get something for her headache. And then she might try finding somewhere private where she could use her glasses unobserved to finish her job.

"Hey, lookee here," one of the three thugs from her cabin sneered. "If it isn't our good ol' roomy, Rachel Katz. How're ya doing, Rache?"

Her head snapped up, seeing all three of her unwanted roommates approaching. "You should address me as either 'ma'am' or 'Cadet Lt. Commander Rachel Katz, ma'am.' You are never allowed to call me 'Rache.'" She grinned dangerously. "Unlike certain other officers who's informality I tolerate, *you* could be sent to the brig if I get too annoyed by you using that name."

"Oh, sorry," The largest of them apologized sarcastically. "Didn't know you were too important to be dealt with as a normal human being in off-duty hours."

Rachel sniffed. "Well, for one thing, I am not off duty. I'm using the lounge as an office to escape from people like you, yes, but only because I need a quiet place to work."

"Oh, I'm sure that's the only reason she needs to escape from us," the last one to speak snorted.

"I think she's scared of us," the first one said. "What do you think, Franco?"

"Oh, definitely, Nathan," the last of them answered back. Something about his tone of voice didn't quite fit, but Rachel couldn't quite place it.

"Afraid of you?" Rachel snorted. Her headache didn't need this. "That's downright hilarious! Why in the world would I be afraid of you?"

"Well, now, that's a very good question, isn't it?" Nathan said. "Why would an *officer* like you be afraid of three ordinary enlisted men like us?"

"She's probably afraid she'll forget what she's supposed to be doing while we're around," Franco joked.

"And just what is that supposed to mean?" Rachel asked, her voice lowering dangerously.

"Well, gee. Here we are, three handsome members of the male species," Nathan said. "And here you are, a slut pretending her Academy standing makes her an officer. I wonder what kind of distraction we might provide?"

Rachel stilled. "Excuse me, but what did you just call me?"

"You heard us," Nathan said, smirking.

It took all her willpower not to strike him, but she held back. She knew he was trying to provoke her into a fight, but she didn't know why. Regardless, she wouldn't give him the satisfaction. She took a deep breath to compose herself. "Leave now or I'll have you arrested for insubordination."

The quietest of the three started to leave. Nathan, however, grabbed him and kept him there. "Hold on a minute, Sergio." He turned to face Rachel. "You can't make us leave, 'ma'am.' This is a public place, and while you might not be off duty, we are. Furthermore, we aren't under your command, so we don't need to listen to your orders anyway."

"Then I'll have you arrested for harassment!" Rachel growled. "Now, leave me alone!"

"No," Nathan said calmly, smirking.

Rachel shut down her hand-comp and slowly stood up, glaring at the three men in front of her. As she stood up, she was able to catch a whiff of Nathan's breath, and detected the strong smell of alcohol in it. *They're drunk. Damn, this doesn't look good.* She glanced around at the lounge. *And it doesn't look like there's anyone inclined to help out, either. I'm in serious trouble.*

"Fine," Rachel said evenly. She picked up her hand comp and started walking away, making sure that she could still see them in the corner of her eye. "Follow me all the way to the security office."

"Oh? Why are you headed there?" Nathan chuckled. "You whoring yourself out for security, too?"

Remember, he's drunk, Rachel thought to herself between clenched teeth. Her headache was killing her, and she just couldn't handle this. *That's the only reason he's being this crude. Right. And if I really believe that, I'll probably buy the next bridge offered to me, too.*

"Hey, bitch," Franco slurred. "Just how do you keep it up? I mean, I gotta figure you're doing everyone in the Academy, but how do you manage that and security, too?"

Franco didn't even see the elbow that crashed into his nose a split second later, sending him tumbling to the ground. A foot stepped on his throat, and he glanced up to see a hard-faced Rachel Katz, still holding her hand-comp, standing over him.

"Oh, I'm sorry," she apologized sarcastically. "I didn't see you there."

She was tackled off of him by Nathan, who charged in to attack once he saw his comrade fall. She dropped her hand-comp as she fell to the floor, but there were other things on her mind.

She kicked out of Nathan's grasp and stumbled to her feet, backing up so the wall would protect her back. Franco was already standing, wiping the blood from his nose and looking downright homicidal. His friends were grinning viciously, and she was starting to wonder just how much of their drunkenness was feigned – they seemed decidedly too steady on their feet to be that drunk, making them all the more dangerous.

"Now, this hardly looks fair," a voice said from behind her three attackers. "It's not very nice to gang up on a lady, three on one." They spun around, and Rachel caught a glance at her new ally. She recognized the renowned Colonel Beccera standing there, grinning. "Now, why don't we even those odd out a bit, shall we?"

Sergio stepped back, seeing the handwriting on the wall. "I'm not ganging up on no-one, old man. I was just drinking with my friends when she up and belted poor Franco."

"Then get the hell out of here," Beccera snapped. "And leave your 'friends' to us."

Without another word, Sergio walked away. Their job had been done, anyway – they'd goaded one of Schubert's friends into attacking them. Now, all he had to do was wait, watch his roommates get pounded into the dust by Rachel and the man in the Army uniform, and let Farmburg know what had happened.

———————————

"Well, the computer said you had an urgent message for me, Sergio. What is it?" Farmburg said from the other end of the comm unit. He hadn't activated the video feature, leading Sergio to believe the man had just woken up.

"Yes, sir. Well, Nathan and Franco took the initiative and tried something," Sergio said. He hesitated. "I want to let you know that I tried to get the others to call you before we started. Nathan, well, he—"

"My time is important. Stop dancing around the subject – something went wrong, correct?"

"You could say that, yeah," Sergio admitted. "Last I saw them, Nathan and Franco were being dragged off to sick bay, to get treatment before they got thrown into the brig."

"Just what the hell did you guys *do?*" Farmburg groaned.

"*I* didn't do anything," Sergio explained. "At least, not after it came to blows. By that point, I knew things were hopeless, and I thought it would be best if one of us wasn't in the brig so that we could let you know what happened."

"Start at the beginning, okay?" Farmburg sighed. "I won't know whether to agree with you until I hear it all."

Sergio winced, but he was fairly certain he had done the right thing. "Yes, sir. Nathan had this idea to go after Schubert by targeting his friends. It probably wasn't a good idea, and I really tried to insist he call and get your approval first, but you weren't there, and Nathan said if we didn't do it right away our opportunity would be gone, so..."

"You're babbling, Mr. Ramsey," Farmburg signed. "Calm down, take a deep breath, and tell me what Nathan's idea was."

As instructed, Sergio took the deep breath and let it out slowly. Then he took another. Finally, he felt ready to continue. "Nathan thought it would be a good idea to pretend to get drunk and start a fight with Rachel Katz in the lounge." He paused. "He figured he'd try the same thing you did to get Schubert in trouble. He said they'd go easier on us if we were drunk, and he was planning on making sure Katz got the first punch in just so that we weren't the aggressors."

"I think I understand," Farmburg replied wearily. "How badly did he step in it?"

"Well, I think Franco really got drunk when he was only supposed to pretend to. At any rate, he got his wish – Katz punched him." For once,

Sergio grinned. "Took a nasty elbow to the face, knocking him to the ground and splattering his nose. It'll probably never look the same again."

"Well, it sounds like things were going according to plan," Farmburg snorted. "What went wrong?"

"An Army Colonel interfered – and don't ask me why he was there, either. Near as I can tell, he overheard everything we said to Rachel, so he knows she was provoked. I ran off after that, but watched him take Nathan and Franco apart alongside the girl. I think Nathan'll end up with a permanent limp, and Franco... well, he didn't look too good, that's for sure."

"And they were arrested, I take it?"

"Yes, sir."

Farmburg sighed. "Well, not much we can do for now. They'll probably just be tossed in the brig until they sober up and given a heap of demerits – they were already badly injured; I wouldn't expect anything worse for them as long as they were convincingly drunk. What about Katz and this Army colonel?"

"They were unhurt, last I saw. They were arrested by the MPs alongside Nathan and Franco, but no brig time for them."

"Well, it's too late to do anything about this, now. Keep me informed," Farmburg ordered, breaking the connection.

Sergio was quite glad that he'd gotten out of it so unscathed – Farmburg had a temper. But he was now the only member of Farmburg's gang left in the cabin – just how long would he remain unscathed?

Chapter IX

EAS Gnat

Burkhard waited by the airlock for the shuttle's crew and passengers to arrive. He glanced over to see one of his pilots, Weber, also waiting for this shuttle.

"...would estimate at least four days before she's airtight," Cadet Lieutenant Christopher Desaix was telling fellow Cadet Lieutenant Wolfgang Schubert as they departed the shuttle. "So we'll be keeping you busy not just running crew back and forth, but also running air tanks so that we can keep the shifts going longer."

"Won't be a problem. It's routine and boring, but I'm not the only pilot," Schubert answered.

"Mr. Desaix, Mr. Schubert, Ms. Flint, Ms. Weber," Burkhard asked. "I need to discuss some things with you."

Chris and Schubert looked at each other in surprise. "Yeah, sure," Chris said, nodding.

The three people who Burkhard had called approached him with curious looks on their faces. "What's the matter, sir?" Schubert asked, voicing the unasked question all of them were wondering.

"It's about your roommates," Burkhard explained.

"No, it's about Rachel," Weber corrected.

The threesome's eyes widened in surprise. "Is she okay?" Chris asked, an unexpected tremor in his voice.

"She's unhurt," Burkhard answered. "She's in a bit of trouble, though."

"What happened?" Chris demanded, stepping up to his Captain, his voice tight and crisp with determination.

Burkhard raised an eyebrow. He'd read all of the records on Christopher Desaix and not a single one of them suggested that he would respond so aggressively. He'd talked to all of the cadets' instructors, and while Morrison had suggested that Lt. Desaix and Lt. Commander Katz had some kind of adversarial attachment to each other, nothing he'd learned had suggested anything beyond that.

"I'm not entirely clear on the details, myself," Burkhard said carefully. He didn't want to make the boy any more agitated than he already was. "As near as I can tell, she and some of your other roommates got into some sort of verbal confrontation. She started to leave, but Cadet Kobe continued provoking her into a fight. My 'Marine' CO, Colonel Beccera, intervened on her behalf. Now two of my officers – Colonel Beccera and Ms. Katz – are being held for questioning in regards to the incident. Since both parties are your roommates, I was wondering if any of you might know something about what sparked all of this."

Chris turned his glare on Schubert, who shrugged and turned to look at another of their companions. "Why didn't you tell him, Lauren?" Schubert asked.

"Not my place to tell, Wolfie," Weber said, a sad grin on her face. "That's your job."

Schubert sighed. "Fine. Alright, Captain, I'll tell you... but realize I can't prove any of this, so there's no point in my testifying."

"It doesn't matter as long as someone explains just what the hell is going on."

"Yes, sir," Schubert said. "But if you don't mind, could we go somewhere to talk about this in private?"

Burkhard wasn't quite sure what to make of the situation. The people involved in this situation seemed to be his best and brightest – Katz was a remarkable tactician if Morrison's reports were to be believed, Desaix was his best engineer, Schubert and Weber were excellent pilots, and Linda Flint was a superior environmental tech despite being an enlisted trainee. They all seemed to know something, but evidently one of them knew more than the others.

"Very well," he finally said. "Mr. Schubert, wait here. The rest of you are dismissed. You may head to the detention area and see how your cabin mates are doing."

With barely a nod, Chris almost ran out of the room in the direction of the brig. With a couple of muttered "Yes, sirs," Flint and Weber followed at a more sedate pace. When they were finally alone, Burkhard turned to his pilot.

"Well, Mr. Schubert. Just why the hell is privacy so important to this whole matter?" he asked.

Schubert winced. "Well, sir, this all started a couple weeks ago at a campus bar. I swear I wasn't drunk at the time – I hadn't been there for more than a few minutes, and it takes me longer than that – but soon I got into an argument with a Cadet Lieutenant Joel Farmburg."

Burkhard frowned. "I believe that I read about this incident in your records. You started a bar fight with the man. You say you weren't drunk at the time, though... so what the hell did he say to you that got you into that fight in the first place?"

"That is what I wanted Chris – that is, Mr. Desaix – out of the room for, sir. See, Farmburg was... insulting him. Sort of."

Burkhard frowned. "You'll have to explain better than that, Mr. Schubert. Just what did he say?"

"It's not so much what he said, as how he said it," Schubert said, hesitating. "He implied, rather crudely, that Chris and Rachel were lovers."

Burkhard nodded. He'd just been speculating something similar, but evidently they weren't. "Go on."

"Even the words themselves wouldn't sound that bad, recited dryly – it was all in his tone of voice. I could tell that he was implying Rachel was 'easy,' insulting the two of them for being attracted to each other."

"And that's when you let the first punch fly," Burkhard supplied.

Schubert nodded. "Yes, sir. Insults to me I could just ignore, but I couldn't stand to hear my friends talked about that way."

"I see."

"The story doesn't end with the fight, though, sir."

Burkhard nodded. If these two incidents were connected, he wanted to know how. "Go on."

"The day of Mr. Orff's party – or perhaps I should say the night of it," Schubert explained. "Someone sent me a message impersonating Captain Anne Morrison, directing me to a meeting with her. When I arrived, her office was closed and locked up, and I later learned that she wasn't even on-planet at the time the request was made. I soon noticed that I was being followed by several large men, whom I've since identified as Cadets

Priest, Ramsey, and Kobe – our current roommates, curiously enough – and Seaman Trainee Jefferson Flay. They claimed they were going to put me into the hospital since I'd put Mr. Farmburg in the hospital. They were apparently his friends, sir, and definitely were out for blood. I'm not entirely sure they wouldn't have killed me."

"How'd you get out of it?" Burkhard asked.

"Ms. Weber and Ms. Flint rescued me," Schubert said. "I didn't know them at the time, but they nevertheless recognized me as a shipmate, and between us we kicked the crap – sorry, sir, I mean fought back against my attackers. We didn't have any proof that the incident happened like we said, though, except for our word, and we were leaving for the *Chihuahua* the next day. Because of that, we didn't report it."

"And so now, you're rooming with three people who tried to kill you, and you think they're trying to stir up trouble with you and your friends," Burkhard concluded.

"Exactly, sir."

Burkhard sighed. "Well, two of them will be stuck in the brig for a few days, and I doubt the third will act alone. I have no say in the accommodations, here, but I'll talk to Captain Sharpe to see if he can do anything about it."

Schubert nodded. "Thank you, sir."

"Now, why don't we join your friends in checking on Ms. Katz, shall we?"

EAS Mouse

Farmburg sat down to organize his reports, wincing. On paper he had long recovered from his hospital stay, but he still had twinges now and then. Perhaps he'd held back a bit too much when he provoked Schubert into attacking him – though, to be fair, the only way to have won that fight would have been to reveal his advanced hand-to-hand training, which 'Farmburg's' background story would not have been able to explain. Schubert was a lot more skilled than he expected.

His small pool of allies hadn't fared much better. To destroy the best and the brightest, he had started befriending the dregs of Academy life: The troublemakers, the idiots, and the petty rogues and thieves which had besmirched the names of every honorable military man since the dawn of time. Unfortunately, the fact remained that they *were* idiots and troublemakers, which made them rather... unreliable.

The Wargame, however, presented more subtle opportunities. By no design of his own, almost a third of the people he had identified as the cream of the Academy's crop were aboard a single corvette, the *Chihuahua*. It would only take a small miscalculation at a critical point to wipe that corvette off the face of the universe, and in a military exercise many things could occur that would be written off as 'accidents.'

His orders from Cygni continued to trouble him. The urgency expressed to him grew increasingly desperate, but his superiors weren't providing the level of support that urgency would normally suggest. A number of the people who were supposed to join him as backup had been detained in Pleiades for some reason, but that only seemed to put his superiors more on edge. One would think they wouldn't leave him relying on idiots like Nathan and Sergio to make these plans happen, whatever was going on in Pleiades. Something was definitely going on that he didn't know about... maybe something that he didn't want to know about.

EAS Gnat

Rachel sighed, rubbing her bruised jaw gingerly. She didn't think it would swell too much, but it was purpling as she sat there. *Oh, well, it was worth it to see that asshole's nose turn into a pancake.*

A hissing sound signified the catches on her cell door releasing. Rachel looked up and was surprised to see Chris coming through the door. She wasn't expecting him back from the *Chihuahua* for another few hours, at least.

"Chris!" she chirped, getting to her feet. "What're you doing back here so soon?"

"There are some microfractures in the hull preventing us from activating life support. Our 'Plan B' if that was the case was to just conduct a quick survey while the Environmental Engineers unloaded their gear, then we would come back and collect the equipment to repair the hulls." He put a finger under her chin, turning it so he could see the purple blot caused by the fight. His eyes tightened slightly. "Are you okay?"

"Yeah, I'm fine," Rachel said, somewhat flustered by the attention. "You should see the other guys."

Chris broke away and looked at his feet. "I'm sorry. I knew they'd probably try something while we were gone. I should have warned you."

"Nonsense. I suspected they were going to try something, too – that's partly why I chose to work in the lounge. I figured I'd be safe in a public place," she said. He looked so guilty, she needed to do something to cheer him up. "It's not your fault."

Chris sighed. "But you didn't guess that this would be their exact plan. Farmburg is on a different transport, though, so I figured they would wait until they could get in touch with him to act. I thought you were safe, but I knew they might have tried this. I could have warned you – I *should* have warned you!"

"Relax!" Rachel said, grabbing his shoulders. "I'm okay. Security is convinced I acted only in self-defense – this won't even go on my record. The only reason I'm still here is that the paperwork hasn't been completed yet for my release."

"Why?"

"What?" Rachel replied.

"They must have said something," Chris said dangerously. "If security believes your attack was a matter of self-defense, they must have said something significant. Why else would you be released so easily?"

Rachel winced. He wasn't going to let it go, was he? "I'd rather not repeat it, thank you. They were rather vulgar."

His fists clinched. "Vulgar language, drink on their breath, stalking you even outside of your cabin. God... they were planning to rape you, Rache...."

Rachel's eyes widened. "No – I mean, yeah, they were drunk, but this was in a public bar. Surely they'd have known they couldn't get away with something like that."

Chris said nothing, and Rachel was starting to feel uncomfortable. What if Chris was right? And now that she thought about it, what would have stopped them if they'd gotten her alone?

"Well, thanks to the Colonel, they didn't," she said matter-of-factly. Chris might have been right, but she would rather neither of them dwelled on that possibility. "When will we be able to move into the *Chihuahua?*"

His jaw set, but the arrival of a pair of their friends stopped him from saying anything.

"Jeez," Flint huffed, panting slightly. Both she and Weber looked out of breath. "What'd you do, fly down here?"

"I know a few shortcuts," Chris said evasively. "Rache says she'll be released soon. They're just completing the paperwork, now."

"So I hear you and our new Marine-for-a-Day, Colonel Beccera, beat the stuffing out of Farmburg's buddies," Weber said, walking past Chris and Flint. "Good job. But how'd you get that shiner? You should've clobbered them before you got it."

Rachel winced. "It was just the start of the attack. I'd just splattered... what was his name? The big guy's nose all over his face, dropping him instantly. Before I was aware of it, though, one of his friends blindsided me and tackled me to the ground. That was the only blow they landed on me, though. Once Colonel Beccera showed up— Chris? Where are you going?"

Chris was making his way to the brig's door. "Back to the *Chihuahua*. They've probably loaded the extra personal air supplies on board the shuttle by now – I want to get that hull patched up."

Weber looked confused for a moment, but there seemed to be some sort of silent communication between him and Chris. "Well, you're going to need a pilot, and I suspect Wolfie's a bit tied up right now. Besides, it's my turn! Get what you need while I prep the shuttle for launch." She turned to Rachel and sighed. "Sorry, girl, looks like I'm going to have to cut this visit short. Linda'll stay with you until you're released, won't you, Linda?"

Flint received a significant look from the woman and nodded grimly. "Yeah, sure. See ya soon."

Rachel watched as Chris and Weber went through the security checkpoints and left. Her face slowly turned down into a frown.

"What's wrong?" Flint asked.

"Why did Chris leave?" Rachel asked. "That seemed so... sudden."

Flint shrugged. "I have my suspicions, but nothing I'd commit to. Did you manage, in all this commotion, to get those cabin assignments completed?"

Rachel smiled slightly. "No, I'm afraid I was somewhat..." she gestured to her surroundings, "Distracted?"

Flint laughed. "Thought so. You'd better finish them as soon as you get out, though." She glanced at the door where Chris had departed. "The repair estimates based on our initial survey suggested it would take four days to make the *Chihuahua* airtight. I've got a feeling those estimates are going to be changing, soon."

Rachel found she was more popular than she had believed, receiving more friendly visitors in the forms of Schubert, Cohen, and even Captain Burkhard before she was released from the brig. She wasn't entirely comfortable about going back to her cabin alone, but Schubert was there to walk with her. When she learned that Nathan and Franco were going to be stuck in the brig for several more days, still, she relaxed considerably. There was that third guy – Sergio, she thought the name was – to watch out for, however.

She waited for Chris to return from the *Chihuahua* so that she could talk to him some more, but as the hours wore on she started to wonder when he was going to return. Finally, she decided to get in touch with Lt. Rappaport.

"I'm afraid I don't know when he'll be back," Rappaport told her. "He hasn't filed any sort of schedule with me."

"Isn't he required to give one to you?"

Rappaport sniffed sardonically. "Yes, but technically he's already given me one. Just not an accurate one – he's moved well ahead of the planned schedule, and he shows no sign of slowing down."

Rachel chewed her lips. "When are you planning to talk to him next, then?"

"I'm going in with the next team of engineers in about a half hour. If he isn't on the return shuttle, I'll have to talk with him regardless. From what I can tell, he didn't take the quantum wheel mechanics into consideration when he was drafting his plans for the refit."

"Good. Could you find out, for me, when he's planning on returning to the *Gnat?* I need to talk with him about a few things."

Rappaport frowned. "Official business or personal?"

Rachel hesitated. "Well, technically it's not official business, but I wouldn't call it personal either, sir."

"Fine. I'll ask him. Could I ask, though, what it is you need to talk to him about?" Rappaport asked.

"I wanted to ask him for some help with questions regarding the... incident... in the lounge, earlier today," Rachel said. She didn't really want to explain, but she felt he needed to know that much.

"Ah, yes – I heard about that. Yeah, I'll let him know you're looking for him," Rappaport said. "I've got a question for you in return, though," he said.

"Oh?" Rachel replied, wondering what Rappaport might want her for.

"I understand you and he are classmates and friends back at the Academy. I've read his file, and I understand he's very good at tactics in addition to engineering. Which is he really more interested in?" Rappaport asked.

Rachel almost laughed. "Chris? Oh, he's definitely more interested in engineering. Or at least, in the technical details of engineering. His hobby is restoring antique electronics. He's scratch-built several things for me based on plans from hundreds of years ago, and he'll fuse old technology with new to produce something better than what's available off-the-shelf. One of his favorite sayings is that 'It may be newer, but that doesn't mean it's better.'" She frowned. "This ship is a dream assignment for him, but I'm not sure he'd really enjoy working on newer ships. He doesn't like quantum wheels, for example. He seems to think that the technology isn't sufficiently debugged for use outside of experimentation."

"There's a lot of that thought going around," Rappaport countered. "I don't particularly like them, myself, but they could be the eventual solution to the deceleration problem."

The deceleration problem Rappaport was talking about involved any ship using a modern fusion drive. Acceleration was effectively instantaneous, but only in one direction – forward. It was usually only possible to fit one such fully-powered drive on any. In order to decelerate, these ships had to make an intricate maneuver, spinning the ship around with reaction control thrusters and then using the main drive in the opposite direction.

The theory was that quantum wheels could reverse this problem by reversing the magnetic wave by which they propelled ships. However, there had not been any success in the attempts to apply that theory, yet.

"I suspect that Chris would agree with you on that," Rachel said. She was unaware of any of the details behind why quantum wheels might solve the deceleration problem, but she knew that it hadn't done so, yet. "But until the quantum wheel fulfills all the promises it claims to be able to deliver in the future, I doubt he'll agree with their widespread use. And I don't think he particularly is interested in solving those problems – I think he'd be more interested in making better use of what we have now."

Rappaport frowned. "What, exactly, are you trying to say?"

Rachel shrugged. "I suppose the best way to summarize my impression of him is that, while he's incredibly talented, he'll enjoy engineering as a hobby more than he would as a career. The same goes with his tactical skills, though, but... well, *because* he enjoys tactics less, I think it would be a better career choice for him. As a tactician, he'd get less... frustrated, for lack of a better word, at having to work on things he doesn't particularly think are that important, or interesting, or useful. If he could keep engineering as his hobby, he'll continue to enjoy it because he won't be forced to do those things he finds too routine. I think *he* would most want to be an engineer... until he actually became one and found himself, say, regularly assigned to re-tune a ship's quantum wheels. A career path which combined the two might suit him best, although I have no idea what job that would be."

Rappaport sighed. "To be honest, I'm not surprised. In fact, I agree with you. But I'm not sure what to do – as an engineer, he's a natural, and I would be a fool not to nurture that. I shouldn't be advising him to ignore that talent. But I agree that he would probably become disillusioned in the end, which could be just as harmful." He frowned. "There is an engineering station on the bridge – once the refit is complete, I'll see to it that Mr. Desaix is assigned there. We'll install some tactical displays or something, and I'll be sure that the Captain includes him as a part of his tactical team. I want him to get experience with both jobs, both the good parts and the bad. I suspect he hasn't seen the dull side of an engineer's career in the Navy, yet. Then we'll see which career path he really prefers."

EAS Chihuahua

Chris sat down, needing to close his eyes for a moment. He was exhausted, having neither eaten nor slept since shortly before the initial inspection of the ship, and a lot of the work he was doing proved to be quite labor-intensive. He couldn't allow himself to take a break, however. For the moment, Rachel's attackers were in the brig, but he didn't know when they'd be released, and he would not rest while she might still be in danger.

There was a tap on his suited shoulder. He opened his eyes, surprised to see Lieutenant Rappaport standing in front of him, looking slightly amused through his own suit's visor. "I'm awake! I was just resting my eyes," he protested,

Rappaport raised an eyebrow. "You know, Mr. Desaix, you're really going to have to learn how to address a superior officer before this is all over."

Chris winced. "Sorry, sir. Didn't mean to be disrespectful."

"I know," the chief engineer said, grinning. "So, how long have you been napping here? You really shouldn't do that in a suit with a limited oxygen supply, you know."

Chris checked his suit's chronometer and air supply gauge. "Barely a minute, and I've got a fresh tank. I just sat down to take a breather."

"Why don't you go back to the *Gnat*? You've been working non-stop for over twenty-four hours, now, and God only knows how long before then you had any sleep," Rappaport suggested. "It's only about a five minute trip back to the ship and your quarters."

"I'm not ready to go back. I need to finish getting the ship airtight and the environmental systems up and running first."

"I thought that was a four day project. You've been working on it for less than a day," Rappaport reminded him.

Chris nodded. "My initial estimate was more on the safe side then I originally thought. So, any news from the *Gnat?*"

Rappaport clearly noticed the diversion, but didn't challenge it. "Not much. Those two goons who were in your room were given three days brig time – the captain's mast Lt. Sharpe held said the sentence would have been much harsher had they not already suffered such heavy injuries."

"Three days? They've already served at least one day, so they'll be out in forty-eight hours, then?"

"Forty-nine," Rappaport corrected. "It'll take an hour to process their release after their sentence is up."

Chris nodded slowly. "That's not very long for assault."

"Yeah, well, Ms. Katz and Mr. Beccera did quite a number on them. I don't blame Sharpe for thinking they'd suffered enough," Rappaport said with some humor.

"Didn't know Rache had any hand-to-hand training," Chris muttered. "Maybe I'll ask her to give me some lessons some day. At any rate, unless there's some business you need to bring up, I need to get back to work."

"As a matter of fact, I do have some business," Rappaport explained. "I was looking over the blueprints you've made for the refit. I don't see any quantum wheel nodes in your plans."

"I haven't forgotten your instructions to include them, sir," Chris said. "And I will. But if I have to use a quantum wheel, I'm going to install it my way. I intend a non-standard configuration of the emitter nodes."

Rappaport smiled slightly. "I am the Chief Engineer, you know. I would appreciate a heads-up if you're planning changes big enough to hide an entire quantum wheel."

"That's just it, sir," Chris said. "We can't put in an entire quantum wheel – not on the stern of the ship. There's not enough room for one in the rear, alongside the primary fusion drive – not unless you want use undersized emitter nodes and re-tune it every other day. So, I thought we should try something unique. It should give us more forward thrust than we'd have had with a more standard configuration, and we might even manage boosted side and reverse thrust as well."

There was a long pause. "Did you say 'side and reverse thrust?'"

Chris nodded. "Yes, sir. Using the pyramid-style emitters, I believe we could install a secondary quantum wheel system that would provide a quarter of the thrust of a standard quantum wheel going forwards *or* backwards, or alternatively a side thrust from both sides about half that of a standard quantum wheel. The solution is actually fairly simple – mount the pyramid emitters on the sides of a ship."

Rappaport frowned. "Oh. You should probably look up the history of the quantum wheel in your textbooks – this won't work."

Chris nodded. "Oh, the concept has been tried before, true, but only with dome emitters. But the pyramid emitters make control so much easier. When we want to provide forward thrust, only those plates facing towards the stern of the ship will be charged. When we want to provide reverse thrust, only those facing the bow of the ship will be charged. If we want to provide side thrust, only the plates opposite whatever direction we want to move will be charged." He gave Rappaport a cocky grin. "And if we want a defensive shield, we charge all the plates at once and use the fusion drive to propel us."

"A shield?" Rappaport exclaimed.

Chris laughed. It was such a simple concept, he had been flummoxed when he figured it out, as well, but the math said it would work. "It won't cover the rear, but the fusion drive provides us some protection, there. And while it won't quite cover the bow, either, we'll have an opening through which spinal-mount weaponry can fire. But it'll protect our flanks better than any armor – the only question I haven't figured out is just how much better."

"But how would this work without crushing the hull?"

"The same way an eggshell does when you squeeze it in your hand – the egg inside is safe because the pressure is evenly distributed. It's not a perfect metaphor, but it's the same principle."

"The 'eggshell' would break, and we'd be vulnerable. We'd lose thrust on that side, and probably lurch violently in the direction of the failed emitter before the pilot could compensate, but as long as the antigrav systems are operating the only remaining danger would be from enemy fire. It should be simple enough to recover maneuverability simply by shutting down the other emitters."

Rappaport nodded slowly. "That sounds... promising. I'll need to look through your design calculations before I give my approval."

Chris hesitated. "I'm afraid, sir, I've already started. Some of the emitters were going to be placed where there were already cracks in the hull, so I figured we'd just seal off those areas and start cutting the bulkheads down in preparation for the emitters. It'll save us several hours getting her airtight."

Rappaport was at once astonished and annoyed. Those sorts of modifications to the ship just weren't made without consulting the ship's *captain,* never mind the approval of the Chief Engineer. "Chris, if you ever do something like this again without telling me first, I'm going to skin your hide... and then I'll have you expelled from the Academy," Rappaport warned. "Do you understand?"

"Yes, sir. I'm sorry sir," said Chris, for once intimidated into remembering the formalities.

"But if your numbers hold up, it was the right *engineering* decision," Rappaport said, "So I'll let it stand for the moment – if I study your math and find a miscalculation, we can still remove those bulkheads. We don't have the parts to build that quantum wheel, yet, and getting the ship airtight and the environmental systems working is more important, so your current modifications can stand as a shortcut to functionality. Now, how much longer until the hull is airtight, anyway? Lt. Katz said something about wanting to talk to you as soon as you returned to the *Gnat.*"

Chris checked his watch. They had been talking for about twelve minutes, and he could make a pretty fair estimate as to how much work the other engineers could manage in that time. "No more than forty-eight hours and fifty-nine minutes, sir."

Rappaport nodded as understanding dawned. Chris was going to get the *Chihuahua* ready for his cabin mates to move in before the men who harassed Rachel were out of the brig if it killed him.

EAS Gnat

"...forty-eight hours and fifty-nine minutes," Rappaport's image on the comm screen said, an amused smile on his face as he repeated the suspiciously specific estimate. He glanced down, and his wrist came into view. "That was about ten minutes ago, Ms. Katz, and he may have revised his estimate since then."

Rachel grimaced. "Thank you, sir."

"I've got work to do, but I said I'd give you a call. Rappaport, out."

The screen went blank, and Rachel cursed. *Damn, he's overworking himself again. I was afraid of that.* She had to try and talk him down from the work. Rappaport had said he wouldn't mind if Chris took off 'early,' given how much he'd already worked, so maybe she could convince him to take a break. Changing the frequency on the comm unit, she tried to hail him.

"Desaix. Go," Chris answered. He sounded tired. He was also acting somewhat distracted – he usually checked to see who was calling him without asking.

"Chris?"

"Rachel!" he exclaimed. He seemed to perk up at her voice. "What's up?"

"I'm told you're not coming back for more than a day," she said. "Are you sure you don't want to come back for a few hours and catch some z's somewhere in there?"

Chris shook his head. "Nah. I'm okay. I've worked without sleep for longer periods."

Rachel shook her head in disbelief. "Yeah, but this has to be more tiring than fixing up a chess clock."

"True," Chris admitted, laughing. "But like I said, I'm okay. Besides, I'm the only one who knows what the complete plan for the refit looks like. Rappaport doesn't even know everything – he's too busy trying to use his regular navy status to speed the requisition through for all of the material we need to get this old girl flying again."

Rachel hesitated. "Are you sure you'll be all right? You sound completely exhausted, already."

"I have to finish this. If I tried to sleep before the life support was functional... I think I'd have nightmares."

Rachel frowned, remembering his problems sleeping. "You can't go through life fearing your dreams, Chris."

"I don't," Chris tried to reassure her. "It's just that, right now, there's a lot on my mind, and I'm pretty sure my nightmares would be worse than usual."

"What's on your mind? The refit?"

The long pause before his reply told her something was off. "Yeah. The refit. That's it. With our inability to establish life support right away, we're falling way behind schedule and that's wearing on me a lot. We've got to make up several days worth of delays, somewhere, and I'm not sure where yet. I hope you're getting those cabin assignments taken care of quickly, because we need more people over here as quickly as possible. I'd bring more of you over, already, but we've maxed out our portable oxygen supplies. I've got to get back to work, now, or I'll be stuck here even longer."

Rachel chewed her lips. "I'm worried about you, Chris. *I* might have trouble sleeping if I'm not sure you're all right."

"I'm all right," Chris insisted. "Trust me."

Rachel wanted to argue, wanted to say that it was obvious he wasn't all right, but she knew that would only make him dig in more. She thought she knew the source of his unrest... and it was her fault. She hadn't been able to diffuse the situation with Farmburg's trio of friends before it came to blows, and now he was blaming himself for not anticipating their attack. The best strategy to avoid future attacks was simply for them to leave the *Gnat*... and that would take finishing the refit of the *Chihuahua* as fast as possible. No, there was no way to talk him out of this.

"Okay, Chris," she finally said, surrendering. "Good night."

"'Night, Rache," Chris replied. "Don't wait up."

The transmission was cut, but Rachel just continued to stare blankly at the comm. She wasn't sure what to do, now, and she felt helpless.

It was then that Schubert came back into the room, followed by Flint and Weber. He took one look at Rachel and frowned. "Hey, Rache, what's up?" he asked.

Rachel shook herself out of her stupor. "Nothing much. Where've you been?"

"Down in Marine country," Flint replied. "Had some things to discuss with them."

"I've got some things I want to discuss, too, Rache," Schubert said, much to the surprise of Flint and Weber. "Can you come outside for a moment."

"Sure," Rachel said, getting up and joining him outside.

Schubert gave her a sympathetic smile. "Okay, you look like you just lost a fight with Chris. What's wrong?"

Rachel snorted. "'Lost a fight with Chris.' I would have to start one to do that, and he was too exhausted for me to even try." She sighed. "He's overworking himself again. Severely overworking himself. He hasn't slept in far too long, and he won't stop working until the *Chihuahua* is airtight. I tried telling him that he shouldn't be working so hard, but then he told me he was afraid of the nightmares coming back to him. I can't talk him out of it, dammit, but he can't keep up this pace. It's not healthy."

"He's gone without sleep before," Schubert replied cautiously.

"Yeah, but not like this," Rachel answered. "You didn't hear how he sounded when he answered the comm. Once he knew it was me he tried to hide it, but I could tell just how tired he was from hello. I don't like it,

Schubert, and I don't know what to do."

"I don't like it, either," Schubert said. "I never have liked it when he's gotten a project into his head and just won't stop on it. But there's never been anything I could do, either. I don't have the right to stop him, and neither do you."

...don't have the right to stop him... Rachel repeated mentally. "You and I might not, but there is one person on this ship who does." She walked over to one of the comms located in the corridor and adjusted the frequency. "Captain Burkhard, do you have a moment, sir? There's something I feel we need to talk about...."

Chapter X

EAS Gnat

Burkhard sighed, rubbed his eyes tiredly, and looked across at the two cadets. "Okay, Ms. Katz. You woke me up so this had better be good – I was having a rather pleasant dream about strangling our so-called 'Acting-Commodore' to death."

Rachel was not normally one to chuckle at such insubordinate humor, but considering what the Acting-Commodore's decisions were doing to her friends she found herself agreeing with the sentiment. "It's Cadet Desaix, sir. He's been working on the *Chihuahua* for," she checked her watch, "more than twenty two hours now without a break. And it was several hours before then that he last slept. I talked to him on the comm a couple hours ago, and... well, he worries me, sir. I've known him ever since his first day at the Academy, sir, and I have never heard him that tired... which, if you don't know him as well as I do, is saying a lot."

Burkhard ran his hands through his hair, shaking his head to clear it. "Excuse me, did you say he's been working for twenty-two hours straight? That's not good. He's liable to make a mistake if he doesn't take a few breaks from time to time."

"No, it isn't good," Rachel agreed. "And I fear it'll only get worse as time goes on. He and I argue about things like this all the time, but this is one time I don't think I can afford to let him win."

Burkhard grinned. "Well, I definitely agree he shouldn't be working without sleep for as long as you claim. I guess I've got to go for a little trip, then."

——————————————

EAS Chihuahua

Chris was really wishing he could wipe the sweat from his brow at the moment. It was collecting under his helmet, and the visor was fogging up – his suit's air conditioner must not have been working at an optimum level. He'd have to take a look at it after he finished this weld.

He finished sealing the small crack in the bulkhead and sighed, shutting off the welder and closing his eyes. He almost dozed off, but caught himself in time, and started checking the various instruments on his suit.

He'd just isolated the problem when two people who he didn't recognize right away entered the mechanical room he was working in. He frowned. No-one else was authorized to be here.

"Chris," Rachel called. "Don't you think it's time to take a bit of a break?"

"Rache?" Chris sputtered, startled. He had been hanging from the wall to repair the crack, but upon hearing her voice he nearly jumped off of it and into free floating. "What're you doing here?"

"I already told you, Chris. I think it's time for you to take a bit of a break. I'm here so you don't blow me off."

"I'm not leaving until I'm done," Chris snapped stubbornly. "Anyway, I didn't think you were allowed to come here. Only the engineering staff was permitted over to work in the biosuits."

"I authorized her visit, Mr. Desaix," Burkhard, the second unexpected visitor, explained. He squinted, looking through the visor of Chris' biosuit at his face. "Are you okay? You're sweating like a pig."

Chris grimaced. "Minor suit malfunction. I'd just localized it to the thermostat when you got here."

"That's because those biosuits aren't supposed to be used for nearly as long as a standard environmental suit," Rachel said. "You, of all people, should know they're not supposed to be worn for more than twelve hours in a row. You've been wearing it for more than double that time."

"It's holding up. There've been a couple minor malfunctions, but I've been able to fix them pretty quickly, and I wouldn't be able to work effectively in one of the more durable environment suits."

"The point is, Mr. Desaix, you shouldn't be working this much in the first place," Burkhard said. "There's a reason the Navy now orders that no-one, outside of actual life and death emergencies, should be working more than two eight hour shifts in a row, and you've already been through three. It wears you out and makes you prone to error. Add the danger of working in a biosuit well beyond its design tolerances, and I'm afraid that as much as I appreciate your enthusiasm I cannot condone your remaining out here for a fourth straight shift."

Chris looked at him, eyes widening. "But... this project needs me here. Mr. Rappaport is too busy working on our requisitions, and he's the only other person who can run this project. Without me, the refit will shut down!"

"Nonsense," Burkhard snorted. "The lack of one person won't affect things that much. And I've reassigned Rappaport back to working on the refit in your place. Our purser, Cadet Ensign Anson Polk, will take care of supply like he's supposed to."

"But Anson doesn't have the clout to get the supplies we need!" Chris protested.

"Neither does Mr. Rappaport," Burkhard said evenly. "Don't worry. We're making other arrangements for those materials as we speak."

"It's unnecessary," Chris said. "I'm still perfectly capable of doing my job. I've worked without sleep for even longer than this with no ill effect."

"Perhaps," Burkhard said. "But you won't this time. You are hereby ordered to return to the *Gnat* and get some sleep. If you do not, you will leave me no option but to get the guards to confine you to your quarters."

"But..." Chris replied weakly. "I guess I don't have a choice, do I... sir?"

Burkhard shook his head, smiling. "No, you don't. That's why they're called 'orders.' Ms. Katz, would you care to escort Mr. Desaix to his quarters? I need to have a meeting with Mr. Rappaport. Return to the *Gnat* and then send the shuttle back for me."

Rachel saluted. "Yes, sir." Grinning at Chris, she said teasingly, "Right this way, Mr. Desaix."

Chris and Rachel were the only two passengers traveling back to the *Gnat* in the shuttle, accompanied only by several dozen expended oxygen tanks. The pilots' cabin, where Weber was flying the shuttle, was closed and locked up. Chris had removed his helmet and was mopping his forehead off with a convenient rag that had been in one of the shuttle's supply kits. Rachel, meanwhile, looked as satisfied as the cat that had swallowed the prized canary. She had succeeded – now Chris would have no choice but to get the rest she knew he needed.

Chris, meanwhile, was constantly glancing in her direction with a betrayed look on his face. Rachel noted his expression, and almost laughed. *I can't believe he's pouting over something as silly as this.*

"Oh, come on, Chris," she protested. "You've lost arguments to me before. Don't be so upset."

Chris sighed. "Yes, I've lost arguments to you. But you actually got Captain Burkhard involved! It's always been just you and me arguing, before – we never brought anyone else in."

Rachel's smile turned a little sheepish. "Sorry, Chris, but I knew I couldn't make you come back on my own. You *do* need the rest, you know."

Chris growled. "You know I'm not going to be able to relax until we've all moved over to the *Chihuahua* and settled in."

Rachel shook her head in exasperation. "You are so frustrating, Chris. You need that sleep – I can see it in your eyes. You're an incredibly valuable resource to the Navy, Chris, and it's important you keep yourself in good shape."

For some reason, that answer rubbed Chris the wrong way. "Oh, so is that all I am? A valuable resource to the Navy?"

"No!" Rachel almost shouted, surprising herself with how hard that accusation hit her. "Of course not. Why in the world would you think I meant that?"

Chris just shook his head. "Maybe I was just hoping for a different answer."

"Well, it *is* the reason I first started looking after you, ya know," Rachel said. "And it still is one of them. Not the only one, though – not any more. We may still argue periodically, but I think we're slowly starting to get along, aren't we?"

Chris said. "I've thought of us as friends for months, now. I'm a bit surprised you only think of us as 'starting to get along.'"

Rachel smiled slightly. "I'd like to point out you don't have to get along to be friends."

"True," Chris said. "But since when haven't we gotten along?"

Rachel laughed. "You mean you've forgotten all the arguments we've had?"

"We've had arguments, yes, but I've always thought they were friendly arguments," Chris noted. "Was I mistaken?"

Rachel hesitated. "I suppose you're right. Though with as many as we've had, it's hard to tell sometimes...."

"I understand," Chris said. "It seems almost every time we talk, we argue. We're arguing right now, after all, aren't we?"

Rachel laughed. "I suppose we are. It's not like our usual arguments, though, is it?"

"No, it isn't," Chris agreed. "Normally, by now, you've gotten pissed off enough that you've let your nose wrinkle in frustration, trying to keep yourself from actually shouting."

Rachel blinked. "I wrinkle my nose?"

"Oh, yeah. It looks pretty cute, actually."

Rachel wrinkled her nose at him. "Cute, huh?" she teased.

"Yeah. Why do you think I get into so many arguments with you?"

Rachel frowned, unintentionally wrinkling her nose again. "I thought it was because you were a stubborn bastard who simply refused to bother with formalities."

Chris laughed. "Well, that, too..."

"I knew it!" Rachel crowed. "And you've admitted it! You do know that I'm going to use that little bit of information against you, don't you?"

"Of course," Chris replied. "But, since I am a stubborn bastard, I just won't care."

"You won't?" Rachel teased. "Then I won't wrinkle my nose for you any more."

"What!? No fair. That little nose wrinkle is the only reason I put up with you, some days!" Chris protested playfully.

"Well, we'll see. If you're good, I'll wrinkle my nose for you whenever you want," Rachel promised.

Chris sighed dramatically. "I suppose that means I won't be allowed to call you 'Rache' any more, will I?"

He looked like such a sad little puppy dog that Rachel just couldn't resist. "Oh, you ham!" she laughed, swatting his knee – the only part of him she could reach strapped into the shuttle's passenger chairs. "Okay, you can still call me Rache, and I guess I'll stop complaining about it. At least when it's you... anyone else isn't allowed, and that includes Wolf!"

"Deal," Chris said, brightening immediately.

"So, are you going to complain about me actually making you get some sleep, now?"

"Of course," Chris grinned. "I always have fun fighting with you... and complaining when you win an argument. But I'll try and get some sleep, anyway, just for you."

"Thanks," Rachel sighed in relief. "I was afraid I'd have to tie you up to get you into bed."

Chris raised a teasing eyebrow. "Oh, wait... can I go for that option, instead?"

They both suddenly realized how daring that comment had been at the same time, and both blushed at the same time. Chris opened his mouth to retract his comment, but Rachel beat him to it.

"Not yet," Rachel said. "You're too tired, and I don't feel up to it. Maybe someday."

Chris looked at her closely for a moment. "Maybe."

"Hey, back there," Weber's voice echoed over the loudspeakers. "You two might want to get ready to dock. If you'll wait, I'll walk with you back to the cabin. It's the end of my shift."

Rachel tapped the intercom button. "Sure thing." She grinned at Chris. "I might need someone to help me if our other passenger tries to run."

Chris laughed. "Come on, let's get ready to dock. We can fight later."

"Promise?" Rachel grinned.

Schubert entered their cabin, trading 'shifts' with Weber. They had agreed to keep a close eye on both Rachel and Chris, but Weber needed to get back to work. It seemed their attention had not gone unnoticed, but Chris was waiting to ask any questions until they were alone.

When they saw that Rachel was safely inside their cabin and heard the water for the shower running, Chris turned to Schubert. "Hey, I need to talk to you about something."

"Yeah?"

"I noticed Lauren was on high alert walking us here," he explained. "Was that your doing?"

"Kinda," Schubert answered cautiously. "Why?"

"Good thinking. I want you to keep it up," Chris instructed. This was definitely an order, and he was definitely not joking about it.

"Eh?"

"Listen, Wolf," Chris said seriously. "I was hoping to get the *Chihuahua* airtight before those thugs who attacked my Rache are released from the brig. Unfortunately, it doesn't look like I'm going to be able to do that. I want you to make sure that they can't even talk to her if I'm not around when they get out."

"Not a problem," Schubert said. Then, something clicked in his mind.

*I can't believe my ears. Did he just call her "My Rache?" How interesting...
I wonder if he even realizes he said it.* "I plan to look after the both of you."

Chris stared at the door to the shower, frowning. "You know, I arranged special permission for her to have extended use of the lounge because I knew they might try something. I thought that would be enough to stop them, but I was wrong."

Schubert snorted. "I'd say it worked well enough. Since they had to attack her in that public of a place, Rache was in a position to defend herself from their assault without repercussions."

"I doubt they were really drunk," Chris replied, a thoughtful look on his face. "I called the guards about the incident while I was over at the Chihuahua. I asked them a number of questions. Yes, the scent of alcohol was all over them. I also saw the surveillance tapes of the incident. Their clothes were soaked in the stuff... but only Kobe was showing any outward signs of drunkenness. Even he seemed mostly in control of himself... no, I think their alleged drunkenness was just a cover story. Unfortunately, security didn't bother doing a blood test on them after they admitted they were drunk. The guards don't expect crewmen to admit to being drunk aboard ship when they aren't."

Schubert frowned. "Okay, so they weren't drunk. Then why did they attack her in public?"

"I don't know, but I doubt the mastermind behind this incident is the same one who managed to set you up before the party. The MOs are slightly different. They're in cahoots, though."

"Farmburg?" Schubert suggested hopefully.

"Never met him, so I can't be sure," Chris said. "We'd better start looking into him. Starting with that incident you've never told me about. Wolf, what really happened at that bar?"

"Ah," Schubert said. "Well, see, I'd rather not."

"I know he said something you think will upset me, Wolf," Chris noted. "I just want to know what that something was."

"I'd still rather not say," Schubert said. "It... you need the context to understand."

"Wolf," Chris said. "I haven't pushed you, before, because I knew you've been afraid of what I'd think of whatever he said, but now I have to insist. We don't have the luxury of sparing my feelings – this is a safety concern, now."

Schubert sighed. "Essentially, they were insulting you and Rachel. What they were saying didn't matter. It wasn't what he said, but how he said it."

"Quit dancing around the subject, Wolf. What did he say?"

"He... he implied that you and Rachel were having, uh, an indecent relationship." Chris frowned slightly, but gestured impatiently for him to go on. "He claimed Rachel was easy, and made crude remarks about the two of you."

Chris shrugged. "He's not the first person to do that – and many people do it to my face. That's okay – Rachel and I can both deal with it, and have. Don't tell me that was the only thing he said. If you started a fight just because he said that, I'm disappointed in you, Wolf."

Schubert sighed hesitantly. "Chris, I honestly think... well, you really do like Rachel, right? If I was into that sort of thing, I'd try my hand at matchmaking the two of you...."

Chris snorted. "Trust me, you aren't the only one. I... might not object to the idea, but I'm not really sure how she feels. I don't really have time to figure her out right now, at any rate."

Schubert laughed at that. "Well, I'm glad to hear it. The two of you are made for each other."

"I wouldn't go that far," Chris laughed. "But I'm not going to say I've never thought about it. But you're distracting me – what, exactly, did Farmburg say about us?"

Schubert frowned. "I don't remember his exact words. He called Rache a 'whore' and you a 'sick bastard' was making me angry, but it wasn't what caused me to plunk him. I'm not really sure what it was."

Chris nodded. "Okay. That's a start. He was insulting me... and Rache." There was a steel in his voice that Schubert had never heard before. "But why was he doing it? Did he just come up to you and start tossing out insults, or what?"

"Well, he was over at a barstool when I'd arrived. He seemed to be intent on his hand comp when I got there, but even though I'd never seen him before he seemed to notice me when I came in," Wolf mused. "I never really thought of it, before, but it seemed as if he was trying to remember me from somewhere. At any rate, I ignored him, ordered a single beer and downed it. When I returned to the bar to get another drink he was talking to an audience of other bar patrons about you guys. Then he started bringing me into it. He grabbed me by the arm and pulled me into the crowd, demanding that I talk about what I knew about the two of you."

"Hmm," Chris said, developing a slight twitch as Farmburg's words were relayed. "When he grabbed you, was he acting drunk? If so, how strong was the alcohol smell on him?"

"Well, he certainly seemed drunk," Schubert said. "His words were slurred and he was staggering about. But the bar itself smelled so strongly of beer that I wouldn't have noticed if there was any on his breath."

"Interesting," Chris said. "Very interesting. Was he acting drunk before he saw you?"

Schubert tried to remember back to that night, but his memories from before the fight weren't very distinct. "He seemed pretty sober at first, I think. Then again he was pretty focused on his hand comp, so it was hard to tell."

"He wasn't drunk either, was he?" Chris said. "No, he wouldn't have been. He must have been waiting for you, or at least someone like you. He wanted to pick a fight, and used getting drunk as a way to escape a court martial for it. In fact, it sounds quite a bit like how Rachel was attacked in the lounge." He paused. "The question is why, though. You say you've never met Farmburg before in your life?"

"Not that I recall," Schubert noted. "He certainly didn't *look* at all familiar."

Chris nodded. "Curious. Well, then... when we've got the *Chihuahua* up and running, let's check into the personnel database. See if there's anything there that'll show what he's up to. This is obviously more than just a simple misunderstanding in a bar, and I intend to find out exactly what's going on." The water stopped running, letting the two of them know Rachel had finished her shower and would be out soon. "In the meantime, Wolf... I want you to arrange some kind of security for us."

"Not a problem," Schubert agreed. "Don't worry, Chris. I've already got plans in place to keep you and 'your Rache' safe."

"Well, that's done," Nathan Priest said, finishing the last line of his release form. "It's about time. How many forms is that, again?"

"Twenty-nine," Franco Kobe muttered dangerously. "Twenty-nine of the longest, most complicated forms I've ever seen. In triplicate. And on paper, too."

Sergio Ramsey, who had shown up to sign them out, grinned wryly. "I think it's supposed to be part of your punishment. We should have gone to Joel, first – he would've figured out something better for us to do."

"Oh, shut up," Nathan moaned, handing his forms to the guard and glancing over at Kobe, who was still working on the paperwork. "You're only gloating because you weren't caught."

Sergio shrugged. "Hurry up. Joel said for me to call him as soon as you got out."

"Not right away," Franco insisted, finishing his last form. "I need to go back to my cabin, first. I want a shower, some clean clothes, and a bit of rest. *Then* we can talk to Joel."

"Fine," Sergio said. "But you'll have to explain to him why you took so long getting in touch with him."

"It'll be worth it just to take that shower," Nathan sighed. "These transports don't maintain their brigs very well. None of the plumbing worked."

Sergio shook his head mockingly. "Geez. And that, on top of having to deal with all of the injuries that one old man and a cute little girl gave you."

"That 'old man' is an Army officer with over forty years of hand-to-hand training and experience. He's probably one of the best in the fleet, and he's pretty well built, to boot," Nathan groused.

"And Ms. Katz is no 'cute little girl,'" Franco added, fingering his bandaged nose gingerly. "She's tough. I'm not sure we could have taken her even if the Army man hadn't interfered."

"Quit being a wiseass," Nathan grumped. "I'm tired of this place, and the more you argue the longer we stay here."

"Then you're both ready? It's about time!" Sergio said. "Let's go. I don't want to keep Joel waiting any longer than we have to."

The trio made their way through the corridors in relative silence. Nathan and Franco had to move slowly, thanks to their injuries, and Sergio had to stay patient as he walked with them. With some determination, however, they made it to Cabin Four, Deck Seven without any stops. Nathan and Franco made no attempt to hide their joy at finally getting somewhere that they could get clean, they surged ahead of the uninjured Sergio and darted inside.

The sight that greeted them brought them up short.

"What the hell?" Nathan exclaimed as Franco cringed in terror.

There were several dozen people present, alongside card games, dice games, loud music, couples dancing, beer, snacks, and more. The sound-proof partition in one part of the room was raised, obscuring several of the bunks, but most of the furniture in the rest of the room had been removed. Their foot lockers weren't readily visible, and even the bunks were nowhere to be seen.

"I'll see your eighty yen, and raise you another twenty," a Marine said.

"Call," a second said, tossing in a chip.

A third approached the new arrivals. "Hey, you here for the poker tournament or the party?" he asked. He was the only one in full uniform, and his rank appeared to be that of sergeant.

"Err, neither," Nathan said. "We live here... or I thought we did."

Hearing that, a feminine hand that had been buried underneath yet another Marine raised itself. Pushing him away, Linda Flint sat up and waved.

"Hey, roomies!" she gasped out, panting. She straightened out her clothes before getting to her feet and walking over to the door. The Marine she had been with looked disappointed, but got up with a resigned shrug and joined some other men who were setting up some tables.

"What is going on?" Sergio demanded, fists clenched.

"Oh, sorry," Flint answered, feigning sympathy. "I thought you knew."

"Knew what?" he replied.

"Hey, when we first came to the cabin, I warned everyone that I was obliged to host a poker game for the Marines once a week," she said.

"*This* is a lot more than just a poker game," Nathan whinged, gesturing to the crowd.

"True," Flint admitted. "See, you were in the brig the whole time, but poor old Chris was just working his tail off trying to get the *Chihuahua* ready for us to transfer there as soon as possible. He overworked himself, so Captain Burkhard ordered him to bed.

"Turns out we're getting the ship up and running faster than Chris feared – she'll be ready in just a more couple hours. It's mostly due to his going above and beyond the call of duty, so we're arranging a surprise commissioning party for him. We raised the partitions around his bed, added some cushioning we got from our bunks to help baffle the sound, and started getting the party together."

Sergio nodded slowly. "Okay. That... *kind* of makes sense. But where's our stuff?"

"Your foot lockers are over there, safe and sound," Linda said, pointing to a cluttered corner of the room. "Locked up tight, so if you want anything out of them you're out of luck. If there was anything else of yours lying around here, we didn't find it."

"Why didn't you guys tell me?" Sergio asked. "I would've been able to help these two prepare for this thing."

"Oh, that's simple," Flint said, smiling dangerously. "We just don't like you."

Chapter XI

Beccera sighed, continuing his stretching exercise as he prepared for his martial arts exercises. If there was going to be one disadvantage to this assignment, it was the lack of a gym in which to exercise. Most naval ships had them, but not transports. Transports, even though they were occasionally called upon to haul large numbers of personnel, were devoid of any of the luxuries most ships had. There used to be one in the *Chihuahua*, but it had been removed in order to make space for the new gravity control system. He would be without a gym for the duration of this assignment.

In place of a gym, he was forced to take his exercise in the cramped confines of his cabin. While this was sufficient for some very basic work, it didn't allow for most of his routine. He was tempted to just let his conditioning go, not expecting to need to be in fighting shape much longer, but he loved the physical activity too much. Which was partly why he'd so enjoyed pounding the hell out of those creeps in the lounge the other day – he'd finally had a chance to cut loose and stretch his muscles.

He was comforted to learn, in that fight, that at least some of the Navy officers knew how to fight. Not the ones he'd trashed, but the girl he fought alongside actually knew her stuff.

A buzzing at the door drew him out of his thoughts, and so he quickly stepped out of his stance. Grabbing a towel to wipe off the nonexistent sweat on his brow, he opened the door.

"Hello, Colonel," a Marine corporal greeted him, saluting promptly. "I'm here to remind you of the commissioning party the Marines are throwing in Cabin Four of Deck Seven and to provide you with an escort."

Beccera blinked. "Party? Oh, yeah. I'd forgotten about that. Give me a minute and I'll join you."

Tossing his towel to one side, he started pulling on his shirt. The corporal looked around with mild curiosity, noticing the katana in its stand lying on the desk. Beccera finished dressing and joined him.

"This way, sir," the corporal said, gesturing with his hand, and Beccera followed him out of the room. "I noticed your sword, sir."

"Oh?" Beccera grunted noncommittally.

"Do you practice much?"

"Not as much as I'd like to," Beccera admitted. "I'd prefer at least an hour a day, but I'm usually only able to practice about fifteen minutes every other day. I suppose it doesn't matter too much, though – when am I likely to actually need it?"

"You very well might, soon, sir," the corporal suggested cautiously. "We're Marines – we use swords all the time."

Beccera looked interested. "I thought they were just decorative parts of your uniform. Aren't they?"

"They're quite functional, sir, and not very decorative at all. Mine is little more than a slab of metal with a monomolecular edged blade on one end."

"Seems rather archaic," Beccera said. "When would you ever use a sword in battle? You normally use sonic weaponry, correct?"

"We do, sir," the Marine answered. "Sonics are a very valuable part of our arsenal. Explosive propellant guns are forbidden aboard warships for any number of reasons. Firearms without explosive propellant ammunition don't even pierce the standard uniform emergency biosuits the regular Navy personnel wear, much less Marine-grade combat armor."

"Okay, I understand that," Beccera replied. "But sonic weapons would work even through most combat armor. So what's with the swords?"

"Well, a dirty little secret about Marine combat is that it's common practice to defend your ship from boarding by evacuating the atmosphere from a room. No air and sound waves can't travel, rendering sonic weapons useless." The corporal grinned half-heartedly. "The defending side is frequently the one hurt the most, because attacking Marines will be better prepared for it, but the losses are usually fewer than permitting their sonic weapons to stay on the field of battle."

Beccera winced. "I'm glad I'm regular Army. I've never had to worry about suffocation on the battlefield."

"At any rate," the Marine said. "Whenever that happens, it often results in a sword battle. Swords won't cut through the armored portion of Marine-grade armored biosuits, exactly, but you can often slice through joint material with devastating effect. Being cut open like that is almost worse than never having put on the suit in the first place, as suits are heavily pressurized to maintain combat functionality. The sudden loss of atmospheric containment will sometimes result in explosive decompression... in other words, you blow up inside of your suit."

"I did not need that mental image," Beccera moaned. "I've seen enough combat to have been exposed to things just as bloody, but that's just a terrible way to go."

"Even if your suit doesn't have an explosive decompression failure, once a sword starts cutting at your joints you start losing air very fast. A few seconds, maybe a minute at most before you're completely out of air. Fortunately for you, sir, you don't need to worry about explosive decompression or suffocation during this exercise. For drills and war games, we're issued special 'practice swords.' Instead of risking death or injury with the air removal tactic, the lights in whatever rooms are affected will be flashing, and using a sonic weapon in those rooms is a foul."

Beccera nodded. "Understood. I hope my sword skills are adequate, although I fear my own practice gives me the tendency to go for the areas which are armored the heaviest."

The corporal shrugged. "I suspect you'll be fine. I saw the recordings of your fight with those two idiots in the lounge. Not bad, there."

"Thanks," Beccera said.

"There were several of our Marines in the lounge at the time," he continued. "We should have been there for you, but we weren't."

Beccera grinned. "That's okay. I enjoyed the fight."

"Nevertheless, sir," the corporal replied, "You earned our respect by stepping in there. You showed us up, which doesn't exactly make us happy, but that was our fault, and we're glad to have someone who is *capable* of showing us up."

"It wasn't your job to help her out, then. Hell, it wasn't *my* job, either for that matter. The Marines have nothing to be ashamed of, there."

"We know, sir." The Marine took a deep breath. "When we heard that an Army officer was going to be our commander, we didn't know what to think. After that fight, sir, we learned all we needed to know. You may not make the most technically proficient Marine, but we know we can pride ourselves on having a CO willing to do the grunt work alongside us, sir."

Beccera was surprised by the comment, but merely nodded. "Again, thank you."

"When this Wargame is over, though, sir, don't be surprised if we go back to hating you as a good Marine should always hate any Army officer."

Beccera grinned slightly. "I wouldn't have it any other way."

"Hey, Rachel," a quiet voice whispered. Rachel blinked her eyes open sleepily, noticing who was leaning over her and shaking her.

"Wolf?" she whispered hoarsely. "What's going on?"

"Shh," he hushed, putting a finger to his lips. "Don't want you to wake Chris."

Rachel nodded and stated to sit up. She blinked, noticing the partitions raised around her. The sound of music and laughter was coming from around the door Wolf came through, and a very light snore directed her attention to where Chris was sleeping on his own bed. "What the..."

"Hush!" Schubert whispered fiercely. "We're not ready, yet. Come with me."

"Just a second," Rachel said, rushing to finish her morning toilette before joining him. She followed him into the rest of their cabin. She was still blinking the sleep out of her eyes when the room hushed at her entrance. She glanced over and saw a sign, letting her know just what event they were celebrating.

"She's ready?"

Schubert nodded. "We got the call two minutes ago. I thought we'd get you up to speed so you can wake up the guest of honor."

Rachel nodded. "How long was I asleep? I thought even with Chris there it was going to take almost a full day, still."

"Ah, well, see," Schubert said, rubbing the back of his head in embarrassment. "Chris was being so... stubborn... that Captain Burkhard decided to include a little extra insurance to keep him asleep. And he figured you'd probably need it as well...."

"Wolf," Rachel warned. "I might remind you that I'm your superior officer, and I don't exactly like it when people dance around the subject."

"Like you'd abuse your power for something like that," Schubert snorted. "Look, Captain Burkhard had you two drugged. It was probably a stronger dosage than he really intended, though. You two were out about twenty-five hours."

"Twenty five!" Rachel exclaimed. "Hell. Well, I guess I didn't really have anything I needed to do except finish up those cabin assignments. Give me ten minutes to work on that, and then I'll go get Chris, okay?" She saw Colonel Beccera walk in along with his escort and changed her mind. "Make that fifteen minutes – I need to talk to the Colonel, first."

Schubert nodded. "Go right ahead. We need about that long to finish setting up, anyway."

Rachel smiled her thanks at him before dashing over to where Beccera and the corporal who had escorted him to the cabin were talking. She wanted to talk with him before he got too involved in the party. "Gentlemen."

"Ms. Katz," Beccera nodded back.

"Ma'am," the corporal added.

"Corporal Etcheverry," Rachel said to the man, "If you'll excuse us?"

"Certainly, ma'am," the Marine said, saluting before heading over to help with the party set-up.

"Okay, Ms. Katz, what is it you want to talk about?"

Rachel hesitated. "Well, sir, there seems to be a slight problem with the cabin arrangements."

Beccera frowned. "I'm not sure I'm going to like where this is going, but go ahead."

"Well, sir," she hesitated. "The housing arrangements aboard the *Chihuahua* are sparse, at best. To put it bluntly, we have more people than we have bunks."

"That certainly sounds like a problem, Ms. Katz, but I fail to see how it concerns me," Beccera said.

"I already have most of the crew cabins hot-bunking at four people to a room," she replied. "Which is rather difficult, since the cabins were designed for one person apiece. I still needed more space for crew, however, so I was forced to have the officers sharing cabins, too. I figured if I assigned two officers to a room, we'd be fine."

"So you need to know if I'm willing to bunk with another officer?" Beccera asked, feeling he knew what was coming.

"Close," Rachel said. "We wind up with one officer who doesn't have another officer for a roommate. We're also one bunk short for enlisted personnel."

"I think I understand, now," Beccera nodded. "You're asking me if I'm willing to bunk down with an enlisted man, right?"

"Woman, actually, but yes, sir. I even have the perfect person in mind... largely because she'd probably spend more of her time cramped in with one of your Marines than she would in your cabin." At Beccera's curious look, Rachel continued, "My roommate here on the *Gnat*, Linda Flint, is in a... fairly intense relationship with Corporal Etcheverry – that young man who escorted you here, today. I suspect they'll be sharing a bunk regardless of where they're officially billeted."

Beccera grinned. "Hmm. So, basically, you're saying I'd be getting probably the only private room in the ship, or more company than I might be comfortable with, depending on where they decide to hang their hats on a nightly basis?" Rachel nodded. "I can deal with that. Not a problem at all."

"Thank you, sir," Rachel said. "With that out of the way, I'll actually be able to finish the billeting assignments before we head over to the *Chihuahua*."

Chris felt lips that were not his own caressing his mouth. At first, he dismissed it as a dream. After all, it wouldn't be the first time. Then he realized that it couldn't be a dream – the one thing which allowed him to separate reality from the dream world was the knowledge he couldn't close his eyes in his dreams. His eyes were definitely closed right now, and still there was someone else's lips on his.

He opened his eyes widely to stare into those of Rachel Katz, just as she broke their kiss. "R-rache!" he exclaimed.

"Good morning," she breathed, her face flushed in embarrassment. "I had to wake you up, and that seemed like a good method for doing it."

Chris sat up, glad he had chosen to wear pajamas that evening. "Don't get me wrong – I loved it – but I have to say, you sure move a lot faster than I would have expected you to."

Rachel grinned at him. "Yeah, well, don't get used to it. This is a special occasion. Time for you to rise and shine."

"Er, right," he said, grabbing a dressing robe and slipping it on under the sheets. Standing up, he started to pick out a uniform from his footlocker when he finally noticed the sound baffles active on their partition walls. "What's going on?"

Rachel laughed. "Go on, get dressed. I'll explain it all in a minute." She ushered him over to the bathroom, stuffed a fully assembled uniform in his hands, and shut the door on him. About fifteen minutes later, he emerged fully dressed. Rachel inspected him quickly, brushed out a wrinkle on his shoulder, and smiled. "You'll do. Come on, let's go."

"Go where?" Chris asked, bewildered.

"Just outside the door," Rachel said, then stopped at the exit. "You first," she said, shoving him through.

He stumbled to a halt and gaped at the forty or fifty people crowded into the small cabin, cheering. With the furniture for eight people condensed into the wall partitioning his and Rachel's bunks from the rest of the cabin, the room was actually large enough for everyone present. In the crowd, Chris spotted Schubert, Colonel Beccera, Weber, Flint, several of the other officers of the *Chihuahua*, and the entire company of Marines.

"What's all this for?" he sputtered.

"It's a party to celebrate our last minutes here on the *Gnat*," Schubert explained over the cheers. "While you were asleep, Mr. Rappaport finished getting the *Chihuahua* airtight... using your plans, by the way. It took him about two hours more than your last set of estimates said you could finish it in, but he got it done."

"But... how long was I asleep, anyway?"

"Almost twenty-seven hours," Rachel said. She hesitated before adding, "You must've been really tired."

"Anyway, we figured it'd be nice to throw a party in honor of this event," Weber explained.

"The ship is hardly ready for combat. We have a lot of work to do, still," Chris said.

"True, but we're only this far this early because of you," Schubert countered. "Just relax and enjoy it. You are the guest of honor, after all."

Chris started to protest, but when Rachel and Schubert jointly sent a glare at him he backed down. "Well... I'm not going to be the one to stand in the way of a good party. Let's celebrate!"

Cheers and laughter followed that statement, and the assembly quickly broke down into several small groups of people enjoying themselves. Dance music started piping through the sound system as fresh food and drink was revealed behind the parting crowd.

Rachel dragged Chris off for a few dances, and Lauren Weber grabbed Schubert. Flint dragged Corporal Etcheverry into the walled-off section of the cabin for a few stolen moments of passion.

The party went on for some time before Chris was able to disengage himself from Rachel. He truly enjoyed dancing with her, but there was something else he wanted to do in the informal setting of the party.

"Colonel Beccera," Chris said, greeting the Army officer during a breather.

"Mr. Desaix," Beccera said. "This is a party, we're from different service organizations, and I'm only a few weeks away from retirement anyway. What say we relax on all the 'colonels' and 'misters' and 'sirs,' okay?"

Chris nodded and grinned. "I prefer it that way, thanks."

"So... Chris, is it? What can I do for you?"

"Well, Andrew—"

"Call me Drew."

"Drew, then. I just wanted to thank you for helping Rachel out in that fight."

Beccera examined the young man closely. "Not a problem, I was glad to do it. Forgive me for asking, though, but why are you thanking me? I wouldn't think it was your place."

Chris grinned half-heartedly. "Well, Rachel and I are friends. Very good friends." He looked to see if the Colonel had grasped what he was saying, and continued when he saw the man nod in acknowledgement. "The thing is, I honestly feel as if I should have done something more to have kept the incident from ever happening."

"You could have?" Beccera asked. "What could you have done? As I understand it, you were on the *Chihuahua* at the time of the incident."

"I was," Chris answered. "But I knew what those idiots were capable of, and I predicted they just might do it. I second-guessed myself, figuring they wouldn't dare risk it. If I'd taken the threat seriously, like I should have, then maybe I could have prevented it."

"Like what?" Beccera asked. "Did you have enough to go on to report it to the authorities?"

"Well, no..."

"Then, could you have arranged to have security tag them wherever they went?"

"Well, not without more justification than my gut instinct, no...."

"Then what could you have done?" Beccera asked. "You weren't here. They were."

"I could have made sure that she and Lauren stayed together," Chris replied. "I might even have been able to bring her with me to the *Chihuahua*, if I thought it was necessary."

"If you'd known for sure, maybe," Beccera said. "But you didn't know, did you? All you had were some educated guesses. Chris, this is meant as a training cruise. Perhaps the first thing you should learn is that you can't afford to blame yourself for what you don't know. If you start falling into that trap, it'll quickly drive you insane."

"Perhaps," Chris replied uncertainly.

"I accept your thanks for defending your lady," Beccera said, giving him a courteous half-bow. "But I won't accept you blaming yourself for this incident, got it? Besides, from what I could tell, she was more than capable of handling herself."

Chris grinned. "I heard."

"So let's move on," Beccera said. "This is a party, Chris. I think we'll all have enough to worry about soon enough, so find your lady and enjoy yourselves for the rest of the evening. Lord knows when you'll get another opportunity."

Chris grinned and nodded, leaving the Army officer to watch him leave. *What an interesting kid. I feel sorry for him, though... I suspect that young Ms. Katz may almost be too much for him to handle. Then again, I thought Kimiko would be too much for* me, *and look how that turned out.*

The party had been over for some time. Flint and the rest of the Environmental Engineering team were the first to be sent over to the *Chihuahua*, with the goal of restoring the antigrav systems as soon as possible. The knowledge that everyone would have to wear magnetic boots for at least the first few days didn't deter the enthusiasm everyone felt about boarding their first ship.

Chris and Rachel were fortunate enough to be going up in the second shuttle, accompanied by several of their classmates, Colonel Beccera, and Captain Burkhard. Weber would be flying them over, but Wolf would be waiting for them at the airlock to take over for the return trip.

"Any hints on who our roommates are, Rachel?" Emily Mumford asked. Rachel was growing to like the Admiral's granddaughter – she was the only one of the network of officers in the command staff that *always* called her by her *full* first name. She was strapped down in a bank of seats beside the Captain and Jeff Cohen, facing Emily, Chris, and the *Chihuahua's* ship's doctor – June Ehrlich.

"I don't think anyone will be too disappointed," Rachel said. "I tried my best, anyway. While things are going to be crowded, I'm confident you'll like your roommates. If you have problems just let me know and I'll see what I can do."

"I want a name," Mumford said. "A full name. I don't want to be surprised."

"Tough," Rachel said, grinning playfully. "You'll find out when you get to the ship, same as everyone else."

"I thought we were supposed to have perks as officers," Jeff groused good-naturedly. "Why do we need to have roommates, anyway?"

"The enlisted have to put up with four people hot bunking a room. The *Chihuahua* wasn't designed for the staffing requirements she now has. Deal with it," Rachel said.

"Hey, I outrank you, Jeff," Mumford said. "And I'm the daughter of one of the highest-ranking officers in our Navy. If I have to deal with a roommate, you do, too."

"I outrank all of you, and even I have to put up with a roommate," Burkhard chimed in. The mild bickering ceased instantly – remembering who they were talking in front of.

"Yes, sir," Cohen muttered, sufficiently chastised.

Chris, however, was never one to be cowed by authority, even if he respected it. Technically, this was an informal setting, and he would treat it as such. Smirking, he said, "So, Rache, why don't you tell us who we are bunking with anyway?"

Rachel fumed at the question, but inwardly smiled. He was in a playful mood, and that realization brightened her own spirits, as well. She couldn't remember him this relaxed since... well, it would have been before their project for Tactics was assigned. Apparently, he really needed all the rest she'd forced him to take.

"Not you, too!" she mock-groaned. "You, especially, aren't getting any favors from me! Not for a long while, at least, after that schedule you set everyone for the refit! I think I'm going to be working harder for this than I did during the physical training section of Academy Boot Camp."

Chris grinned. "You scratch my back, I'll scratch yours. You tell me who I'm bunking with, and I'll get you your pick of assignments on the *Chihuahua*."

Rachel just sputtered, and everyone else laughed. Burkhard grinned. "Hmm, I don't know if you're in a very good position, Mr. Desaix. She hasn't submitted to the political influence of Ms. Mumford, what makes you think she'll take your bribes?"

It's not like he doesn't already know who he's bunking with, Rachel thought. *He has to realize I'd know better than to separate him and Wolf. Maybe he just wants to see my nose wrinkle again.*

She tested that theory, and the sparkle in his eyes convinced her that was the case. Wrinkling her nose again, she said, "It'll take a lot more than that to get me to violate my own rules, buster," she snapped playfully.

"Oh, well. Guess I'll have to think of something else," Chris mused. "I have to wonder what the Colonel did to get you to tell him who he's bunking with."

"Might have something to do with him saving her from some drunk thugs the other day," Cohen suggested mildly.

"Please stop," the normally soft-spoken chief surgeon assigned to the ship, Doctor June Erhlich (whose rank of Lieutenant Commander was a courtesy, as she was actually a member of the civilian auxiliary) said, a twinkle in her eye as well. "It took a team of several doctors, myself included, just to reconstruct Mr. Kobe's nose. I'd hate to have to treat the lot of you by myself, should you push her too far."

Chris flinched slightly at the reminder of what he saw as a personal failure, but didn't lose his humor. "Oh, well, guess I'll just have to wait."

Rachel patted his leg. "Don't worry," she said in the same patronizing tone one would use to comfort a child. "It won't be much longer."

"Well," Chris said. "You told me you wouldn't tell me who *my* roommate is. Would you tell me who someone else's roommate is, then?"

Everyone knew the answer would be no – even Chris – but Rachel wanted to keep the conversation going. Besides, she was curious. "Whose?"

"Hmm, good question," Chris said. "Now, we already all know about Colonel Beccera and Linda Flint. I have a couple ideas for who might be my roommate, too. So, maybe I should just ask who your roommate is, then."

"Mine?" Rachel squawked.

"Yeah," Chris replied. "Yours. You did remember to assign yourself a room, didn't you?"

"Of course I did!" she cried in outrage, and the others in the shuttle started chuckling at the bickering couple. "But why do you want to know who else is in my room?"

"Simple curiosity, of course," Chris said. "I'd just like to know."

Rachel grinned. "Okay, Chris, I'll tell you," she cooed.

"You will?" he said, a bit surprised.

"Sure I will! But you'll have to wait until we get to the ship. It's not public knowledge yet, after all."

"Prepare to dock, everyone. We're here," Weber's voice interrupted.

"Well, looks like I'll be finding out soon enough," Chris said. "And remember to turn on your magnetic boots before you unstrap – there's no gravity at the moment."

"Oh, yeah," Cohen said, reaching down to flip the switch. "I'd forgotten about that."

A soft "thoom" of energy indicated the activation of the magnetic lock which sealed the shuttle to the *Chihuahua*. It took a moment before they could finally board the ship, but everyone, even the Captain, rushed to the door once the airlock indicated it was secure.

Most went straight to the nearby computer to look up their cabin assignments. Captain Burkhard was in the lead, of course – no-one wanted to deny him the first glance. "Hmm... looks like I have to bunk with my exec. Well, that makes sense," Burkhard said.

Rachel noticed Chris just standing behind the others, not bothering to head to the computers. "Chris? Don't you want to know where you're bunking?"

Chris nodded. "Yeah, but I met Wolf on his way out to the shuttle. I know who I'm bunking with, already, so I'll let the others go first."

Rachel grinned back. "I thought you wanted to know who was bunking with me, though."

Chris chuckled. "I do... but I also want you to tell me who it is, like you said you would. I figure that's a good enough way to learn."

"But the computer's right over there!" she exclaimed. "Why do you need me to tell you?"

Chris shrugged, winking at her. "You said you'd tell me, so I'm waiting to hear the name of the person straight from your mouth. You aren't going to back out of a promise, are you?"

Rachel fumed, wrinkling her nose at him to show that she was still having fun with the argument. "It's no trouble to check the computer. Just look it up!"

"It's even less trouble than looking it up on the computer."

"Oh, just drop it," Weber huffed, stepping between them on her way to the corridor. "She's bunking with me. Quit your bellyaching and move on."

Chris blinked, then looked at Rachel. "What's her problem?" he asked in a whisper.

"Not sure," Rachel answered, her voice also hushed. "Maybe I'll find out tonight. Wanna join me for dinner at 1900 hours?"

"Sure thing," Chris said. "I'll comm you to confirm."

"See you later, then," she said, waving as he ran off.

"So you finally quit your flirting," Weber growled as she stepped back into the entryway. "Come on – I want to head on over to our cabin."

"Nothing's stopping you, you know," Rachel shot back. "You don't need me to go with you."

"Yeah, well, since you two were *so* discreet when you were talking about what's wrong with me," Weber said sarcastically, "I figured I might as well wait around so you can interrogate me."

Rachel winced. "Sorry about that. You just aren't acting like yourself, though." She paused, and grabbed the cord attached to her footlocker.

Weber started leading her out of the waiting room and down one of the corridors. She'd been to the cabin a couple times on previous transport jobs, so Rachel trusted she knew where she was going. "There's really nothing you can do anything about. It's a personal matter."

"Try me," Rachel said. "I'm a better listener than I look."

Weber sighed. "I suppose you're going to keep bugging me until I do, aren't you?"

"Of course. And I'm pretty persistent, too."

Weber gave a half-hearted chuckle. "Yeah, I noticed.'"

"Well, since you admit that, you know you have no choice but to 'fess up!" Rachel teased.

"All right," Weber sighed. "It isn't like it was something you wouldn't be able to find out through the grapevine, anyway. And you just might understand – after all, pretty much everyone around here knows how much trouble you and Chris have had."

Rachel blinked. "What about Chris and I?"

"You think no-one else has noticed the crush you two've had on each other for the past several months?"

The other woman almost choked. "What are you talking about? Yeah, there's been a bunch of silly rumors, but they were utterly groundless! Really!"

Weber smirked. "Really. Then what was that dinner invitation about?"

Rachel flushed slightly. "That's a fairly recent development. The rumors have been going on pretty much since we met, though – and they *have* been groundless, up until a few days ago."

"If you say so," Weber said doubtfully. "Even your friends have been saying you two've flirted with each other for months. I heard it started when you were assigned to be partners for some tactics project...."

"You shouldn't believe everything you hear," Rachel said.

"Not everything, no. But there's often some basis in truth behind these kinds of rumors...."

Rachel flushed, and decided to just let that argument stand where it was. "Um, are you going to explain what *your* problem is, or am I going to have to get 'persistent?'"

Weber sobered up instantly. "Well, maybe I'd better tell you, after all, considering what the rumor mill is like. Better that you know what's fact and what's fiction."

"Good choice," Rachel said.

"Essentially, I made a move on Wolfie," she sighed. "It was at the party. We'd been dancing. I was just about to suggest we find someplace a bit more private when he practically ran away from me! Claimed he had to use the bathroom, and I never saw him again until clean-up."

Rachel frowned. "Hmm, that doesn't sound like him."

"Anyway, that's all that's bothering me. I just wanted to get out of that airlock without having to meet up with him again."

Rachel nodded. "Well, I don't know what's going through Wolf's head, so I don't know what to say. It might not be as bad as you think – he might really have had to use the bathroom, for all you know."

"He might have," Weber said. "And if you really believe that, I've got a planet to sell you. We're here."

That last comment was followed with a wave to the door marking their cabin. Rachel grinned slightly and keyed in her own password, opening the door and heading on in. She found that most of her heavier pieces of luggage had already made it down there. She quickly locked her footlocker down by the unused bed with magnetic seals and started to unpack.

"Hey, Rache," Weber said softly. Rachel blinked – she couldn't remember that she'd ever heard the other girl speak so quietly before. Turning around, she saw that Weber was fidgeting around nervously, unable to meet her eyes.

"Yes, Lauren?"

"When he comes over tonight, could you... could you ask Chris if he knows why Wolfie...." Weber begged.

"Ran off?" Rachel suggested. When Weber nodded, she grinned. "Not a problem."

"He ran off?" Chris laughed. They were in the Chihuahua's mess hall. With the gravity off, the only things to eat were the rather unappetizing dehydrated chunks of what claimed it was beef stroganoff, which had to be eaten by hand. They were trying to ignore the flavor through conversation. "Oh, that's rich."

Rachel restrained herself from smacking him. "Hey, this is serious – Lauren's really hurt by this."

"I'm sure she is," Chris said, still smiling. "But I think she completely misunderstood what happened."

"Well then, enlighten me, oh knowledgeable one," Rachel huffed, annoyed.

"Simple," Chris answered. "Wolf isn't against the idea, trust me. In fact, I get the impression he's rather attracted to her. That isn't the problem at all."

"Then what is?"

"He's absolutely terrified of her. In fact, he's never been so scared of anyone in his life. I suspect what happened was that he was going to suggest the same thing, realized who it was he was talking to, and got out of there because he thought she'd kill him if she knew what he was thinking."

Rachel blinked, then laughed. "Oh, that *is* funny. I never would have thought Wolf was *afraid* of her. He strikes me as a pretty fearless person."

"He is, usually," Chris explained. "I think, though, he's in awe of her fighting skills. According to him, she 'descended like an avenging angel' upon those idiots who attacked him."

"Heh. I'll let Lauren know that," Rachel chuckled. "I suspect she'll decide to descend on *him* like an avenging angel, too, once she knows. And she won't take any prisoners, either."

Chris nodded, but then decided to change the topic. "So, what job did you get?"

Rachel glared at him. "Don't you know? I thought you were in charge of that."

"Well, I would have been if I hadn't been drugged up at the time," he said, glaring right back at her playfully. "Instead, Rappaport took the job. He just pulled down the list of assignments and wrote a random name generator program to match people with jobs."

"Oh," Rachel said. "Well, that explains the assignment I got. For a while there I was convinced you were playing a bad practical joke on me."

Chris frowned. "How bad is it?"

"I was assigned to the 'waste recycling team.' I hope that isn't what I think it is...."

"No," Chris chuckled. "It has nothing to do with any aspect of the janitorial program. Waste recycling is typically just driving a big cart around, picking up whatever parts are left over when one job is complete and re-filing them into storage."

"Oh," Rachel said. "Well, that's a lot better than I feared. Still, it sounds kind of dull."

"Well, I'm afraid most of the jobs you ignorant non-engineers can do are rather dull," Chris teased. "If it gets too boring for you, let me know. I'd asked to get an assistant, but I wasn't assigned one. It'll still be boring work – all you'll be doing is taking notes when I tell you to, or maybe holding some tools or something. Still, we could chat as we worked, and I might even be able to teach you a few things to make it more interesting."

"I'll consider it," Rachel replied doubtfully. "But I know how obsessed you get working on these projects, and from what I've seen I'm not sure you'd even remember I was there."

Chris laughed. "That's just what Rappaport said when he told me he couldn't give me an assistant."

"See? I'm not the only one who thinks you're too obsessed."

"Maybe, but I wouldn't forget about you – honest!" Chris protested.

"Well, I'll consider it... but not right away. As boring as waste recycling sounds, I think I'll give it a shot." Rachel grinned ruefully. "I don't want anyone accusing me of shirking my responsibilities. So, what job did Wolf get?"

"Well," Chris said. "He's a special case. He's the primary pilot for the work shuttle. When we don't need a shuttle in service, though, he's got a nice cushy job testing certain pieces of software for functionality."

Rachel bit into a particularly crunchy piece of her beef stroganoff and nearly gagged. "I can't wait until you guys get the gravity generator functioning, if for no other reason than that means the kitchens will become functional. I hate this freeze-dried stuff."

"Not part of my job – that's environmental's task. Talk to Linda – she seems to be doing better with it than Wayne. He's so obsessed with the small details he's letting the big jobs go." Chris shook his head. "I think that we're finding that some of our more highly-touted people aren't as good as they were marketed to be."

"That's to be expected," Rachel said. "We are just students, after all. A lot of people who do well in school do poorly on the job; a lot of people who do poorly in school are incredibly good when it comes to real-life situations. Figuring out which is which is the whole point of this exercise."

"Still, I'm afraid of what's going to happen when one Cadet Ensign Wayne Evans is given a time-critical assignment, like restoring life support before we all run out of air." He shook his head. "On the plus side, he does understand the artificial gravity system unlike anyone else in the fleet. By the time he's done, we'll probably have the safest antigrav ever built."

"This is going to be one of the best ships ever built, period, by the time you're done with her," Rachel said. "I've heard about some of the modifications you're making. Quantum wheels on the sides to create shields and increase maneuverability? We'll be able to outrun anything in space, at a minimum, and we might even be able to protect ourselves if we do get caught."

Chris shrugged. "It isn't that great. We can't fire through the shield, ourselves, and we've got some holes in our coverage. Furthermore, these quantum wheels probably won't be strong enough to completely shield us – the best we can do is weaken the blow if someone shoots a particle cannon at us."

"We're still safe from rail guns. And our armor is adequate to keep those weakened particle cannons from doing serious damage."

"Maybe," Chris shrugged. "We won't know until she's been tested. And I hope to get her ready to test before the three weeks are up... which means we'll have to finish ahead of schedule."

"Oh, no," Rachel said, her face falling. "Don't tell me you're going to be going without sleep, again?"

Chris shook his head. "No, I probably won't. I'll pull more than my fair share of shifts, but Rappaport's going to be doing the same so I'll have time to rest." He sighed. "Well, I'll have time to rest if I don't have to spend all of it in fabrication."

"What's wrong?" Rachel asked. If there was anything she could do she would, she would – she wasn't going to let him get into a position where he'd self-destruct if she could do anything about it.

"We've sent a number of requisitions in to the tenders. The equipment is vital to our refit plans, and there's sufficient stores for them to easily provide supplies to every ship, but the question is whether the Commodore will let us have it or not. If he hadn't arrived to the system late, we wouldn't have been permitted the supplies to make the ship airtight."

Rachel nodded. "Yeah. He seems to be so concerned about getting those battleships functional he's going to make it impossible for us smaller ships to get fitted."

"Not impossible," Chris said. "Just difficult. If we don't get those supplies... well, we'll have to fabricate them ourselves. We can do that, but it'll take more time than we can afford."

"Is there anything I can do to help?" Rachel asked, still hoping that he wouldn't have to work too hard.

Chris sighed and shook his head. "Not unless you've got access to the storage bay of a tender."

Rachel shook her head. "Sorry. But if I can think of anyone who does, I'll let you know."

"Rappaport seems pretty confident about getting those supplies. I don't know how he could be, considering what we know about the Commodore, but he said something about getting Colonel Beccera involved. Maybe the Colonel has connections, somewhere," Chris mused.

"Maybe," Rachel said doubtfully. From what she knew of him, she didn't think the Colonel would have any connections that would matter, here, but the only other reason she could think for him to be involved was too outlandish. After all, the Wargame hadn't officially started, yet, so who would he be raiding?

Chapter XII

Chris knocked on the door for Jacques Rappaport's office and went on in without waiting for a response. To his surprise, there was already a meeting going on between Rappaport and Colonel Beccera.

"Ah, Mr. Desaix," Rappaport began. "We were just talking about you. A bit surprised you came before we called, though."

"I wanted to ask about the supply problem. We're about to run out of some important parts, so if we don't get that equipment by tomorrow we'll have to start fabricating them ourselves."

"That's just what Mr. Beccera and I wanted to discuss with you. Please, sit down. This is going to take a bit of explaining."

Chris did as Rappaport suggested, wondering just what was going on. "Do you have some news about our requisitions?"

"I do, indeed," Rappaport said, smiling like a shark. "Here, take a look."

He handed Chris a hand-comp with a list on it. After checking through the list for a minute, Chris frowned. "This isn't even close to what we need! We might get another day or two's leeway with it, but we might as well start fabrication now because we'll need those parts eventually, anyway."

"I know," the chief engineer said, still smirking.

"There's something you're not telling me," Chris said.

"Just a plan we've been working on to get those supplies," Rappaport answered. "Care to fill him in, Mr. Beccera?"

"Thanks to that friend of yours, Ms. Katz, we were able to get in touch with a contact on board the tender *Don Quixote*. He can give us the access codes to the main supply room," Beccera began.

I was joking, Rache. But thanks for coming through, Chris thought. "Okay, but what good would that do us?" His eyes narrowed as he thought about it. "Or are you planning a raid?"

"Got it in one," Beccera answered. "I figure we can get five minutes before security will notice our presence and send down forces to stop us, but I'm going to need someone to come along with me who knows exactly what we need. I'm told only you or Mr. Rappaport could do that by sight, so I need at least one of you."

"I'll go if I have to, Chris, but I'd like it if you went instead," Rappaport said. "I think the mission would do you good. I can't order you to go, though – this isn't exactly in the rules, you know."

"Don't sugarcoat it, Jacques. Listen, Chris. Think hard about this. If we get caught, there's a good chance we'll get court-martialed."

Chris frowned. "I can't say yes to that. I won't say no, either. In fact, I can't exactly sit on this, now that I know we're planning it. It's not worth letting any of the people here get thrown out of the Navy just to get a ship ready for a simple war-game. I've got to talk to someone about this."

Jacques' eyes widened. From the records, Chris seemed to be relaxed enough on the letter of the law that he would accept this kind of job as necessary. Now, if he carried through with his threat, they couldn't enact the plan at all. "Mr. Desaix, please, reconsider..."

Chris shook his head. "I said I won't sit on this. I didn't say I wouldn't take part in the action, however." He looked Rappaport straight in the eyes. "I'd like to schedule a shuttle flight to the *Don Quixote*. I want to talk to Captain Anne Morrison – one of the observers and my tactics class' teacher – and I'd rather not have that conversation over the comm system. I'm pretty sure that if we asked if some of our Marines could perform a small exercise in infiltration and detection, she'd be glad to make use of our services."

Rappaport blinked. "What?"

"He means he's going to talk his teacher into covering our asses," Beccera grinned.

"Exactly," Chris said. "If I won't get thrown out of the Academy for this, I'll gladly take the job."

There was silence as Rappaport weighed the idea, staring intently into Chris' face. Finally, he nodded. "We'll have a gap in the shuttle schedule in about forty-five minutes. You can take her out to see the observers then." He paused. "I just hope I don't regret this."

"Let me get this straight," Captain Morrison said. "You want my permission to steal supplies from this tender?"

Chris nodded without hesitation. "Yes."

"Under the guise of a training exercise?"

"Yes."

Morrison nodded with surprising calm. "And just how badly do you need these supplies?"

"If we don't get them, we won't be able to get the *Chihuahua* commissioned until after the Wargame is half over. With them, we'll finish well ahead of time."

She sighed. "Okay, I think I understand the situation. Let me talk to Admiral Mumford about this. I don't have the authority to allow this, but he might. And he can go over Green's head, if necessary."

Chris nodded. "Thank you, ma'am."

She nodded. "By the way, how's the crew we assembled shaping up so far?"

"It's still too early to tell," Chris said. "Some of my fears were confirmed about one or two of them. I won't mention names, but there are a few people who've been at the top of their class in engineering theory but who get too bogged down in the details in real life situations. Likewise, I've found a few enlisted people who would make better officers than I do. I've kept close contact with Rache, Wolf, and Lauren Weber since the party, and all three of them seem to be a cut above on the job."

Morrison gave him a questioning eyebrow. "Anyone there you wish you'd left off of your list entirely?"

"Not exactly," Chris said. "There are a few people who I wish we'd never given any authority to, and one person – Jonathan Rosebaugh – who, though knowledgeable, should be locked up for his and our safety. I suppose we've got a good crew, overall."

Morrison nodded. She had hoped he'd take the opportunity to discuss the lounge incident with her, but he hadn't. "Okay, Mr. Desaix. Thank you for the gossip, but I need to go schedule a meeting with the Admiral."

"Thanks," Chris said.

She got up and left the room. Chris sighed, leaning back in his chair with his arms behind his head. "Like I thought, we'll get permission."

"How do you know?" Beccera, who had accompanied him, asked curiously. "The Admiral still hasn't had his say, yet."

Chris shrugged. "She wouldn't have bothered meeting with Admiral Mumford if she didn't know he'd say yes. Looks like we'd better start planning this little exercise."

"I already have it planned," Beccera laughed.

"I would like a chance to see the plans, first, though. I don't want to get 'killed' before the Wargame even begins."

Beccera pulled out a data cartridge. "Here. I figured she would ask to see the plans herself before she gave approval to the idea. You might as well use the time we're waiting to read them."

"Thanks," Chris said, slipping the cartridge into his hand-comp. He spent a few minutes going through the file, a frown growing on his face as he read. "This won't work."

"What?" Beccera asked. He knew he wasn't entirely familiar with shipboard combat, but his Marines had checked its feasibility for him.

"Well, maybe that's a bit strong," Chris corrected himself. "But I don't particularly like our chances with this plan. I think we should go in wearing our helmets in airtight position from the start – no sense in losing someone when they flash the lights to indicate the air's gone for sake of a moment's discomfort. Also, you're relying too much on surprise. Surprise is always a very good thing to have, but you can't afford to rely on it too much. But the real kicker is this." He pointed to a highlighted map on the screen. "In order to maximize your chance of surprise, you're taking this entry point. It may prevent the easiest form of detection, but it lengthens the time we could be under fire significantly, and it doesn't hide us from several other forms of detection."

"Then what do you suggest?" Beccera said, looking speculatively at Chris.

"Let's not bother worrying too much about hiding ourselves once we're on the *Don Quixote*. We're inevitably going to be detected at some point, no matter what we do – and once we're detected, we'll have five minutes to finish our job and get out of there, at most – so we're better off minimizing how long it takes to get the cargo from the hold into our transport. We just disguise our shuttle, which you were already planning to do, and come in right at the freight-management equipped shuttle bay. We speed up the transfer of cargo, and we're placing ourselves further away from the bulk of the ship's on-board security forces."

"I agree with that, in theory," Beccera said. "I've raided a few supply depots before, and I know it's usually preferable to cut the distance you'll be carrying the supplies. But I'm not sure that's true in this instance. From what Mr. Rappaport says, we need more than five minutes to get all the supplies we need. I was trying to increase the amount of time we have to go through that supply room. Security is three minutes away from the airlock in our plans; it only takes three minutes more to get the cargo from that storage area to the shuttle than it would to go through the freight-equipped bay."

"That leaves no margin for error, though. Don't tell me that an Army officer with more than thirty years experience is completely discounting Murphy's Law?"

"No," Beccera replied. "But Murphy can screw us just as much wherever we go in."

"True," Chris said. "But there aren't as many things he can do once we already spoil it for him. Just crash the party, send the ship into confusion, and grab everything we can." He paused. "If we had another shuttle feint a separate raid, wouldn't that be better?"

"Well, yes," Beccera said. "But we don't have another shuttle, so that's out of the question."

"What if we could make them *think* we had another shuttle?" Chris asked. "Get security running to take care of a threat on the other side of the ship. That would extend our time by a few minutes."

"How?" Beccera asked.

"Well, we'll need to add someone else to the team – Yannis Langer. He was a computer specialist even before he joined the Academy, and he's even better at it now. We can send him aboard the Don Quixote on some pretense and have him throw the computers for a loop before we even get there. Once he gives the word, we move on into the docking bay and get things done, there. He'll be able to cover his own tracks, and we'll make Murphy's job that much harder for him."

Beccera frowned thoughtfully. "How good is Langer?"

"He hacks into the Academy mainframe on a regular basis without detection," Chris said. "I don't know of anyone else who can do that, though. Those things are locked up tight."

Beccera raised an eyebrow. "And just why does he break into the mainframe? Does he change his grades or something?"

It was only then that Chris realized what he had admitted to. "Um, no, he doesn't need to. He does nothing which violates academic ethics. Besides, the grades are kept on a separate system, even if he tried. He has been known to snatch certain people's sealed personnel records, though. Rache thinks I don't know, but she used him to look me up one day."

"Hmm," Beccera said. "I suppose we can overlook that admission, since we have no evidence outside of your word. But I would suggest that you make sure Langer is willing to help us with this."

Chris nodded. "I don't know him too well, but I'm pretty sure he will be."

"By the way, why was Rachel checking out your sealed records?" Beccera said, curious. "She doesn't strike me as the sort of person who would violate regulations like that."

"She was the one who got us the access codes, wasn't she?" Chris countered. "She's just full of surprises."

"Just how did you get those access codes, anyway?" Chris asked at dinner that night.

"Oh," Rachel began, wiping her lips. It was the first dinner they'd been able to have together since the antigravity system had been activated, and she'd found she'd gotten used to eating in a zero G environment a little too well. She actually struggled with some of her utensils, and she was dripping food on her uniform periodically. Still, it was worth it just to have good food once more. Too bad the standard issue rations weren't exactly 'good food.' "One of the regular Navy officers on board the *Don Quixote* used to work with my parents in the Orbital Guard. As it happens, he had access to the supply rooms and was willing to give me the access codes. I owe him a bottle of whiskey when we get back to Earth, though."

"I'll gladly pay for it if this all works out. It'll be well worth it," Chris suggested.

"So will having you not wear yourself out fabricating the needed parts," Rachel retorted. "And *I'm* the one who made the deal, so I'll take care of the purchase. Besides, I'm as anxious to be part of the Wargame as you are."

"How about we split the cost?" Chris said. "I'd feel guilty otherwise."

"Well, if you insist," Rachel said airily, having no intention of splitting the cost at all. "So, how's the refit coming, otherwise? I must say, I was glad when the gravity came on and I could finally take off my magnetic boots."

"It was entirely thanks to Linda we got the gravity working last night," Chris noted. "Evans would've spent another several days fine-tuning it. Linda pointed out that most of the things he wanted to do were best done after it was activated."

"Well, we all knew Evans was much more of a theorist than a practical engineer when we made up the crew lists," Rachel mused. "I suspect he'll probably be placed somewhere in Research and Development when he graduates – with the reports he must be getting, Personnel should know to leave him off of shipboard assignments."

"He'd probably be good at R&D," Chris agreed. "But that doesn't help us, now, does it?"

"Is anyone else giving you any trouble?" Rachel asked. "I know we were given a pretty good crew, at least on paper. Paper doesn't always translate into results, however."

Chris smirked. "Just Jonathan Rosebaugh," he said. "And his problem is more that he's a complete and total klutz than anything else. He's an asset to any team when he's not dropping his tools into the delicate wiring."

Rachel winced. "I heard he's managed to do that twice, already."

"Three times," Chris corrected. "That we know of. The first time was during the initial survey, but most people didn't start counting until the atmospheric controls were set up and the crew came on board. He's only done it twice, since then."

"He sounds as bad as you feared," Rachel noticed.

"He is," Chris said. "In fact, most of my worst fears about these people are coming true. Wayne's too technical-minded, Jon's too much of a klutz, and so on. You're actually one of the few bright spots – I was afraid you'd be as stuck-up about things like saluting as you are in the Academy, but you seem a lot more relaxed than I thought you'd be."

"Me? Stuck-up?" Rachel said, a little hurt. "Is that what you really think of me?"

Chris sighed. "Not really. I always knew that if you were really as stuck up as you acted, you really *would* have reported me for insubordination like you always threatened to during our arguments. You just seem a little... overly concerned about proper uniforms, saying 'sir' all the time, things like that. I never would have thought you'd be as lax on the rules as you have been recently. I would've figured you'd protest a raid like the one we're planning, but instead you helped initiate it."

Rachel felt relieved. "I've always been more relaxed on the rules than you seem to think. But I also think you had better start following a few more of the customs of the Navy. In the future you might not always find people quite as reasonable as your teachers and Captain Burkhard have been when you've forgotten to address them properly. One of your superiors might decide to throw you in the brig for insubordination if you keep doing that."

"I'm too busy to remember things like that!" Chris protested. "I haven't heard many complaints."

His companion raised an eyebrow. "You haven't heard *many* complaints? Doesn't that mean you've heard some?"

"Just a couple," Chris said. "And they weren't really serious or anything – mostly just teasing. And you've been the one to make half of them!"

Rachel let her head fall into her hands. "What am I going to do with you, Chris?"

"I dunno," Chris said, lips twitching with restrained laughter. "But I suspect you'll figure something out." He took a sip of his drink and sighed contentedly. "So, how is your job in Waste Recycling going?"

"Oh, it's okay," she said. She hoped she was convincing, but it was hard not to feel her mood shift at the question. "It's just a little boring."

Chris frowned. "You sure that's all you've got to say about it? You don't sound so sure of yourself."

"The job's fine, I promise," Rachel vowed. She was schooling her face as strictly as she could – she didn't want to worry him when there really wasn't anything wrong at all.

Chris nodded. "So, how are your co-workers?"

She flinched, knowing he had her. "Well, they're fine..."

"Rache, tell me."

"Really, they're fine," she insisted. "It's just... well, I'm the only officer on the entire team, but because of my position I'm under their command. They like lording it over on me because of that, giving me silly orders, that kind of thing. Nothing too bad – I can handle it."

Chris frowned. "I think I'll have a talk with them about that. Who's your team leader?"

"Oh, please don't," Rachel huffed. "I'm fine. I'd much rather deal with things myself then cause problems inside your engineering teams."

The watch Chris was wearing beeped, and he looked at it with a frown. "I can't do anything about this right now – I've got to get ready for the raid – but we *will* be talking more about this, later. Dinner, tomorrow?"

Rachel sighed. She didn't want him to get involved in her problems, but it looked as if he was going to insert himself in whether she wanted him to or not. Still, she didn't want to turn down dinner. "Sure. Same time, same place."

"Your personnel record says you've completed the basic hand to hand courses, but haven't had any training with sidearms yet. I'm assuming that you've never used a sword, then?" Corporal Etcheverry asked Chris as he was handing out the equipment.

"You'd assume wrong, although I admit I've never even used a modern sword," Chris retorted. "I'm a member of the Society for Creative Anachronism. Well, I was – I haven't been to a meeting in ages, but I've had some training with a saber and have won a few of the lower level competitions at medieval festivals. I am not exceptionally skilled, by any means, but I'm able to handle one without cutting off my own legs."

"Hmm," Etcheverry said. "I'd like some time to evaluate your skill level, myself, but we're on a tight schedule. If this were a real combat situation, I wouldn't issue you a weapon until you'd passed a qualification test. Since it's training rules, with practice swords, I suppose I'll provisionally accept your self-assessment. Try not to get yourself killed."

Chris chuckled. "If things work right, we shouldn't need weapons at all."

Beccera came into the shuttle, a grim expression on his face. "Okay, people, we've received word that Mr. Langer is in place. We leave in precisely fifteen minutes. We hope to have at least ten minutes to collect the goods, but probably won't have much more than that. Mr. Desaix, I trust you know what you're supposed to do?"

"Go in, point out what we need to the Marines, and help haul things out with the antigrav pads," Chris listed. "Oh, and keep myself alive until we're all back on the shuttle."

Beccera nodded. "Correct. Etcheverry!"

"Sir!"

"Has everyone been issued their sidearms and blades?"

"Yes, sir," Etcheverry said. "Twenty sonic stunners, twenty one practice swords issued, sir!"

Beccera raised an eyebrow at those numbers, until he saw Etcheverry gesture quickly at Chris.

"Very well. Okay, people – this is a very important mission, but don't go getting yourselves 'killed' even though this is just an exercise. The *Chihuahua* only has twenty Marines and it needs them all."

"Yes, sir!" the collected Marines chorused.

"Good. Now, strap yourselves in. Ten minutes 'til launch."

Chris boarded the shuttle and strapped himself down. He wasn't entirely sure what to do with his sword, and mimicked the Marines by laying it on the floor under his feet. He hadn't been lying when he'd said he could use a sword well enough not to cut himself, but he wasn't entirely comfortable with the idea of using it in battle. He was more comfortable armed for this raid than not, though.

He also didn't feel comfortable getting involved in the chit-chat and laughter between the Marines, which ceased abruptly once the shuttle undocked and started moving. Things got so quiet that the hum of electric current running through the overhead lights could be heard.

"One minute 'til docking," Wolf's voice echoed loudly throughout the passenger compartment. Chris stiffened – he wasn't quite sure he should have volunteered for this assignment. He just prayed he didn't freeze up at a crucial moment.

With a metallic clunk, the shuttle connected with the *Don Quixote*. Beccera was the first out of his seat, gesturing silently for the others to hurry and get ready themselves. Chris nervously unhooked himself from his seat, grabbed his sword, and stood up. As he joined the line-up he found himself in the center of the group, surrounded by a wall of Marines.

The alarms were already sounding by the time they went in. The alarm messages, however, indicated they were still undetected.

"This in an unscheduled drill!" An announcement began. This was a live person's voice, and not the synthetic voice of the computer alarms. "Academy personnel to respond only."

What followed a mere thirty seconds later, however, was a series of synthesized recordings that every person in the Navy learned about very early on... and never hoped to hear.

"Security breach on the Bridge. All available Marines, to the bridge."

"Warning – critical failure of life support systems. Repeat, critical failure of life support systems."

"Collision alert! All hands, brace for a collision!"

"Looks like Langer did his job well," Chris mused.

One right after another, alarm systems sprang up. Hidden among them was the security breach at the supply room – mentioned, but very quietly underneath all the loud warnings of imminent danger. The computer systems mentioned a crisis in every room on the ship, and the supply room was the least of the worries for the crew of the *Don Quixote*.

It would take plenty of time for the security forces on board the tender to respond to the more dangerous possibilities... at least, that's what Chris and Beccera hoped.

"Okay," Beccera said, entering the access codes Rachel had acquired to open the supply room. "Time to do your thing, Mr. Desaix."

"Huh?" Chris asked blankly. Becerra gave him a sour look before he remembered just why he was there. "Right, let's go. And bring those grav pads – there is no way we could do this in the time we've got without them."

The Marines followed him in and he started pointing out various things that needed to be picked up. He checked crate after crate, deciding what to keep and what to toss.

"Hydrogen collector assembly – we'll need one of those, and it's a priority, so load it up fast. Semiconductors, hundred count. We'll need thirty of those boxes, but we don't have much time. We can hold off on those until later. Quantum wheel nodes... way too big to load aboard the shuttle. Computer components – grab as many of those as we can, but hold off on that until the end, since we can make do with what we have if necessary..."

Chris continued babbling out instructions, rapid-fire, assigning priorities for loading on the fly. Without even realizing it, he had taken over the Marine unit, not even allowing Beccera a chance to assign the proper sentries before he sent everyone off in various directions.

Beccera grabbed two of the shuttle-bound Marines at random. "Drop off your loads, ASAP, and then take sentry positions. Don't go back in there – we can't afford to have you drafted into the collection parties again."

"Yes, sir," they answered, grinning slightly at the whirlwind activity behind them as they rushed off to do as ordered. Quickly as they could, the Marines started filling the shuttle's hold up. Beccera kept a watch on time, but didn't even need to. Chris seemed to have some sort of internal alarm, so before Beccera could even give him the two-minute warning he had let everyone know to load up for their last trip. Once the last of the Marines had taken their last load, Chris tossed several boxes of semiconductors on his own grav pad and started heading out, Beccera and the two sentries following him.

They didn't quite make it back to the shuttle before they were intercepted by the *Don Quixote's* Marines.

"Damn," the lead *Don* snarled. "There really *is* a security breach.

Bridge! Air evac, Corridor 3a, ASAP!"

"Affirmative, Marine. Be advised, Admiral Mumford has personally confirmed that this is a genuine unscheduled drill, so war-game rules apply. Stun equipment only."

"Understood," the *Don* said, seeming to relax slightly. "Helmets on, boys – we don't have too long before we evacuate the air."

"Well," Beccera growled. "They're better than we thought. Marines! Lay down some cover fire, and remember your suits ARE active."

Powerful sound waves, so strong as to distort the air around them, flew outwards towards the *Dons*, and return fire came quickly. That lasted for only a few seconds – with no success – before the lights started flashing to indicate the simulated evacuation of all oxygen in the corridor.

"Swords!" the lead *Don* Marine ordered, pulling out his own practice sword. Chris, Beccera, and *Chihuahua's* two Marines also drew their swords, preparing to defend themselves.

Beccera's pair of Marines charged into the fray, hoping a nearly suicidal charge would help spring the more important twosome free. Much to their surprise, however, the assembled *Dons* fell back. The Marines stopped their charge, seconds before a flanking force poured out of a side corridor where they would have been moments later.

"Fall back!" Beccera ordered through his suit radio. Chris knew that it was already too late. In an instant he came up with a way to save them, prying open a panel on one of the walls. Before anyone could ask him what he was doing, he crossed a pair of wires and waited.

"Containment doors closing," a computerized voice announced. No-one would have heard it, had the atmosphere really been evacuated, but since it was just a drill everyone did.

"What the—" the *Don* Marine started, before an airtight door slammed shut in his face.

That left it a more even fight. Beccera and his two Marines faced off against four of the *Dons*. Chris gave the grav pad a push, knowing that the inertia would get it to their shuttle even if they didn't, before turning his attention back to the fight. Beccera was faring well, though he seemed to have found himself fighting two enemy soldiers by himself. He failed to notice, however, a third *Don* charging him from behind after breaking free from his own fight.

The sword blow, which would have struck right in the back of the neck joint in Beccera's suit, was parried away by Chris' practice blade. In a matter of moments, the engineer was able to take advantage of the surprise his arrival generated and slash across a shoulder joint, forcing the Marine to back off and "repair" the simulated leak in his suit. The surprise allowed Beccera to finish off one, than the other, of his dueling partners.

Now outnumbering their opponents, the foursome from the *Chihuahua* made short work of the *Don Quixote's* remaining Marines.

"Not bad," Beccera grinned. "Seems you were competent with that sword, after all, Chris."

Chris hesitated. "Not really. Just lucky enough to take my opponent by surprise."

Beccera chuckled. "Sometimes a little luck and a little skill is all it takes. Now, hurry up — we've got to get out of here before they get through that door you put in their way."

———————————

"Well," Rappaport reported later that day, speaking on behalf of Chris and Beccera. "We will still have to fabricate some things. Those quantum wheel nodes were just too large to load, according to Chris, but we got most everything else we'll need. We'll probably be a bit low on replacement parts when all is done, but we'll have a functional ship for the start of the Wargame."

"Good," Burkhard said, nodding. Turning to Beccera, he said, "Were we found out?"

Beccera grinned. "No. Green believes it was a regular Navy action, and apparently that's how Admiral Mumford set it up. Even if we'd lost men in the raid, we still would have had them back for the Wargame. Turns out we're good enough that we didn't need to take him up on the offer."

Burkhard nodded. "Remember, be careful not to let anyone who doesn't already know what happened how we got those parts. If someone protests...."

"We'll be careful," Chris said. "But it's unlikely we'd have to get rid of the parts, even if someone found out. Admiral Mumford has given us written permission to keep all items acquired in the raid, regardless of whether we were discovered or not."

"Even the Admiral may be called on to explain himself if we have to produce those orders. Some people already think we're being favored by him because we have his granddaughter on board," Burkhard warned. "Captain Morrison explained a few of the possible issues to me while we were watching your 'exercise.' Green is nothing if not a master of service politics — if he felt that Admiral Mumford's favoritism was usurping his authority and decided he wanted some retribution, he could very easily turn several upper level members of the Admiralty against Mumford. It's too much to expect absolute silence about this incident, but let's try and keep the talk down enough that Mumford doesn't have to step in and protect us. Got it?"

Chris and Beccera shared an uneasy look, and the old Marine stepped forward. "Got it, sir. We'll keep the rumor mill quiet."

EAS Mouse

Farmburg studied the video records he had obtained on the 'daring raid' that had supposedly been conducted by the regular Navy. He had a suspicion that assessment was incorrect and wanted to know exactly who it was. It had taken some effort to hack into video logs of the incident, but he felt confident they would be worth it.

Even if it was just an exercise, there were a lot of Academy officers who would come down hard upon someone they felt 'cheated' to get an advantage. Internal rivalries like that would help to fracture the disciplined unity that the Earth Alliance Navy had enjoyed for centuries. Sowing that kind of internal dissension was one of the reasons why he had been inserted in the Academy in the first place.

After several hours of reviewing the footage he was about to give up, but then he noticed a discrepancy. A shuttle had left tracking only a minute before the raid occurred. It was tagged as coming from one of the colony stations orbiting the system's primary planet, but backtracking the shuttle's course that didn't seem likely. He checked to see if there were any visitors logged into the station at the time who might have altered the records.

The Chihuahua, he thought furiously. *Damn! This isn't good. They're the one ship I can't do anything about right now.*

His plans tentatively called for the destruction of the *Chihuahua* in the last days of the Wargame as an 'accident' in an effort to take out the Academy's best and brightest. If that bit of sabotage was timed to occur shortly after revealing this bit of news, would it cause more internal conflict among the Academy students, or would it be better to let the crew of the *Chihuahua* live and struggle with ostracism and derision from their fellow classmates for the favoritism shown them?

Probably the former. Most likely, people would think that someone felt so strongly about the Chihuahua's 'cheating' that they had taken revenge. Everyone would be pointing fingers and accusing their fellow students of the crime.

Which, as long as he wasn't discovered as the actual saboteur, would be a good thing. But, regardless, when would be the best time to begin the operation? If he started rumors now then chances were the actual incident would be largely forgotten by the time the *Chihuahua* was destroyed, even if some resentment remained. Timed so far apart, though, it would be harder to connect the person who originated the rumors with the saboteur, making things safer for him. If necessary, he could admit to starting the rumors, but he couldn't admit to being the saboteur.

The other possibility was a bit more risky, but could have greater impact in the long run... if it worked. He would have to continue investigating, to find more solid evidence, harder to explain away evidence of the Chihuahua's involvement. He might even be able to connect the raid with someone higher up, which might cause resentment and strife among the Admiralty should one of them take offense for the favoritism.

He would have to limit how much time he could spend on that investigation, though. The rumors could be perfectly timed to allow the outrage over the supposed 'favoritism' to peak amongst the ranks. That would give him until the day before he orchestrated the *Chihuahua's* destruction. It would take some doing, but he was sure he could manage it. It was definitely a risk, though – the information just might not be there to be found, and the closer the two incidents were to one another the harder it would be to hide his connection to both of them.

Farmburg was not a risk-taker, usually, but the rewards just about equaled the risks in this case. He just couldn't decide.

"Hey, Joel," Jefferson Flay called. He was the man he'd put in charge of the failed assault on Wolfgang Schubert before that party. Of his 'flunkies,' he was probably the most competent... but that wasn't saying much, in Farmburg's opinion.

"Yeah, Jeff?" Farmburg said, assuming a face of interest despite still being absorbed in his decision.

"I just wanted to return that hundred yen I borrowed from you, yesterday," Flay said, tossing a coin his way. "I gotta get to work. See you."

Farmburg caught the coin in mid-air and stared at it for a moment. Shrugging, he flipped it into the air, and watched it fall to the ground.

"Heads," he whispered to himself once it had stopped spinning.

Well, that was one vote for waiting.

Chapter XIII

EAS Chihuahua

"Hey, Chris!" Rachel shouted over the din of the cafeteria crowd, waving him over. "Over here!"

Chris held back his smile until he was close enough for her to see it. "Hey, Rache," he said. "Seems a bit busier here than usual."

Rachel nodded. "There's something of a victory party for your 'raid' going on, as far as I understand things. I was invited, but I didn't want to go. Do you want to pick up some food and take this to one of our cabins? It's getting a bit too loud to talk in here."

"Good idea," Chris said. "I'll get it. What do you want?"

"Well, considering we're running out of the fresh food we collected from the *Gnat* when we got gravity up," Rachel said, "I'll take anything that hasn't been reconstituted or freeze-dried."

Chris' lips twitched with restrained laughter. "I'll see what they've got. We won't have to wait too long to get away from the freeze-dried stuff, though. We're due for a shipment of fresh food from the planet in about three hours. As I understand it, it's the first time this colony has ever sent food outside of their own hydroponics gardens."

"How is the planet's food? Do you know?"

"Better than what we're using right now, but I doubt anything they've got will ever be listed as a top quality ingredient by the Interstellar Gourmand's Society. At least, not for many years to come."

Rachel shrugged. "As long as it isn't this reconstituted crap we've been living on recently. I wonder if our own hydroponics bay will grow anything edible before the war games are over."

Chris shrugged. "I doubt it. Jonathan Rosebaugh was pulled from the rail gun project to work on it."

Weapons techs usually had no technical duties when they weren't engaged in the service or operation of the weapons, yet they took up a large portion of any ship's crew. For that reason, they were often given the day-to-day assignments that didn't require a specialist – things like maintaining the food supply, cooking, janitorial work, and so on.

Rosebaugh had proven himself to be a hazard to himself and others in the massive reconstruction projects that were taking place. He was competently skilled, but clumsy, leading to several instances where dropped tools or similar accidents had created safety hazards. For that reason, when Captain Burkhard had taken Chris and Rappaport aside to ask for someone who could be spared to set up a hydroponics bay, the first name out of both of their lips was the errant weapons tech.

"Hey, maybe he'll be able to actually manage," Rachel said doubtfully.

"Maybe," Chris said. "We'll see. Be right back."

Rachel waited impatiently for his return with their meals. She'd missed lunch and was fairly close to starving. She wondered vaguely if it really would matter to her if Chris could get 'real' food or not.

"Hey, Rachel," Weber said, walking over to her out of the throng of party-goers. "I thought you weren't coming."

"I'm not here for the party," she replied. "I'm waiting for Chris to get back here with our dinner."

"'Our' dinner?" Weber asked, smirking. "You guys have been eating together pretty much every night. I know you mentioned you two are kinda dating, now, but it's starting to sound serious."

"Perhaps," Rachel admitted. "At least, it's more serious than I thought it'd get before the Wargame was over. I've been trying to keep him from overworking himself by getting him to have dinner with me each night, and it's been working, but it's helped our relationship tremendously. It's not a hot-and-heavy romance, yet, but... well, it's nice." She forced a grin, hoping to change the topic. Babbling on about her love life was not how she intended to spend that evening. "By the way, how're you and 'Wolfie' coming along?"

"We've talked through some things," Weber sighed, not sounding all that happy about it. "I think he's still scared of me, but it's hard to say.

There isn't much chance to explore things with him – when I'm here, he's flying the shuttle. When he's here, I'm flying the shuttle. Thanks to that damned shuttle, we've barely been able to see each other. Rappaport tells me the number of flights we have are going to be tapering off soon, but I haven't seen any evidence of that yet."

Rachel shrugged. "Chris told me that the last of the shuttle work we need will be completed tonight. At least, until they start putting in the quantum wheel, which won't be until everything else is finished. You'll have plenty of time together after that."

Weber beamed at her. "Is that so? Well, then, I suppose I'd better start getting ready to go Wolf-hunting tomorrow."

Rachel laughed. "Lucky you. I've only got my horrible job in 'Waste Recycling' to look forward to, tomorrow."

"And dinners," Weber reminded her.

"And dinners." Rachel grinned self consciously.

"How interesting are those dinners?" Weber asked. "You say this relationship hasn't gotten hot-and-heavy, yet, but how it is really?"

Rachel shrugged. "We haven't had a moment alone since the party. Not really, anyway. We eat here, in the cafeteria, and work in completely different places."

"So, you're waiting until you can get him alone before you test his prowess in the sack, huh?" Weber smirked crudely.

"*What!?*" Rachel sputtered. "I... I'd never... *We'd* never...."

Just then, Chris strode up carrying two trays of food. They both were covered, but he seemed to know whose was whose.

"Hey, Rache. Here's your dinner," he said, handing her one of the trays. Noticing her expression, he frowned. "Something wrong?"

"No, nothing, thanks," she replied, taking it with a smile. She mustered up enough composure to turn one last glare at Weber before returning her attention to Chris. "Well, I guess we'll be eating in my cabin. Since Weber's about to go on duty, Wolf will want yours to sleep in."

Weber leered. "I don't expect to be back for a while. You two can have it all night, if you want."

Chris missed the comment, but Rachel certainly didn't. "Come on, Chris," she ordered, blushing furiously as she stormed away.

He blinked at her retreating back. "What was that all about?" he asked.

Weber just laughed. "Well, don't just stand there – go after her and maybe you'll find out."

"I haven't had a chance to ask about the raid, yet," Rachel noted as they entered her cabin. "I know it was successful, but I haven't heard anything else, yet."

"To be honest, it was mostly a blur to me," Chris admitted, setting a tray down on a small end-table by Rachel's bed. They'd eaten in the cabin before, and Rachel had always insisted on using the desk, leaving Chris to fend for himself. Weber's desk was occupied, so he chose to sit on one of the beds.

Rachel frowned slightly, Weber's earlier comments about "testing his prowess in the sack" made the sight of him sitting on her bed feel somewhat awkward. She might really like Chris – though she still couldn't quite believe it, sometimes, when they got into one of their (increasingly infrequent) arguments – but she wasn't the sort of girl to leap into bed with a man just because they were starting to get along.

"I think it's about time I relinquish my desk to your dining," Rachel noted, trying to quiet the memory of Weber's words. "You get too many crumbs on my bed."

"I do not!" Chris protested, though he looked amused. "Then again, it's a lot more comfortable to eat at your desk, I believe, so maybe I'll accept my punishment for a crime I didn't commit, and count my lucky stars."

"If you say so," Rachel said, not meeting his eyes. To be honest, Chris was telling the truth. She made her own way to the bed and realized she didn't really feel much better taking his place. One of them was still on the soft, warm sheets that might just be big enough for two, if they held each other pretty close.

Deciding to distract herself from those thoughts, Rachel decided to bring back the original topic. "You aren't dodging my questions that easily, Mr. Desaix," she teased. "What happened on the *Don Quixote?*"

Chris shrugged. "Things went by so quickly, it was pretty confusing. I dunno how to describe it."

"Try," Rachel said. "I've heard you actually got into a sword battle at one point."

"Towards the end, yeah. But only very briefly," Chris noted. "I surprised someone and stopped them from striking Beccera in the back, using the distraction to cut him down. But I couldn't have stood up to them in a real fight – trust me. I'm terrible with a sword."

Rachel smiled. "So what? That just makes your achievement that much greater. An unskilled, barely trained engineer defeating a promising

Marine cadet. You should be proud."

"I'm not exactly upset about my performance," Chris reminded her. "I'm just saying it wasn't really a big deal. Actually, I'm just glad that I didn't freeze up when the action started. I had a serious attack of nerves on the flight over."

That rung a small alarm in Rachel's mind. "You mean, like you sometimes do in your nightmares?" she asked hesitantly.

"Yeah, kinda," Chris answered, fidgeting. "Normally, in my dreams, it's a lot worse... and so is the situation my nightmares place me in. No-one's life was really at risk in this one. I still fear I could freeze, one day, in more dangerous circumstances."

Rachel frowned. "Chris, this may sound like an odd question, but do your nightmares ever include your freezing during an engineering crisis?"

Chris considered that question briefly. "Hm... not that I can recall. I don't always remember my dreams."

Rachel nodded. "I thought so. Chris, I want you to answer me honestly about this... do you honestly believe you're a better engineer than a tactician? Now, before you answer, I'm not asking which one you'd rather do. I'm asking which one you'd be better at, ignoring things like your personal enjoyment or your nerves."

Chris paused. "I'm not sure. I've been told I was good at tactics since my days fighting war games with the SCA, but...." He shrugged. "It doesn't really interest me. Um, hey, shouldn't you start eating before your food spoils? I went to a lot of trouble finding you things that I thought you would like."

Rachel hesitated. It was an obvious attempt to change the subject, but he was right – she was letting her meal go to waste. She wanted to get her point out, first, though. "Chris, what is it about tactics that gives you nightmares, anyway? If you make a mistake or freeze up when we have a major reactor breech, we're all dead, so that's not all that different from making a tactical mistake. What is it with your tactics classes that gives you all these nightmares that you don't feel when you're practicing your engineering?"

Chris didn't have an answer to that. "Rachel, what do you expect me to say? I like engineering. I suppose I like some aspects of tactical training, too, but... I just don't know. All I know is that I enjoy engineering, and it doesn't give me nightmares."

"I wish I knew how to stop your nightmares. If we could, I think you'd be better off leaving Engineering as your hobby and working primarily as a tactician in the Navy," Rachel sighed, starting to take the cover off her tray of food. She was going to say more before she finally saw what was on her plate. "Dear God, how in the world did you manage to find *that?*"

There, on her plate, was real sushi – fresh sushi, including what looked like real crab rolls, fresh tuna nigiri, and smoked salmon in a hand-roll. In addition to that, there was an avocado salad and a soup of some sort.

Chris grinned broadly. "When we were hiding our tracks for the raid, we had to head over to the station orbiting the planet. I was able to buy a small box of supplies while we were there, and kept it all on ice for the trip. I took it to our chef and asked him to make it as a surprise for you. The crab and the tuna are real, the salmon is actually a similar native fish found on this planet's surface, and the avocado... well, I don't really know where that came from. The soup is, unfortunately, just an ordinary dried variety, but I figured you wouldn't mind that with the other things I got."

"Oh, thank you!" Rachel said, completely forgetting her prior train of thought. "I can't believe you managed to do this."

"Well, I was curious about this planet's food supplies, myself," Chris noted. "Rice has taken to the surface of it fairly well, and both native and Earth-based fish thrive in the oceans. Vegetables have kind of struggled, as I understand it, which is why I'm so surprised by the avocado, but it seems to be pretty decent from what I can tell. Like I said, it isn't prize-winning yet, but I've tried it and it ain't bad."

Rachel selected a pair of chopsticks from the various utensils she had been given and immediately delved into the sushi. "Oh, this is good. Who is the chef? They should be on the job full-time, if this is any sample of what they can do."

Chris laughed. "Dr. June Ehrlich, believe it or not. She'll likely be too busy as our doctor to be a full-time cook, but I wouldn't be surprised if she winds up getting the job part-time, since everyone seems to be working two jobs on this boat. While she was in the Academy's medical school, she earned a bit of spending money as a cook in the reserves. She even won some armed forces competition about a dozen years or so ago before retiring to private practice and the civilian auxiliary."

Rachel took another bite and sighed. "Oh, this is so good. Where did you get the soy sauce and the wasabi?"

"Well, it's not real wasabi, but it comes from the local gardens and seems close enough," Chris noted. "As far as the soy sauce goes, I have a personal supply. I prefer it to salt in most cases."

Rachel nodded. "I think I remember that from the few times we've eaten together at the Academy. This is the first time I've seen it out since we left for the ship, though."

"Well, we never had anything worth using soy sauce on," Chris said.

"Yes, the food we've had has definitely been too poor to waste a resource as precious as that on," Rachel admitted.

"Agreed," Chris said. "I don't waste good resources on trash. Which reminds me..."

"Yes?" Rachel asked, wondering why he'd just drifted off like that.

"Remember how we were discussing your problems with your coworkers in that 'Waste Recycling' job," Chris said.

"Yes?" Rachel wasn't sure if this was yet another attempt to change the subject or what.

"Like I just said, I don't waste good resources on trash, and you're definitely a good resource," he grinned. "You're wasted collecting trash, so—"

Rachel had her problems with her current job, but she didn't want him doing anything that might get him in trouble. Visions of him launching an operation similar to the Don Quixote heist danced in her head. She had to stop him before he tried something dangerous. "Chris, I know I've had my complaints, but I'm okay with it. Really."

"Relax, I'm not about to get Langer to hack your personnel file and get you transferred or anything like that," Chris said. Was he reading her mind? He gave her a cheeky grin before continuing. "I have more legitimate ways of helping you out. Remember me saying I needed an assistant?"

Rachel nodded slowly. "Yes, I remember something like that."

"Well, I talked with Rappaport. If you check your messages, I think you'll find a change of assignment notice."

Rachel spun to the wall-mounted computer by her bed and directed it to open her e-mail. Sure enough, there was a message addressed from Lt. Jacques Rappaport, Chief Engineer, directing and requiring her to accept a new assignment as Cadet Lieutenant Christopher Desaix's new personal assistant.

She raised an eyebrow. "I'm your personal assistant, now, am I? You realize this gives me an even better opportunity to keep an eye on you? You aren't going to be working even *two* straight shifts if I have anything to say about it."

Chris smiled. "Well, we'll just have to see about that..."

Rachel sighed. It might have been uncomfortable working on the Waste Recycling Team, but at least it was better than being bored all the time... as she was, now, since Chris never involved her in anything. True, this was just her first day and they were both just getting used to the adjustment, and he did think to chat with her from time to time as they were moving between one assignment and another, but he didn't seem to really need her.

"Hey, Rache," he called. "Come here a minute."

Rachel started in surprise. That was the first time he'd spoken in the twenty minutes since they arrived in the heart of this mechanical section that she couldn't decipher the function of.

"Coming," she said, leaping up from her seat and rushing over to where he had his head buried under some computer component.

"You know how to use a circuit tester, right?" his still-headless voice asked.

"Uh, well, not really," Rachel said.

That got him to shove his way out from under the circuitry and look up at her in disbelief. "You're kidding me. It's one of the first things they teach you in the basic maintenance course everyone at the academy is required to take!"

Rachel laughed nervously. "I was planning to complete that requirement next semester."

Chris shook his head, sighing. "I guess I'll have to see if I can get you up to speed, okay?"

"Uh," Rachel hesitated. "I might be a hopeless case. There was a reason I've been putting off taking that course."

"Well, I can try," Chris said, shrugging. "After this shift, though. In the meantime, let me show you how a circuit tester works, so you can work while I finish up here."

"If you really want to risk giving me this kind of job," Rachel said. She did want something to do, but she wasn't sure she should be entrusted with anything important... and she definitely remembered Chris mentioning that it was important.

"Unless you've got the klutz factor of Mr. Rosebaugh to go along with your lack of knowledge, you shouldn't have any trouble."

"Well, I'm not that bad, at least," Rachel admitted with a smile. "Okay, so how does this thing work?"

He picked up a nearby device. It looked pretty simple – there was a slot, a button, and a pair of small LED lights.

"It may look like one of my antiques, but it's not – this really is the modern design for a circuit tester. They probably haven't changed it because it's so simple even an idiot can use it – and you're no idiot, so this should be fine. You take the device to be tested..." he held up a computer part she couldn't readily identify, "and plug it into the slot. Press the button, and wait a few seconds for one of the lights to come on. If it's red there's a problem. Set it aside so I can see if it's salvageable. If it's green, the device is okay; just hand it to me when I ask for it. I need everything in that stack tested. Think you can handle that?"

Rachel nodded. "Easier than I would have thought."

"Try it," Chris asked, handing her the tester and the computer part.

Rachel re-enacted Chris's demonstration with success. "Green light. It works."

"Good," Chris said, burying himself under the computer, again. "Give me that board you just tested, okay?"

"Sure thing," Rachel said, making herself busy. Okay, maybe she wasn't going to be quite as useless as she feared. There was still the threat of those engineering lessons he had planned, though. There was a reason she had put off that basic maintenance course. Hopefully this wouldn't be too bad.

Schubert sighed as he staggered his way into his cabin. He had finally completed the last of the mind-numbing trips back and forth in the shuttle for the refit, and was nearing collapse. He had the rest of the day off, and then he'd be starting his new job as a software tester the next day. He didn't quite know how frustrating that assignment would be, but he figured it wasn't any worse than piloting a shuttle. He may love being a pilot, but after a while shuttles drove even the most enthusiastic pilot into boredom.

"Hello, Wolfie," a feminine voice said. "Long time, no see. I fell asleep waiting for you."

There was only one person in the galaxy who had ever called him 'Wolfie,' so it wasn't too hard to guess who it belonged to.

"Lauren?"

"Still scared of me?" she asked. "Or can we... talk?"

Schubert swallowed. "Talk?"

"Mm hmm," Weber purred, cocking her head and batting her eyes seductively. "Talk. Of course, there are a number of ways to talk...."

Schubert started slowly backing up. He liked women, but this one just terrified him for reasons he couldn't put into words.

Weber's well-shaped form rose from the bed, letting the covers slip off, revealing that she wore a particularly skimpy nightgown and not much else. She grabbed a thin robe and slipped it on over her shoulders. "I just want to make sure you aren't scared of me, any more. That's all."

"Right," Schubert said, trying to think of how to get out of this situation with his dignity still intact. While entrancing, she was even scarier half-naked. "Chris gets off any moment, and I'm pretty sure he'll be coming down here pretty soon—"

"Nope," Weber said. "He and Rachel are going to be sharing my cabin for the night. I doubt they'll have quite as nice a... 'talk' as I hope we will, though. Rachel said he was only over to give her a crash course in engineering. Poor girl thinks that makes for a good date. I think we both know what makes for a better date, right?"

Wolf's progress backwards was stopped with a *thunk* as he found himself stuck in a corner. Weber continued to move towards him, a grin spreading on her face.

"Since your roomies stuck in my cabin, it seems I'm going to be stuck in yours tonight." She leaned forward, and captured his mouth in a kiss. "Whadya say we make the most of it?"

Rachel winced. A tiny electric spark from the malfunctioning device Chris was teaching her to repair shot up in front of her eyes, nearly blinding her. "I don't think this is going to work, Chris."

"Well, it might if you remembered to connect the power to the circuit instead of leaving it exposed as a live feed," Chris noted dryly. At her embarrassed look, he added, "Don't get too stressed out about it. I've met people who've made worse mistakes, and they were professionals."

Rachel sighed. "That may be, but I'm just not getting the hang of this. I don't think I've got what it takes to be an engineer."

"I'm not trying to make you an engineer," Chris said softly. "Just someone who can breeze through their Basic Maintenance class."

Rachel glanced at the broken device she was holding and sighed. "Just what is it that I'm supposed to be fixing here, anyway?"

"It's the electronics package for one of the shock chairs. We probably would just get rid of them if this ship were being re-commissioned for regular duty, but we don't have the time or the resources to switch them out for more comfortable chairs. It's the only thing I found portable enough to teach you with."

"You couldn't find anything easier to handle?" Rachel sighed.

"Oh, come on. It's not that bad," Chris said. "Let me show you what you did wrong. It's pretty simple to fix from this point."

Rachel yawned, waving him off. "Not right now. If I don't get some sleep soon, I won't be any good tomorrow."

"Okay, if you insist," Chris sighed. "I might as well turn in, too, then. Where am I supposed to sleep, anyway?"

Rachel blinked at him. "Huh?"

"Well, I'm staying here tonight, right? At least, that's what Lauren said the deal was," Chris explained, scratching his head tiredly. "She didn't want me using her bunk, though, so I figured you had an idea for what I should do."

Rachel groaned. "Oh, hell. Not another matchmaking scheme. Why won't that woman let me set my own pace in this relationship?"

"You didn't know about this?" Chris asked, astonished.

"I knew she was going to be out all night," Rachel sighed. "I didn't know where, or that you'd be locked out of your cabin tonight. Like I said – it's another matchmaker scheme of hers. She keeps trying to get me to 'speed things along' with you, and it's giving me a bit of a headache."

Chris hesitated. He didn't really see the need to "speed things along," since they didn't really have much time to themselves, but he wouldn't have objected if things between them got a little more physical.

"Are you really that upset at the prospect of us sharing a room?" Chris asked.

Rachel glared at him. "Look, Chris. I like you, but I'm not ready to share a bed with you just yet. Lauren figures I need a push. She sticks you in my cabin and forbids you from taking the only free bed. Oh, I guess I have no choice but to offer to share a bed. Right. I'm not looking for a fling with you, Chris. I want to take this slow, and we aren't anywhere close to that, yet."

"We're working towards it, though... aren't we?" Chris asked, suddenly unsure of himself.

Rachel deflated. "Well, maybe. Not today, though."

"Of course," Chris agreed. "But someday?"

"Like I said, maybe," Rachel answered softly. She shot him a playful look. "I'm still not entirely sure I can put up with you, yet."

Chris laughed. "Well, there is that. At any rate, that leaves us with a problem tonight. I'm a man of my word, and won't take her bed, and we're not ready to share yours. But I could point out a little loophole, here: Lauren only forbade *me* from using her bed... she didn't say anything about you, now did she?"

Rachel blinked up at him owlishly, and then laughed. She stepped over to him and gave him a kiss. "Oh, I suppose that will do, at that."

Chapter XIV

EAS Chihuahua

"So," Burkhard asked at the daily staff meeting. "What's the status of the refit?"

"Well," Chris answered. "There are a few bells and whistles that need to be taken care of, but for the most part we are done except for the quantum wheel. We still need to find some pyramid-style nodes."

"Got 'em," Rappaport answered smugly. "And they'll be powerful, too. While you've been busy with everything else, Chris, I've secretly been adding on to your side-mount quantum wheel, idea. Ran it through the simulations, and figured we could actually include battleship-sized nodes without compromising our power distribution requirements or size limitations. It should make your shield idea a bit more effective."

Chris frowned. "That might complicate things with the emitters. I'm not sure we have the parts to make emitters that size."

"Taken care of," Rappaport replied. "I had to do a lot of horse-trading to get them, though. As things stand, we'll be practically out of replacement parts, so the first thing I'm going to do once the refit's complete is set up a fabrication shop and put most of our staff on that." He shrugged. "The local planetary authority is willing to make deals that can give us the raw materials we'll need. A good thing, since Commodore Green won't let us have anything more than we've already taken. He was rather annoyed we got to keep the parts we acquired on that little raid of yours."

Still somewhat stunned, Chris turned back to his captain. "Well, then, sir, I'd figured on several more days to fabricate those nodes, but if that's all been taken care of... we should be space-worthy later this afternoon."

"Excellent!" Burkhard clapped. "Do you two think your staff can manage without you in this final stage?"

"Chris isn't needed," Rappaport answered before the younger man could. "The only tricky thing is the nodes, and that's my job. I can keep an eye on those 'bells and whistles' while I work."

"Good!" Burkhard said. "You've both got forty-eight hours of leave in thanks for all the overtime you put in for the refit. Chris, yours starts the moment this meeting's over. Jacques, obviously yours will have to wait until you're done."

"Thank you, sir," the two engineers chorused.

"Mr. Orff," Burkhard continued. "Your report, please?"

"Well, sir," Orff, who had yet to fully realize his duties as the ship's executive officer in the chaos of the refit, began. "Given that we have some, uh, new equipment to test out, but don't have any Academy ships to fly against, the Wargame officials will be loaning us the regular navy corvette *Tarantula* from the Regular fleet to help us test our systems and drill against. They may also loan the Academy other ships for exercise purposes, as well, until more of our forces come on-line, should we need them."

"Good work lobbying, Mr. Orff. I think I'll keep you as our liaison to the Wargame officials until after our shakedown cruise. Ms. Katz, you'll be acting as my executive officer until then."

Rachel, a little overwhelmed, nodded. "Thank you, sir."

"I doubt you'll be thanking me when you realize just how much work that means you'll have to do," Burkhard said, his eyes twinkling. "You've got forty-eight hours leave, too, so you're fresh when we start that shakedown. I think that's all for today. Any other business? No? Then you're all dismissed."

The gathered officers started milling about the room, some getting involved in quiet conversations while others made their way out of the room as quickly as possible. Chris slowly made his way over to Rachel. They'd been making plans for another engineering lesson after the meeting, and with his unexpected leave he was hoping she might consider a short trip planet-side for some fresher food then what was available on board the *Chihuahua*. One of the 'bells and whistles' Chris had mentioned to

Burkhard was a new food-storage system, since they had quickly discovered that many of the kitchen refrigeration systems were not fully functional. Because of that, the crew was still on rehydrated rations. On the plus side, though, the otherwise incompetent Jonathan Rosebaugh was proving to be an excellent gardener, although his greenhouse was still weeks away from producing fresh food.

Still, to get the really good stuff, you had to leave the ship, and Chris suddenly had a lot of free time on his hands.

---

94 Ceti, Orbital Colony Station

Rachel glared at the shock chair electronic package as Chris pulled it out of the luggage they'd taken with them to the station orbiting the only planet in the 94 Ceti system. "You know," she grumbled, "I'm really starting to hate those things."

Chris smirked. He had invited her to join him for a little vacation... but hers would be a working vacation. "Hey, you're getting pretty good at fixing up these things, and each repair you've made has taught you something else. At this rate, you'll be able to ace that Basic Maintenance course next semester."

Rachel sighed. "Maybe. I still don't understand how these things make the shock chairs work."

"Simple," Chris said. "It regulates energy collectors which absorb the kinetic energy that is produced by the acceleration of the ship, redirecting that energy from the chair's occupant. It puts any surplus power it generates into the emergency life-support batteries. And there's no 'maybe' about it. With what you've learned already, you are probably better at engineering work than the 'Chief Engineer' of the corvette *Ishmael?*"

Rachel's eyes widened. "What? How is that possible?"

"Thanks to my lessons, you now know a little bit about real engineering," Chris noted. "The *Ishmael* is the one of the ships in the Academy fleet which has an Academy student as a chief engineer instead of a reservist or a regular Navy officer. I know the guy – his name's Mark Taira. He's a Junior, but he only recently switched from a major in International Relations to Engineering, and like yourself hasn't taken the Basic Maintenance course, yet. The *Chihuahua* is very lucky – almost all the engineering staff assigned to us are actual engineering students who have either experience or training in engineering. A lot of the people who are working as engineers in the rest of the fleet are as bad at engineering as you were a week ago when we started this, and only function by using prefabricated parts. Whoever assigned Mark to be a part of the *Ishmael's* engineering staff was an idiot, though, because he's a Cadet Lieutenant Commander, and was the highest ranking engineer aboard. Which made him the Chief Engineer... and has led him to call me every night asking what he needs to assign his people to do."

Rache blinked. "So, you're actually organizing two refits?"

"Well, sort of."

"So, is the *Ishmael* going to be as good as the *Chihuahua* when all's said and done?" Rachel asked, amused, as she picked up the offending electronics package and started diagnosing it.

"Hardly," Chris snorted, leading her down the corridors of the station. "I wouldn't trust Mark to try putting in a whole new cold fusion plant, even if a Phoebe class corvette could handle one. It's got a quantum wheel and an old-fashioned fusion reactor, which means it's got about the worst power-to-drive set-up that we ever produced. *Ishmael* should be as good as an unmodified Phoebe-class corvette can be, though."

Rachel shrugged. "Well, if you say so. The Phoebes are the newest class of ships the Academy has on its side, so they should be the most advanced, but if you're sure it's not as good as we are...."

"No, the *Chihuahua's* the newest class of ship," Chris noted. "We've practically rebuilt her. Sure, we kept the old fusion drive and the fusion reactor. We also added a quantum wheel that doubles as a shield – which no-one else has – and a cold-fusion plant. We upgraded the computer systems until they're the equivalent of the modern top-of-the-line systems. Add in Wayne Evans' tweaks to the standard gravity control system, and the *Chihuahua* is probably the most advanced ship in the entire Earth Alliance. Only thing I'd change about her if I were designing her new is the rail gun broadside and the crew compartments. And if you were to replace the rail guns with the more modern ones – the double-barreled shots that use one less person per gun – we'd be able to kill both problems at once. That, though, would require several months of dry-dock time and major modifications to the hull's exterior, power distribution systems, and internal bulkheads. Maybe if the ship is preserved for the Navy's use following the Wargame, someone'll think to do that. I've made notes for the record to that end."

Rachel chewed her lip. "Were there any modifications you suggested to him, at all?"

Chris shrugged. "Like I said, Mark isn't the best of people to put in charge of a refit like this. I made a few minor suggestions, but I doubt it'll amount to anything. The only major modification I would recommend would be to his quantum wheel's dome-emitters with pyramid-emitters. That's a pretty standard modification, but I'm not even sure he'll be able to do *that*. But he will be ready in time for the Wargame, that's for sure."

Rachel smiled. "Well, that's good. So, there are engineering crews led by engineers who aren't even as good as me. Can you think of any which have engineering staffs better than ours?"

Chris thought for a moment. "On the Academy side? Well... possibly Commodore Green's *Sirius* could put together a better crew, though he has just as many Mark Tairas as he has Jacques Rappaports. He got the best he could, but he was filling out the roster for a battleship and not a tiny old corvette. He asked for me, too, by the way, but I was already assigned to the *Chihuahua*."

Rachel smiled slightly. "I'm glad you're here. I think you made us a lot more effective then you would have made a battleship, and I'm glad we have this time to spend together."

"So am I," Chris said, grinning. "I'd hate to have to work on a battleship, myself. But that reminds me, we're going to have to share a cabin tonight."

Rachel snorted. "Again? That's, what, the fourth night this week?"

"Yeah," Chris said. "We've got my cabin, this time, and I hope you'll forgive me for saying I'm very glad. Last time they left it in a terrible mess." He sighed. "Enough chit-chat. We need to eat and have what fun we can, before the Captain pulls you away from me."

"Well, we've still got a day. Maybe we should see if we can rent a couple rooms tonight, so we can avoid both of our cabins on the ship," Rachel suggested.

"Maybe," Chris said. "Or maybe we should just rent one... we're used to sharing a cabin, after all, and I'd rather not have to fork over the yen to pay for multiple rooms in a place like this."

Rachel paused. "Maybe. As long as there's two beds, I guess that'd be all right."

Chris froze. "I wasn't suggesting that we, uh..."

"I know, Chris, I know," Rachel said. "I was just trying to be clear."

"Well, okay," Chris said, relaxing slightly. "I'm letting you take the lead on that, just so you know. But for right now, I don't want to waste our time off in transit between this station and the ship, so I still suggest we bunk here. But we aren't going to be doing anything during our leave until you've finished fixing this last electronics package."

Rachel laughed. "And what'll you do if I refuse?"

Chris considered that for a moment. "Hmm... maybe this."

With that, he attacked her, tickling her along her ribs. Rachel gasped, laughing, and started running away. "Hey!" she cried. "No fair. You aren't ticklish!"

Chris chased her down the corridors. "You just haven't found out where I'm ticklish, yet. And anyway, I won't let up until you promise to do your work!"

Unseen by the two, Farmburg, disguised and dressed in civilian clothing, watched their merry romp. Perhaps the rumor he'd used to get Schubert so mad at him was true after all. He'd have to think about this, and see if there was any way to use it to his advantage.

EAS Chihuahua

"Captain Wendkos," Burkhard said, greeting the commander of the *Tarantula* as he came aboard the *Chihuahua*.

"Captain Burkhard," Commander Martin Wendkos replied, shaking hands with the younger man. "I understand you're going to need my services, soon."

Burkhard nodded. "Yes, but not right away. We'll complete by the end of tomorrow, but I'm giving the crew some leave afterwards while we take care of some administrative details – they've earned it with the time they've put into getting this ship spaceworthy. But after that, and running a burn test on our newly modified engines and power systems, we'll need someone to monitor our shakedown cruise and to drill against. There may be a snag, though – I'm not sure a corvette is a fair match up against our ship."

"Oh?" Wendkos asked.

Burkhard smirked. "Uh huh. I know our crew size rates us as a corvette, but with some of our modifications we're better armed and armored then any corvette in the Navy. One of our cadet engineering majors came up with an intriguing idea. Our chief engineer took his plans and modified it just a trifle, and while we haven't finished testing it yet... we're pretty certain it'll work. We just don't know how effective it'll be."

"And I'm assuming you won't tell me what this secret system is?" Wendkos asked, rolling his eyes. "So you want me to try and expedite the release of other ships to test your ship against?"

"I'm hoping we can officially get re-rated as a pocket frigate when we're done," Burkhard noted. "So, yeah... I'm going to want to test myself against them. But there was another issue I wanted to discuss."

"Yes?" Wendkos said, still looking like he didn't quite believe the whole 'pocket frigate' idea.

"Well, I was hoping we could keep our test results secret from 'Commodore' Green."

Wendkos frowned. That was an especially unusual request, and one he wasn't sure he could grant. "Any particular reason why?"

Burkhard smirked. "Well, let's just say I don't trust him to know how to use our ship properly once he finds out how much we've upgraded it. I'd like to see how effective she really is before discussing the matter with him."

Wendkos considered Burkhard's reasoning, and with what he knew about Green it made sense. "I suppose I can understand that, but how do you plan to keep these tests secret? Green has to know that she's had her shakedown cruise, after all," Wendkos noted.

"Come into my office," Burkhard said leading the way down the corridors. "As long as you're willing to help, I have a few ideas which should work...."

Chapter XV

EAS Chihuahua

Burkhard took his seat in the captain's chair, smiling. Finally, he'd be able to see what his ship could really do. In theory, it would be simultaneously one of the oldest and most advanced ships in the Earth Alliance Navy... but in practice, well, he'd been waiting to see.

At the moment only a skeleton crew was on board while they tested the systems. The rest had been sent to stay, briefly, on the Tarantula. They would be returning once the engineers were convinced the ship wouldn't explode, but they hoped to confirm that before the next scheduled shift change. The initial burn testing for the hardware had been completed, and now it was time for the first live engine tests. There were some things about these engine tests he wanted to keep a secret, however.

"Mr. Schubert," he called. "Fusion drive only, slow burn – 5% power, accelerate to 2000 kps, if you please. Course... give me a slow arc around the sun."

"Aye, sir," Schubert answered, slightly disappointed. He wanted to see what the *Chihuahua* could do, but reluctantly agreed that their first flight out should be a little more cautious than normal.

Chris stood by at the engineering liaison station. Rachel, from her position at tactical, walked over to him with a slight grimace on her face.

"Chris?" she said softly, wanting only him to hear.

"Yes, Rache?" he answered, concentrating mostly on the display in front of him.

"I'm very proud of this ship you rebuilt for us," she said. "But if one of your little innovations goes wrong, I want you to know I'm going to kill you."

Chris grinned. "And if nothing goes wrong?"

"Well, I'd like to take you to dinner," she replied. "But I suspect the rest of the crew will want to do that, too. So, why don't we talk about a suitable payment later?"

"Tactical!" Burkhard called.

Rachel quickly snapped back into her position. The delay, fortunately, went unnoticed by the Captain. "Yes, sir?"

"I want you to let me know the second our sensor profile goes out of sight from the rest of the fleet."

"Yes, sir!" Rachel shot back crisply, mentally berating herself for her earlier inattention. She started keeping a close watch on her monitors, making sure she would not have any more slip-ups.

"Sir," Mumford said. "Regular Fleet Corvette *Tarantula* is hailing us, sir."

Burkhard nodded. "What're they saying?"

"Her captain is inviting us to a race when we orbit back around."

He raised an eyebrow. "Is that so? Well, I don't think I want them to know our full capabilities yet, but I suppose we could arrange that. Just acknowledge them for now, though."

"Aye, sir," Mumford said, turning back to her console.

"Engineering, Sir," Chris said. "Lieutenant Rappaport's compliments, and he recommends we start testing the engines at higher output."

"Acknowledged. Mr. Schubert, as soon as Ms. Katz informs you that our sensor profile has disappeared from view, open her up – maximum burn on the fusion drives."

"Yes, sir!" Wolf snapped with satisfaction.

"Sir," Mumford said, frowning as she listened to something through her ear piece. "Signal from flag. They... I don't understand it, sir. Something about us not having filed a proper flight plan?"

"Bullshit," Burkhard snapped under his breath. Louder, he said, "Inform them that I filed that flight plan almost twenty-four hours ago, and that they should have it. It's message..." He pulled out a hand comp and taped on it for a bit. "Message Chihuahua-10535 Beta."

Mumford repeated his words, and waited for a response. A few moments later, she turned back around and said, "Sir, Commodore Green has specifically asked us to stand down. He claims the forms were not properly filled out – apparently, our flight plan is not specific enough. He wants a track record in addition to waypoints."

Burkhard couldn't help himself – he gawked at her. "You're kidding?" he said. "I filed all the standard flight plans. He isn't entitled to ask for more."

"No, sir," she agreed. "But he's... fairly insistent."

"I have a suggestion, sir," Chris said. "Emily, inform the Commodore that we have no way of estimating our track with any accuracy until we've fully calibrated our engines. Until then, he'll have to make do with waypoints."

"Sir?" Mumford asked, seeking confirmation from her Captain.

"Hell, go ahead. Let's hope he buys it."

Rachel stepped over to whisper in Chris' ear. "Is that true?"

He shrugged. "Yeah. Oh, sure, our estimate might only be off by a few dozen meters either way, but that's not how *I* would define accuracy."

Orff looked at his captain with some uncertainty. "Sir, why are you so concerned about Commodore Green knowing our flight plan? He is our superior officer, so shouldn't he have a right to know what we're doing?"

Burkhard grinned. "Little lesson for you on the life of a corvette commander. Corvettes – as well as frigates and most light cruisers – are designed for independent command. Which means we aren't supposed to be as micromanaged as, say, the captain of a heavy cruiser or battleship would be. The fact that 'Commodore' Green is demanding to know this much about our plans when all we're conducting is a general test run does not, to be polite, bode well. A fleet commander just can't control that many things on his own, and has to learn to properly delegate... and it doesn't seem as if the 'Commodore' knows quite how to handle that part of his job. And I'd really rather not allow anyone to know what we can do until it's too late – by Wargame rules, there may be regular Navy spies in Green's officer core, so reporting everything too him would reveal too much. We won't even be going all-out against the *Tarantula*... although I think using our shields would be a good idea. It'll make the Regulars think twice when they encounter one of our corvettes out on a scouting expedition... and they're not likely to realize we're the only ship equipped with one." He paused, grinning sardonically. "Another piece of advice – don't do what I'm doing now. Telling your subordinates that a superior doesn't know what the hell he's doing is not a good idea if you want a good career. It'll hold you back from promotions, like it has me."

"Message from Flag," Mumford interrupted. "Commodore Green has authorized our flight, but advises that we are to give him best-guess flight paths in all future missions. Waypoint records will not be sufficient."

Burkhard sighed. "Well, that makes perfect sense coming from him. We'd better get all of our real testing done today. Mr. Schubert, continue on course to sensor shadow point, 2000 kps."

"Aye, aye, sir."

"Yeehaw!" Schubert cheered alongside most of the bridge crew, conducting a hairpin turn. The fastest military ships on record were the Alligator class corvettes, which were able to maneuver at an incredible 0.23c in normal space. Even without the quantum wheel to supplement their fusion drive, they had just clocked 0.26c. It was a new speed record.

"I think this is the speed we should report to the Navy list," Burkhard suggested abruptly over the cheers, quieting them down. "Just in case the Regulars decide to use it for 'intel.' But why don't we see what we can really do? Mr. Schubert, open up the quantum wheels. Assuming you think they're ready, Mr. Desaix."

"Aye, sir. Engineering is ready," Chris acknowledged. Burkhard may have been the captain, but this flight was primarily an engineering test. For a brief moment, Chris would be in command.

Chihuahua continued accelerate while turning circles, seeking the velocity at which the ship was no longer able to maneuver. The crew waited, curiosity mounting.

"By God," Schubert whispered. "We're almost at 0.29c, and we haven't even started to lose control."

"Slow acceleration," Chris advised. "Our debris collection systems has not been cleared to handle your average piece of space dust past one third c. I'm not anxious to discover what thousands of tiny projectiles will do to our hull at relativistic speeds."

The debris collection system was a mild magnetic and gravitic wave which redirected and collected small particles of space dust, ostensibly to mine space for the raw materials needed to increase the endurance of a ship before it had to resupply. It had been developed many hundreds of years before, in the early ages of space flight on Earth. As technology advanced, it was discovered to have a more important function: Protecting a spacecraft from space dust and debris as it traveled through the cosmos.

The problem was that, unlike the high-intensity field created by a quantum wheel, certain speeds overwhelmed the system, disabling its ability to collect the debris fast enough and prevent it from colliding with the hull. The breaking point (with some margin for error) was discovered to be just under .40c, with most safety protocols directing acceleration stop at 0.33c for safety purposes, though such limitations had never been an issue among maneuverable vessels – only unmanned test vehicles accelerating without care for maneuverability had ever reached such speeds. Improvements were being made in the devices all the time, but the tests never exceeded that speed.

Weapons manufacturers took these numbers as their standard. Modern rail gun, sometimes called a RKE or "relativistic kinetic energy" weapons, were tested to target ships traveling at that speed. The device used a magnetic field to fire armor piercing rods at speeds above 0.33c. The *Chihuahua's* own rail guns were pretty small, shooting DUMs (Depleted Uranium Munitions) which were only 18" in diameter, and only shot them at 0.40c. The *Tarantula* was one of the newest corvettes around, and had the much more modern (and amusingly named) DUDS (Depleted Uranium Directed Strikes). Her broadside rail guns could fire larger diameter rounds – 20" – and target a vessel traveling almost half the speed of light. The single bow chaser mounted rail gun she carried shot things a little slower – just fractionally over the 0.40c limit – but was able to fire 48" shot. Commodore Green's elderly *Sirius*, however, had serious issues with its broadside armament: Her 60" rail guns weren't able to fire rounds any faster than the minimum speed to qualify as an RKE – 0.33c – which allowed them be turned away by some of the more modern debris collection devices.

"Turning failure!" Wolf cried just before he could respond to Chris' orders. "Shutting off the drive and measuring top speed. We come in at... holy! Well over 0.30c. Almost 0.35c, in fact."

Silence met that statement on the bridge of the little corvette, until Chris sighed. "And I was hoping we'd actually have the maneuvering power to reach the collectors' limits."

EAS Sirius, Flag Officer's Suite

"Let me get this straight," Acting-Commodore Green said, looking over Lt. Commander Burkhard in their first face-to-face private meeting. Reading through the man's files, Green knew he was a bit of a hot-head with a penchant for taking his superiors to task when they screwed up. Burkhard had received numerous reprimands, and was once (for about a week) busted down to a noncom after complaining about a tactical error the late Admiral Brussey made during an exercise. Later, after he had cooled off, Brussey realized that if a mere lieutenant had been able to find a hole that big in his plans, either he was getting too old to direct a fleet properly or Burkhard hadn't been promoted high enough. Covering all his bases, he restored Burkhard's commission, retired, and as his last official act promoted the man up to lieutenant commander, where Burkhard had sat for the eight years since.

The truth was, everyone liked Burkhard, and thought he was a brilliant officer. Most of his superiors, however, felt he lacked the proper discipline to be considered for promotion. As almost everyone in the regular Navy who served on the Academy side of the Wargame was promoted just for participating, someone obviously was trying to get him a back-door promotion.

Still, Green felt he needed close supervision. Certainly the man was a brilliant tactician, but tactical aptitude would mean nothing in the upcoming Wargame. No, Green wasn't going to win. His best chance of showing that he could be successful as a Commodore was in proving he had the ability to keep his fleet neat, orderly, and well disciplined.

Unfortunately, he'd been saddled with a maverick in Burkhard, and Green wasn't quite sure what to do about him. Especially now, after having met him and deciding he actually liked the guy, too.

"You've completed most of your major tests with a single test flight," Green continued. "But you need to practice against another warship for the purpose of assessing some of your newer systems, and so you plan to have a friendly duel with one of the regular Navy's ships."

Burkhard nodded. "Yes, sir."

Green frowned. "I'm not sure I like that idea. I've read the report of your test run. I'm not sure revealing that your ship has set record high speeds is a good idea. Couldn't you wait until one of the other ships is ready? I understand the corvette *Inkadh* will begin its own shakedown run in a couple days."

Burkhard grinned proudly. "She will, but only because I sent several teams of my engineers over to help them out. The cadet responsible for my new system designs, Mr. Desaix, believes that he can fine tune their fusion engines to a point where they'll be even faster than an Alligator class corvette. But the *Inkadh* will still be in a testing phase for several days after she's completed, and won't be available for the necessary dog fighting simulation which we require until after the official start date of

Wargame hostilities. Besides, our speed will be revealed by the new Navy list coming out shortly. No secrets there."

Green nodded. "I suppose that is correct."

"Also," Burkhard continued. "I'm interested in how she'll fair against regular Navy ships. I think that when you combine her unusual weapons load out with her remarkable speed, plus a few surprises my engineers have in the test phase, my ship may be able to take on a frigate in a fair one-on-one fight and come out on top. The only chance I'll have at even seeing a frigate for practice combat, though, is if I can convince the Regulars to let me have a stab at one."

Something in Burkhard's tone made Green suspicious. "What 'surprises' are you talking about?"

"Well," Burkhard huffed. He'd hoped to avoid mentioning any of the major modifications his crew had made, but he'd known he'd likely have to reveal a few of them. "Among other things, we have a dual power generator -- in addition to our fusion reactor, my engineering team was also able to rig a secondary cold-fusion reactor in a separate area."

Green raised an eyebrow, but showed no other signs of surprise. "Intriguing, but hardly a military advantage unless you count how much that likely adds to your potential speed. What else?"

Damn, he's shrewder than I thought, Burkhard thought. "Well, I suppose I have to let the cat out of the bag. We think we've developed a potentially functional energy shield technology."

Green's left eye twitched. "As in, the holy grail that our weapons and defense manufacturers have been trying to develop for eons?" Burkhard nodded nervously. "And you were planning on giving away this advantage already *why?*"

"I want to intimidate them, sir," Burkhard explained. He was about to explain some of his strategy, and he figured it might go over Green's head. For that reason, he decided to take his most deferential tone -- no need to upset the man any further than necessary. "At the end of World War II on Earth, the United States of America had just developed the atomic bomb. They only had two of them stockpiled, but President Truman figured the cost of an invasion would be too deadly for them to try a conventional campaign. So, Truman dropped both of them, hoping desperately that the Japanese would surrender before he had to reveal that we were several months away from being able to drop any more.

"I plan to show off my ship's shields, and make them think that all of our ships have them. I believe it was Sun Tzu who said, 'Appear strong when you are weak.' Well, we're definitely weaker than our enemies, but perhaps we can make them think we're a lot stronger then we actually are... and intimidate them into error."

"Why shouldn't we hold you in reserve -- keep you as a secret weapon?" Green asked, secretly shoving the data chips with the titles that revealed he was boning up on his tactical knowledge. When discussions changed to military strategy, Green always grew nervous. Something Burkhard was quick to notice.

"Well, sir, we aren't really powerful enough to make much difference. We're just a lone corvette, so even if our modifications made us as powerful as a battleship, which is ridiculous, it's just one ship. And when they open their campaign and find that our other ships are unshielded, they'll probably be able to guess that we've only got the one shielded ship. If we demonstrate the shield to them and flaunt it, we may be able to intimidate them into giving us more time to get ourselves ready. As I understand it, six of our battleships and at least one, possibly two, heavy cruisers will not be ready for combat at the start of the Wargame. It'd be nice if we had the time to finish those, don't you think?"

"The moment that one of our other ships engages them, they'll know we're just bluffing," Green noted.

"True," Burkhard admitted. "But that may not happen for some time if we're lucky. We may only be able to buy a few days... hell, they may realize we're bluffing right away and give us no time at all. You can never predict what your opponent will do with any certainty, but at least you can try. In a sense it's strictly a textbook maneuver, provided your textbook has the heading of 'psy-ops.' But we do need to do something. There is no way we'll have our entire fleet operable by the start of the Wargame, and we'll need any extra delays we can get to finish up as many ships as we can."

Green finally conceded the point with a nod. "Okay, you've convinced me. But your ship will be the only one allowed in the 'neutral' system until our fleet is at full strength. I want to minimize the chance that our bluff will fail as much as I can, so you'll be responsible for all recon of neutral territory, initially. And if you get in trouble, well, it'll be your job to get out of it, because we won't be able to help you."

"Yes, sir," Burkhard said, secretly pleased. He'd wanted independent command, and now he was going to get it. He just hoped his ship's modifications were really as effective as he imagined they'd be, or his command would be short lived.

"Now, there's one other thing I don't quite get in your initial request," Green noted. He pulled out a form and read from it. "'In the interest of secrecy, no after-action report will be filed.' Explain this, especially if you're hoping the action will intimidate the enemy."

"Well, that statement was somewhat... inaccurate," Burkhard explained. "I might file an after-action report, but it'll be bogus. If things don't work as well as they should, I'd rather not let the Regulars know that. I'd rather they base their assumptions on what they'll see, and hope that they'll opt to err on the side of caution in their estimates of our performance."

He just pulled that one out of his keister, Green thought. *He doesn't trust me to lead him properly. Well, I don't like it, but his explanation is sound. I won't call him on it... this time.* "I'll accept that. However, I want you to come brief me personally -- there may not be a written after-action report, but you can give me a verbal accurate one."

Shit. I'm not sure I can get out of that one. "Of course, sir. Anything else?"

Green pursed his lips in thought. "No, you are dismissed." Watching Burkhard go, Green nodded. *Well, I think I'm beginning to understand the warnings about him, now. I wonder how he'd act if he knew I was ordered to evaluate him for promotion, myself?*

EAS Chihuahua

"Five minutes to game-time, people," the loudspeakers announced. "Finish up your coffee and prepare to go to battle stations."

Beccera frowned. Looking at Deborah Culp, his secretary, he realized that she wouldn't be able to help him. Glancing at the Marines in his command, he called the one who looked the least occupied.

"Corporal Etcheverry, can you come here for a moment?"

"Certainly, sir!" Etcheverry replied, snapping to attention.

"Mr. Etcheverry, I've got a small question for you."

"Yes, sir?"

"Well, I've been gradually familiarizing myself with Marine procedures as I work through this assignment, but... I'm a trifle uncertain as to just what my job is when we go to battle stations. It isn't in any of the literature I've been able to find...."

"Understandable, sir," Etcheverry said, grinning slightly. "Since it's not written anywhere. Officially, there is no set station for the Marines in combat, barring a boarding action. Our duty is to be prepared to leap into action at a moment's notice. However, by custom, we're on call to perform various services: Rescuing trapped casualties, clearing the way for damage control and engineering teams to make repairs, and similar emergency services. As our CO, your job is to direct us to said emergencies."

"So, I'm essentially a dispatch officer?" Beccera groaned. "Sometimes I wonder if this job was worth it. Well, given that this is just a simulation, what are the procedures for us today?"

"Well, in a standard combat drill – which would include combat simulations such as the Wargame – the drill is to find the most efficient way to handle these emergency situations. It's essentially a test of our response time, even if the time to complete those operations is partially simulated.

"However, this isn't a standard combat drill, today. This is a shakedown cruise in a combat simulation. Because so much of our equipment is still untested, there's greater likelihood of *real* damage needing to be locked down, not just a simulation. So for us, the battle stations call won't be a drill... and the same applies to the people in engineering.

"The computer won't generate any simulated emergencies for us to respond to, since that could put us out of position for a real emergency. Instead, the computers will estimate times for our response based on our personal performance records, and on average response times for a combat-able ship. We will actually be even less active than either real combat or a standard drill, but it's necessary."

Beccera just shook his head sadly. "Figures. The last assignment of my career and even the simulation is simulated. They managed to find me the one field command that's actually a desk job."

Etcheverry snorted. "Well, this is just the shakedown. When the Wargame starts, don't be surprised if we actually get called on to make some kind of boarding action, considering *this* set of officers."

The old Army officer raised an eyebrow. "From that tone of voice, I have to believe you don't think much of this ship's command crew?"

"Don't get me wrong," the Marine said, waving his hands in denial. "I suspect we have the best officers and crew in this entire rag-tag little fleet of rookies. What I mean is, they're all young, all extremely innovative, and all just a tad overconfident in their abilities. I gotta figure they're not going to overlook any resource this ship has, however small it is... which means they aren't going to let something as valuable as our Marine unit go to waste. It happens in every one of these Wargames, and every time it winds up with the Marines being eliminated early. When you add that to just how, uh, creative our current rookies have already proven to be, and I'm pretty sure you, me, and just about every other Marine on this ship are going to be finding new ways to get killed off before too long."

Beccera didn't have a chance to respond before the alarm klaxons started sounding. "Battle stations, all hands to battle stations. Commencement of combat drill has begun."

Etcheverry sighed. "Well, that's our cue. Good luck, sir, and I hope you *don't* have to call us to action, this time."

The bridge of the *Chihuahua* hadn't exactly been the most organized of places when the expected alarms sounded. The chaos wasn't anyone's fault as the situation was very odd – there were almost three times the normal number of people, and half of them were conducting a drill while the other half were monitoring various systems to ensure the drills didn't become legitimate emergencies.

Chris, normally assigned to be the only engineer on the bridge during the call to battle stations, was surrounded by three others who were there only for their eyes. It wasn't humanly possible to keep a constant check on all of the monitors which needed looking after in this assignment, and all four of the engineers were constantly reading off any change in any reading at all while they worked, however insignificant. As they were frequently talking over each other, it was impossible for anyone else on the bridge to make out what any of them were saying. Rachel distinctly hoped that they didn't have a crisis requiring one of them to address someone on the bridge crew – no-one would be able to hear them at this rate.

Schubert was not happy, either. He had been benched as primary helmsman for this drill in favor of Weber, who he routinely traded off with for the job, and had instead been placed in the navigator's slot. Usually, at battle stations, both jobs were quite important. The primary helmsman's job, during battle, was to enact evasive maneuvers and follow the directions of the Captain as best as they could. The navigator, in the same circumstance, was to keep track of each target's movements with the intent of trying to predict their actions. In time, his calculations would be quite helpful to the Weapons Control Officer, in this case Lieutenant Luke DiMarco, when targeting their shot. If there was some crisis and weapons control went out of DiMarco's hands for some reason (his death or injury, the computer console being destroyed, etc.), Schubert's calculations and predictions would be utilized by the ship's artificial intelligence system to take over weapons control and lay down its own firing patterns.

Unfortunately, Schubert found this to be his weakest skill when it came to helmsmanship. He had a hard time getting into his opponent's mind, and often fed predictions into the computer based on what he would do and not what he saw his enemy doing. Weber was a wiz at it, and really should have had this job – something she agreed with – but the captain had overruled both of them. As he reminded them, this was just a shakedown exercise, and the crew needed a shakedown just as much as the ship did. It didn't keep Schubert from muttering under his breath about the whole thing, but at least it helped him understand why he was given that job.

Navigation and Engineering weren't the only bridge stations which seemed to be a bit less organized than a ship at battle stations should be. Cadet Commander Orff was arguing with Ensign Cohen over which seat was supposed to be whose during battle stations. It seemed, when battle stations assignments had been handed out, they had both only been given 'bridge' as their station. Both of them were supposed to take what were known as the 'redundancy stations,' being the backup for the captain and the backup for the tactical officer when at battle stations. The problem was that these redundancy stations, while identical in their initial construction, had not been refitted identically when the Chihuahua was being restored.

Lt. Diana Tarbell, who was the backup weapons control officer for the shift, just shook her head at the two and took one of the touch screen stations so that she didn't have to get involved in such a silly fight.

"Mr. Orff," Burkhard called sternly. "We're about to go into combat. I would appreciate it if my first officer were doing something more productive than arguing about where to sit." Orff nodded and grudgingly turned the preferred chair over to Cohen.

"Looks like the Captain was right about this being a shakedown for the crew as much as the ship," a voice said from Rachel's side. She looked up to see Emily Mumford standing next to her, holding out an earpiece. Rachel gave it a curious glance and took it from her hand, but clearly had no idea what to do with it. "I guess you've never used one of these before. This is tuned for you specifically. I'll be relaying relevant damage control and weapons control chatter over to you as the battle progresses. You don't need to do anything as long as I'm 'alive,' but if something goes wrong you may need to adjust things manually. This dial will put you on different channels – engineering here, damage control, weapons control, Marine dispatch, and sickbay."

"Thanks," Rachel said, taking it from her. "Jeff and Rob don't seem to get along too well, do they?"

Emily nodded. "Wolf's annoyed, Lauren's unhappy because Wolf is annoyed, and the captain's unhappy because we can't seem to settle down. In fact, I'd say the only person on the bridge who looks happy right now is Chris, just having a ball in his little cocoon of engineers."

Rachel glanced over at him and let an appreciative smile grace her face. "Yeah, he looks like he's in his element right now, doesn't he?"

Mumford glanced at the tactics officer for a moment, a bit surprised at the softer tone of voice. "Well, maybe not the only one."

A light blinked on Rachel's console, and she coughed. "You'd better get moving." Raising her voice so it could be heard over the din, she announced, "Everybody, sit down and shut up! Entering firing range of *Tarantula* in thirty seconds. Training mode confirmed; battle computers report synchronization established with the *Tarantula* for simulated weapons fire."

"Tactical display if you please, Ms. Katz," Burkhard ordered crisply.

The bridge crew finally centered their attention as Rachel directed a graphical representation of the *Tarantula* to the main monitor – not a picture, as both ships were moving so fast that no-one would have seen more than a streak of blurred light if they were to show the actual visual image of either ship, but a three dimensional graphic which would show various readouts such as energy output, estimated damage, estimated surviving crew, and so forth on display. The image also turned to roughly demonstrate just what part of the scanned ship was being presented to them at the moment. Rachel, however, didn't need to look. She'd had the same image on one of her own monitors since making initial sensor contact with the *Tarantula*.

It looked like and acted an awful lot like a picture, though, and currently, it was heading in at an intercept angle, bow first. A slight flash came from the bow, causing an alert to sound on Rachel's tactics platform.

"*Tarantula* firing bow chaser, sir. Single forty-eight inch fixed-mount rail gun, in his case, sir."

"Thank you, Ms. Katz. I am aware of how a Hornet class corvette is armed." Burkhard said. "Were we 'hit?'"

"Negative, sir," Rachel answered after a moment's hesitation. "That appears to have been a 'shot across the bow,' sir. We're still out of range of his particle cannon turret or any of his broadside rail guns."

Burkhard snorted. "Arrogant prick, asking us to surrender before combat maneuvers have even begun in a *drill*. All right, time for Operation Bluff to begin. Are capacitors charged for the particle cannon?"

"Yes, sir," was Rachel's reply. Usually, it would be Chris' job to monitor that bit of information, but for the duration of the systems tests he had yielded the responsibility to her as tactical officer.

"Very well. Let's try out these shields, shall we? Mr. DiMarco, I want you to prepare a heavy firing pattern with our particle cannons for a ship facing the bow. Ms. Katz, let me know whenever any additional weapons, either ours or theirs, comes into optimum range. Mr. Schubert, monitor their flight patterns as usual, but let me know if and when they seem to have figured out about the hole in our defenses. Ms. Weber, bring us in to close range, but keep the gap in our shields away from them until the last moment."

"Aye, aye, sir," came several voices around the bridge.

"Ms. Verne," Chris' voice suddenly piped up, though his gaze refused to leave the monitor. "Are there any reports coming in at all, and if so are any of them near the interior housing of the quantum wheel?"

"No, sir," Carol Verne replied, her voice wavering. She didn't like having attention called to herself, and as everyone had gone quiet so that Chris could hear her response the entire crowd on the bridge was now focused on her. As the Damage Control Officer, she would get status updates on certain electrical failures before the engineers did. She also received casualty reports. "The only thing I've heard so far, sir, came from sickbay. A weapons tech burned himself while calibrating a rail gun, but there was no report of any defects in that weapon to cause it."

Chris sighed. "I suspect we can make do without Rosebaugh."

Verne flinched. "How did you know it was him, sir?"

"Educated guess." Chris answered. "I need to know, priority one, if there are any reports of fluctuations or turn stress damage coming from around the quantum wheel housings, before you even send the repair teams. Unlike the weapons, which are all practice rounds and light shows, we're running live shields during the exercise. If something goes wrong with them, we may have to shut down the shield immediately to prevent a disaster. We have failsafe devices, but obviously they haven't been tested under live combat-related stress conditions."

"Understood, sir," she squeaked. Rachel was quick to notice Verne's relief when no further questions came her way.

"Coming up on the extreme range of their broadside rail guns, sir. We'll be in our particle gun range before we're within optimum range of their broadside, however," Rachel noted. She knew what Burkhard was planning, and felt that was an important point to make.

"Acknowledged. Have they opened fire with anything since that chaser round, yet?"

Rachel hesitated. "Not exactly, sir. They have been firing far-side rail guns, sir, but not at anything on my scan. I've been wondering if I'm seeing things, sir."

There was a pause before Burkhard laughed. "Oh, tricky, tricky. Minefields, Ms. Katz. He's laying a minefield. Ms. Weber, make certain that we do not cross any area in a firing line from their far side broadside. If we do, we lose."

"Yes, sir," Weber acknowledged, slightly altering her projected flight path. "Sir, if we continue to close range at this angle, we will be unable to avoid the mines without directing the quantum wheels to speed our deceleration and turn after the first pass."

"Then we'll have to get them on the first pass. Mr. DiMarco, do you have that firing pattern ready yet?"

"I... think so, sir. I still have no tracking from Navigation as to the *Tarantula's* projected maneuvers, sir."

"There's no data to make a projection *from,* sir," Schubert noted before Burkhard could reply.

"I agree," Burkhard nodded. "Feed him what your own plan would be, if you were aboard the *Tarantula,* Mr. Schubert."

"But—"

"Just do it, Mr. Schubert. There's nothing else to base a predictability pattern on."

Schubert sighed, and typed some keys quickly. "Sending best guesstimate... now."

Luke DiMarco looked over the numbers coming into him and frowned. "Sir, this isn't exactly textbook."

"That's what I would do," Schubert insisted.

"Yes, sir," DiMarco sighed. "Firing pattern altered based on the new data. Helm may need to anticipate temporary AI override – brief being sent now. Waiting orders to fire."

"Brief received," Weber answered, and then considered it carefully. "Can I tweak the AI responses slightly?"

DiMarco laughed nervously. "Please. I'm not exactly comfortable with those numbers, myself."

Weber fussed with it for a moment. "AI prepped."

"We'll be hitting their optimum particle cannon range in fifteen seconds," Rachel called. "Our own will be five seconds after that."

"Ms. Weber, at precisely one second until *our* optimum firing range, change course to present bow full-on against *Tarantula*, and activate Mr. DiMarco's firing program," Burkhard ordered. "Everyone else... standby."

"Sir!" Rachel called. "Incoming fire, particle cannon, top shot staggered from bottom."

"Brace yourselves!" Burkhard barked.

Nothing happened. "We're hit!" Rachel noted. "Simulation shows the shields held, sir. If it were a real shot, we might have been shaken, but—"

She didn't have time to finish explaining before Schubert's call of "Fire pattern Alpha initiating!" echoed across the bridge,

There wasn't immediately the telltale mechanical grind of turrets turning nor the electric drum sound of a capacitor releasing a shot, however. Instead, the ship spun in what appeared to be a wild version of the Immelman turn, keeping its shield to the *Tarantula* as the other ship also began some sort of maneuver charging almost directly at the *Chihuahua* before ducking under it. The result was to keep the shield pointed at the *Tarantula* until the very last second, when suddenly all of the particle cannons fired simultaneously, intercepting the other corvette at point blank range when it passed the bow.

"Coming to all stop!" Weber called. "If we didn't get him, we're a sitting duck."

Rachel didn't say anything for a moment, gaping at the figures she saw on the readout. She knew it had been possible, but she wouldn't have believed it if she hadn't seen it.

"Ms. Katz?" Burkhard prompted.

"Sir, that would have killed a frigate. Probably something much bigger than a frigate, in fact," she said. "A little Hornet class corvette, sir? She's gone."

"Captain of *Tarantula* hailing us, sir," Mumford called from across the bridge. "His exact words, uh, aren't repeatable, sir. Essentially, he acknowledges the kill and requests to know just what we did, sir."

Burkhard laughed. "Tell him if he'll take our bridge crew here to dinner at the station, his treat, I'll explain everything."

Chapter XVI

EAS Chihuahua

It had been a wonderful victory celebration, with all but a handful of the officers and crew of the *Chihuahua* given the night off. After a few minutes of post-dinner socializing, Chris had managed to drag Rachel away for some fun. The terraforming station orbiting 94 Ceti wasn't exactly a tourist trap, but it wasn't completely Spartan, either. Among some half-decent dining joints and a number of simple shops selling various trinkets and clothing which had sprung up in the station's commercial sector, there were also a number of facilities which one might conceivably wander to on a 'date-like thing,' as Chris had described it. While they both had decided against heading to one of the many low-gravity dance clubs which seemed quite popular in the local dating scene, they found that they were both interested in a local Shakespearian theater (which, sadly, didn't have another show until they were supposed to be back on duty), a museum displaying various archaeological finds from the planet surface (which turned out to have its entire display closed for cleaning), and finally a zoo dedicated to the native wildlife.

Given the earlier disappointments, neither of them were very hopeful when they found the little zoo. As they neared the entrance, however, they found that they had hit the jackpot. Much to everyone's surprise, there had been a considerable amount of native life on the planet when Humans arrived. The Earth Alliance had, in fact, investigated the system many centuries before attempting to establish a colony, and until relatively recently it had been set aside as a form of nature reserve. It had only been released to colonization because of an urgent need for new colonies in Earth Alliance territory following the loss of several worlds in a war against the 16 Cygni Confederation.

Enough life prevailed that the terraforming project was really nothing more than a study to determine which species of plants and animals from Earth could co-exist with the native wildlife, and which species of native wildlife were hazards to humans and their crops. It was for this reason that the colonization of the planet was taking so long – 94 Ceti had been in the 'terraforming process' (a misnomer for sure, in this case) for three decades, and so some of the species on display were about as well studied as any animal from Earth itself was. Several of these more heavily studied species, including the salmon-like fish that Rachel had eaten as sushi several days before, were labeled as 'safe for off-planet export.'

The couple made their way through the rest of the zoo without incident. Well, almost without incident – one of the fire-breathing 'millipedes' on display in the insect house burned some of the stubble off of Chris' face, although he wasn't really hurt. They quickly decided together to move on from the zoo after that.

Not wanting to return to the *Chihuahua* right away, they found a small coffee bar where they could sit together and talk. They started chatting about the zoo trip, but soon ran out of things to say. An awkward silence started to descend upon them as the conversation broke down.

Not wanting to give up without a fight, Rachel decided on a desperate ploy.

"Why don't you tell me something I don't know about engineering?"

Chris shrugged. "You actually know quite a bit, already. You'd ace that Basic Maintenance course by now, and probably pass an equivalency test for the Freshman and Sophomore level Engineering courses with what I've taught you. If you want, I'll see if my academic advisor can work out an Engineering minor for you. What more do you want to know?"

Rachel snorted. "I think I'll stay away from a possible career in engineering. I'll leave that to you."

"You might enjoy it, actually," Chris said. "I've noticed that you seem more and more interested, the more I teach you. Otherwise, why would you even ask to find out more?"

"Well, that's because it's *you*," Rachel explained, blushing slightly. "It's been rather repetitive work, but I've enjoyed those few nuggets of wisdom you toss in on occasion. I wouldn't like it as a career, but I might be willing to join you in some of your hobby work from time to time."

Chris smiled softly. "I think I'd enjoy that. So, you still want me to explain something about engineering you don't know?"

"Yeah," Rachel answered, nodding. "Something like, say, why the particle cannons can only fire once every fifteen seconds. Or why cold fusion plants are more effective than standard fusion plants. Or even why we can't miniaturize a decent propulsion system small enough to create a fighter class. Or—"

"I get the idea," Chris laughed. "Okay, I suppose there are a lot of engineering principles which aren't explained simply by studying a shock chair's electronics package. Let's take those questions in order, then, shall we?"

"Well, if you want. I was really just listing a few examples, so if there's something else you'd rather—" Rachel began.

"They sound like good enough suggestions to me," Chris intervened, hoping to head her off. Much to his surprise, she had developed the nervous habit of babbling whenever she tried to express any curiosity about engineering to him. "Okay, the first one was about the limitations of a particle cannon, correct?"

"Well, I was a bit more specific than that," Rachel corrected, "But I suppose that would be more of what I was trying to get at."

Chris nodded, and coughed slightly. Rachel suspected he didn't know it, but whenever he tried to teach her something he always cleared his throat before letting out a long lecture – something which she knew several other professors at the academy did. Vaguely, Rachel wondered if he would become a teacher one day.

"There are two main factors limiting a particle cannon, both of which contribute to the slow rate of fire," he began. "The primary problem comes from the 'backwash' caused by the shot – when firing with enough power to be effective against modern ship armors, a particle cannon overheats quickly from the tremendous amount of charged plasma it shoots out. Usually, it takes about fifteen seconds for a cannon to cool off between shots, so at most we can fire four shots a minute. The secondary problem is that it's impossible to send the necessary power to the cannons without a heavy pulse-power capacitor bank, and a fairly large one at that. When pulse-power particle cannons were first built, you could realistically fit, at most, four capacitor banks in the housing of the cannon. The size of these heavy capacitor banks have gone down a lot in recent years, but by the time you've shot the cannon four times with the proper cooling period between shots, the first capacitor bank will have recharged."

"So even if you were able to speed up the cool-down period, you would still need to increase the number of capacitors in order to improve the rate of fire," Rachel concluded. "You would have to redesign a modern ship in order to increase that number. But if you retrofitted older ships that were designed for these larger capacitors, I would think you could add more. Using modern capacitors, how many could we fit into the *Chihuahua's* cannons?"

"In the *Chihuahua's* time, you practically needed a whole room for one single charge. Now, for the same effect, you only need something slightly larger than a dinner plate. It's hard to say accurately unless I took some measurements, but I imagine we could squeeze in several hundred. Most modern ships still use somewhat less advanced capacitors, though, since they're cheaper and need replacement less frequently. Probably about two or three dozen of that standard. There really isn't any point in doing so, however, with the overheating issues."

Rachel's nose scrunched up as she thought hard. "Has anything ever been tried to reduce the cooling time? It goes without saying that great tactical advantage could be had if you could fire six times as fast as your enemy."

Chris shrugged. "A few things have been tested over the years. Most involve using more heat resistant materials or some kind of coolant tubes, but nothing seems to really reduce the time between shots without rendering the weapon ineffective. Fairly recently, some improvements in metallurgy have reduced the frequency of the 'unbushing' phenomenon – where a particle cannon had to be taken offline for repairs because of heat-induced metal fatigue in the focusing tubes. I'm going to be replacing the *Chihuahua's* tubes with modern ones, myself, assuming we can get our hands on some. I hope to get *Chihuahua* purchased back into the regular Navy when this is all over, and small fixes like that will help."

Rachel considered her knowledge of engineering very limited, but as she considered what Chris had taught her she realized it wasn't very limited at all – just very specialized. That specialty seemed to her as if it might provide an answer to the cool down problem. It wasn't possible that she was the first to think of it, though... was it?

"You know," Rachel began slowly, "the shock chairs I've been working on must have been developed for the same sort of problem. Humans couldn't survive the G-forces a ship's acceleration would release on them, so a system had to be developed that would bleed off the kinetic energy a person was exposed to without obstructing his vision or his ability to work at his workstation. The resulting development would absorb excess kinetic energy and transform it into storable energy. Could such a system be developed to work on the heat energy that potentially could damage the particle cannon?"

Chris laughed. "Actually, I suppose I was wrong – there was a more useful system developed from those experiments. The shock chairs were developed based on a failed design to eliminate the heat problem in particle cannons. It doesn't work – the electronics are too sensitive. It didn't reduce heat enough to protect them, and so the system failed after just two or three shots."

"Has it been tried recently?" Rachel asked, curious. "You know, using modern heat shielding materials? I mean, if they've improved enough to eliminate 'unbushing,' wherever that term came from, then maybe they could have improved enough to protect the electronics package of a shock chair-type system. And if power was reduced to, say, 80% of what we currently fire, wouldn't that further reduce the heat backwash?"

He stared at her for a long moment. "Are you sure you don't want to be an engineer?"

Rachel blinked. "Huh?"

Downing the last of his now cold coffee, he stood up. "Come on – we have to get back to the ship. We've got work to do."

"We do?"

"Yeah. You, me, and the entire engineering staff. We've got to set up a fabrication shop for newer, smaller, more efficient capacitors, we have to start adding heat shielding to several of those shock chair electronics packages you've been fixing up, and we've got to modify my replacement plans for the focusing tubes."

"You mean *my* idea?" Rachel asked, bewildered. "But... surely... I'm not... aren't you even going to test it first?"

"I'll have to the moment we get back, just to prove to Rappaport, it can work. I don't need to test it, though," Chris said cheerily. "I always say our best technology is rooted in the past. Even I make the mistake of not adapting past theories to modern advances, however. You've never had it ground into your head from day one that such a system can't possibly work, though, so of course you'd think of it."

"I don't understand," Rachel answered in a daze. Chris guided her up out of her seat by the arm and led her out of the coffee bar.

"That's okay," Chris said, pulling her into his arms and giving her a quick peck on the lips without even thinking about it. "You and I just invented and designed the biggest leap in particle cannon technology since they were developed into a practical weapon. However, we won't have time to get it ready unless we start right away."

Rachel groaned. "This is why you hated me in class, isn't it? Because I always found a way to make you work, even when you had leave or were on liberty. Great, now the entire engineering team is going to have it in for me."

"I don't think so," Chris laughed, almost dragging the young woman with him as he raced to their shuttle. "For a project like this, I suspect most real engineers would be glad to give up their leave."

"Next time I start complaining about your laziness," Rachel said, collapsing into her chair, "Remind me of this moment. I never knew how much work you engineers did. The test didn't take long, but fabricating the heat shielding for those electronics packages took forever!"

"We aren't done, yet," Chris complained, pacing in front of her. "We still need to make the new capacitors – I figure that we can make them small enough, with the new cooling system, to fire six shots a second. That'll be a near continuous stream of particle cannon fire to the naked eye, but we'll need to manufacture three hundred and sixty very small capacitors to get it to work. However, Jacques ordered us out of the fabrication section so that the environmental techs can manufacture some more important consumables, and we can't continue until we get back there. Since I'm being shipped off to the *Superb* before then, I'll just have to finish during my rest breaks. You don't need to join me for that, though – you've done a good enough job. You really are getting to know engineering yourself, now – better than some of my staff here on the *Chihuahua*."

That sent alarm bells ringing in Rachel's mind, but she held her tongue. She resolved to speak with Burkhard quietly about Chris' decision to work through rest breaks as soon as she could. In the meantime, though, she could see to his getting enough sleep prior to starting another tough job.

"Go to bed," she said softly, reaching up to squeeze his hand and stop his pacing. "Your temporary transfer will come in just six hours, I'm afraid."

"Get to bed, yourself," Chris admonished. "You'll be getting your own call at the same time."

Rachel's eyes widened. "I'm not coming with you, am I?"

Chris chuckled nervously at that. "I wish. No, you're getting another assignment. Mark Taira – you remember me mentioning him, right? The so-called Chief Engineer of the *Ishmael,* even though he knows nothing about engineering? He asked Burkhard if I could come over to his ship and help him finish the refit after the one person in his crew who could act as his technical advisor injured herself and went on medical leave. This was after I had been given my assignment to work on the *Sirius,* and Burkhard was going to decline, but I suggested that I might know someone who might be able to help. Someone I'd been tutoring in Engineering."

A frown – along with an unintentional nose wrinkle of the kind Chris seemed to like about her – appeared on Rachel's face. "Don't tell me you volunteered *me?*"

Chris winced. "Well, I was planning on asking you about it, first, but Burkhard kind of pressured me for an answer on the spot. Um... sorry?"

"And just when were you going to tell me about this?" Rachel asked, glaring at him.

"We were working on the heat shielding fabrication when Burkhard asked," Chris explained. "I was going to tell you as soon as I could, but I haven't had a real opportunity."

"Well," Rachel huffed, somewhat mollified. "I suppose I'll forgive you, then. But whatever made you believe that I was capable of doing something like this?"

Chris snorted. "Trust me, Rache, you're good. You've learned enough about engineering in the past few days to pass several of the same placement tests I did when I applied to the Academy. You just haven't realized how to apply the lessons I've taught you outside of those electronics packages you've been practicing with. That's what this is about – I was going to ask you to do it as a sort of final exam for the training I've been giving you – a test to see if you can apply my lessons outside of our 'classroom.' Don't hesitate to call me if anything goes wrong, though – I don't expect you to know everything. I'll even arrange for a special comm frequency so that you can talk to me directly."

"I don't know," Rachel said uncertainly. "I was under the impression that what you've taught me so far was fairly specialized. How—"

"No, what I've taught you is the basic principles you'll need using some very specialized examples," he said. "And this assignment will help you discover that."

"I... well, I suppose I'll find out, won't I?" Rachel sighed. "But if we're going on assignment in six hours, I'm going to need some bed time. And so will you – if I hear you haven't taken at least five hours of sleep yourself, well... if you ever thought you've seen me mad, you'll know just how wrong you were after I'm done with you. Got it?"

Chris' laughter as he turned to leave with a farewell wave was all the answer she got.

EAS Superb

Rachel had a hard time believing it, but Chris had been right. Her limited understanding of engineering was enough, when paired with her understanding of logistics and command, was good enough to direct the more experienced engineers aboard the *Ishmael* to the appropriate problem areas, and to determine which areas the less experienced engineers could handle. In other words, she was able to temporarily handle the job of a chief engineer, even though she might not have been the best or most knowledgeable engineer aboard. Then again, maybe she really *was* the most knowledgeable engineer aboard – this particular group of engineers was pretty much entirely freshmen and sophomore level, and she had yet to find anyone who really knew more than she did.

When she thought about it, she realized it wasn't so strange, after all. Freshmen and Sophomores rarely had classes outside of the core curriculum mandated by the Academy – they might have taken one or two basic-level courses in their intended major, but rarely more than that. She had put in over forty hours of engineering training under Chris' tutelage, many of which were spent while acting as his 'assistant,' or perhaps 'apprentice' would be a better description, during *Chihuahua's* refit. That was approximately the same amount of time as she would have put into a fifteen-week (three one-hour sessions a week) Academy course on basic engineering, and under more practical circumstances. She even knew a thing or two many basic engineering students didn't... especially when it came to certain things, like a particular just-developed experimental weapons system.

After a few encrypted comm session with Chris, Burkhard, and the Captain of the *Ishmael,* she managed to direct the engineering crew into making many of the same modifications to their particle cannons that they were making aboard the *Chihuahua.*

It wasn't complete. There was no way the appropriate number of capacitors could be fabricated before the regular deputy chief was restored to duty. She wasn't sure if the present staff could handle such a task unsupervised. That meant her efforts were likely to go to waste, but at least the particle cannon was as functional as the standard design.

Unfortunately, she couldn't explain the purpose of the modifications to anyone in order to maintain the secrecy Chris, Burkhard, and the captain of the *Ishmael* seemed to find important, so it would be up to them whether any further work would be done on the cannon. Just in case, she left instructions in a securely encrypted file. With those instructions, the weapons upgrade could be completed within a day's worth of work provided the raw materials were available. But now it was all out of her hands.

It had been exhausting work, and left her little time to think about how tired Chris had looked when he left for the *Superb*; it had been quite apparent that he hadn't rested very well in the six hours she had ordered him to catch up on his sleep. Hopefully it was just that, and not that 'nocebo effect' condition bothering him again.

The moment she made it back aboard the *Chihuahua*, Captain Burkhard had sent her right back out again – to the *Superb*, with orders to "retrieve Cadet Lieutenant Christopher Desaix and his team," ostensibly to co-ordinate a new repair effort on his 'home' ship. That the repair effort in question was really replacing a few burnt-out light bulbs wasn't mentioned in the orders. And the real reasons for his retrieval – to force him to take some much-needed rest and to then complete the particle cannon modifications – wasn't even hinted at. She wanted to talk with him, but the 'immediate need' described in the orders she carried to the *Superb* wouldn't allow her any time for small talk if she were to maintain her cover.

Commander Jonathan Daniels, captain of the *Superb*, met her just outside of the airlock. "Orders, please, Ms. Katz," he demanded, sounding as if he had either just woken up or was in desperate need of getting to bed.

"Yes, sir," Rachel replied, handing him the official copy of the orders with the rehearsed stiffness of an unpleasant formality.

Commander Daniels looked over the papers briefly. "Huh. The singing engineer, huh?"

That surprised Rachel, as it certainly wasn't one of the many questions she'd anticipated him asking. She didn't even think Chris could sing. "Singing, sir?"

The captain snorted, looking more alert. "Well, after a fashion. I find the practice undisciplined, but then he is just a first year cadet. We'll drill it out of him before his four years are up."

Somehow, Rachel doubted that. Chris was nothing if not stubborn... although she still wasn't entirely clear on the singing part. "Curious, sir. I'm not just one of his fellow shipmates, sir, but his dorm supervisor at the Academy, and I've never heard him sing."

That brought a chuckle out of the old captain. "Well, he's only singing one song... over and over and over again. When I asked him about it, he claimed he felt 'inspired' given where he'd been transferred. I suspect you'll understand when you retrieve him. He's in Engineering room three, on deck four. As bad as his singing is, I'll be sorry to see him go. He's actually managed, with just one day's work, to put us on schedule for completion by the start of the Wargame. As things stand now, we'll probably be the only battleship battle ready when the Wargame proper starts."

"He's good," Rachel admitted with pride. "I don't think even he knows how good. Thanks to him and Chief Engineer Rappaport, we're going to be flying the fastest ship in the Navy... and that's not the only major improvement they've come up with. The sad thing is, he's an even better tactician. Admiral McCaffrey has taken a personal interest in getting him to aim for a second major in tactics, or at least complete a minor in the field."

"I've heard about him," Daniels admitted. "His solution to McCaffrey's contest was the talk of the town when it happened. But after seeing him in action in Engineering, I don't know if his desire to be an engineer is really any serious problem. He'll make a major contribution in either field, I'm sure. Given that it's peacetime, he'll probably have a better chance of being remembered for his engineering innovations than for his tactical ones."

"True," Rachel admitted. She had never thought of it that way, before. She could easily see the public, during peacetime, wondering what good a master tactician was without an enemy to fight. They likely wouldn't ever see him as anything more than a peacetime soldier. A low ranking one at that, probably, considering that Chris lacked the innate understanding of fleet politics to advance in a peacetime Navy. However, as the inventor of the shield system they'd incorporated into the *Chihuahua* (and the co-inventor of the particle cannon design, although Rachel was still hoping he'd take all the credit for that one and leave her out of it), he would likely be remembered for quite some time.

Daniels gave her a hard look – one which made Rachel realize just how sharp the man could be. "I find it interesting that you have these urgent orders to retrieve an engineering team for 'emergency service,' yet you allow yourself to be delayed for a chat with me."

Rachel forced herself to shrug casually. "I'm not one to tell a superior officer he's talking too much, sir."

It was perhaps a bit presumptuous for her to say such a thing, but it got a laugh out of the *Superb's* captain anyway... and allowed her to escape from a dangerous question without lying to him.

"Yes, yes, of course. Ms. Katz, in the future, please do not be afraid to tell me if I'm interfering in your duties. Now, go and fulfill those duties, will you?"

"Yes, sir!" Rachel answered, snapping off a technically perfect salute with ease before turning towards the lifts.

"Oh, one more question... just what is it that needs 'emergency service,' anyway, Ms. Katz?"

Rachel hesitated, if only for a split second. She wondered if he'd guessed the real reason for Chris' recall. There wasn't any need to lie, however... a half-truth might be enough to get her out of this predicament.

"I'm not really an engineer, sir, but I think it has something to do with the particle cannons."

Daniels gave her a hard stare for a moment, but she refused to flinch. "Very well," he finally said. "Dismissed."

"Yes, sir!" Rachel said, nearly bolting from the area in an effort to get away before he asked a question which would force her to lie to him.

Captain Daniels, who just happened to be a relative of Burkhard by marriage, and who had already been briefed as to the real, unofficial reasons for the orders, simply smiled at her retreating back. His brother-in-law was right; Rachel was a tough cookie to crack. A few minor slips here and there, but otherwise a very creditable effort on her part to maintain the legitimacy of the official orders. He made a mental note to inform Burkhard of her successfully completing that particular stress-test.

Chapter XVII

EAS Superb

Much to Rachel's surprise, Chris was, indeed, *singing* as she approached his assigned work station. She also heard voices which must have belonged to several of the *Superb's* crew joining him, although many of them sounded off-key. As she listened to the lyrics of the archaic tune, she soon realized just what had inspired Chris – and apparently a chorus of others – to sing.

> *"The wind was rising easterly, the morning sky was blue.*
> *The Straits before us opened wide and free*
> *We looked towards the Admiral, where high the Peter flew,*
> *And all our hearts were dancing like the sea.*
> *The French are gone to Martinique with four and twenty sail,*
> *The Old Superb is old and foul and slow;*
> *But the French are gone to Martinique, and Nelson's on the trail,*
> *And where he goes the Old Superb must go!"*

Rachel waited, listening to the unfolding ballad of how the "Old Superb" continued to sail to Martinique and fight the French with the rest of Nelson's Navy despite her poor condition. As more of this modern-day *Superb's* crew joined in on the chorus, Rachel couldn't help but smile and shake her head. Somehow, the idea of Chris knowing this particular song didn't surprise her in the least, even though she actually had no idea as to what his usual taste in music was. It somehow just... fit him.

Apparently, the crew of the *Superb* loved it, too. Every time the "Old Superb" was mentioned, a rousing cheer came up from the people who weren't singing. In Rachel's mind, it sounded just like the atmosphere one would expect in a port city's tavern during the time of Nelson's wooden ships, only with more ozone from heated electronics and less wood smoke.

She stepped into Engineering Room Three, where the loud cacophony of untalented singing was drowning out all the sounds of the work that was actually taking place. Work crews were carrying large heavy-duty wiring conduits and support structures all around the room, at least three separate teams were digging through circuitry along one wall, and Chris and his team were all fabricating more wires and circuits to add to the repairs already complete.

Taking a deep breath to wipe the smile off her face, Rachel assumed the most professional air she could muster. It would be hard to hide behind official orders if she was laughing when she delivered them.

"Lt. Desaix," she called stiffly, standing ramrod straight at attention, when the singing seemed to reach at least a temporary pause.

"Yeah, Rache?" he answered without even looking up. After a moment, he blinked and focused his attention on her. "Rache? What are you doing here?"

"New orders," she answered simply, handing him the same official copy which she had shown to Commander Daniels. "You and your team are needed aboard the *Chihuahua*. Rappaport and the rest of the engineers will remain here, however."

Chris read the note with an eyebrow raised in curiosity. "That's odd. I thought everything was in hand when I left. What do you all need me for? Did something break?"

Rachel tried to keep her nose from wrinkling in frustration – really she did – but she couldn't help it. Why did he have to ask that question?

She resorted to the same cover story that she gave the *Superb's* captain, in hopes that she'd be able to recover without any additional emotional displays. She reminded herself that she was representing the entire crew of the *Chihuahua,* and took a deep breath. "Well, I'm not an engineer, but I believe it has something to do with the particle cannons."

Chris smirked. "Not an engineer, huh? I wonder if the crew of the *Ishmael* would say the same thing."

"Who've you been talking to?" Rachel asked timidly, letting some of her professional demeanor slip.

"Well, I haven't heard about any major disasters," Chris snorted. "And you didn't call me in a panic, so I figure you were able to handle yourself."

Rachel nodded hesitantly. "While Lt. Commander Taira might be completely unskilled as an engineer, the rest of his crew knows their jobs. I just had to know enough to manage them."

Chris snorted. "I'm more surprised that Taira's engineering was competent than I am to hear that he wasn't. *Chihuahua* was very fortunate to get the engineering team it did, I suppose, but I wish that there were a few other smaller ships which were given the resources that the big battleships were. If the Academy has more than half a dozen ships in service by the end of the 'peacetime,' sequence, I'll be astonished."

"Maybe we won't," one of the other engineers in the room said, overhearing, "But you can bet the *Superb* will be ready!"

Cheers answered the man, and so did another round of singing, although this time Chris didn't join in. Rachel shook her head as she quickly dragged him from the engine room and headed toward the docking section.

"What is that song, and just how the hell do you know it?" Rachel asked. "It certainly doesn't sound like it was written any time in the last few hundred years, that's for sure."

"It wasn't," Chris grinned. "It's part of a piece written by Sir Henry Newbolt and set to music by Charles Villiers Stanford in 1904 called 'Songs of the Sea.' My late father sang it a few times with the Epsilon Eridani Symphony Chorus a couple years before he died, and I've memorized every one of his performances. He often dragged me, my mother, my two uncles, and all of my siblings together so he could have 'dress rehearsals' in addition to the Chorus' regular practices."

Rachel winced. That would be a bittersweet memory for her, to say the least, but Chris didn't seem affected by it. "When did he die? It says in your service record that you're an orphan, but—"

Chris stiffened. "With the exception of my older sister – who I have never gotten along with – my entire family was killed in the Azumah Station Incident."

Rachel shuddered. The *Azumah* Station had been the intended replacement for the *Roman Brown Expedition* Station – the oldest colony station still in service. Epsilon Eridani's two colonizable planets had been a part of humanity's earliest efforts to colonize the stars, and the colonial waystation had been maintained as a habitat for hundreds of years since the colonies grew independent of it. The *Roman Brown Expedition* station was still quite functional even in its old age, but despite the fact it would mean uprooting almost a million inhabitants the Epsilon Eridani local government decided to scrap it for a newer, more state of the art facility – the proposed *Azumah* Station. Resettlement had begun, and almost half of the *Roman Brown Expedition's* population was on the *Azumah* when the accident happened.

Azumah Station had included a number of unique innovations, some of which had never been fully tested. Among them was a newly designed artificial gravity system that did not rely on rotating the station. While spacecraft had been using smaller artificial gravity fields for centuries through various scientific innovations that were still way over Rachel's head, 'rotational gravity' (really the application of centripetal or centrifugal forces, depending on your perspective, by rotating habitable containers in one of several configurations) had been the only way to provide large artificial habitats such as space stations anything even close to a simulated gravity. These systems worked, but they required people to live on the "edge" of the stations for full gravity – there was a lot of wasted space in the middle of these stations, which some engineer somewhere found unacceptable.

The *Roman Brown Expedition* had relied on rotational (or centripetal) gravity for centuries, and the people living on it were quite satisfied with the set-up. This new, station-sized artificial gravity design (whose marketing people sold it with the phrase "No gaps in your gravity!"), seemed unnecessary. At least as far as colony stations were concerned, the artificial gravity system was – as Chris had often described such technology – a system which was newer, but not necessarily better.

In the case of *Azumah* Station, it was also quite hazardous. The new system had been tested and applied in small scale, such as with spacecraft (many of which already had reliable artificial gravity systems, though those were impractical to expand to something the size of a space station), and even the older systems had never been tried on something as large as a colony station (costs were far too prohibitive). The result was that all the previous tests failed to account for one particular burden to the system – the natural gravity of something massive enough to house dozens of the largest spacecraft to ever have had an artificial gravity system installed.

The defect was not immediately apparent, as the construction crews spent over a year after the station's completion before finalizing the installation. Most families, however, were splitting their time between their *Roman Brown Expedition* station suites and what were supposed to be their new homes aboard *Azumah* Station. Many employers had already moved their facilities on board the new station, so almost half of the population of *Roman Brown Expedition* had moved across or at least were regularly commuting to the station when the artificial gravity generators came on line.

In a huge ceremony televised all across the Epsilon Eridani system – including on *Roman Brown Expedition* – the generators were activated for the first time after being completed on time and, shockingly, on budget. Most of the remaining citizens of *Roman Brown Expedition* were watching the event, as it was to be a landmark of the plan which would culminate in their all moving to new homes. It was supposed to be the ceremonial conclusion to a prolonged and, many felt, unnecessary ordeal. The *Roman Brown Expedition* was, by decree, going to be decommissioned one year after the *Azumah's* gravity system went on-line, as long as it proved satisfactory.

What the people who were watching saw, however, met no definition of the word 'satisfactory.' The antigravity generators came on, and the effect of the new artificial gravity on a facility large enough to create a small moon-like gravity field of its own was seen – namely, that as the gravity of the object the device was operating on increased, so did the effect of the anti-gravity generator... exponentially.

People watched in horror as their spouses, parents, children, friends, and neighbors were all turned into a gelatinous mass. Things got worse as the artificial gravity generator survived the initial catastrophe. *Azumah* imploded, and as it did it got denser and the gravity field intensified even further. The *Roman Brown Expedition* station was also damaged in the incident when the *Azumah* Station turned – for a few brief but devastating seconds – into an artificial black hole, yanking *Roman Brown Expedition* out of orbit. Only the fact that the artificial gravity generators finally died when their power systems failed saved the entire Epsilon Eridani system from destruction.

Nearly half a million people aboard *Azumah* station had died in a matter of seconds. *Roman Brown Expedition* suffered nearly a quarter of a million casualties itself, and the station was rendered unsafe for continued habitation... and evacuation of the survivors was initially believed to be impossible. The more 'primitive' form of artificial gravity that the Roman Brown Expedition had been using for hundreds of years – rotating the station to produce centripetal force – had been disrupted as the temporary black hole *Azumah* became yanked it out of its traditional orbit. Many of those wounded by the initial incident died slowly without any medical help available, and many survivors started rioting and looting causing even more deaths.

Compounding the problem was the damage that *Azumah* had done to the planet it had been orbiting. Tectonic plates had actually been shifted by the strong force of gravity, launching a record number of earthquakes and volcanic eruptions all across the surface. Cities were devastated, floods took out much of the coast, and electronic communication was disabled for weeks.

The other Epsilon Eridani settlements survived largely unscathed, and after a bit of rebuilding the system once again became the second most important set of colonies (both politically and economically) in all of the Earth Alliance. The death toll was enormous, however, and the displacement of over a million additional people left scars that were still being felt today.

Not all of the tales were tragic, however – some were of heroism. A group of high school students aboard the *Roman Brown Expedition* managed to access an abandoned station maintenance corridor from their school's campus (built on top of what had been, prior to the establishment of the system's planetary settlements, an old fabrication plant) and stabilize the station's rotation and orbit, allowing rescue operations to begin. They had also managed to establish rudimentary communications, but none of them knew how to properly direct a rescue operation, and their misdirection nearly cost the rescuers several ships before someone more qualified was able to take over. No-one blamed the teenagers for that, however. Many people wanted to decorate them as heroes, but no-one had ever divulged the names of those young men and women to the press.

"My God," Rachel finally said. She was starting to put a few puzzle pieces together regarding her classmate and friend.

Chris ignored her and quietly stepped to a comm panel on the corridor wall, pressing a button to activate the microphone. "Engineering Team Chihuahua Two, report to the shuttle in docking bay... Rache?"

"Docking bay four," she said absently, still working through her deductions. "Wolf should have her prepped for launch by the time we've returned."

Chris nodded, then strode down the corridor. It took her a moment to figure out he was heading on down without her, but she caught up with him almost half-way to the shuttle. She tried to think of something to say, but she couldn't. She had no idea how to.

Surprisingly, she didn't have to. "My nightmares didn't start until after... *Azumah*," Chris noted, breaking the silence between them. "I'd had a few before then, of course; everyone does. Nothing really serious, though – just silly stuff, like those dreams of showing up in class naked and things like that."

"Chris, you don't have to—"

"The nightmares I had during the *Azumah* incident were my first encounter with the nocebo effect. At first, I thought I was just finding injuries I missed during the initial incident, but that idea didn't make any sense for long. When I realized what was happening to me, I became as afraid of sleep as many others in the station were of the doom which seemed to be upon us. So, to distract myself, I started trying to figure out how we could save myself and the rest of the population on *Roman Brown*. We were trapped in the classroom section of the station, and several of my classmates found out what I was doing and joined in.

"You probably know that it was my tactical knowledge for a war-game scenario which got me into this accelerated program at the Academy and gave me my Lieutenant's bars. What was *not* made was that I got my engineering scholarship to the Academy for having fixed the orbit of the *Roman Brown Expedition* station."

Rachel gasped. This was too much. Chris was the mysterious, un-named student who led the team that saved the *Roman Brown Expedition's* people.

"But why—"

"The nightmares actually went away when I got the station stabilized. They came back when I screwed up traffic control for those rescue flights, and damn near got both the people of *Roman Brown Expedition* and all the rescue personnel killed. I didn't know my limits, and a lot of good people died because of it." He sighed. "When I say that I'd rather not study tactics as a career path in the Academy, I have my reasons."

Rachel winced. "Look, Chris... I can understand that, but you were only, what, sixteen when that happened? That was several years ago, and you're an adult now. You can't throw away a great talent – and your talent for tactical planning *is* great – just because you weren't perfect at it when you were in high school!"

Chris shook his head. "I—"

"Stop!" Rachel said. "If you're going to say one word about your nightmares, you can forget it right there. The only real cure for your nightmares will be to confront them. So then maybe, just maybe, you will be able to sleep without pain again." She reached out and softly stroked his forearm. "I think we both would be glad if that were the case."

"I already agreed to take the study seriously. I'm not sure I'll keep at it, but nightmares will no longer stop me." Chris shook his head. "But that doesn't mean I don't have my reasons for being a bit... reluctant."

Rachel sighed. "Yes, I suppose you do. Chris, I'm sorry. I knew you grew up on Epsilon Eridani, but I never even considered the fact that you would have been involved in that disaster."

"Yeah, well, I don't make it a point to mention it to people," Chris chuckled halfheartedly. "I'd be grateful if you did the same, okay?"

"Sure, Chris. If that's what you want, I'll keep quiet about it."

"Now, come on. I think I'd like to get in on the 'emergency repairs' I'm being recalled to complete, and I'd also like to hear all about what happened on the *Ishmael*."

EAS Chihuahua

Upon exiting the shuttle to board the *Chihuahua*, Rachel and Chris were met at the airlock by Captain Burkhard. He looked a bit frazzled, and the moment he saw them his finger crooked out beckoning them.

"Ah, Ms. Katz, Mr. Desaix. About time. A word, if you please?"

The two looked at each other in surprise. It sounded like they were in trouble with the Captain, but neither of them could think of anything they had done which might have raised his ire.

"Certainly, sir," Rachel answered for both of them after a moment's hesitation. They followed Burkhard into a small storage room, where he appeared to be hunched over a hand comp.

"Could you, perhaps, tell me about your recent leave on the colony station?" he asked after a moment.

Chris shrugged, sharing another puzzled glance with Rachel. "Nothing really notable happened. Rache and I went out for coffee. I've been tutoring her in engineering basics, and just gave her my 'final exam,' so it was kind of a celebration. Actually, it was thanks to that discussion that I figured out the whole rapid-fire particle cannon design."

Burkhard hummed dismissively. "Yes, yes – not an issue, and you're not fooling anyone. I don't care if you students are dating or not, and neither will anyone else – all the rules about fraternization and the like are usually ignored as a matter of course, provided no-one gets married inside the same chain of command and no-one on active duty gets pregnant.

Keep that in mind, and you'll stay out of trouble."

Rachel blushed. "Yes, sir!"

"There is something a bit more serious to worry about, however. Did you encounter Cadet Lieutenant Joel Farmburg while on the station?" Burkhard asked stiffly.

Chris and Rachel glanced at each other in surprise. "No, sir!" Rachel snapped.

"How about a crewman named Jefferson Flay?"

"I don't know anyone by that name, sir," Rachel replied, shaking her head.

Chris nodded in agreement. "I remember that his name was linked to the assault on Mr. Schubert a few weeks back, but that's all I know of him. Even so, we didn't encounter any other naval personnel at all. I doubt we could even have met him without realizing it, unless he was someone dressed in civilian clothes, perhaps... could we see a picture, sir?"

Burkhard glanced at a hand comp and sighed. "No, that won't be necessary. It's just your word against his." He paused. "However, I should warn you that the two of them have lodged a complaint against certain members of this crew – the two of you, included – for stalking him. To that end, except on official business, I am restricting all personnel to stay off the colony station during any times he should be aboard."

"Yes, sir," the couple chorused.

"Dismissed." He watched them leave, the concern clearly written on their faces. He looked once more at the complaint report in the hand comp. He hadn't believed Farmburg's complaint from the start. There was definitely something suspicious going on, but he had no choice but to treat the complaint as credible until it could be disproven. Burkhard sighed – this whole Farmburg business was getting out of hand. Perhaps he needed to speak to their Academy instructors on the matter and decide on a next move.

Looking at past records relating to Farmburg and the Academy, Burkhard now suspected there was a conspiracy targeting some of the best and the brightest students, and he was at the center of it. His motivation was as yet unclear – it could merely be a case of someone attempting to 'get ahead' by removing the competition. If so, Farmburg would be dealt with once the evidence was more conclusive, but Burkhard suspected more sinister possibilities. It was something he resolved to look into, soon. For now, though, there was little that could be but sit and wait.

Chapter XVIII

EAS Chihuahua

The next day, the modifications to the *Chihuahua's* particle cannons were completed. It didn't take too long afterward to prepare the ship for another test run. The crewmembers on shore leave were recalled to the *Chihuahua*, with just one day left before the Wargame was supposed to start. That meant it was inspection day.

The Naval Corp. of Engineers' Inspection Committee, which was officially required to certify every ship as spaceworthy before they could be formally commissioned (or re-commissioned, as the case may be), had sent in several teams to check the Academy's work, and the Chihuahua was able to claim a slot in the first wave of inspections. Burkhard was at the airlock and ready to meet the inspectors, trying his best to hide a smug grin.

"Captain Morrison," he said, greeting the woman who had put together his crew accompanying them. "I wasn't expecting you to be here for the inspection. How did you come to attend?"

Professor Anne Morrison shrugged. "I asked. I'd like to see how my favorite students are doing with an old clunker like this."

"It's hardly an 'old clunker,' now," Burkhard coughed, trying to hide his laughter. In point of fact, with all the work his crew had done and all the modifications the engineering team had accomplished, the *Chihuahua* was one of most advanced ships in the Navy, despite its aged origins. He desperately wanted to keep that as a surprise, for now, however.

"All these ships are 'old clunkers,'" one of the inspectors sighed. "Hodge Coles, Assistant Chief Naval Constructor and the man in charge of all the inspection teams in this fu— ahem, that is, silly affair. How you academy types expect to even compete in this Wargame boggles the mind, considering what I've seen today. Only six ancient battleships and three corvettes completed against forty two ships, including fifteen top-of-the-line battleships. Most of the 'completed' ships I've seen from your side aren't exactly in tip-top shape, either – I'd say only the *Superb* and the *Ishmael* are what I would normally consider battle-ready."

Burkhard openly smiled. "Well, Mr. Coles, you may not have been aware of it, but my crew and officers assisted in the completion of both of those ships. And it wasn't like I'd send my engineers off to finish other ships before I thought my own was ready. If you and your inspectors would come with me?"

"I didn't mean to imply that your ship wasn't battle-ready before I even started inspecting it, Captain Burkhard," Coles said, nodding respectfully. "But the quality of most of the ships I've seen today has given me a rather pessimistic expectation on that regard."

"That is no surprise," Burkhard snorted, guiding the inspectors down the corridor. "Only battleships had access to the tenders, and most parts requisitions by smaller ships were denied in favor of them. There wasn't enough time to get many of those Sirius-class battleships fully battle ready, even with those advantages. In my opinion, it was a waste of resources on the Academy's part. I'm amazed that *Superb* was finished, even with my crew's help, to be honest, much less the five other battleships."

Coles nodded, pulling out his hand comp and a stylus to take notes. "Was there anything you wished you could have done that you were unable to, because of the lack of a tender?"

Burkhard nodded. "Yes, a few things. Mr. Rappaport, our Chief Engineer, said that all we would have required was six hours with a tender, and we might have been able to find a solution to the staffing problems we started with."

That caused eyebrows to be raised by all present. "Staffing problems, Mr. Burkhard?" Captain Morrison asked. "I thought I gave you one of the best staffs in the fleet."

"You did," Burkhard agreed. "The fault wasn't yours; it was the ship's. There wasn't enough interior space for the amount of crew we needed – especially in the medical area. In fact, we've only got one ship's doctor on board, despite the usual two doctor requirement."

Coles wrote something into his hand comp. "And just what did your chief engineer have in mind that would help with this problem?"

"Mr. Rappaport believed that six hours would have been long enough to re-cut and reseal the rail gun bays, which would have allowed us to replace them with more modern, double-barreled rail guns. This would give us both heavier firepower and fewer required weapons techs, and given us enough extra space to expand sick bay. He believed actually replacing the rail guns might not have required the tender, however, as long as we had the parts."

Coles raised his eyebrows appraisingly. "An interesting modification. I imagine that would make this ship almost competitive with modern corvettes."

Burkhard chortled. "Competitive? Oh, I imagine we're quite competitive with modern corvettes as it is. Indeed, we're hoping to convince the navy to buy her back into the service when the War Games are over. The *Chihuahua* has had a number of... unique, shall we say, modifications."

"They would have to be pretty significant for me to suggest that the Navy re-commission a 150 year old ship into active duty," Coles warned, not liking Burkhard's boasting. In fact, had the ships' captains not been instructed to critique Commodore Greene's decisions, some of what he'd been saying would have qualified as insubordination, which rubbed Coles the wrong way. "I can certainly see why limited resources might have been refused a ship like this. I wouldn't have bought her into the Navy even when she was first built."

"I wouldn't have, either," Burkhard agreed. "But I'll let our engineers explain what we did during the refit. Mr. Desaix, the cadet responsible for most of the refit designs, should be present when we reveal the surprises."

Morrison goggled at that. "Mr. Desaix? You mean the tactics student?"

Burkhard hesitated. "I know he's done impressively in the tactical sims, but I have yet to talk with him much on tactics, although our Marine CO has worked with him on one occasion. I do know he is a rather brilliant engineer, however."

Coles snorted. "I've known good engineers who could deal with tactics, but not brilliant ones. The brilliant ones are typically too flighty to deal with something like that."

"He's pretty flighty," Morrison agreed. "I gather he barely sleeps, and he's not exactly a model officer. He also, uh, distrusts a lot of modern innovations. I imagine it must have been like pulling teeth to get him to include the quantum wheel I saw installed as we were shuttling in."

"At first, yes," Burkhard agreed. "But he talked himself into it."

"Talked himself into it?" Morrison repeated. "What in the world does that mean?"

The door Burkhard had been leading them towards opened, revealing the main engineering section with all of the engineers decked out in their dress uniforms, from the burgundy red jerkins with black jean pants to the black deerstalker caps which had universally replaced the color-coded beret system just two years before (someone in the logistics bureau had apparently been bored... and a fan of Sherlock Holmes). They were lined up, at attention, lead by Chris Desaix, most fighting to hold back smiles. Rappaport was nowhere to be seen.

"Ah, good to see you again, ma'am," he said, addressing his tactics instructor. "Welcome aboard."

"Thank you, Mr. Desaix," Morrison said, greeting her student, mildly amused. In the entire time she had known him, he had never been that formal with her or any other instructor she knew. Something was definitely up. "I heard that, somehow, you were convinced to allow quantum wheels and the like aboard your ship, and in fact convinced yourself to accept them. Just how did that happen?"

Chris shrugged. "I wouldn't have installed quantum wheels as our primary drive system, ma'am. Classic fusion drives are still significantly superior to them for most applications. You might note, however, that we have reconfigured the standard quantum wheels for side-mount applications. This allows for certain other improvements in our design."

"Such as?" Hodge Coles asked. "I've been told that you were responsible for certain 'modifications' which make your Captain believe this ship is competitive with current corvettes. I'd be grateful to know just what I should look for that would make this piece of junk worthy of purchase into the modern Navy."

"Yes sir. We developed a few unique systems for the *Chihuahua,* which may be useful for the rest of the Navy as well."

"What sort of 'unique systems' are those, Mr. Desaix?" Coles asked, looking down his nose at Chris condescendingly. "I do not appreciate the run around we're getting on that."

"Most significantly, we melded the side mount quantum wheels into a shielding system which covers over eighty percent of the hull from particle cannon and rail gun fire," Chris replied. "Particle cannons might be able to penetrate those shields with enough concentrated and sustained firepower. It would take a fleet to do that, however; a single ship would be unable to without another modification we've developed – a near-streaming particle cannon system. I was tutoring one of my fellow cadets in engineering, and she happened to point out how an old, long-discounted concept could work if done using modern materials. I took the idea and ran with it."

Coles couldn't believe his ears. Two of the longest-sought-out concepts in military technology, developed by a bunch of academy students during a simple war-game. *If* they worked as well as was claimed.

"I have to admit I'm skeptical." He finally said. "If they do work, I want to make my own estimates as to your their effectiveness."

Chris shrugged and nodded. "A good place to start on those estimates might be the sensor logs from our recent combat drill with the *Tarantula*. Regardless, I think calling this a 'corvette' is a bit of a misnomer now that we're done with her. Even when other ships get shields and near-streaming particle cannons, we'll still have a heavier weight of fire with our particle cannons. Rail guns, in ship-to-ship combat, are going to become... less important, although still useful in some situations. Based on her current combat potential, I think the *Chihuahua* would rate as, say, a pocket frigate in the modern Navy."

Coles was getting more and more frustrated at the seeming arrogance of everyone on board this ship. The Navy had been trying to develop shields and streaming particle cannons for centuries – and even if this ship had some new prototype design, it was his job to value their effectiveness, not their job to assume it worked right out of the box.

"We'll see," Coles said, taking a deep breath to maintain his calm. "Again, I'd like to see these systems in action."

"As you wish, sir," Chris agreed. "But I don't want to test them nearby. While we have, of course, filed initial reports on our designs with the Navy Weapons Development Board and received their estimates, we haven't shown the Fleet side of the Wargame everything we can do. Only the members of this crew and possibly Commodore Green are fully aware of the improvements."

Burkhard was already walking over to an intercom. "Mr. Orff, please prepare the ship for another shakedown cruise, to start in thirty minutes. Mr. Coles would like to see us in action."

"Yes, sir," Orff's voice came back.

"In the meantime, let's get the rest of this inspection over with first, shall we?" Burkhard suggested.

EAS Natsugumo

"Mr. Farmburg," Commander Barbara Meier, captain of the Academy Frigate *Natsugumo,* called. "I understand you volunteered to escort the observer from the Cygni Confederation to the foreign observer's pre-Wargame dinner on the *Don Quixote?*"

Joel nodded. "Yes, ma'am."

"Any particular reason why?" she asked.

It was not an unexpected question. There shouldn't be any reason for Joel Farmburg to have an interest in anyone from Cygni. As a Cygni Confederation operative, however, Farmburg needed to meet with him. He was overdue for word from his handlers, and that could mean a change in plans. Were his people still planning on starting a war with Earth?

In short, Farmburg needed another reason for volunteering, which anyone but a complete incompetent would be prepared for. Not being a complete incompetent, he had one ready.

"I have a legal matter – civil law – to attend to, ma'am, and I heard that one of the Advocate Generals is attending the Wargame and will be observing from on board the *Don Quixote.*"

"And so you volunteered for the first shuttle run to the *Don Quixote* you could find," Meier sighed. "We really need you here, Mr. Farmburg – the Wargame starts the day after tomorrow, and we're at least two days away from completing our refit. If we delay much longer, we'll miss our window for bringing in the inspectors."

"My apologies, ma'am," Farmburg said regretfully. "I signed up without realizing we would be at this crucial of a stage when it came time to make the run. By the time I realized just what the situation was, it was too late to cancel."

"Very well," Barbara sighed. "You're dismissed. You can take shuttle three to the colony station, where a Mr. Dane Myles will be meeting you for the journey to the observation ship. Spend as little time as possible on this assignment, Mr. Farmburg, and maybe I won't have to issue a reprimand for your poor judgment."

Joel swallowed. He certainly didn't want that. While he didn't let himself appear unnaturally talented as an Academy student, he never allowed himself to do anything which would be serious enough to appear in his official records as a reprimand. He needed a near spotless record to do his job properly, after all.

"Yes, Ma'am. I won't let you down, ma'am."

"See that you don't," Captain Meier snapped, turning away from him in annoyance. Of all her officers, Farmburg was her least favorite. She couldn't tell why, exactly – he always seemed to do his job fairly well – but something about him rubbed her the wrong way.

With a nod, Farmburg was off. He'd have to move at peak efficiency, and hope that Dane Myles did as well.

At least he'd finally be getting word from home.

EAS Chihuahua

While he still didn't believe everything the *Chihuahua's* crew was telling him, Coles had to admit that she was better outfitted then he had anticipated. Especially when it came to the things that the engineers hadn't mentioned earlier, like the increase to her top speed and maneuverability that the unusual quantum wheel configuration provided. What bothered him, however, were the shields – they obviously worked against rail guns, given the tests they ran, but he wasn't entirely sure about the crew's estimate on their effectiveness against particle cannons. He would like to ask the crew for further tests, because he couldn't believe the numbers they were giving him, but he'd been forced to cut his inspection short prematurely.

"I don't know," he said. They were in the middle of his final assessment debriefing, and he was ostensibly giving the *Chihuahua's* people a final opportunity to make their case. In truth, he'd already made up his mind and was trying to justify his decisions to them. "We'll have to take the specs of this system and study it some more before we can give an accurate estimate of just how much stopping power it has. I'll also make sure the patent applications get entered properly in your names."

"Thank you, sir," Rappaport agreed. This was the first time he'd met the man who was the *Chihuahua's* chief engineer. And he was only present, now, because Coles insisted. "But please ensure that Mr. Desaix and Ms. Katz are the only ones listed on those patents. I was not responsible for either innovation."

"The final numbers will take some time and testing to calculate. Time we don't have, with the Wargame starting tomorrow," Coles continued. "I'll have to provide some sort of preliminary guesstimate for the simulation. I'm afraid that I'm going to have to lowball the amount of firepower we'll allow those shields of your to absorb. I'm going to say a direct, concentrated strike of all the particle cannons of an Argus class battleship will be able to penetrate the shield and do some damage, and work our figures from that estimate. If your numbers are accurate, it will be more powerful then that, but for the purposes of the Wargame..."

"You don't want to give us an unearned advantage," Rappaport agreed, keeping the hand he'd been using to restrain Cadet Desaix out of sight. "I completely understand, Mr. Coles, and I consider that an... equitable solution. Thank you, sir."

"Now, if you'll excuse me, I'm off to inspect the *Sirius*. Commodore Green insists that we clear his flagship next, even if there is still some work ongoing. so you can have at least seven battleships in time for the opening action. Oh, and assuming things work as you have anticipated, Mr. Desaix, I do anticipate buying the Chihuahua back into the service as a pocket frigate, as you recommended."

Chris was momentarily startled, but quickly recovered his tongue. "Yes, sir. Thank you, sir, Mr. Coles."

As Coles left the room, Rappaport released his unseen grip on the younger man. "Hodge Coles is a good man, Mr. Desaix. I hope you realize that."

"He doesn't show it, sir," Chris snapped.

"Yes, but he's a good man, nonetheless. Nothing he said was to insult you or the shield system. To be honest, I think he was low-balling us because he is an engineer himself, and knows how frequently experimental systems can go haywire in the field. The fact he allowed the streaming particle beams to pass, unchallenged, is remarkable. You should take it as a compliment.."

Chris hesitated before nodding. "I will, sir."

"Good," Rappaport replied. "Now, I hope you see just why a little patience and diplomacy might be a good thing, now and then? If you'd been a bit more humble in the initial presentation of the shield systems, I doubt he would have felt the need to rub you the wrong way."

"If you say so, sir," Chris said doubtfully.

Shuttle, in transit to EAS Don Quixote

"So, you're Joel Farmburg, are you?" Captain Dane Myles, the man assigned to observe the Wargame by the Cygni Confederation. There was a time, once, when each invited nation would send a minimum of three officers for every Wargame, and those officers would frequently be of flag rank. As long as the event had been running, however, the spectacle was gone and most nations had dropped the number and importance of the delegation sent.

A lone Captain wasn't unusual, anymore. In fact, it was generous – Iota Draconis, for example, sent a Lieutenant as their highest ranking observer. On the other hand, a few nations continued to treat this as a major event – the relatively tiny nation of the Larkin Triumvirate sent three full Admirals. Then again, the Larkin Triumvirate, also known as 'Larkin's Folly,' was a bit of a special case.

Back in the early days of colonization, when everyone and anyone was heading to the stars to set up their own colonies as empires, three brothers of the rather wealthy Larkin family financed an expedition to the star known as 9 Puppis A, which afterwards came to be known as Larkin's Star. Long distance observation had indicated that there were planetary bodies in orbit around the star, and that those planetary bodies were solid masses (and therefore were terraformable) but little more was known about them when the expedition left. As it turned out, there were actually three planetary bodies that were terraformable, but each was no larger than Earth's moon. This worked out reasonably well, as each Larkin brother had his own planetoid to rule, but the tiny size of the three planets meant they weren't good locations for empire building. Also, natural resources were very limited, as there were few mineable ores in the system as a whole. In spite of this, the three brothers decided they would form three separate 'kingdoms,' one for each planet.

At the time, there were hundreds of these 'interstellar empires' being born, since just about everyone who could afford an expedition wanted their own planet to rule. Many wars of conquest broke out between these empires in the rush to grab vital resources. Larkin was no exception, save that their wars were between the children of the three brothers, and the battles were all confined almost entirely to within their own single system. The small size of their three planets was what saved them from being trampled by the expansion of their neighbors. Who wanted three tiny, feuding planetoids when there were so many greater prizes to be won?

The three kingdoms of Larkin eventually noticed that powerful empires were expanding around them on all sides, and it was only a matter of time before someone's attention turned to their system. A treaty was written to resolve their differences, the three leaders of the respective worlds agreed to share power, and thus Larkin became a triumvirate. As it turned out, the large civil war they'd been involved in for so long had given them significant military experience, and united, they had become powerful enough to fend off several assaults from other systems.

Their unique political structure led to certain peculiarities, however, such as the decision to always send three admirals to the Wargame (one representing each planetoid). This sounded impressive... until one realized that, due to a prolonged period of peace, Larkin no longer had any significant military to speak of. They had eight 'admirals' to command their 'fleets,' but only two dozen ships to manage – four frigates and a flock of cutters.

Nevertheless, those three admirals were treated with all the respect due an officer of flag rank from any nation. Meanwhile, Captain Dane Myles, whose rank actually put him in charge of more firepower than all three admirals combined, was treated just as any ordinary ship's captain.

A lone escort, and a mere cadet lieutenant at that, seemed beneath Captain Myles, but he would deal with it as diplomatically as he could.

"Yes, sir," Farmburg answered him. "Cadet Lieutenant Joel Farmburg, here to meet any and all needs within my authority that you may require of me."

Myles paused. That was one of Cygni Fleet Intelligence code phrases – which meant this 'mere cadet lieutenant' might be a Cygni officer. That changed some things, but he'd better not give the game away.

"Thank you, Mr. Farmburg. I won't require more from you then your authority grants," he replied, giving the countersign.

"Let us hope your authority and my authority grants us sufficient latitude," Farmburg replied, giving the final confirmation. "If you'll follow me, sir?"

Giving a subtle nod, Myles followed the supposed cadet, gesturing his farewells to his fellow observers (including the three bickering Larkin Triumvirate admirals) as each of them followed their escort to their respective 'private' shuttles – each observation team being granted one shuttle (with accompanying Earth Alliance pilot) for the duration of the exercise. Curiosity was making it difficult for him to maintain his usual stoic air of indifference, but he bit off any words he wanted to say until they were both in the shuttle with the airlock secure.

"So," Myles sighed, taking his seat next to the pilot's chair after the pre-flight communication was completed. "Mr. Farmburg, is it?"

"Not really, sir. Lieutenant Commander, Cygni Fleet Intelligence." A subtle pressure in their chests indicated that the shuttle was in motion. "If you want my real name badly enough, you'll have to check with your superiors. But of course you know that."

"Of course," Myles agreed good-naturedly. "Now, why did you initiate contact? You're deep-cover, right?"

"Yes, sir," Farmburg agreed. "So deep that I haven't been able to get in touch with my handler in almost a year, save for burst transmissions where I can send out my reports. Which means I need info – policy info."

"Ah," Myles acknowledged. "You mean, 'how close are we to war?'"

"More or less," Joel admitted. "And if there are any specific people inside of the Earth Alliance I should be keeping a close eye on."

Myles thought about it for a minute. "Well, I'm not really prepared to give you a real briefing, given that I'm out of the loop, myself. However, I suppose I can give you some information which you may not have access to living outside of Cygni."

"Anything would be appreciated, sir."

Stroking his chin, Myles considered just what he knew and organized it all in his mind. "Well... I suppose that the Earth Alliance is still our biggest enemy, but much of our decision on whether to pursue a war footing against them is resting on the results of this Wargame. We have no real guide as to just how good their Navy is, and we're completely ignorant of the capabilities of their new Argus class. If our battleships can stand against theirs in a head-to-head battle evenly, then we're in pretty good shape to attack. The Earth Alliance Navy is stretched too thin to defend all of their planets, so we should be able to assemble an attacking force large enough to overwhelm any of their planetary defenses except for those around Earth itself. However, if the Argus class is reasonably close to what their PR claims, we would be much better off going against one of our targets – likely either the Virgin Planets or Iota Draconis. Larkin might also be a secondary target, regardless of who else we fight, simply because they'll be easy to raid and because they claim to be allied to all of our other potential targets – whether those powers agree with them or not."

Farmburg raised an eyebrow. "Last I heard, Pleiades was our primary alternate target. What became of that?"

Myles shrugged. "I don't have all the details, but in the last few months something has been happening in Pleiades that has Fleet Command downright terrified. Almost all our spies, and those we'd identified as spying on them from other powers, have... disappeared. There has been nothing in the press about this. The last report from before the disappearances mentioned something about an unusual build-up of state security forces, notable for wearing full power armor, complete with helmets, even when planetside. There was also a large amount of construction in the military sector, especially the Navy, but secrecy there was too tight for us to penetrate even before we lost most of our assets. Second-hand data retrieved from Larkin, which we believe – to our shock – is the only foreign power who still has agents in Pleiades, indicates they've started adapting some undisclosed advanced technology to their fleet. We think they're preparing for war, but we don't know why or with whom."

Farmburg frowned. "All of the intel inside Pleiades has been stopped? That's... unusual." The word he really wanted to use was 'disturbing.' Farmburg made a mental note to look into the Pleiades situation within Earth Alliance spheres. However, that was getting off track – he needed to bring things back to more relevant topics.

"Does our leadership know whether Earth Alliance suspects anything – either of us or of Pleiades?"

"They always expect us to do something," Myles answered. "They devote many of their intelligence resources against us, and our own sources in their embassy have noted that they're worried. They've had a fleet patrolling just outside of our space for quite some time, trying to project power against us. They're as aware of the tactical situation between us as we are, and are hoping their performance in the War Games will convince us they're too much trouble to go to war with. Their focus has been turned towards us so much that they've practically ignored their other borders. But they don't seem to know how close we are, either."

"So, in other words, they know we *are* coming, but not *when* we're coming."

"Correct."

Farmburg sighed heavily. "I'm greatly concerned with this news about Pleiades. I'm hesitant to start a war with Earth without knowing what they are planning."

Myles shrugged. "It's not my position to create policy, nor is it yours. We just follow orders."

"I realize that. My concern is just that my communications from Cygni have become so spotty that I have to guess if there's a change in policy and whether that change would effect my orders. If the situation in Pleiades is as unsettled as it seems, my more... active espionage efforts may work against our best interests."

Myles shrugged. "I have never been involved in the clandestine service, so I don't know what it's like to be out of communication with my superiors for so long. I might have the same concerns in your position. So, what do you think our policy should be?"

Farmburg hesitated. "We raid and plunder, in the tradition of our pirate ancestors, but we don't occupy any territory outside of our own. We are not conquerors. Pleiades, however, is a different story – they're imperial in nature, despite being a confederation. And they're on a war footing. If we take out Earth's navy, I wonder how they would react? Perhaps they might target only other power capable of challenging them?"

Myles nodded. "Perhaps it would be better if we waited for Pleiades' move. I'll send your analysis up the chain of bureaucracy, and see if they can get word down to you about what to do. In the meantime, make preparations to act quickly against either Earth or Pleiades, depending on what orders you receive. And God help us if those orders lead us into folly."

Chapter XIX

"Captain Burkhard, I know we discussed this earlier, but it's a flag officer's prerogative to change his mind," Acting-Commodore Green sighed. "I hadn't realized we would be so behind in preparation before the Wargame. We only have nine battleships and three corvettes ready to participate at the moment, and I must have everything I can stay here for defense. I cannot afford to send out anyone until we can present a show of force. The *Natsugumo* will be ready tomorrow, as will two of the other battleships, so maybe then—"

"Before you make a final ruling," Burkhard interrupted. "I think you need to consider something: *Because* we're so understaffed, we must develop a little subterfuge to make our enemies think we're more ready than we truly are. I recommend that we send all three corvettes and one battleship – let's say the *Superb,* since I've worked with her Captain during the refits – to take up a position inside of the 'neutral' territory. If there's a superior force present, we'll jump out fast. If our forces are nearly equal force, we'll arrange to have *Chihuahua* take point and skirmish with one of their corvettes to, ah, intimidate them, while holding the rest of our ships back so that they can maintain the illusion that they also have shields. If there's an enemy presence that we feel we can easily handle, we'll encircle them to prevent any chance that one may escape and then wipe them out. If there's no enemy force, the *Chihuahua* would be the ideal ship to fly into *their* territory for a scouting mission – with her shields and at our maximum speed, we should be capable of avoiding combat while still flying close enough to get a good idea of how they're forming their groups, all the while projecting a sense of strength and confidence in our own forces."

Green narrowed his eyes angrily. He knew, already, he wouldn't win a debate over this plan if he allowed one – he couldn't out-think a master of tactics like Burkhard on the tactical front, and he didn't really have enough force to do things by the book if he expected to put in a good showing early on. Burkhard's insubordination by interrupting him was a challenge to his authority, however, and it couldn't be ignored. Green weighed his options briefly before coming to a decision.

"I suppose that might work, Mr. Burkhard. However, I will not let you be in charge of the, ah, expedition. Captain Daniels will be in overall command of the squadron, with orders not to stay in the system if even a single battleship is present. The *Superb* is no match for an Argus, or even a lesser battleship in the Navy's forces. I don't want to risk the *Chihuahua* by having it go up against a battleship on its own just to have a chance to 'skirmish' with a Fleet corvette."

Burkhard held his gaze for a brief time, but took that in stride. He hadn't asked for command of the squadron, and knew he wouldn't have been given it anyway as he was the most junior commanding officer in the Academy fleet. Having someone even remotely competent in charge, like Daniels, would be better than he had hoped. As to the battleship restriction... well, it made sense in this case. Perhaps Green was better at tactics then he thought. Or perhaps he was just trying to keep some control of the situation. Either way, it was a reasonable decision.

EAS Superb

"Hello, ladies and gentleman," Commander Jonathan Daniels began once all four captains and their staff were seated. The *Superb*'s conference room was large enough (and Task Force One was small enough) that each captain was able to bring their entire tactical staff as well as each ship's official observer without crowding the table, so at the moment his position as task force commander looked more impressive than it really was. "By now, you're all aware that what we've got on our hands is little more than a scouting mission. I've reviewed the specifics of Commodore Green's orders, however, and have decided to... expand on them a bit, if there are no objections?"

Lt. Commander Terry Christopher, of the *Inkadh*, looked a little hesitant, but Burkhard smiled and even Lt. Commander Trevor Kushner, the *Ishmael's* captain, seemed confident in the idea. The staff officers, for the most part, mimicked their respective captains.

"None from any of us, sir," Burkhard said after a moment.

"Before this meeting begins," Chris Desaix said hesitantly, looking at his hand comp and not at anyone in the room. "If the intent of Green's orders was to prevent the Fleet from learning how few ships have been refitted with *Chihuahua's* upgraded capabilities, I have some information that I just learned from these briefing papers that may expand your options a bit. While we don't want to risk your taking fire and revealing how rare our new shield technology actually is, I think the *Superb* should be able to open fire as well if it attacks suddenly and from a distance. I made some of the preparations to incorporate *Chihuahua's* 'special' particle cannon modifications into the *Superb* while I was assisting your engineers, here. By the time we get into Fleet territory, you could have some 'enhanced' particle cannons available."

Rachel tried to hide her wince. Chris was present as a courtesy, only. He had no official position on the tactical staff, despite deserving it, but here he was speaking out of turn to the task force commander himself, without any attempts at military courtesy.

"My apologies, sir," Kushner said, addressing Daniels and drawing attention away from Chris. "I should also report I arranged to have similar preparations made on board the *Ishmael*. I have no idea how long it would take to complete them, but perhaps our own borrowed engineer, Ms. Katz, might know?" he motioned questioningly.

Rachel flushed slightly, being put on the spot. "Well, sir, I got the emitters and heat sinks completed, but not the capacitors or external fittings. You didn't want to let anyone know what I was doing for security purposes, and it's impossible to hide the installation of those parts from any outside observers. The weapon can fire, as is, but for safety purposes I locked down the system, preventing it from attempting to operate as a streaming particle cannon."

Chris grinned slightly. "Well, at that level it shouldn't be a problem. If all three corvettes share the fabrication work between them, we should be able to have the streaming particle cannons done for *Ishmael* in under an hour, as well."

That was news to most people in the room – and a bit confusing, as well, since most of the junior officers had no idea what the special modifications were to the *Chihuahua*. A slow murmuring started among the crowd, and Daniels looked rather annoyed at the interruptions. Burkhard, though, was grinning widely.

"Streaming particle cannons on both your flagship and another corvette – that is worth our time, don't you think, sir?"

Daniels rolled his eyes. He had come to expect such a lack of discipline, being related (by marriage) to Burkhard, but he hadn't expected the man's officers to be just like him. Unlike some in the Navy, however, he wasn't so uptight about discipline that he let it get in the way of sound judgment, but verbal reprimand was in order at the very least.

"Of course, Captain Burkhard," he sighed. "However, in the future, I would appreciate it if you and your officers remembered the formalities. Everyone here will have their say, in time, even if we retain the order and discipline most navies – *including* our own – proscribe."

"Yes, sir," They answered in unison.

"Very good. That being said, your information suggests that we are more battle-ready than I expected, which may change our plans." He noticed one of his more disciplined officers fidgeting, and sighed. "Captain Christopher, do you have a comment?"

The captain of the *Inkadh* nodded his head. "Yes, sir. I hate to say this, considering the condition of our other ships, but I have yet to pass my ship through inspection as 'battle-ready.' We are, however, flight-ready. Work is in progress, and if we had another few days we'd probably be up to battle-ready standards."

Daniels nodded. "I was informed of that by Commodore Green, but don't worry. While I can't give you that much time to finish repairs, your part in the plan should keep you out of combat. I have another task for your ship:

"Despite being a contemporary of Phoebe class ships like Kushner's *Ishmael*, your *Inkadh* was a unique design. While your engineers report states that much of your internal electronics had to be replaced to get her spaceworthy, your ship still has her original sensor package. Is that correct?"

"Yes, sir."

Daniels nodded. "Most modern sensor suites concentrate on improving short to medium range ships sensors at the cost of long-range sensors. The current doctrine replaces these long-range sensors with coordinated multi-ship arrays, allowing for more resolution and detail the more ships are included. However, the long range sensors on board your ship have been left untouched from the old doctrine, where ships would be better equipped for independent action rather than fleet activity. *Inkadh* was designed to be an independent scout, so her long-range sensors were high-end even under the old doctrine. Your one ship's sensors might not be as good as we could get if we had a dozen ships to co-ordinate with, but they are far better than anything we have. I daresay, they are better than we could manage even with a coordinated sensor scan using all of the ships in this first strike expedition."

The *Inkhad*'s commander relaxed and nodded appreciatively. "Yes, sir. Thank you, sir. But what if a Fleet ship approaches my position before our other ships can react?"

"Then you are ordered to flee. We may have a few tricks up our sleeve, but nothing Fleet has is fast enough to catch you at a run."

"Yes, sir."

"Now, I think that's a good lead-in to why I'm making a slight modification to Commodore Green's orders," Daniels said. "If we did not find a Fleet presence in the neutral system, the *Chihuahua* should make a quick run through their 'home' system as well. *Chihuahua's* scanners, however, are not ideal – for all her other advancements she has a basic modern sensor package, which in a single ship is best used for close to medium range tactical assessments. If the *Inkadh* could make one sensor pass, even at extreme range, it should be able to direct the *Chihuahua* on where to focus those more detailed short-ranged scans. *Inkadh* is incapable of defending herself, however, so *Superb* and *Ishmael* must also be present to provide cover should we jump into a bad situation and need to make a hasty retreat.

"Of course, no matter what precautions you make there is always the chance of something going wrong. I would like to introduce my tactical officer to brief us all on what we know about Fleet facilities. Cadet Lieutenant Turk, if you would?"

Turk wasted no time, stepping up to the front of the room. However, his eyes were not on the crowd as they should have been, but instead were locked on his hand comp. "We all know that this exercise is supposed to give the Academy enough ships to outnumber Fleet to make up for Fleet's ships being newer and more advanced warships. However, the Academy has not been able to complete the re-commissioning of all of its ships, so at the moment the number of Fleet's forces are rather intimidating. Breaking it down, Fleet has fifteen battleships, fourteen heavy cruisers, four frigates, and eight corvettes. The corvettes are split evenly between

Hornet and Alligator class ships; the frigates include two Ventures, one Raven, and one Ptolemy class; the heavy cruisers are mostly Valkyries, though there are two Allegro class; and finally, the most diverse group, the battleships: We must deal with two Terrible, two Rhino, two Corona, two Saratoga, and seven Argus class battleships." With that, he paused dramatically. It wasn't news for anyone present, however.

"I think we were all well aware of the ships in the Fleet list, Lieutenant Turk," Daniels sighed impatiently. "We've all read the Navy list. I believe we're much more interested in the other facilities available to them."

The officers all came alert at that statement. As far as anyone else knew, there were no Fleet facilities outside of the ships – while all three stars in which the war games were taking place had been claimed for colonization by the Earth Alliance, only the system in the Academy's sphere of influence had been developed enough to hold anything other than marker buoys, as far as they knew.

"Yes, sir," Turk said, flushing. "In a move which surprised both Fleet and Academy forces, K1 Enterprises, the manufacturers of the Valkyrie class heavy cruisers as well as many civilian ventures, used the Wargame as leverage to help win a bid for a construction contract. They were able to immediately launch one complete colony station – which was assembled during the period that our forces were refitting our ships – in exchange for the contract to also build the next five new colony stations over the next five years. Commodore Green was briefed on this three hours ago and passed the information directly to us.

"We are not certain what else was provided to them with that station, save that a 'Norn' class colony ship deployed it and is part of it, and the package deal the Navy received includes multiple satellites as well as some support ships that this Norn class vessel carried into the system."

Chris started. "Excuse me, Nat, but did you say this was one of K1 Enterprises Norn class colony ships?"

Turk, looked decidedly ruffled at being addressed rather familiarly as 'Nat,' nodded stiffly. "That is what I said, yes."

"Then I may be able to provide some more information," he answered back regretfully. "In the summer before I joined the Academy, I interned with K1 Enterprises. Some things I can't tell you about because of a non-disclosure agreement, but I can give you a *few* specs that were only known to K1 employees."

Several people shot Chris sympathetic glances. K1 was an up-and-coming company with an excellent reputation both as an employer and as a successful ship builder, but everyone knew what working there meant. As part of the legal settlement following the Azumah Station Incident, the company which was responsible for the disastrous gravity generator design had been dissolved and all its assets seized. The seized assets were used to create K1 Enterprises, a corporation held in trust for the victims and their families in partial compensation for their losses. K1 also was saddled with a 10 year hiring restriction, during which it could only employ survivors of the disaster and their extended families.

"Go ahead, Mr. Desaix," Daniels said.

Chris stood up and joined Turk at the front of the room. Typing a few commands into his hand comp, he plugged it into the conference room's main computer system. The display screen in front of the table immediately flashed with light and started showing several illustrations.

"I may have only been an intern, but I worked in the public relations office for the sales teams, providing technical documentation for their presentations. That meant I received early estimates for many statistical aspects of K1's proposed projects. Among the presentations I worked on was the Norn class. The exact statistics I have may be a bit dated, and was certainly sanitized by K1 Enterprises' administrators to only put this prototype in the best light, but what information I do have is probably more accurate than anything we can currently get from the public record.

"Some of you may not know what, exactly, a colony ship contains; the Norns are the first production-grade colony ships launched in nearly twenty five – excuse me, thirty, now – years. Colony ships are intended to move into orbit over a planet, 'unpack' themselves, and then act as orbital cities. These orbital cities are to provide housing, large-scale aquariums, large-scale terrariums, laboratories, manufacturing facilities, and so forth.

"Sometimes terraforming equipment is kept separate from the populated colony ship, but in the Norn's case it was included as a selling point. Terraforming equipment is not meant for combat, of course, but someone skilled in improvisation could, without damage to the facility, make tactical use of a few things: Explosive and implosive devices capable of altering planetary landscapes might be included, but I doubt such a use would be authorized for a simple exercise, even one as significant as the Wargame. Of far greater concern is a device intended to ionize or de-ionize existing atmospheres. With little effort, this device could be used as a massive EMP generator, with enough power to even tear through the electronic shielding employed by modern spacecraft. I am... uncertain how the Chihuahua's new shield systems would react to such a device.

"The Norn colony ships were planned to have another unique feature, however: They came with a set of parasite ships capable of both atmospheric and interstellar flight. While not intended for military-grade combat, those parasite ships include several armed cutters equal to most Orbital Guard ships. In addition, a Valkyrie class cruiser is contractually required to be delivered to the Navy with each completed Norn sent on a colonizing expedition. I suspect this means the *Dragon* has finally been completed, after a long construction delay. She had been slated for Epsilon Eridani's defense fleet, but it is possible she was delivered to the Navy to be a part of the War Game.

"The prototype Norn-class Colony ship – if this is, indeed, the prototype – will be unpacked into one main station and several satellite facilities. The *Yggdrasil* is the name of the orbital city section. The remaining orbital facilities included would be the terraforming satellite *Skuldr,* the farming satellite *Verthandi,* and the *Urdr* – a 'natural biolab' satellite, a new concept by K1 Enterprises, which should allow scientists to preserve and study indigenous flora and fauna and determine which can be re-introduced to the planet's surface once the terraforming process is complete."

As he spoke, images projected from his hand-comp at timed intervals. No-one at that table cared about this 'natural biolab' satellite, but he was in a rhythm, now. This was a presentation which, at least at one time, he must have rehearsed often enough to get the timing exactly right. Rachel noticed that his voice took a slightly different tone as he spoke, one which gave him the air of professionalism he often seemed to lack whenever he was acting as an officer.

"Many of the included parasite ships are superficially similar, but each is equipped differently depending on the assigned task. Three freight shuttles were equipped for terraforming service. These are the *Thor,* the *Odin,* and the *Loki.* A fourth, the *Marler,* is available as an option.

"Likewise, three utility shuttles were also included – these designed largely for a payload of passengers and not equipment. As you can see from the diagrams, they are able to travel in the extremely dense atmospheres you sometimes find on pre-terraformed worlds. They are equipped to clear potentially dangerous wildlife from landing areas and act as command and control facilities for landing parties. *Yggdrasil's* are the *Freya,* the *Peorð,* and the *Brunhilda.*

"Finally, we come to the three armed cutters. Just like standard Orbital Guard ships, they are armed with a single-barrel particle cannon and a 12" rail gun, both turret mounted. K1's documentation claims those cutters can maneuver even at speeds of .21c, but I happen to know that number was incorrect. Those claims were based on a prototype armed cutter, the *Mjolnir*. The original *Mjolnir* was redesigned after its engines had to be ejected during a test flight, however. While sturdier and less likely to explode, the *Mjolnir II* is incapable of maneuvering safely when traveling any faster than .17c. This means they are on par, speed-wise, with the *Inkadh*, and are even a little faster then *Ishmael*. The three of these ships designated for the *Yggdrasil* are the aforementioned *Mjolnir II,* the *Sleipnir,* and the *Valhalla.* Despite the reduction in maneuvering speed, these ships will be the fastest available to Fleet forces."

"Of note, the prototypes for these cutters – despite the sales literature – did not have any interstellar capabilities installed as of the end of my internship at K1 Enterprises, though the techs were working on it. Also, as they were intended to be crewed by civilians, I am not sure they will be employed in the Wargame. I suggest we request clarification from the Wargame's current arbitrator as to whether they are legitimate targets or not."

"The base is," Captain Morrison piped in from her observer's position. "But I haven't heard anything about the parasite ships, either way. I wasn't even aware the base was equipped with them."

The slideshow style presentation behind Chris returned to the initial image, and it soon became obvious that he was done talking. Rachel almost felt like giving polite applause for his performance.

"Well," Daniels sighed, standing up. "Would you mind copying that presentation over to our files for study?"

Chris shook his head. "Nothing I said was covered under the non-disclosure agreements I signed, so that should be no problem. Some of it may be a bit dated. You may be able to update some of that information if you can find K1's sales brochures."

Daniels stood up. "All very interesting, but now we need to decide what to do with this new information. We will adjourn for twenty minutes. Captains, please be prompt; junior officers may attend to other duties if required. Mr. Desaix, I do not expect you to return. You and your teams are directed to co-ordinate the work on any of the particle cannons we can get streaming-ready, post-haste. Meanwhile, I will get in touch with Admiral Mumford on board the *Don Quixote* with the question about whether those armed cutters should be considered legitimate targets. The rest of you, feel free to head to the officers' wardroom to pick up some refreshments. We'll get down to the nitty-gritty when you all return. Thank you, all."

Daniels left immediately, but Chris fiddled with his hand comp for a few moments first. As the tactical team of the *Chihuahua* stood up and started to mingle with the other officers, Rachel leaned over him resting her elbows on his shoulders.

"I'm sorry you're going to miss the rest of this meeting," she said to him softly. "But that was a great presentation."

"Thanks," he replied with a grin. "Glad I never purged that presentation from my files."

"How did anyone get a cutter to move the same speed as a corvette, though?" she asked.

"By designing the smallest, fastest corvette they could... and then removing all of the mission-unnecessary gear to reduce mass. Things like broadside rail guns, non-turreted chase armaments, and anything required for long-term deployments like bunks and kitchen facilities, since cutters aren't expected to be deployed for much longer than one or two shifts. It's still the largest cutter ever built, however – her engine is the same size and diameter as the *Chihuahua's*."

Rachel raised an eyebrow. "So, basically, she's an under-armed corvette incapable of interstellar travel or the ability to sustain a crew overnight?"

"Yep," Chris said. "She's all speed and little else."

"Please tell me this wasn't your design," she sighed. "I would hope you would make something a bit better than that."

"He was an intern!" Cohen laughed. Langer and Orff, the last two members of Burkhard's tactical team, joined in with a chuckle. "No matter how good an engineer he is, who'd trust an intern with such a design?"

"No," Chris answered Rachel, ignoring the laughter. "I designed the utility shuttles instead, although not for this project. K1 had an internal contest for the design of a lightweight Army landing craft open for any employee, with possible prizes available. I was informed that, due to costs, it did not meet the requirements of the assignment my boss sent my plans – and me – to Project Norn, where it was adopted after some modifications." Finishing with his hand comp, he stood. "Now, if you all will excuse me, I have to get started."

"Need any help?" Rachel asked sympathetically, shooting a glare over at the now dumbfounded Cohen and Langer.

"Nah, this is child's play. What'd you password the lockdown on the *Ishmael,* by the way?"

"The password won't do you much good by itself – I encrypted it. I'd better go with you."

Chris shrugged. "If you want, though the encryption protocols you're familiar with are standard enough I could decrypt it myself."

Rachel hesitated. If she were honest with herself, she was hoping to use this as an excuse to get out of the meeting ahead, but the excuse did seem a bit watery.

"Go," Burkhard said. "You two head on back to the ship. One of you should relieve Mr. Schubert, who has been patiently manning the *Chihuahua*'s conn despite his many protests that he never, ever wanted to take command. I figured he needed the experience, even if he insists the command chair makes him break out in hives."

Chris laughed, nodding to Rachel. "He's right. Wolf's probably going stir crazy, by now."

EAS Colony Station Yggdrasil

Vice Admiral Lee Craig, the commander-in-chief of the Fleet side in the Wargame, looked around at the command team she'd been given for the exercise. It was a good bunch – the best of the best, in fact – but she still felt something was missing. Perhaps it was the lack of a 'civilian' representative – Governor Geraci was returning to 94 Ceti with the *Yggdrasil*'s arrival, and the civilian director of the station was too busy with set-up procedures to come to the meeting – but Craig didn't think that was it.

The war room of the *Argus* was filled to standing room only – quite a feat, considering the luxuries afforded the ship the Navy's latest, greatest warships were designed after. Rear Admiral Honeycutt, Commodore Chapelle, and Commodore Klingler all stood at the head of the table, flanking Lee as she allowed everyone the few minutes of gossip time she figured they would need before she settled them down to start the meeting. As she waited, she surveyed the crowd, trying to figure out just what it was she was missing.

Most people in the room were chatting, laughing, and smiling confidently, all unconcerned about their place in the Wargame. The one notable exception to that rule, however, was Captain Martin Wendkos of the *Tarantula*. He looked thoughtful, and appeared to be muttering to himself as he looked around, but beyond that Lee couldn't tell anything about the man's state of mind. Lee refused to allow any doubt to show on her face, but Wendkos has submitted a report on the Academy forces that disturbed her. Curiously, Wendkos was the only person who hadn't brought his executive officer to the meeting – it wasn't mandatory, but it was expected. Especially since a part of the meeting was to go over the reports on the Academy testing Wendkos and the *Tarantula* had just completed.

Wendkos' report was just about the only thing that gave her any doubt about the Wargame's outcome. Everything was coming up roses for the Fleet side, especially since the Yggdrasil had arrived. Three more ships for their side – even if they were just lowly cutters – were a great help. One of the cutters had some technical flaws (an electronics package necessary for interstellar flight hadn't been installed before shipment, and wouldn't be until the Wargame was complete), but so far that was the *only* problem to arise with the Norn station prototype. Nothing had arisen regarding the regular Fleet warships, either, so things were looking good.

Something was still bothering her, however.

Deciding that an appropriate amount of time for socializing had been granted, Lee cleared her throat meaningfully. Within seconds, everyone was quiet and either sitting or standing at attention.

"At ease," Lee said. "Get comfortable, everyone. We're too crowded for formalities, today, and we've got a lot to cover."

The sound of feet shifting as people adjusted themselves accordingly could be heard for the next few seconds, though few people actually looked 'comfortable.'

With a nod from the Vice Admiral, Flag Captain Ivan Zettler (Craig Lee's Chief-of-Staff) stepped forward to officially begin the meeting.

"On behalf of Vice-Admiral Craig," Zettler began, "I would like to welcome you all for coming. While this is the official strategy meeting, attendance was optional for all but a few of you. We're please to see so many of you decided to attend."

In truth, Zettler was not complimenting everyone for coming, but admonishing Captain Wendkos of the *Tarantula* for not producing his exec. That calculated reprimand was not something Craig had or expected Zettler to give. Lee would have to take the man aside in private to discuss the matter with him. Zettler was a new addition to her staff, replacing – of all people – the very man who was currently in charge of the Academy Fleet, 'Commodore' Green. Zettler had come well-recommended, and was known for being able to take the initiative without having to wait for orders, but he still needed to be familiarized with her command style.

"I would also like to thank Commander Kip Skudra of the *Tarantula*," Lee intervened, hoping to negate the sting of Zettler's words. "Who wanted to come, but who I personally ordered attend to a certain detached assignment."

Zettler winced. "Yes, well... with this number of people attending today, we'll skip the introductions. Most of us know each other, anyway, but when called upon please let everyone know who you are and which ship you are attached to. Admiral?"

Lee stood from her chair at the head of the table, steepling her fingers behind her back in a nervous gesture. She hated speaking before large crowds like this, but that was a fear she had to keep silent even from her closest associates if she wanted to be taken seriously. She had long since developed the habit of locking her hands together out-of-sight in order to keep them from waving about.

"Most of you, I suspect, think this year's Wargame is going to be a cakewalk for us," she said, casting her gaze around the room. The trick was to make every officer think that she was talking directly to them without making herself more nervous by locking eyes directly with them. "I admit, at first, I thought the same. Recent reports suggest things might not be so one-sided, however. I believe we must proceed with a more conservative, cautious strategy than I had originally hoped for."

That drew a few brief murmurs from the crowd. Save for the crew of the *Tarantula*, not a single man in the Fleet had any reason to believe that there was any need for a 'conservative, cautious approach' to these war games. They had been looking forward to the freedom an aggressive strategy would allow them, a freedom rarely allowed in most exercises.

"Zettler, the rundown?" Lee said.

"As of right now, we're unsure how many ships the enemy has managed to re-commission. As old as the Sirius class is, they've probably had to fabricate replacement parts. With that sort of delay, the number of completed ships may be in the single digits. There is, however, the possibility that the ships which are completed may be more dangerous than anticipated."

It was Craig's turn again, but thankfully it was only to introduce the only person with first-hand knowledge of just why the Academy fleet might be 'more dangerous than anticipated.'

"One Academy corvette, the *Chihuahua*, was completed early enough for combat drills," Craig began. "With no other Academy ships in commission, they requested we send a few ships to practice with. The controlling officers of the Wargame felt that it was a reasonable request, and directed me to send them a corvette. I sent Captain Wendkos and the *Tarantula*, and he brought back some rather alarming intelligence. Captain Wendkos?"

Wendkos stood up slowly. From his expression, it was plain to see he was feeling a bit spooked.

"My *Tarantula* is one of the newest ships in the fleet. The Hornet class was produced using the same technological architecture as the Argus class battleship – in fact, every piece of advanced technology adopted for the Argus class was tested, first, in Hornet class corvettes like the *Tarantula*. The *Chihuahua* is over a century old, and any attempts to refurbish her should have been limited by the obsolete architecture in her structure. Therefore, in terms of class performance, there should have been no comparison. "

"However, this was not evident during the drill," Wendkos continued, activating the holographic projectors to provide a rotating three-dimensional representation of the ship he had encountered. "The *Chihuahua* clearly has undergone extensive modification, as demonstrated during our combat drills. Visual observations alone showed that they had replaced the antiquated sensors with modern systems. The new sensors give them targeting and tactical systems up to modern warship standards. Furthermore, the addition of the hydrogen collection towers, seen here, indicate the inclusion of a cold fusion reactor inside the ship. More unusual, however, was the addition of quantum wheel emitters... but on the side of the ship, not on the rear, while the fusion drive was retained.

"As it turns out, that was their greatest innovation. She was incredibly fast – the fastest warship I've ever seen, and I am not naive enough to believe they let us see her top speed. She also came to a dead stop faster than just about any ship I've ever heard of. None of those are the important facts, however. What *is* important I can sum up in just six words: They have working energy shields."

Murmurs arose at that information, many of them in disbelief. Craig understood the doubt. She had been just as skeptical until she reviewed the logs of the action herself. She had a better perspective than anyone else on the situation – she knew 'Commodore' Green better than any of the people present, which gave her a pretty good idea of just what state the Academy fleet was in.

"A thought, Admiral?" the battleship *Yamato*'s captain interjected, receiving a nod from Craig to continue. "This is a Wargame, after all, so any weapon effects are being simulated by computer. Could their shields be just a simulation instituted by the control cell as a handicap to even the odds?"

"No," replied Craig, once more taking her place at the forefront of the table. "The existence of this shield technology was confirmed not only by the testimony of Assistant Naval Constructor Hodge Coles, who is in charge of estimating weapon and armor effectiveness for all Wargame simulations, but also by sensor logs from the *Tarantula*. The *Chihuahua* was running live shields – not some simulated handicap. The good news – at least from a Wargame perspective – is that we know there are weaknesses to the shield system. Moreover, it's unlikely that every Academy warship has been equipped with it. We'll still need to use caution before engaging in any sort of action, however, until we learn which ships have it and which don't. Consequently, before we can start any large-scale operations, we need to ascertain just what the state of the Academy is. We need intelligence badly.

"To that end, I have asked Commander Kip Skudra, the exec of the *Tarantula*, to officially commission the Orbital Guard cutters *Valhalla* and the *Sleipnir* for the duration of the Wargame. We will be sending these ships into both the neutral and the Academy systems as scouts. We believe a simple external scan of each ship will provide us with the necessary information, as our technical analysts believe the side-mounted quantum wheel nodes act as the shield emitters. Once we have that information, we can make our plans accordingly."

The sounds of whispered conversation between captains and their officers rose and fell, but to her surprise no-one was asking any questions. As Zettler dismissed the meeting, Craig took a deep breath. The hard part was out of the way – now all she had to do was fight a 'war.'

Chapter XX

"Captain, I'm receiving an odd transmission," a voice called through the intercom. Commander Kip Skudra, now the acting-captain of the *Sleipnir*, could not identify the voice on the intercom. None of *Sleipnir's* crew were regular Navy, having been 'loaned' to the Fleet by the newly formed colony's Orbital Guard along with the three armed cutters. Being addressed as 'Captain' was an event Skudra had long looked forward to, but he was rather disappointed with this, his first command. Nevertheless, he was resolved to command her to the best of his ability.

"A transmission? Who from?" Skudra's ship had been the only presence in the neutral system since they arrived. His surveillance mission expired in only two more hours, and if he made no contact before that deadline he was to return to Fleet space for further instructions. His crew was to comm him the second any hint of another ship was detected. It shouldn't be possible for someone to get close enough to transmit a signal without his having a warning of their approach, first.

"It... it appears to be a remote buoy, sir. Pre-recorded transmission, sir – a looping message on repeat. We didn't see it until the transmission began."

A buoy? Why would they be getting a transmission from a buoy? For that matter, how did a buoy get placed there before they arrived, anyway?

"Put it through. And give me the whole thing, from the top."

"Yes, sir," came the voice from the end, followed by an electronic click as the transmission was being set up for him.

The voice on the other end was one he wasn't familiar with, but he recognized the authority indicative of a command-grade officer behind it. His comm system automatically started running voice-print software, and within a few seconds displayed a tagline indicating that the voice was Commander Jonathan Daniels, Captain of the battleship *Superb*. The speaker wasn't important, though – it was the words which followed that caught his attention.

"Attention, *Sleipnir*. This is Task Force One of the Academy Forces. Our orders were to destroy any 'Fleet' ship we encountered in this system, but Admiral Mumford informed us to regard the *Yggdrasil's* cutters as armed civilian craft on Fleet's side rather than 'regular' Naval vessels. With this in mind, we used our discretion to bypass your ship. Consider yourselves lucky.

"By the time you hear this, you will have failed what we assume to be your mission – that is, to scout out enemy ships and give advanced warning of any approach to your home fleet. Because, as of this moment, Task Force One is currently in your home system, engaging in operations... and it is too late for you to stop us.

"Sorry about that, but we thought you might enjoy a consolation prize. Therefore, please allow the Ad-Hoc Sirius Symphony Chorus to regale you with a lovely ballad to demonstrate that we hold no grudges against you."

The speaker left for a moment, and soon an odd synthesized music started playing, a very ancient form of music. The words accompanying it were a tune Skudra had never heard before, but were so hauntingly upbeat that he couldn't help but feel humiliated.

"The wind was rising easterly, the morning sky was blue,
The Straits before us opened wide and free..."

Skudra couldn't help but listen to the entire refrain of *Old Superb* before turning off the speaker. A wrenching feeling was forming in his stomach. He wondered if allowing the Academy fleet the opportunity to deliver this kind of taunt was enough to cost him that better command in the future.

EAS Colony Station Yggdrasil

Vice-Admiral Lee Craig was in a meeting with the Yggdrasil station's director going over some last-minute logistical details when the alarm sounded. The meeting also included a simulated electronics fault that was jamming in-station communications, and coincidentally Lee was unable to contact her people to find out what the alarm was about. She didn't have to wait for an answer, however, as one of the civilian colonists burst into the room, panicked.

"Excuse me, Vice-Admiral, Director Morisato, but I think this could qualify as an emergency," the colonist said between gasps for air. "Long-range sensors are detecting a squadron of Academy ships infiltrating the system."

Craig's eyes widened. Her greatest strategic advantage in this war was her knowledge of Acting-Commodore Green's tendencies. Green, she knew, stuck precisely to the book for tactical problems. The book would definitely not approve of any sort of sortie into the Fleet system at this juncture. And yet here they were.

"Please tell me it's not a large force – half of our ships aren't able to move until we're done with the last-minute set-up of the *Yggdrasil* station!" Craig said, unable to rein in her frustration at being caught off-guard.

"I was reporting to the Director," the colonist snorted. The glare that the Vice-Admiral sent him in response caused him to swallow some of that civilian flippancy. "But I might as well let you know, too. It appears to be just four or five ships, though at that range we can't be certain of their numbers. Tracking seems to indicate that it's a single battleship and three or four corvettes. Only one of the corvettes is moving, but it's coming extremely fast. Too fast to safely maneuver, I'd say."

Well, that fit the Commodore Green she knew a little better. He would never agree to any large-scale operations against them, at this stage of the war, but he might be talked into authorizing a scouting mission if his subordinates were persistent enough. Failing to anticipate such an operation might have been a slight failing on her part, but she could easily turn this mistake into a victory.

"Too fast to maneuver, eh?" Lee mused. "Not a bad idea to try and speed through our ranks before we can react, but I think it's going to be 'fatal' for whoever is aboard that corvette; we've spotted them too early. Message to all ships on watch status: target the projected flight path of that corvette, and open fire as you bear. Director Morisato, does this station have any form of command and control facilities?"

Morisato nodded. "Yes, ma'am. I don't believe they're up to military standards, and they still require some post-deployment set-up, but they should be sufficient for viewing the action."

The Vice Admiral nodded. "Very well." She turned to the colonist and asked, "Could you get in touch with the rest of my staff on this station and ask them to meet me in the command and control center, ASAP?"

"Sure thing, boss!" the colonist chirped, disappearing before Craig could say anything in reply.

Shaking her head, Craig addressed the station director. "Mr. Morisato, I think when this is all over you need to talk to your people about protocol. I understand he's a civilian, but 'boss' is not the proper form of address for *any* naval officer... much less a flag officer."

EAS Chihuahua

At the precise moment a certain buoy started transmitting to the *Sleipnir,* Academy Task Force One initiated their synchronized operation in Fleet space. All four ships emerged from hyperspace at extreme sensor range, with sensors scanning outward as soon as they were through the temporary rips they had created between normal space and hyperspace.

An open data feed was immediately forwarded from the *Inkadh* to the *Chihuahua,* and in less then a minute Rachel Katz, with Captain Morrison 'observing her work' over her shoulder, had managed to plot an optimum safe path through the enemy ships and orbital structures. And just like that, the *Chihuahua* was off.

"Well?" Burkhard asked.

"My sensors show they're reacting as expected," Rachel said after a moment. "Although they're being more subtle about it then I would have thought. And only about half of their ships appear to be prepped for action – I'd say they were a touch overconfident."

"Not surprising," Burkhard muttered.

"Rache, could you send me the real-time data on the *Yggdrasil* station?" Chris asked from his position as the bridge engineering liaison. "I would like to see just how much of the post-deployment set-up has been completed. Oh, and I'd like to see if they've made the modifications necessary to turn their terraforming station into an EMP weapon."

"Copying the data to your terminal," she replied formally. She made a mental note to reprimand him later in private. Calling her 'Rache' when they were off-duty might be... allowable, but she had *both* of their careers to think of now that they were involved... and if there was one thing that she could do to improve both of their careers, it was making sure that he addressed her properly when on duty, at the very least.

"Time to the first turn?" Schubert asked from the helm.

This was Cohen's responsibility from the backup tactical position, but for some reason he didn't respond right away. Rachel looked in his direction for a split second, seeing him looking awfully confused.

"Mr. Cohen?" Burkhard prompted.

"Sir... I'm not sure what to make of it. I... I think I'm experiencing a terminal malfunction. I... the data isn't making sense."

Chris looked up. "Should I check it out, Captain?"

Burkhard nodded. "Go ahead. Ms. Katz, please take over for Mr. Cohen until the problem is resolved."

Rachel clucked, but checked the data anyway. The reason for having two tactical officers on the bridge at once was more than just to provide redundancy – it was to allow the tactical officers to concentrate on just one or two points of data at a time, and to forward more precise results to the needed people. However, it was not unreasonable for her to assume both jobs, in this case – just unexpected.

"One minute until we hit the nearest ships firing arc, so... first turn in forty-five seconds, mark."

"Son of a bitch," Chris muttered from Cohen's station. "Sir, we have a *simulated* malfunction on the sensors, tracked to a virus introduced by the Wargame control committee, signed Hodge Coles. We're apparently scheduled to have a variety of malfunctions over the next two days, and this is one of them... and there is nothing we can do as a preventative measure for them. This 'simulated malfunction' concept is a potential navigation and safety hazard, goddammit! I do understand the need to simulate unplanned defects, but not this kind, and not so early out of port! Give us a few days to see what she's really like, first!"

Burkhard coughed, and Anne Morrison shifted uncomfortably. Both were in silent agreement with the cadet, but neither were exactly comfortable with his lack of professionalism. "Mr. Desaix, please watch your language while we have a guest on the bridge," he noted, pointing to Captain Morrison. "That said, is there anything you can do to fix it?"

"Sorry, sir. I've already done what I can – I gave it the 'pass code' and my student id number. It says I have to remain here for three minutes, enter it again, and then the station will be 'released.'"

Burkhard sighed. "Well, it can't be helped. Return to your own station – we'll have Mr. Cohen handling that malfunction.

"Yes, sir," Cohen said, flipping a few switches.

"In the meantime, best guess for when to turn, anybody?"

"By running the numbers for dead reckoning, and assuming no unexpected ship maneuvers by the Fleet, I think we turn in ten seconds," came from Rachel's position. "Five. Four. Three. Two. One... mark!"

EAS Colony Station Yggdrasil

"I'm *still* having trouble believing what I'm seeing." was the greeting Vice-Admiral Craig received as she entered the command and control room, already occupied by Captain Zettler and a few civilian workers.

"Status?" the Vice-Admiral snapped.

Zettler snapped to attention. "It appears, ma'am, as if the approaching ship is traveling at a speed of over 0.3c in normal space and *turning* at the same time. The remaining ships continue to hang back, observing."

Craig's eyes widened, but only for a second. "Well, we knew they'd developed some pretty impressive tech in the Academy. I wonder if this is another one of Cadet Desaix's inventions?"

Morisato, standing at Craig's side, blinked. "Desaix?"

"He's being credited, according to the Wargame control cell, with the development of shield technology and other unspecified advances." With a rueful grimace, Lee continued, "It appears as if we've just seen a demonstration of one of those unspecified advances."

Morisato coughed. "Yes, ma'am. I thought that name sounded familiar. If he's who I think he is, I'm quite familiar with Mr. Desaix. As an intern, he was on the development team for this station."

Lee turned to the man for a moment, raising an eyebrow. "How much does he know? I would think, as an intern, his access to much of the classified technology would be limited, but if you know him personally...."

"Only by reputation, ma'am," Morisato sighed. "K1 offered him a long-term contract, but he was determined to join the Navy. Him turning down the deal was big news in the rumor mill when it happened. He was heavily involved in some of the satellites and ancillary vehicles – designed one of them, in fact – but I doubt he knew much more than what the promotional material stated about the station itself. I think there was more to him then I knew, though, because there were classified documents in his personnel records I was not given access to. I have no idea what those records dealt with, but I'd assume they had something to do with the Azumah Station Incident."

"Just my luck," Craig muttered. "My one opportunity to lead the Navy in the Wargame comes when the Academy has a bloody engineering genius available to design things like shield technology and impossibly fast ships."

"Ma'am," Zettler called. "We've identified the corvette as the *Chihuahua*... and she's coming directly for this center."

Craig winced. "Crap."

EAS Chihuahua

"Captain," Chris said from his engineering station. "Now that the simulated malfunction has been corrected, I was able to evaluate our current situation. The dead reckoning turn was closer than we had any right to expect, but it still put us slightly off course. If we follow our intended flight plan, the *Chihuahua* will get within firing range of *Yggdrasil* station."

Burkhard turned to him. "How serious of a problem is that likely to be?"

Chris shook his head. "Not a problem, an opportunity. *Yggdrasil* station has a command and control center which would be an excellent target – both for the damage to system defenses and the potential to hit significant personnel. With a very minor course correction, this command center will pass directly within our firing arc. We may pass within the range of an EMP blast if we do, but only if they've completed modifications to the terraforming satellite. Based on the current data, I don't believe they have."

Burkhard nodded and hummed to himself in thought. "Feed the target over to Mr. Cohen and let him calculate the course correction. Copy it over to Ms. Katz so that she can evaluate any threats you might have missed. Mr. Schubert, I expect you to be ready to maneuver at a moment's notice."

"Standing by," Schubert answered, having plotted the course change on his board before Cohen's corrections had arrived. He'd worked it out for himself the moment Chris had started speaking.

"Make the correction. Mr. DiMarco?"

Cadet Midshipman Luke DiMarco, the Weapons Control Officer on duty, shifted uncomfortably in his seat. "I think I've got a usable firing pattern already plotted, but I'll need Mr. Cohen's course corrections to be sure."

"Sent," Cohen noted.

"Plotted," Schubert shot back almost instantly, noting with a glance that Cohen's data matched his own.

"Making minor correction... and ready, sir," DiMarco answered crisply.

"Fire when in range."

EAS Superb

Commander Jonathan Daniels noticed that his tactical officer, Naval Reserve Lieutenant Thomas Eure, was gaping at his readout. Sighing, he decided to figure out what had the man in such a state.

"Report!" he snapped.

Eure shuddered slightly, turning to the *Superb's* captain. "I think Burkhard is insane."

Daniels raised an eyebrow. He might have expected that of a younger cadet, but a reservist was supposed to have had enough training to avoid such undisciplined statements.

"Explain," he finally said.

"The *Chihuahua* is actually strafing *Yggdrasil* station. In doing so, they're putting themselves in the firing lane of the EMP satellite and possibly as many as a dozen warships – they're going to get themselves 'killed,' pulling a stunt like this, sir," Eure explained.

Daniels sighed. If he hadn't known Burkhard, he might have agreed with Eure. Knowing Burkhard, though, he figured there was some plan in mind that was more likely to work than not. That assumed Burkhard was in charge, however – the Wargame Control officers were known to 'replace' the regular captain at certain strategically difficult moments, just to gauge how well the junior officers stepped up to more senior tasks in a crisis. Daniels thought it was a little early to for them to start that kind of thing, though.

"The *Chihuahua* is a rather impressive ship with a rather impressive crew. They may know something we don't," he said. "And I would suggest that you not call one of my in-laws insane in my presence."

Eure winced, realizing his mistake. "My apologies, sir. I was... taken by surprise."

Daniels sighed. "Of course. Just remember not to do it again."

EAS Chihuahua

"Enemy ships are about to lock weapons onto our flight trajectory," Rachel warned. "Estimate fifteen seconds."

"Mr. Schubert?" Burkhard snapped.

"Ready, sir," Wolf shot back.

"Begin maneuvers in five seconds," Rachel said. "Three... two... one...."

EAS Superb

"Enemy ships are firing on the *Chihuahua,* sir!" Lt. Eure reported. "She can't avoid... Uh, never mind. I..."

Daniels waited, but nothing further came from his tactical officer. "Well?" he prompted.

Eure shook his head in disbelief. "Sorry, sir -- too much happening at once. The *Chihuahua* dodged crossfire by decelerating to a complete stop in the three seconds of time it took for the incoming fire from the enemy ships to reach their trajectory. Then, they went back to full acceleration... after launching a rail gun assault against the command and control section of the *Yggdrasil* station. They've now managed to speed out of firing range before anyone was able to lock a new firing solution on them."

Daniels shook his head. Very little surprised him about that particular corvette, and nothing surprised him about what his brother-in-law could manage.

"As I said, Mr. Eure," Daniels finally sighed. "She is a rather impressive ship."

EAS Colony Station Yggdrasil

Vice-Admiral Lee Craig continued to gawk at what the sensor readings told her, no longer able to maintain any visible sense of composure. "The reports... We had advance warning about that technology, we knew about the personnel well enough to prepare for them, and still... "

A cough came from behind her. Spinning around, Craig was greeted by the contrite expression of Assistant Chief Constructor Hodge Coles, who had just arrived for his final inspection of the *Yggdrasil* station for the war games an hour earlier.

"I just received a transmission by this system's chief Wargame Control Officer, from on board the *Hippopotamus*-class tender *Fruit Bat.* He wanted me to relay a message, as no Control Officers have been assigned to the *Yggdrasil* Station just yet."

Lee nodded, gesturing for Ivan Zettler and Morisato to come up beside her. "Go on, Mr. Coles. How bad is the 'damage' he's assessed?"

"No offense, ma'am, but I'm afraid that is no longer your concern," Coles sighed. "Everyone in this command and control station is a KIA-casualty, for the duration of the Wargame. No exceptions, although civilian employees such as Mr. Morisato may resume their normal civilian duties provided they avoid roles supporting naval personnel or functions."

"I'm sorry, say that again?" she goggled.

Coles laughed bitterly. "Ma'am, if you believed that being the commander in chief of the Regular Navy forces would grant you some form of immunity from the casualty lists, I'm afraid you're mistaken. I believe the quote that he gave me was, 'Sometimes, in a real war, important leaders are killed right off the bat. The Navy must learn to cope with that in a drill, so that when it happens in real life we are prepared.' And so, ma'am, I fear you have been 'killed.'" His next laugh was entirely genuine. "Actually, ma'am, think of it this way – until the Wargame has ended, one way or another, you get a paid vacation. From here on out, it's Rear Admiral Honeycutt's war to fight. You are welcome to continue to observe, however."

EAS Chihuahua

"Mission, completed, sir," Rachel reported as the *Chihuahua* outran all pursuers to reunite with the rest of the task force. "And we still have a secret or two we haven't shown them."

Burkhard grinned fiercely. "Well, now – I suspect even 'Commodore' Green will have a bit of praise for that, even if we didn't quite go 'by the book.'"

Part III

The
Promotion
of Pawns

Chapter XXI

61 Cygni, Orbital Drydock

"Ambassador," Captain Tager said in greeting, as Noriko Goldsmith entered his office on the *Valkyrie*. They were still all still stuck in 61 Cygni, so he was a bit surprised to receive a visitor. "To what do I owe the honor of your return to my ship?"

Goldsmith hesitated, glancing around. "Captain... Is your ship ready to fly? I mean, in an emergency?"

Tager considered. "Well, the quantum wheels haven't been fully re-tuned yet, and there are some other maintenance issues we would like to take care of, but in a pinch we could get the ship underway in a couple hours. Why?"

"Where is Vice-Admiral Breslau's fleet? And how quickly can we rendezvous with them, assuming you left as soon as possible?"

"I'm not sure where he would be at this time," Tager replied. "He was given free reign to navigate his squadrons where he felt appropriate, and was only required to make check-ins at certain locations. I wouldn't be able to catch him even if I knew where he was, though. I could make it to one of those rendezvous points in few days, however. Again, why?"

"It may already be too late, but we have time critical intelligence that must be delivered to his squadron and to Home Fleet," Goldsmith said. "And I think you'll see why time is of the essence when you hear what that information is...."

Sol System, Earth Orbit, EAS Mohawk

Admiral Ken Pratchet sighed as he completed the last of his paperwork for the evening. This particular set of paperwork was supposed to have been done by Captain Theodore Bradford of the *Camel*, who was in charge of the escort forces for the science expedition which had left for Pleiades just hours before. It should not have been his job at all, but in some convoluted way – partly due to the massive manpower drain brought about by the Wargame – he was the only person left with the authority and knowledge to complete it.

He sipped on his coffee and looked outside of the observation deck of his flagship, the Argus class battleship *Mohawk*. Normally, these massive windows were covered by thick doors and the exterior image was a motion-reduced projection instead of a genuine view of space. However, that was only when the ship was moving – while in a station-keeping orbit and not on alert status, those doors could safely be opened. The view was quite popular – especially for those inevitable young couples that developed on co-ed warships with thousands of crewmen. There were some token regulations made in an attempt to keep fraternization from damaging the performance of the crew, but it was kind of hard to prevent a little bit of romance from developing in a service branch which had grown on the backs of a pre-FTL Navy employing sublight ships to get to the stars. When centuries of Naval tradition required its members to 'to procreate in sufficient numbers that the ship can be manned and maintained for several generations of flight,' rules against fraternization were hard to bring back.

Pratchet was neither young, nor (since becoming a widower) part of a couple, yet he had definitely been in need of some stress relief when he received the word that Bradford had left without completing most of his required paperwork. The observation deck was suitable for his needs, although he was a little ashamed at chasing away a couple of blossoming young lovers just so that he could relax a bit. Nevertheless, he loved looking out at the stars and the colors of the universe.

He saw something odd when he looked up this time, however. He quickly reached over and pressed a comm button. "Admiral Pratchet to the Bridge."

"Bridge, here, sir."

"I'm down in the observation deck, and I'm seeing what looks like either a meteor shower or a large number of ships approaching. I wasn't informed of either, so I'd like to know what's going on."

There was a long pause. "Sir... I'm not picking anything up on the passive scanners, so I assume it's a meteor shower of some kind. I'll go to active to confirm, however, if you would like."

"Proceed."

Another pause. "You'd better get up here, sir. I've asked the corvette *Pike* to confirm, but... I think we have a bloody armada incoming."

Earth Alliance Naval Academy, Admiral's Office

"Admiral McCaffrey!" a panicked aide cried, storming into the Admiral's office in the Academy facilities. "Sir! We've got an emergency, sir!"

McCaffrey snorted, glancing up at the man. "Lieutenant Hrkac, calm yourself, take a deep breath, and explain. Considering where we are and what we're doing, there's hardly much chance of your emergency being so vital that you give yourself a heart attack trying to deliver it."

Wade Hrkac, the Flag Lieutenant assigned to the (nearly empty, at this time) Academy Head Office, didn't pause to take a breath as ordered, nor did he calm down. But his words explained exactly why in a heartbeat. "Sir! There were no plans for the Wargame to have any operations in Earth orbit, were there?"

McCaffrey frowned. "Of course not. Why?"

"Because that is the only alternative explanation for the large fleet which was just seen in orbit. Sir, Earth fleet is under attack!"

McCaffrey stood up, horror dawning on him. "Under attack? By who?"

"We don't know yet, sir," Hrkac explained. "The war room is being set up as we speak, and Admiral Pratchet is relaying transmissions as close to live as possible."

"Lead the way!"

McCaffrey had only been to the Academy's earth-side command and control center a few times in his career – it rarely was run by anything other than Academy officers and their immediate supervisors as part of their training, even if it was as fully equipped as any other Naval stations C&C center – so he needed Hrkac to guide him. Otherwise, he probably would have sprinted there faster then the lieutenant.

"Admiral on deck!" the call went as he stepped inside. There was a mere skeleton crew available at the Academy due to the Wargame.

Nevertheless, in the short time since the attack, the staff had managed to find people to man each station. But not a single one stood to attention or even flinched when McCaffrey entered the room – they were all too busy, or too absorbed in what they were seeing to notice.

"Report!" he demanded, ignoring the slight. This was a situation where infringements of the rules of protocol could be forgiven.

Captain Jyrki Ahonen, the current Chief of the Watch and a former staff member of McCaffrey's, stepped up and saluted him. "A large force of ships, apparently employing stealth technology the likes of which we are unfamiliar with, has entered Sol system, bypassing outer defenses and approaching Earth orbit. Admiral Pratchet on the *Mohawk* was the first to see them, and he sent the *Pike* to investigate. *Pike* was destroyed before it could complete its report."

McCaffrey grimaced. "Size of force? Origin?"

"Origin unknown. Pratchet will be sending down a size estimate at the first opportunity, although he warns us it will not be precise. Even with active scans, we're having a hard time detecting them."

"Pratchet's transmission coming in now, sir!" a petty officer McCaffrey didn't recognize called.

"Put it on speakers. We should all hear what we're dealing with," McCaffrey snapped.

"...will be relaying this feed straight to command, live, until the battle is over," Pratchet's voice was saying. "They are already inside our defensive perimeter. We're trying to organize the fleet into formation, but it may be too late. Too many ships are using skeleton crews because personnel are on liberty, and some ships even have cold engines. By the time we're all maneuverable, they'll be through our line.

"This is what we know of their numbers: As of the latest count, they have approximately fifty battleships, forty frigates, and seventy cruisers. That means we're vastly outnumbered, but we should have enough battleships to match theirs if we can get together. Outside of their advanced stealth systems, they haven't displayed anything to make me believe their ships are any better than ours, so we stand a pretty good shot of matching them in a stand-up fight. If anything, they're a bit below us technologically – we detect no quantum wheel signatures. A shame – that would allow us to penetrate their stealth, better.

"However, they also are escorting at least a hundred troop transports – enough to deploy approximately five million soldiers and all of their equipment. It is vital that Army Command musters forces, now. Our initial targets will be these transports."

"Tactical display on main screen," Ahonen called over the sound of the transmission before McCaffrey even thought about it.

The situation shown on the large display panel wasn't pretty. The plotted positions of the known enemy ships showed they were definitely on an attack run. Home Fleet was completely disorganized. Fortunately, most of the Home Fleet – even the unarmed museum ships – were starting to show signs of movement. The museum ships were just scurrying for cover, of course, but the rest of the fleet... well, most people would think they were running away, too, to be honest.

McCaffrey, however, knew Pratchet's tactical preferences fairly well, and caught it after seeing the course corrections each ship was making. "Good thinking, Pratchet," he mused aloud. He was saying this aloud mostly for the benefit of the junior officers, who were increasingly nervous as Home Fleet appeared to flee. "Slingshotting around the moon will let you attack those troop transports in the rear."

The minutes ticked by as the war room staff watched silently, transmitted reports from Pratchet and other officers the only sounds anyone noticed. The maneuvers McCaffrey predicted had begun in earnest, but slow-moving stragglers were left to fend for themselves and wound up being easily overwhelmed by their attackers. Vice Admiral Walter Chan, in his Cleopatra-class battleship *Netzahualcoyotl,* fell trying to build a strike element with four of the other aged Cleopatras and two Valkyrie class cruisers which could not join the rest of the fleet. The names of the destroyed ships – *Netzahualcoyotl, Hecate, Darwin, Raleigh, Danae, Vampire,* and *Proteus* – started scrolling across the screen in stark red lettering, joining the corvette *Pike* as victims of this assault. Before the mass of the Earth fleet could begin its counterstrike on the troop transports, other ships joined that list – the battleship *Revenge,* the light cruisers *Mole* and *Consort,* and the frigate *Leopard.* McCaffrey's eyes latched onto that last one – one of his favorite nephews was on board that ship, serving as the first officer. It was highly unlikely anyone survived its destruction.

"Now beginning counterstrike," Pratchet's voice intoned. "We... oh my God!"

"Sir!" Lieutenant Hrkac, now sitting at one of the monitoring stations, called. "We've just detected more ships hiding in the sensor distortion of the troop carriers. Over a hundred of them – another fifty battleships, seventy heavy cruisers, possibly more."

McCaffrey's eyes widened. "What? How is that possible? Who the hell could muster one hundred battleships for a single battle?"

"Continue the assault!" Pratchet's voice echoed over the comm system. The open channel now also relayed the cacophony of voices from a dozen bridge personnel all trying to talk at once, some quite agitated. "Those troop carriers are our top priority, even over our own survival!"

It got hard to follow after that, as transmissions started overlapping. Pratchet could still be heard barking orders over the comm system, but his words became indistinct among the other voices. Meanwhile, the tactical display continued to show the battle as it progressed. Rear Admiral Percival Leeming and his flagship, the *Corona*, had command of the point, but the entire squadron he was commanding was wiped out in minutes after being caught in the trap. Battleships *Corona, Tripoli, Freedom, Niagara, Horne,* and *Coronado* joined the list scrolling at the bottom of the screen. The smaller ships were not spared – the corvettes *Carp* and *Octopus*, the frigate *Roanoke,* and the heavy cruisers *Sylph* and *Kronos. Niagara* and *Horne* were the first of Earth's proud Argus-class battleships to ever be destroyed, which slammed McCaffrey's morale harder than he thought possible.

The death of Admiral Pratchet hit even harder, the Mohawk vanishing from the tactical map seconds before his voice cut off. Pratchet's death caused at least one of the younger officers in the war room to break down crying. Many others had oddly detached expressions on their face. McCaffrey was only able to function because his long active duty experience had left him on automatic.

Command of Home Fleet then fell to Vice Admiral Lonnie Hornblower, but she and her flagship *Grizzly Bear* were destroyed before she even knew she was in charge. Only one flag officer in Home Fleet, aboard the flagship *Antelope,* remained alive by that point: Rear Admiral Jacques King. King, however, did not assume command – whether because she didn't know she was, or because she had frozen in the growing horror as so many others in the room were, no-one could say by that point.

There were still some remaining moments of bravery left for Home Fleet. Captain Duncan Black, of the *Skjoldebrand,* saw that no-one was taking charge and did so himself. He organized an ad-hoc squadron of nearby ships and pressed the assault on the troop carriers, taking out several of them. He actually rammed his battleship through one troop carrier, taking significant damage to his own ship but remaining in action despite it. McCaffrey spared a moment to look at the stats, and saw that already at least half of the troop ships were gone. Even one was too many, though – twenty troop ships could carry enough to match the largest organized Army on earth. Five could establish a significant beachhead and hold it for years. One could potentially hold out long enough for reinforcements to arrive from whoever the attacker was.

The battleship *Ranger,* commanded by Capt. Gustavo Eccleston, took over when *Skjoldebrand* was destroyed. By now, only thirty-four of the ninety-nine warships which had started the day as a battle-ready Home Fleet were still able to fly at all. The reason for King's lack of response was now known – the *Antelope,* while still able to fly, was nevertheless little more than a hulk. As it became clear that no-one was officially in command, the fleet went into an 'every man for himself' mode. *Ranger* organized a small core force consisting of the battleships *Boadicea, Alamo,* and *Ceres,* the heavy cruiser *Valhalla,* light cruisers *Wolf* and *Terrier,* the frigates *Panther, Jaguar, Constellation, Phoenix*, and *Falcon,* and the tiny corvette *Bee.* That core, small as it was, proved effective once in formation, and continued destroying as many troop carriers as possible.

McCaffrey wanted to do something. He wanted to officially put Eccleston in charge of the fleet and end the disorganized scramble that a lack of flag officers was causing, but by that point there was no way to make a fleet-wide transmission. That they were even able to receive all the tactical data they were getting – both on their own forces and on the enemies – was something of a marvel, considering how much electronic interference the battle itself was producing. The people inside the Academy's war room were helpless to do anything except watch the names of the ships scroll down, each representing hundreds or thousands of lives. The silence in the war room was intense.

"Alert the students." McCaffrey barked, desperate to do *something,* even if he couldn't save his comrades in space. "All cadets left on base are ordered to report to the disaster shelters and await further instructions. Issue sidearms with live ammo to all personnel, on my authorization."

Sirens started blaring throughout the Academy compound, but no-one in the war room flinched. Their gazes were locked on the main screen as more and more ships were destroyed. The frigate *Victory* had picked a fight with no fewer than five of the enemy battleships, apparently hoping to draw some of the attackers off of *Ranger's* squadron. Remarkably, it was able to destroy one of them before succumbing to defeat, itself. Idly, as if in a trance, McCaffrey thought that a certain Mr. Chris Desaix's belief that the *Venture* class frigates were the best ships in the Navy was proving to be true. Unfortunately, the 'pride of the fleet,' the Argus class, was not faring as well. The *Guerrico* and the *Nimrod,* the only surviving members of that class in Home Fleet outside of the *Ranger,* were swarmed by a host of smaller ships and were being picked apart, unable to respond effectively.

Eccleston's core of ships were not unscathed – the battleship *Ceres* was destroyed shortly after the *Victory* fell – but it was also growing as other ships recognized it as the only organized unit remaining and joined him in formation. The battleships *Midway, Ticonderoga,* and *Terrible* replaced the fallen ship... at least for a time.

Some of the Fleet ships, damaged beyond usefulness, began to make their withdrawals. The battleship *Invincible* was destroyed trying to retreat, but a few made it far enough away to jump out into hyperspace. The corvette *Leech* and frigates *Java* and *Mallard* made their escape that way. The *Boxer*, a light cruiser whose weapons and hyperdrive were completely destroyed, had found a hiding spot that the nameless enemy apparently couldn't see it from. Every man in that war room felt dismayed whenever one of those ships made a run for it, but no-one could blame them.

The enemy was taking significant losses, as well. Before being wrecked by a powerful concentration of rail gun fire, the cruiser *Guerriere* killed six ships, including one cruiser and three troop carriers. Though crippled in the end her hull remained largely intact, and McCaffrey prayed that her crew would live through this battle.

Eccleston's core force seemed to escape the brunt of the damage, but others unable to join him were being wiped out with regularity. The heavy cruiser *Dragon,* under Captain Ernie Duval, tried to collect the light cruiser *Ram* and three surviving frigates to cover the retreating museum ships. They were crushed rapidly, however – giving more then they took, but just as dead as if they had remained separate.

Finally, the last ships not already destroyed or crippled joined up with *Ranger* and took positions in formation. McCaffrey looked at the board indicating numbers, and saw that all but two of the troop ships were destroyed. There was a virtual wall between Eccleston's small force and those two troop ships, however, and there wasn't any chance of piercing it to get to them. McCaffrey sighed – it wouldn't be pleasant, but Earth could hold out against two troop ships.

"Can anyone get a signal up to *Ranger?*" he asked softly. He wasn't sure who he was asking, but he figured someone would be able to answer him.

"We've been working on that since the battle began. It took a while, but we can make single ship transmissions now, sir," Captain Ahonen replied somberly.

"Then send this to Eccleston on my authority. 'Mission complete. Army can take it from here. Retreat.' Then get the weapons chief on line and have him start issuing those sidearms."

There was a brief pause as everyone realized just what McCaffrey was saying. Earth probably could survive an assault from two troop carriers, yes, but it would not be easy.

There wasn't really any other choice, however, and everyone there knew that. "Yes, sir," Hrkac replied from his station. "Transmitting now. They're receiving... and replying."

Eccleston's voice was garbled, both by electronic interference and by the sounds of his ship breaking apart around him, but it nevertheless conveyed they message he was trying to send.

"Not one enemy soldier will set foot on Earth. Court-martial me if you like, Admiral, but we're not done yet."

Thus began what could only be described as a suicide charge into the teeth of the enemy force. *Boadicea,* a century old battleship of the Cleopatra class, was the first to fall. She had stood in the line fighting just as fiercely as if she were an Argus or another premiere battleship, taking punishment as great as the newest and most advanced battleship could manage until her aged frame finally couldn't handle it any more. The *Venture* was crippled and fell behind her fellow ships. Every cruiser, heavy and light, found itself taking on three battleships, and every frigate at least one.

Only the battleship *Ranger,* the frigate *Jaguar,* and the light cruisers *Terrier* and *Wolf* survived the charge through the line. *Ranger* spun to provide a rear guard and was quickly destroyed, making Eccleston's potential court martial moot. Not that anyone would have dared press charges against him at that point.

His efforts had bought the other ships time, however. One last ship remained between the three survivors of Eccleston's charge and the two troop carriers... but that one ship was a battleship. *Jaguar* rammed the battleship nose to nose, both ships exploding in brief, silent flashes of fire as their internal oxygen burned out. *Terrier* and *Wolf* both collided with enemy ships as well, running through the broadsides of the two troop carriers. The transports were destroyed, but the two light cruisers were not. *Wolf* was disabled, however, and *Terrier* probably couldn't escape. It spun, as well, limping over to cover its comrade in a final show of defiance, bracing itself for destruction.

The battle, however, was over. Once the troop ships were gone, the attacking fleet seemed to hover in indecision for several moments. After a long, tense moment, the enemy fleet disappeared, just as mysteriously as it had come.

The battle was over. And, astonishingly, Home Fleet had won.

Both surviving ships of it.

Chapter XXII

Sol System, Orbital Guard Station Alpha

The Naval Liaison Office's conference room on board Orbital Guard Station Alpha hadn't been so active since it had been carved out of an old storage room some three years before. It also just happened to be about the only place Admiral Michael McCaffrey could host such a meeting in the immediate aftermath of the battle now coming to be known as either the Seventeenth Battle of Earth or the Home Fleet Massacre.

The first thing McCaffrey had done, once the shock of knowing the sudden battle really was over, was to send out rescue efforts. The Orbital Guard had already begun operations, but he made sure every shuttle he could get his hands on was aiding them in the recovery efforts.

Saving the *Guerriere* quickly became a number one priority. Evacuation of the ship would have been the best course, but after an Orbital Guard cutter had stabilized their orbit, established a temporary power supply, and made partial repairs to the life support system, her crew refused to abandon her. They began making hurried repairs – the rumor was that there would be a new fleet assembled shortly to retaliate against this aggressor, and they hoped to be a part of it. The chances of that happening, McCaffrey knew, were near zero – not only was the *Guerriere* unlikely to even be able to move on its own for the next several weeks, but the rumor was wrong. At least until they knew more about who they were dealing with, the only fleets they intended to assemble would be defensive in nature. Taking away that hope, however, would be cruel, and he refused to do that.

The *Wolf* was salvageable but would need considerable time in dry-dock. Her crew abandoned ship in the life pods, although a cutter had towed the wrecked light cruiser into a stable orbit as well. Once rescue operations had calmed down enough, they would tow her into the surprisingly untouched repair and construction yards still in orbit around Earth. There, a more complete assessment would be made.

The crippled *Antelope* was the only battleship to survive the action. Rear Admiral King, however, had not, nor had any of her bridge crew. The entire command and control section had been opened up to the void of space, and the only functional center to run the ship from was down in engineering. However, after restoring power, engines, and life support without external assistance, it was in better shape than most.

In the best shape, however, was the frigate *Venture.* By the time rescue forces had been dispatched in her direction, she was mobile – her crew had been working non-stop to get her repaired. Even the *Terrier,* the only ship to stay in the fight all the way from beginning to end and survive in what might be considered battle-ready condition, had not been able to repair herself to that extent. Then there was the *Boxer,* which emerged from hiding after makeshift repairs returned it into fighting condition. Little by little, the surviving pieces of Home Fleet were brought together.

The Orbital Guard wasn't having much luck finding escape pods, however. They continued to scour the wreckage, hopeful that someone was alive still, but the chances were already very small. Literally millions of people had been on board those lost ships, but fewer than twenty life pods were sending out their beacon signals.

McCaffrey's nephew was not on them. The body of that nephew, however, had been recovered, along with the bodies of thousands of others. The remains of those people who had been identified were processed just as they had been since the days of generation ships, where storage space was precious: A form of cremation that reduced the ashes into an artificial diamond. Thanks to the practice, the older tradition of using diamond rings to propose marriage had fallen out of favor. Instead, diamond rings and other pieces of diamond jewelry came to mean something else. McCaffrey now had four such diamonds on his person, all worn in the form of stud earrings in his left ear.

With a sigh, he took his seat. Surrounding him was the best staff he could assemble from the surviving units. Most of the usual higher-ranking officers in the Navy were at the Wargame, and Commodore Bernhard Haas was busy working with the Orbital Guard in rescue operations, which left few officers for this council of war. There was just one flag officer left in his little assembly, Commodore Oli Jokela of the Navy Yard, and as a dockyard officer he looked decidedly out of his element. The man was a career desk officer in his eighties, and just about everyone else in the room but McCaffrey were in their twenties and thirties.

Captain Ahonen and Lieutenant Hrkac accompanied him from the Academy. Jokela came from the base. Captains Alton Fraisse, Stephan Boone, and Wayne Hoch, and Commanders Mia Spirit and Sophie Lindt, came from their ships – the *Wolf, Boxer, Terrier, Guerriere* and *Venture* respectively. The *Antelope's* representative was her chief engineer, a Lieutenant Commander Matthias Arnason, and a few of the captains brought their first officers as well. In all, fourteen people populated the small room, and every one of them had disbelief etched in their faces. The unthinkable had happened and now they were the ones who would be in charge of recovering from it.

"Well, I'm afraid we're it," McCaffrey began, taking a seat at the head of the table. "At least until the civilian representatives get here. We'll have to start this meeting without them. Let's start with contingency planning."

"With what?" Arnason asked gruffly, scratching away some flecks of dried blood on his day-old beard. His words were slurred. Temporary stitches had been placed to hold a gash in his cheek together until a doctor could take a better look at him, and it was affecting his speech in a most distracting manner. Everyone knew that every word he spoke pulled painfully on those sutures, but he continued on as if he hadn't been hurt at all. "How are we going to respond when all we've got is a bunch of crippled ships? I'm thinking we would be better off trying to figure out why they spared our few remaining ships and retreated. Yeah, we got their troop transports, but without reinforcements the path to landing on Earth is open for anyone to fly in. And I'm not even sure bringing the reinforcements directly here is a good idea – the fleet they had left might be waiting to ambush whoever we bring in."

"Reinforcements are already on their way," McCaffrey said. "I dispatched one of the star drive-equipped Orbital Guard cutters, the *Tapir,* as a messenger. They are headed to the Wargame, and whatever is available will be either returning to Earth or reinforcing other strategic positions. If they're waiting for us to bring in more ships, they've got it. Which means we'll need to come up with a contingency plan if luring those ships here is their goal, and additional plans for preparing ourselves if it is not."

"At this point," Ahonen chimed in. "We don't have much to go on. We have no knowledge of who it was who attacked us, why they attacked us in the first place, or why they retreated after we destroyed their troop ships. What we do know is that they have a tremendous lead in some technological areas, especially in stealth and targeting systems. But none of that tells us who they are, what they want, or what we can do about it."

"We've been expecting trouble from the Cygni for some time," Lindt snapped. "I'd lay odds it was them, but they'll just deny it, which will make *us* look like the aggressor if we retaliate."

McCaffrey's eyes hardened. "People... I know we're still all in a state of shock from this surprise attack, but throwing up our hands and saying 'there's nothing we can do' is not an option. Nor is baseless speculation as to who attacked us. There are concrete things we can work with, so let's go over what we know. My first thought, when I heard about the attack, was that they were exploiting the hole in passive sensors that allowed unpowered ships to coast by on inertia undetected, but that proved to be wrong. No matter how much power they were generating or what they were doing, every passive scan detected nothing from these ships. So, from now on, all patrols will be running constant active scans. Even the slightest blip will be cause to send out the alarm.

"Many of our early losses came because we couldn't get the men to battle stations and the ships into formation before they were in battle. That was a consequence of our peacetime doctrine. We always believed that passive sensors would give us enough warning to assemble our forces. This doctrine must be scrapped, and a new one must be established to deal with this new enemy.

"Finally, we know that they have at least... how many enemy ships do we know survived, Mr. Hrkac?"

Hrkac blinked for a moment, surprised at being addressed directly by the Admiral, but quickly checked his hand-comp for the data. "We detected seventeen battleships, twenty two frigates, and thirty one cruisers that we could not count as 'killed' in the after action report. There may have been others we did not detect."

Commander Spirit whistled. "I didn't think we did that well. According to those numbers, we killed them almost two to one, plus got rid of all the troop ships."

McCaffrey grinned darkly, though it didn't meet his eyes. "See, ladies and gentlemen? Looking back on it, we performed admirably. We were surprised, outnumbered by more then two to one, and started the battle well out of position, yet we still managed to destroy them two to one. What we need to do, however, is prepare ourselves to face at least twenty battleships, thirty frigates, and forty cruisers... because we know they've got at least that many."

"With what?" Arnason snorted. "Even if all the survivors can be repaired into fighting shape, one battleship with half a dozen smaller vessels would be wiped out in moments."

McCaffrey nodded. "Indeed. Commodore Jokela, what are the chances you might have a solution to this?"

"Me, sir?" Jokela replied, startled.

"Yes, you. You command the Naval Station. That means you would know the status of all ships which are still under construction or being fitted out. You would know better than any of us how quickly we can launch more ships."

Jokela hesitated. "Well, that—"

"Before you answer, consider the following: The Civilian Authority has just authorized an emergency spending bill that gives us what amounts to unlimited funding to aide in the recovery for the next three months. They have also authorized a draft, so your theoretical personnel limitations are the number of human beings inside of Sol System, although admittedly not all of them would be skilled labor and few have anything resembling Naval training. The only restriction we've got at the moment, in terms of finishing those ships and building new ones, is how fast can your Navy yard operate?"

Commodore Jokela's eyes widened as he heard those conditions. "Sir, we've currently got twenty-two ships fitting out for duty or otherwise close enough to completion that we can start assigning crew. That means we've got the parts for them all set aside, at least, and we could launch all twenty two within a few weeks, given unlimited budget and labor. Only five of those ships are battleships, though. We can also repair damaged ships, as well, but even so the most we would have would be thirty-one ships, of which only six would be battleships. I don't think there's a snowball's chance in hell that six battleships could stand up to twenty, or that thirty one ships overall could stand up to ninety. I suppose we could quickly assemble the materials to build another couple of battleships and maybe a few frigates and corvettes during the three month period that bill allows, but that's it."

McCaffrey nodded, not surprised. "And if we purchased into the Navy some of the merchant fleet and Orbital Guard cutters currently in orbit? How much of what's here is solid enough to refit and modify into warships?"

Jokela winced, and several others shifted uncomfortably in their seats. The idea they were desperate enough to bring in civilian ships was uncomfortable, to say the least. "We might be able to convert a few cutters into corvettes, sir, but... but there's no way the hull of your average merchantman or pleasure cruiser would stand up to the fire of even the smallest warship. Maybe, with a lot of armor plating, a few of the civilian transport ships and pleasure cruisers that are already equipped to defend themselves against pirates could be turned into something that would make good commerce raiders, but I'd rather spend the labor and materials on new warships. It takes a lot more to make a warship then to stick guns on her, Admiral."

"I know that," McCaffrey snorted. "But we're talking desperate measures, here, gentlemen. We need hulls, and like it or not our merchantmen are the only thing we've got until we can gather the materials for something better."

Spirit hesitantly raised her hand. "Sir... if it's hulls you want, I might have an alternate idea. It'll take a lot of work, but I think it'll be better for everyone if we can manage it. And Mr. Jokela's right, sir – even as a desperate measure, I don't think converted merchantmen is the way to go, if I may be so blunt, sir."

McCaffrey looked at her silently. Given her performance in the battle, he was inclined to listen to her, but he wasn't exactly happy about having his plans questioned. However, she'd more than earned the right to speak, so he'd give her a chance. "So tell us your idea."

"Sir, after each Wargame, most of the Academy side's ships are mothballed. The location of the mothballed ships is usually kept secret and need to know – it's possible even you might not have been apprised, sir," she began. "But I happen to know where at least one batch of 'Wargame' converted ships are, along with many other mothballed ships that could be re-commissioned far faster than any civilian merchantman could be converted. And it's only about twenty minutes hyperspace travel away...."

EAS Chihuahua

"Mr. Orff seems capable of running your battle plans pretty well,

Conrad," Anne Morrison said softly to the *Chihuahua's* captain as the simulated battle raged on around them. "I suppose your being a 'casualty' isn't going to hurt the crew's performance too much."

Burkhard sighed. It hadn't been a very good few days – not only had he been listed a 'casualty' and reduced to the role of observer alongside the Academy instructor early on, but word had leaked out that his ship had been behind the supply raid on the tenders, and speculation was heavy that Admiral Mumford had been favoring the *Chihuahua* for special treatment because his granddaughter was on board. It was making them an unpopular ship.

He had hoped to resume command early despite his 'injuries,' but after those rumors surfaced – which, despite their malicious origins, were perhaps more on target then either the Admiral or Burkhard would care to admit – he didn't dare carry them out.

"I fear what would happen if he got distracted, or if the conditions changed. I'm convinced he's smart enough, but not that he's enough of a quick thinker for command. He bickers with his 'underlings' over things he feels his rank should entitle him to, whether it really does or not. He follows orders well, yes, and can carry out a plan, but I suspect what we've actually got is another Commodore Green in the making – efficient, but constantly requiring guidance of one form or another."

"Well, we could test that theory. You're 'hospitalized,' and 'fighting to survive,' but that frees you up to become a distraction if you want. You're now an 'observer' and can order tests of certain individuals. In fact, I suggest you try distracting various crew members, just to see how they respond."

Burkhard grinned and glanced around the room looking for a decent target. He would get to Orff, of course, but only in due time. Distracting the acting captain's support staff would be much more useful for the moment.

"Mr. Desaix," he called.

Chris didn't bother looking away from his monitors. He did, however, reply. "Aren't you dead?"

Burkhard snorted. "Not yet. But I'm supposed to be the annoying distraction of a wounded man screaming in pain or something like that. At any rate, I'm supposed to make some sort of attempt to distract you."

"Ah. Proceed, then," Chris said absently, typing something on his keyboard.

"If we manage to get the *Chihuahua* purchased into the Navy, I suspect they're not going to let us keep her name. So, what name would you change her to?"

"I don't see why they wouldn't keep the name," Chris said, his attention still focused on the monitor. "It's perfect for her. And they've allowed sillier names in the past."

"Perhaps. But if they were to choose a new name for her, what name would you give her?" Burkhard asked.

"Easy. The *Virginia*," Chris replied.

"Why is that so easy?" Burkhard asked, a little startled at how quickly he was able to come up with the name.

It was not Chris but Rachel who answered him. "Sir, haven't you read up on your pre-spatial military history?"

"Um... not recently," Burkhard replied. This wasn't going quite as he'd planned. They weren't distracted, but now he was.

"During the American Civil War on Earth," Rachel began, not losing track of her own instrumentation as she talked. "One side of the war, known commonly as the Confederacy, developed a new type of warship: The ironclad. They raised the hulk of an old ship, the *Merrimack*, that had been what we might today call 'mothballed.' They gave her a new propulsion system, new weapons, and then clad her in iron armor plates. She was the first ever ironclad warship to fight a battle, and they re-commissioned her the *Virginia*."

"And we are a ship that was pulled out of mothballs," Chris continued for her when she became too busy at her tactical station. "Given a new, modern propulsion system, new weapons, and we're now the first... um, shieldclad, I guess you could call us. The parallels are all too apparent."

"So what happened to her?" Burkhard asked. "I faintly recall reading that this 'Confederacy' lost that war."

"Abandoned and destroyed to prevent capture when her port was evacuated," Chris replied. "Before that, she had proven herself effective against the normal wooden vessels of the time, and stalemated her only fight against the Union's own ironclad vessel. Neither side had a weapon prepared that could penetrate the other side's armor."

"The Union's ship in that battle was also innovative for the time," Rachel added. "It was scratch-built, and used the very first turrets ever operated in combat. However, it was poorly designed for deep water ocean travel, and sunk in a storm without ever seeing action again."

"I doubt the Fleet has managed to develop its own *Monitor* since finding out about our existence, however," Chris concluded. "So we don't have to worry about that one."

Burkhard's head turned from Chris to Rachel and back again as the speakers changed. Finally, he glanced helplessly at Captain Anne Morrison, whose shoulders were shaking as she tried to hold in her laughter. "Right. Mr. Orff!"

"Sir?" Orff replied.

"What are your thoughts on the name of the ship?" Burkhard asked, deciding to keep the distraction as mild as possible at first.

"I think... What was that, sir?" Orff asked, looking over at his 'injured' captain and blinking to try and clear his head. "Is that really the right thing to be talking about right now, sir?"

"For me, yes it is," Burkhard explained. "So, your thoughts?"

Orff looked rather uncomfortable. "I... well, I don't know, sir."

"New contact incoming!" a muffled female voice reported. It wasn't Rachel speaking, but it did come from the general location of the tactical station.

"Well, give me an answer, dammit!" Burkhard snapped. "Or the whole damned mission will fail!"

"Mission? What mission?" Orff replied, horribly confused. "I... what is all this about, sir?"

"Don't ask me. This is all your fault!" Burkhard shouted, getting into the spirit of things and deciding to have a little fun with it. "I need an answer, and you're wasting precious seconds asking me why I'm asking you what I'm asking of you, so you better give me an answer that justifies asking a question!"

"Huh? Sir, I can't follow—"

Suddenly, an alarm went out across the bridge. A recorded voice started repeating the words, "Collision alert! Collision alert!"

Orff spun to look at Rachel. "Ms. Katz, why didn't you warn me before this? I—"

"My apologies, Mr. Orff," Anne Morrison intervened primly from her spot standing next to the aforementioned female cadet. "I seem to have sat on the collision alert button."

"But—"

"However, you were warned of a target incoming, and ignored it to answer Mr. Burkhard's questions... when you should know perfectly well that your captain is 'incapacitated.' Now, that target warning should probably have been confirmed, but—"

Morrison was unable to finish her lecture before an entirely different cry came from across the bridge. "Transmission from Flag, sir," Emily Mumford's voice called out, silencing the cacophony.

Orff looked at her, knowing he shouldn't repeat his mistake and let the people who weren't officially there distract him again. "On speakers."

But Mumford shook her head. "We're on stand-down. 'We' meaning not just *Chihuahua*, sir, but the entire bloody Wargame. Something big just happened... I think the Wargame is being cancelled. Captain Burkhard, you're being asked to contact the Flag securely."

Orff's eyes widened. "But... what's so big that it could cancel The Wargame?"

Burkhard and Morrison shared a dark look. There was only one thing they knew of which would cancel The Wargame... and that was a real war.

Alpha Centauri, Orbital Guard Cutter Pangolin

"Talk about a graveyard for old ships," Lieutenant Hrkac said, surveying the scan results. The assembly Admiral McCaffrey had called was currently on a chartered private vessel, to avoid diverting any of the ships that were still engaged in rescue and recovery operations or undergoing significant repairs. It had, indeed, only taken twenty minutes of travel time to get to the dumping area Commander Spirit had mentioned.

"I didn't think we returned to Alpha Centauri after we advanced past the need for hyperspace jump gate technology," Captain Ahonen remarked in amazement.

Prior to the invention of a practical hyperdrive small enough to be mounted inside of a ship, there were 'doors into hyperspace,' as they had been promoted. These hyperspace jump gates could open and close doors into the only practical method for interstellar travel... but, in order to work, a jump gate would have to be installed at both the entry and exit point for all travel. It required the use of generation ships, traveling – as the name would imply – for generations towards the targeted star and building the gates before a new route could be opened. Alpha Centauri was the location of the first prototype jump gate exit, and after that became the launching point for many generation ships.

"Well, the old waystation was abandoned," Mia admitted. "And so were the jump gates, although some of them might still be floating around – the one in Sol is, after all – but we've been sending decommissioned warships here for hundreds of years. There used to be a small shipyard here, as well, but I believe that was abandoned. The only security left for this place is that no-one knows it's here save for a few very high ranking members on the Wargame Committee... and the people responsible for transporting ships to be mothballed, such as yours truly. Not that security is all that important. Who's interested in a bunch of old, mothballed, obsolete warships that have been largely stripped of anything worth keeping, anyway?"

"We are, that's who," McCaffrey said.

"Is that a generation ship?" Hrkac blurted out, amazed, as he saw one particularly well-worn vessel. "My God, this is the stuff of ancient history here."

McCaffrey surveyed the fleet around them. Yes, everything here was old and it was all *entirely* obsolete... but there was a lot that could be exploited, too. Every Wargame ever was a practice for re-commissioning ships like this, and every Academy student had experienced the Wargame once in their schooling. Yes, some of the ships, like Hrkac's generation ship, were too old to be of any kind of practical use, but there were still the hulls of a number of corvettes, frigates, the classic 'starships of the line' which once filled the role of modern battleships but would now only be considered a light cruiser, heavy cruisers, and even a number of battleships. Most of the battleships were undersized, but a few weren't. There were a few of the Cleopatra class, sisters of which were still in commission in the modern Navy. Sirius class battleships such as those used by the Academy in the current Wargame could be seen. Nothing here was particularly exciting, but there was enough to build up an emergency force to deter another attack by the fleet which had limped away from the battle, if they had just a little time.

"It doesn't matter," he said finally. "All that matters now is getting this stuff home and to start building. Their hyperdrives have probably all been stripped, though, so we're probably going to need to bring in a few interstellar-capable tugs, and it will take a while to get them back to Earth."

Commander Spirit hesitated. "About that, sir... I have another idea, if you're willing to risk it...."

Chapter XXIII

EAS Don Quixote

"Are you sure they requested that I come, too?" Beccera asked, astonished, as he followed Commander Burkhard to the shuttle bay. "Or was it a general 'all regular officers above a certain rank' type of order?"

"Your name was specifically mentioned in the communiqué we received," Burkhard replied grimly.

"But... what possible need would there be for me in a meeting like this?" the Army colonel asked, unable to believe his ears. "I mean...Hell, do they expect me to storm a planet or something? That I can do, if I have an Army unit or three, but we don't. What are they interested in me for?"

"I don't know," Burkhard snapped impatiently. "I don't know anything! Just that they've suspended the Wargame... and about the only thing which could make our Navy do that is war or major disaster. So, something's going on. Maybe you're being recalled or something, but I just don't know."

Beccera grimaced. "My apologies. It's just... I'm as startled by all of this as you are."

Burkhard shook his head, sighing. "No apologies necessary, Drew. If anything, I should apologize for snapping. This whole situation has me a bit edgy."

"As you say, no apologies necessary. So... we don't know anything. Surely you have your suspicions, however. What do you *think* is going on?"

"I think there's a war going on," Burkhard replied grimly. "And I think no-one's quite sure what to do about it."

"And I think we're going to be late if we don't get moving," Captain Morrison said from the entrance to the shuttle bay. "Hurry up, guys, I've been waiting here five minutes."

"My apologies, ma'am, it was my fault," Beccera said. "I needed a few minutes to get ready for travel."

"Well, you're here, now, so get on board!"

"Yes, ma'am!" Beccera agreed, saluting.

Burkhard grinned slightly as he followed the Army officer and the observer through the door. "Don't you outrank her?" he whispered, curious.

"Err, yes," Beccera replied. "But I think if I just pretend otherwise, things will go much smoother."

The shuttle ride over to the *Don Quixote* was about as tense as any shuttle ride the trio of officers had been on. Even Weber, piloting for them, was silent as she flew. All three officers knew by now that she loved to talk up a storm when piloting.

They were met at the airlock by a woman with bizarre tattoos, cat-like eyes, and what appeared to be natural emerald-green hair. That combination of features instantly identified her as an inhabitant of the Iota Draconis colonies. A side effect to the genetic alteration done to counter poisons in the atmosphere of a particular colony world gave them the unique hair and eye features. The tattoos came from tradition: When settling Iota Draconis as the first politically independent extra-solar colony in human history, the colonists decided to mark their independence by calling themselves 'Dragons' and tattooing certain patterns on their bodies that gave them a more draconic appearance. Accepting the tattoos eventually became a rite of passage for those entering adulthood, though patterns had changed over the centuries to become something far different than the original. The women of Iota Draconis were also prized as lovers all across the galaxy. As another effect of the genetic alterations made them release a pheromone with particular sensitizing effects when in the heat of the moment. It made them a frequent target for kidnapping. Iota Draconis women now rarely left their homeworld because of the phenomenon.

"Hello, ladies and gentlemen," the foreign observer from Iota Draconis said, bowing in greeting. She gestured for them to follow her, and together the four of them left the airlock in the direction of the conference room.

"I am Second Taii – the equivalent of your Commander rank – Seiroku Ildryn. The staff of this ship was running short of guides, and I was asked to bring you to the meeting. I will be attending, as well. My sympathies for your loss."

"Our loss?" Burkhard asked. "You must know more about this meeting that we do. I'm afraid we don't know quite what it is we lost, yet, Ms. Ildryn."

Her eyes flashed – with what emotion, none of the trio could say. "I'm afraid my people are traditionally addressed with their given name last. You should address me as 'Ms. Seiroku,' or rather, 'Mrs. Seiroku' in my case. Alternatively, you could address me as 'Taii Ildryn,' but only in situations where rank matters."

"Thank you for the education, Mrs. Seiroku," Burkhard replied. "But that doesn't tell me what it is we've lost."

"It is not my place," she hesitated. "But I suppose you'll hear of it, anyway. There was a surprise attack on Earth itself by an unknown enemy. Employing tactics and technology heretofore unseen, your entire Home Fleet was decimated. Earth Alliance forces 'won' the battle, as the enemy retreated when its last troop ship was destroyed, but for the moment Sol System is virtually defenseless."

Burkhard and Morrison froze. Beccera, as an Army officer, didn't know enough about the composition of Home Fleet to fully comprehend the impact of that statement, but he knew it was significant. A question came to mind, however. "And just how did you happen to come by this information before we did?"

Ildryn flushed. "I was with the first officer of this ship when it was reported. I... assumed you had been told."

"What were you doing with the First Officer?" Beccera asked. The way this woman was acting was sending all sorts of alarm bells into motion in his head, and he was sure she was covering up something.

Her flush grew. "We were... um, in his stateroom. Do I need to explain further?"

"Are you married?" Beccera asked, digging deeper.

"Yes, but—"

"Mr. Beccera," Burkhard snapped in a broken voice. "Taii Ildryn's... infidelity... or whatever was going on in that stateroom, is completely unimportant at this point. Assuming her report is correct, we have a *much* more serious matter to deal with."

"I'm just wondering why the 'Second Taii' would be having an affair if she is happily married," Beccera replied. "Dragons are known for using sexual favors as a method of gathering intelligence, so—"

"Colonel, at least a quarter of a million of our military personnel have just been killed," Burkhard interrupted harshly. "In one battle. At least forty percent of the ships in our Navy have been destroyed. I think that is more important than ferreting out a small-time intelligence agent of an allied power!"

"Small time?" Ildryn protested, offended.

Burkhard rolled his eyes. "Taii Ildryn, please... I don't care if you're a spy or not at this point, or whether you're small time or the most important spy in the history of Iota Draconis. Just lead us to the meeting."

"I am not a spy," Ildryn insisted, gesturing for them to follow her regardless. Her gaze pinned down Beccera. "And those particular rumors are greatly exaggerated."

Beccera shrugged, neither agreeing nor disagreeing but acknowledging the rebuke. "I am only repeating what I heard," he said, neglecting to mention that he had heard that bit of information every time a security briefing was made by anyone in any of the intelligence branches he'd ever worked with – civilian or military; loyal to the Earth Alliance or a declared foreign agent. All of them mentioned had the same warning. And, after hearing of an attack on Earth, anyone with unexpected information would arouse his suspicions, regardless.

"There usually is some truth behind any rumor," Ildryn admitted. "And there may be with this one. I, however, only know that it is exaggerated, and that whatever may be true regarding this rumor has nothing to do with me."

"If you insist, Mrs. Seiroku," Beccera replied, watching her face to see if his gentle jab at her marital status would cause any reaction.

Her flinch showed that it did, and finally an explanation came forth. "I am legally a married woman, Mr. Beccera. However, my husband is a victim of Castergyne's Disease and has been in support for over four years. I cannot remarry until he dies. I have no intention of divorcing him under these circumstances, but neither do I feel any moral compunction to remain celibate, as I am virtually a widow. My relationship with the first officer is already known by your intelligence organizations, and neither of our governments have objected. The only function I have with regard to the intelligence agencies of either of our nations is to occasionally pass their communiqués with each other back and forth secretly. I suppose I could be a leak, yes, but I'm a 'controlled' leak... and everyone knows it."

All three Earth Alliance officers winced. Castergyne's Disease was a horrible, incurable illness that would trap a person inside their own body. Brain scans showed that the brain was still active, but they also showed no indication of any connections to the body's senses or control over the body. On life support, the person could live as long as their brain did – rarely longer than one year, but at least one case lasted for seven years before dying. Breakouts usually occured because of contaminated vegetables, and it was nearly impossible to detect before symptoms started to develop. There had been some recent discoveries that might allow for effective treatment if it was caught early enough, but they were still experimental and provided no hope for those already in long-term care.

"My apologies, Taii Ildryn," Beccera finally replied into the silence which followed. "We still don't know who it is who attacked us, and perhaps I am acting somewhat paranoid, but that doesn't give me the right to judge your morals or to suspect you of using your sexuality for spy work. I am sorry about the loss of your husband."

Ildryn nodded stiffly in acknowledgment. The silence that followed remained awkward until they finally entered the conference room.

"Ah, finally," were the words that greeted the foursome. Admiral Mumford was standing in front of the assembly, which was comprised of every captain and flag officer from every ship in the system, including the foreign observers from Iota Draconis and the Larkin Triumvirate. Notably absent were the observers from Cygni and the Pleiades Confederation, as well as the small number of minor powers who had managed to send a delegation that year. "Taii Ildryn, welcome. Mr. Burkhard, Mr. Beccera, Ms. Morrison, please take your seats – you're the last to arrive, and we have much to cover."

"Our apologies, Admiral," Burkhard replied respectfully, taking his seat along with Beccera, Ildryn, and Morrison.

Mumford just nodded at them, then turned his attention to the rest of the crowded room. "Let's begin, then. By now, you all probably have heard that Earth has been attacked. Details are sketchy, at best, but here is what we know so far."

As Mumford recounted the reports sent out from Earth on the attack, people around the room grew stiffer and more quiet. Any attack on Earth would have been bad enough, but the destruction of Home Fleet was a far worse situation than anything those present would have imagined. When the Admiral finished reading from the dispatches, the whole room waited in silence for some explanation that might help them understand what had happened.

Vice Admiral Lee Craig, who had moved to the *Don Quixote* as an observer after her 'death' in the Wargame, was the first to break the silence. "We don't know who did this, you say, but can we narrow it down a bit? Who has enough power to manage something like this without being noticed? Who could build this many ships and concentrate them into one force without anyone seeing them do it?"

"Those sorts of questions are exactly why I asked the observers from the Larkin Triumvirate and Iota Draconis here," Mumford explained. "Obviously the Cygni are one possibility. However, while we knew a threat from them was building, our intelligence estimates indicated that it would be quite some time before they were ready to implement any plans. Six months to a year, at least. And while they have this kind of power, we doubt they could develop this level of technology and build this large a fleet using it in secret. Our intelligence sources inside Cygni are quite considerable, and we're confident they would have heard something. However, our sources outside of Cygni are almost nonexistent, which is why we've made secret intelligence-sharing treaties with the Larkin Triumvirate and Iota Draconis. The circumstances have forced us to make that intelligence sharing a little less secret then we'd like, but I will still ask everyone here not to mention this treaty outside of this room.

"With that in mind, I'm going to ask Taii Ildryn, from the Federal Republic of Iota Draconis, and Admiral Kris Orpik of the Larkin Triumvirate up here to give us the briefings each was asked to prepare. Sir, Ma'am?"

Ildryn left the trio from the *Chihuahua* to stand in front of the room. She looked fairly comfortable with the spotlight, but that was to be expected of a Dragon – their society promoted the development of people who could rarely, if ever, be bashful or shy in the presence of others.

"Well, our best intelligence indicates there are only five powers with enough capacity to build a fleet of the size that attacked Earth. Those are my own Federal Republic of Iota Draconis, the Pleiades Republic, the 16 Cygni Confederation, the Virgin Planets of 70 Virginis, and the Earth Alliance itself. I'll assure you that my people had nothing to do with this, and you obviously didn't attack yourselves. That narrows us down to three. Your own people are the specialists in Cygni, and they don't believe those pirates were responsible for this attack. Cygni may be allied to whoever the attackers were, since we know they were considering their own assault on the Earth Alliance, but my people have no information either proving or disproving that theory.

"When we signed the Joint Intelligence Treaty seven years ago, the Larkin Triumvirate was given the responsibility of data collection on Pleiades – we do have some sources of our own, but largely in the civilian sector. However, my people have been steadily investigating the Virgin Planets for many decades, and I can report extensive findings on them."

"In terms of their physical capacity to produce an invasion force, the Virgin Planets are probably near the top. Contrary to their published census, multiple sources are reporting that they have the second highest civilian population in the known galaxy, surpassed only by the Earth Alliance itself. In terms of planetary numbers and territory, they are fourth, behind the Earth Alliance, Pleiades, and 16 Cygni. In terms of raw resources, they are second only behind Iota Draconis. However... after that, things start to lead away from the conclusion that they could possibly be the attackers.

"Their political system has been rather... mixed. Within the past five years, they have gone from an empire, to an absolute monarchy, to a democratic republic, to a socialist republic, and most recently to a constitutional feudal monarchy with a collection of vassal states. Whether this latest change will stabilize the country or result in a civil war, we can't say, but the kind of planning required for the attack on Earth would have taken more planning than a nation this unstable to have managed. Nevertheless, it is conceivable that they could be the ones responsible. Any questions?" Ildryn asked.

"If they are not the aggressors," Commander Daniels began. "What are the chances that they – or at least one of the vassal states being formed inside their, ah, kingdom – could side against Earth?"

"At least as remote as their being behind the attack," Ildryn answered without hesitation. "No *single* faction inside of the Virgin Planets could provide enough firepower to be a threat in such a war effort, and until they have stabilized politically – even if just temporarily – it is unlikely they would be willing to involve themselves in foreign adventures as a collective entity without some provocation."

Colonel Beccera stroked his chin and raised his hand for the next question. "Taii Ildryn, I'm a veteran of a small war resulting from a similar situation. You say it is unlikely that they would get involved in our war, but what about the possibility of us being drawn into theirs? If some of the feudal states wish to aide us and ally with us, and others wish to fight against us, and still others wish for a state of 'armed neutrality,' how likely is that to cause a civil war? And how likely is it that we will be required to aide them?"

"A good question," Ildryn replied, mulling over his words briefly. "A very good question. I have no direct analysis in regards to that, but I do know that they have fought nine civil wars in the past century. All nine have been fought internally, but each time there was such a war private foreign nationals were hired as mercenaries or privateers to fight alongside them. My guess is that they would not call out for aid directly, but would be willing to purchase some... and their history suggests they would not look for any *causus belli* unless direct military force from a foreign power were to side with any one faction. Any other questions?

"You say that no single faction could provide enough firepower to be a threat. But what about economic, political, or other non-military aid?" Burkhard asked.

"Another good question. I would not be surprised if one or two of the vassal states did make deals under the table with, well, anyone, if they believed it would somehow be of benefit to them. They are all looking for advantages against each other, and a secret trade deal or the like would do that. It is something we will certainly keep an eye on. Now, if there are no more questions, I will turn the floor over to Admiral Orpik."

The Larkin Admiral did not look nearly as comfortable as Ildryn. Larkin was considered a backwards civilization of backwards people doing backwards things, and even their most noble and powerful people were often treated as if they should be humored rather than respected. Admiral Orpik was not considered one of their most noble and powerful people, but he was being asked to give a presentation to a bunch of foreigners who would undoubtedly think poorly of him. Any other time, Beccera would feel sorry for the man, but things were far too serious for him to care at the moment.

"Ahem, yes, well," Orpik began, shifting uncomfortably. "We were charged by the Joint Intelligence Treaty with the unenviable task of keeping an eye on the Pleiades Republic. It's been a rather difficult task, to be sure, and we have no definitive answers for you. Pleiades has been trying to hide something of great significance over the past few years. Many of our agents' lives were lost attempting to pierce the wall of secrecy around this undertaking with no success.

"Their Navy has been involved in some kind of military build-up, though the ships we're seeing them produce do not match the design of the ships in the assault on Earth. The reasons for the build-up are unclear, and there has been no corresponding build-up in other service branches. In fact, much of the construction appears defensive in nature, mostly involving upgrades of sensor stations, defensive platforms, and so on. But its unusual. Most nations typically start defensive upgrades either with their perimeter worlds, to try and provide early warning, or in the heart of the political center, to protect the government. This build-up focuses on neither. Instead, they seem to be building a number of ships in their outer worlds, but have little or no construction going on in their capital system.

"Internally their government is tightening controls over local jurisdictions, and appears to be undergoing some sort of internal purge of political opponents. The number of openly armed personnel belonging to either the 'Pleiades Republican Internal Security Services' or their 'Worlds' Internal Security, Pleiades Republic' has increased exponentially, and several government officials have gone 'missing.' This points to some sort of political strife, possibly a coup attempt, but as of yet we've seen no evidence to suggest such a thing has occurred or is being threatened. We have also come to the conclusion that most of the changes are being brought about by a rather unlikely source – their science director, a Dr. Ian Karlsson. His office has been granted unusually high levels of power, and he has been exercising that power throughout the government and not just inside the scientific community.

"We believe that, like the Virgin Planets, the capacity for the Pleiades Republic to build such a force as attacked Earth *may* be possible, but their focus is too internal for it to be likely. However, we are less sure of this assessment than Iota Draconis is with the former. Furthermore, there is one thing which seems to point in Pleiades favor as your attacker: During the attack on Earth, an advanced stealth technology was employed that has not been encountered before. Dr. Karlsson's focus, before he became the science director, was in stealth technology. For this reason, I would say that they are a good candidate for your attacking power. If they were your attacker, however, their motivation is unclear – there has been no indication they had any hostility towards Earth or any other foreign power."

Beccera felt a twitch in his gut. His wife's family was from Pleiades, and she was on her way there, herself. If Pleiades was complicit in the attack on his own home world, than this war could be more personal than most. Which, considering Earth had been so badly hit, seemed to be a horrible thing to say, but he couldn't deny it was true. "Was the scientific expedition to Pleiades launched before the attack?"

"It left a few hours beforehand, yes," Admiral Mumford said from his seat to the left of the podium. "The captain of the expedition left early. It's a fortunate thing he wanted to rush out and avoid filing some paperwork or they would have been caught up in the attack. We find it unlikely the expedition would be targeted, regardless of Pleiades' stance with us, as the scientists were invited to appear. They might be asked to surrender upon arrival, and as unarmed ships facing a sizable foreign navy they would certainly do so, but we see little threat to the lives of the scientists unless someone does something exceptionally foolish."

That did little to relieve Beccera's fears, but there was at least some comfort to know that Kimiko had not been caught in the initial attack. "Thank you, sir."

"Any more questions?" Admiral Orpik asked.

Captain Philip Yates of the heavy cruiser *Valkyrie*, one of the regular Navy warships, raised his hand. "Yes, sir. You've said that much of the build-up in Pleiades appears defensive, but that construction has not been taking place in their home system. Does that mean the shipyards we know are located there are quiet?"

"There is considerable construction going on in the Alcyone system," Orpik admitted. "It is difficult to ascertain how much of that construction is being done by the military, however. Much of what we do know in the way of military construction in their home system seems to show they are engaged in refitting old ships, not constructing new ones. In their other systems, we have been able to identify construction work orders belonging to thirty one different warships: Ten battleships, six heavy cruisers, seven light cruisers, and eight frigates. This is about double the pace they usually have for replacing retiring warships."

Yates followed up with another question. "Have you been able to verify, then, that they are retiring warships at their usual rate?"

Orpik nodded. "Our intelligence is based primarily on official sources: Namely, the classified version of their own Navy list. It has been showing the names of older warships removed at their typical rate, and we have no reason to believe that those lists are inaccurate. It is possible, however, if they are attempting some sort of secret build-up, that their Navy list is being manipulated."

"Any more questions for Mr. Orpik?" Mumford asked, stepping up after a brief period of silence. "No? Then, I guess we've heard what we know so far. Now, on to what to do about all of this mess. Colonel

Beccera, please come up here."

"Me, sir?" Beccera said.

"Yes, you. Up here, now."

"Yes, sir," he replied, stepping up to the podium. Commander Burkhard and Captain Morrison joined him.

Mumford pulled out a jewelry case, opening it to reveal the silver star warn by those of the rank of Commodore. Quietly, so that the rest of the conference room couldn't hear them, he said, "Burkhard, Morrison, you should witness this. Mr. Beccera, I'm appointing you Acting Commodore. You will take command of one half of the Academy-controlled forces and—"

"Sir?" Beccera exclaimed, unable to maintain his usual discipline. Even the other Naval personnel present seemed rather disturbed by this news. "But... but I'm an *Army* officer!"

"With wartime experience. And you were the highest ranking command-line officer across the entire Academy side of the Wargame, regardless of service. *And* you're listed on the Navy List as second in command to Green, who is being assigned to other duties. You may be weak on Naval tactics, but to be honest you're probably better qualified to be a Commodore then the man we *actually* put in charge of the Academy forces." Mumford made a face and looked around, noticing Green sitting at the table. He really hoped that Commodore Green hadn't heard him say that. "Don't anyone repeat that last bit, please. And don't worry, Drew, this is just a temporary position. Your command will be sent to rendezvous with Vice Admiral Marvin Breslau's squadron outside of 16 Cygni. We'll give you the co-ordinates at which you should be able to join him. His fleet has three flag officers in it, but enough ships were pulled from it for the Wargame that it is currently composed of just one squadron.

"That will allow Read Admiral Hawkeye Fulton to assume command of your squadron once you make the rendezvous. Their job will then be to ascertain the culpability of Cygni and report back to Earth for further instructions. Your job is mainly that of supervising the other officers during the voyage, which will, for many of them, be their first commands in a wartime situation." Mumford grinned somewhat wryly. "You're playing nursemaid on a milk run, in other words. Your Naval experience, or lack thereof, won't really enter into it. Your fleet's captains will double as your staff for the duration. Frankly, every officer capable of even temporary fleet command who isn't already in charge of a comparable force will be sent elsewhere."

Burkhard, who had come up with Beccera, frowned. "Sir, are you saying you're sending the Academy ships into the war? Ships manned by cadet crews who haven't all completed even their basic coursework? Ships in such poor condition that few, if any, of them would be allowed in a modern navy?"

"There are sufficient regular and reserve officers on board each ship to give crash course training to whoever needs it," Mumford replied. Subtly raising his voice so that the rest of the conference room could hear him, he continued. "But let's face facts: Almost half the Naval officer corps has been wiped out, along with about 40 percent of our ships. We may face another attack on our homeworld at any moment, and we're at the point of desperate measures. Which brings me to some of my other news: A draft has been instituted, and budgetary limits have been temporarily loosened. Academy and training programs are being shortened across the board, and we're buying those hulks that the Academy captains managed to get running into the fleet, regardless of their overall condition. We'll try and get your ships sufficiently outfitted to make assignments something less than suicidal, but for the most part, you're on your own."

"Realize, ladies and gentlemen, that whatever reserve personnel might have been sent to replace the current Academy crews are already spoken for – some to speed training, some to help repair what's left of home fleet, and some to replace those killed in action. Yet these ships have to be manned, because we need to replace our losses as quickly as possible... and the Academy crews are all that we have. The cadet and trainee rankings each Academy student and enlisted crewman currently holds will be made an 'acting' rank as of this date. Captains, it will be up to you whether or not those ranks should be approved as permanent promotions. Until further notice, the internal organization of your ships are entirely in your hands. You may promote people, demote people, make people officers or drop them down to non-coms at your discretion. Your own acting ranks are now yours to keep, but that still may mean some of the cadets 'outrank' you until you reorganize, so keep that in mind. No current Academy student should be put in a department head or similar command position if it can be avoided. I suggest you complete any necessary reorganization en route back to your ships."

Burkhard was shocked at that news. He knew the scale of the loss Home Fleet suffered was unheard of, but until that moment he had not realized how much it would affect even the personnel and logistical situation. "Yes, sir," he replied quietly.

Even Beccera, whose knowledge of the numerical strength of the Navy could fit in a thimble, was unable to argue against his temporary placement after hearing that. He finally reached out and took the rank pins being offered him, staring at them slowly. "Sir... if I am to take command of the Academy ships, what will become of Commodore Green's command?"

"It'll be split up," the admiral replied dismissively as he turned his attention back to the assembly. "Captain Morrison, come forward."

"Yes, sir," Anne Morrison said, leaping out of her seat and heading up to the Admiral's side.

Pulling out another set of rank pins, he said, "I'm officially promoting you to Commodore as of this moment. This is a permanent promotion, unlike Beccera's."

Morrison took only a second to recover her composure. If Mumford was drafting Army officers to command a fleet, he certainly wouldn't discount her for a simple problem with occasional fainting spells. "Yes, sir!"

"You will assemble a squadron of five Academy battleships, plus whatever support craft may be spared, to reinforce the defenses at Epsilon Eridani," Mumford ordered, then pulled out yet another case, this one displaying the gold stars used to denote Admirals of all levels. "Commodore Kosuke Babel is currently in command there. Although he doesn't know it yet, I have promoted him to Rear Admiral, effective immediately. I hope you will be good enough to give these to him. You will answer to him and be his second in command. With your ships, he should be able to fill out two squadrons, and you are to command one of them."

"Yes, sir!" Morrison replied briskly.

"Commodore Green will be taking the remaining Academy ships to reinforce the new Home Fleet, and Vice Admiral Craig will similarly take those Regular Navy ships involved in the Wargame and do the same. I will take the observer ships to our station on Il Aquarii and organize a defense force there until I can be relieved. Il Aquarii is still our third largest shipyard, and must be protected just as Earth and Epsilon Eridani were."

"Sir," Commander Jonathan Daniels interrupted. "What about other systems, such as the colonies we are currently stationed in? Are they going to be left entirely undefended?"

Mumford swallowed. "Many planets are currently indefensible," he replied slowly. "Those which do not already have some defensive force around them will be forced to fend for themselves. It is our hope that the enemy – whose motives are still unknown – will ignore the smaller worlds in our region, but if they do not... there is nothing we can do but promise to come back for them when or even if we can."

"Have these colonies been warned of this?" Burkhard asked. "So that they may prepare as best they can, if nothing else?"

Vice Admiral Lee Craig stood up at that. "There are no Navy ships to spare sending out these dispatches, and there are no civilian ships in this sector. Two of the three Orbital Guard ships attached to the *Yggdrasil* station, however, are capable of interstellar travel, as are some of their other parasite craft. They will be sent to nearby systems to spread the word as much as possible, under the circumstances. I have already spoken to Director Morisato about this, and he agreed to lend them to us for this purpose. It's our hope that some of the colonies they contact may have ships that can aid in the process, sort of like an old-fashioned comm tree."

"Are there any more questions?" Mumford asked from the front of the room. "If not, then you are dismissed. Godspeed, gentlemen, and let us hope that we all survive this war at least long enough to know who it is we're fighting."

Chapter XXIV

"I hope you understand, Mr. Orff, just why I'm not promoting you all the way to acting-commander," Burkhard said, looking at the man who was – officially – his first officer.

Each of the cadet officers had been given a private meeting with Burkhard, Beccera, Rappaport, and Dr. June Ehrlich – the four regular fleet officers on board and the staff physician – to discuss the news. In most cases, the young men and women were heartbroken by the news about Earth. Letting them all know that their 'Wargame' rank was now an acting rank, which Burkhard then confirmed, provided them with something positive from each meeting (cold comfort that it was). Burkhard couldn't leave Orff as a full commander, however, which must have felt like a further slap to the face.

Orff had to have known he would be 'demoted,' though it was clear from the expression on his face he was far from happy with it. He was able to make himself say the right things, at least. "Of course, sir. Going from an Academy student straight to Lt. Commander is stretching things far enough; giving me command rank before I even graduate would be pretty extreme. And as captain, you should outrank your junior officers, after all."

"Thank you," Burkhard said. "Now, since the schedule is tight, would you please co-ordinate with Ensign Polk – who is still our purser, despite the re-org – to make sure that we have all of the supplies needed for an extended mission? We'll have to leave within the next two hours, and this is our last chance to obtain everything we'll need for the next three months. It wouldn't do to run out of food on our first real mission, after all."

"Yes, sir," Orff replied, leaving the *Chihuahua's* tiny conference room to find the logistics officer.

"I'm surprised you're keeping him in the position of your first officer," Beccera, now sporting the silver stars of the commodore's rank on his Army uniform, just under the golden eagles of his colonel's rank. It wasn't a regulation way to wear the rank, but then his situation wasn't exactly covered in the regulations. "I know you were unhappy with him."

Burkhard grimaced. "Well, I hope he never has to take command of the ship in a crisis, but he's capable of handling an exec's duties fairly well. He can keep watch when nothing serious is going on, he knows how to delegate properly when executing my orders, and he runs the administrative side of things efficiently – he does all the paperwork better than I do. I'd rather have Ms. Katz as my first officer, to be honest, but I think she's too valuable in her tactical position, and Orff... just isn't any good anywhere else."

Lieutenant Rappaport sighed. "Well, I could always give you Mr. Desaix to take Ms. Katz's place, if you like, and Mr. Orff could be placed somewhere else where he won't cause any trouble."

"And rob us of our best engineer?" Burkhard laughed coldly. "You and he are just about the only people on this ship who really know engineering. Everyone else, while quite talented in their chosen field, is either untrained or a specialist. I've already given him watch duty, and that will tie him up enough as it is. Maybe when the rest of your team is all caught up in their training, I'll consider it, but in the meantime he needs to work with you getting everyone up to a reasonable standard."

"I also have another job in mind for your engineering staff, if you can handle it while running the ship and training everyone at the same time," Beccera said. "I realize my role as Commodore is largely that of a figurehead, but there are a few tactical matters I imagine are the same whether you're Army, Navy, or Marines."

"Of course, sir," Burkhard replied, emphasizing the 'sir' a little bit in order to show that – however much of a figurehead the man may think he was, Beccera was still officially his flag officer.

"This would be an ideal project for Mr. Desaix, actually," Beccera continued. "It involves both tactics and engineering. If he wants others to work with him – such as Ms. Katz – I strongly encourage you to allow it, provided this doesn't interfere with their other duties."

Burkhard and Rappaport shared an amused grin. It was good to find something light to think about on a day like this. "I may agree to that, sir, if you'll tell me what the project is. And, sir... just a point of protocol: As a flag officer you generally don't order specific people on the ships under your command. One of the tenets of naval etiquette is that you ask the captain, and he'll determine which people from the crew are best suited to carry out this task."

"Of course," Beccera replied, shaking his head ruefully. He might be new to the business of being a naval officer, but he clearly understood how command structures worked. He hoped he wouldn't have to get too used to this whole flag officer thing. "Well, anyway... I may be a bit behind on *naval* tactics, but I imagine it's important to follow the rule 'know thine enemy' regardless of which service branch you belong to. We'll be receiving a copy of any data we can find on the attack, shortly, and I would like a team to go through these records. Determine just what it is we're facing, what their tactical abilities are, what kinds of weapons they have, just how effective their stealth technology is, that kind of thing. I imagine it would take people well versed in engineering and tactics to get anything useful. I realize this won't give you enough to make anything definitive, but I imagine any amount of analysis would be a step in the right direction, and it'll be all we have to work with until the boys from Earth can give us something more to go on."

"Of course, sir," Burkhard said. "I'll draft orders to that effect right away. Anything else?"

Dr. June Ehrlich, who had been listening from the side without comment, spoke up. "I would recommend that we start calling in the regular crew and interview them, not just the officers, sir. The crew is small enough we should be able to meet with everyone over the next few days, and it would give me a chance to assess whether anyone needs counseling after this tragedy."

"Of course, Dr. Ehrlich," Beccera replied graciously. "Mr. Burkhard, if you would call in the next person?"

"Of course, sir," Burkhard said. He looked at his list, made a checkmark beside Orff's name, and started a new list. Pressing a button on the comm, he said, "Chief Petty Officer Flint, please report to the conference room on the double."

The tiny stateroom ostensibly belonging to Schubert and Desaix had become something of a lounge over the past few days, and this day – despite the attack that had so drastically changed all of their lives – was no exception. It was far more somber than usual, but there was still a definite clubhouse atmosphere in the air.

Couples were huddled together. Wolf was holding Weber as they were stretched out on his bunk. She was crying into his shoulder, having just learned that her older brother and both parents had been killed in the assault. Corporal Etcheverry sat in the one chair the room provided, Flint sitting on the arm of his chair. Rachel and Chris were together as well, sitting on his bed as they shared a mini-comp analyzing the attacker's technology and tactics. Lt. Cmdr. Mumford, Ensign Cohen, and Lt. Diana Tarbell – one of the weapons control officers – had joined them.

This was the team intended to assess the enemy's capabilities. Langer was supposed to join them later, but he was on the bridge with Orff and Polk while the ship was preparing to get underway. That would normally be Rachel's job, at this time of day, but watches were being reorganized to better distribute veteran officer oversight. Conveniently, that same reorganization allowed the bulk of the team as much free time together as possible.

In many ways, they were the ideal team for the job. Rachel and Chris were perfect for analyzing both the tactics and the engineering in general, and each of the others could provide differing perspectives. Weber and Schubert would have insights into the demonstrated maneuverability of the enemy ships compared to most Earth Alliance ships. Etcheverry could provide the "out of the box" perspective of a layman, as well as insight on the kind of information a ground forces officer like Beccera would find useful for their report. Mumford, though far from having the sort of expertise that the experience granted to most communications officers in the Earth Alliance Navy had, was easily the most knowledgeable person on the *Chihuahua* when it came to signal analysis. Tarbell understood weapons analysis better than anyone else on board, and had the added advantage of a basic foundation in engineering through her class work. Flint, a genius when it came to environmental systems, had already begun running rather impressive calculations for a rough estimate of how many crewmen the ships were designed to support based on the atmospheric mix and density that each ship revealed when they were destroyed. When all that had been done, Cohen and Langer would be able to take all the analysis and run it through the computer to collate the data and look for unexpected correlations.

The truth, though, was that this small group of Academy cadets always been the core team that kept *Chihuahua* running during the brief time they had been a crew. Of all the Academy students who had launched from Earth bound for the *Chihuahua*, this small group were the people who had proven to be the most ready for real duties, who could have set foot on any ship in the fleet and be a strength to the crew. There were others in the crew who contributed, many of whom were good at their jobs, but these were the people who made the ship work and set the tone of the crew's character.

Burkhard must have recognized that when he assembled this analysis group. None of them missed the implication that this report was something their Captain felt was important. They recognized that many teams across the Earth Alliance would be studying the same data, but with something this critical the redundancy seemed only fitting.

Chris was looking rather stressed as he read the reports. His glasses were off his face and he was rubbing the bridge of his nose when he finally broke the silence which had been plaguing the room since he started the review. "Well," he said. "I'm stumped."

Heads from everywhere in the room turned to look at him at that. "Stumped about what?" Rachel asked.

Chris didn't answer directly. Instead, he turned to Tarbell with a question. "Di, if you saw a battleship firing single barrel sixty inch broadside rail guns, how old would you say it was?"

"From a battleship?" Tarbell replied, surprised. "More then a century, at least. The Sirius class battleships we were refitting during the Wargame were equipped with them, and even the more modern Cleopatras don't have anything smaller than sixty two inches."

"I'd say about two thirds of the ships Home Fleet fought were equipped with hundred year old weapons, then," Chris replied. "Yet those stealth systems... I've never seen anything like them, before. They're so advanced I can't even figure out what technology they were based on. They also were better with precision targeting, I think. Emily, in order for a ship to hide in the active sensor shadow of another, how close does it have to be?"

She clucked under her breath as she did the mental math. "Pretty close, depending on the range. Based on what I read of the range the hidden fleet revealed itself from behind those troop carriers, I'd say no more than a hundred yards."

"A hundred meters distance between hundreds of ships, with no collisions?" Chris mused. "No chance they managed that without some way of sensing where their partner ships were, yet there is no way they could use active sensors without revealing their position. I'd say that's pretty conclusive, then – there's a way to see them with passive scans, at least at short range, with sufficiently advanced sensors. Sensors we don't have and they do, which means their sensors are better than ours. However, while they have all this extremely advanced electronic warfare stuff, there is zero advancement anywhere else. In fact, my guess is this stuff was grafted on to mothballed ships, similar to how we added the shields and modified the particle cannons on board *Chihuahua*. Only they didn't bother with corvettes, and went straight to the battleships and heavy cruisers."

"If that was the case, the ship configurations should be in our database, and we should be able to identify who it was easily," Rachel pointed out.

"Which just adds to the puzzler, because they aren't," Chris mused. "Unless... unless something has been done to them to confuse the computer's ability to identify them unaided." He grimaced. "Which means we'll need to take the images of the attacking warships and compare them – by eye – to every single ship design for the past couple of centuries from every nation in the known universe." He paused. "The computer might be able to prioritize the list of comparisons for us, but it'll still take a while. I think we need to ask Yannis to bring lunch with him when he comes by."

Chris Desaix stepped on the *Chihuahua's* bridge in a capacity other than that of an engineer. He hated that, but the new dynamic that the surprise attack on Earth brought about forced him to accept extra duties. His regular station was the engineering console, but now he needed to accept additional roles.

The reorganization of the watches also re-ordered duty stations. There were now four six-hour watches instead of the three eight hour watches they'd had earlier. Christopher Desaix would now be taking command of one of those watches. Everyone took two shifts a day – usually with rest shifts in between – and his second one would keep him in engineering, but having him in a 'command' slot for six hours each day was something he hadn't ever expected. Chris wasn't sure what to make of it.

Obviously, Burkhard was at the top of the chain. He took the First Bridge Team, which consisted of Rachel at tactical, Schubert at the helm, and Mumford at communications. That was it. No-one else was needed on the bridge when not at battle stations – not even at the engineer's station.

Orff would take command for the Second Bridge Team. He had Weber at the helm, Cohen at tactical, and Polk at communications. Mumford was the only person on board who specialized as a Communications Officer, but the members of the logistics team were supposed to cover for her whenever she was off duty.

It was when Rachel took the third shift that things got a little weird. When the crew requirements had been set down, the staff was set for just one layer of redundancy, with no plans made for the possibility of four separate bridge teams. Langer, who was a computer tech nominally attached to both the engineering and tactical sections, wound up not at tactical – as would be expected – but at communications, allowing Mumford to spend her second shift training Polk and a few others to eventually take over the role. Tarbell, the weapons control officer, shifted to tactical, but she'd probably need Rachel to give her some on-the-job training if that became a permanent position. Finally, Schubert stepped up for his second shift – there was no-one else who could take the job outside of he and Weber, and no-one was available to train anyone else. Once there were others available for the tactical position, the hope was that Rachel – who was a qualified pilot in civilian circles but couldn't fly a military vessel due to her eyes – would be able to let someone else take over her tactical shift with the first team so she could start training new navigators, as Wolf and Weber were too busy with other duties to train them. Eventually, after a three month deployment, it was hoped that crash courses like these would complete the training that they were supposed to be getting in Academy classroom settings... and if they managed to avoid too many combat situations, that might be possible. Of course, as they were heading into potentially hostile space, so that relatively peaceful cruise did not look very likely.

Then there was the fourth bridge team, which Chris was in charge of. In terms of where he was listed in the chain of command, there were three other people whose rank entitled them to take command ahead of Chris. Lt. Commander Emily Mumford, who was too busy training her replacement to take on a shift, was one. Lt. Commander June Ehrlich was another, but her rank was largely an honorary one, and she was incapable of running a watch. Finally, there was Chris' superior in engineering, Lieutenant Rappaport, who probably should have been promoted to Lt. Commander when the Academy promotions were converted over.

Chris had expected Rappaport to take the watch command, so when it went to him he was shocked. When he protested the assignment, asking Burkhard the reason he had given the fourth watch, all that he got as a reply was a cryptic, "Don't think we've stopped evaluating students just because the Wargame was cancelled."

It wasn't until he received the crew assignments for his watch that he understood. His 'tactical officer' wasn't a commissioned officer at all – it was Petty Officer Jonathan Rosebaugh. In other words, while sitting at officer of the watch, Chris would have to teach the tactical position to someone who had zero practical competence in the field... and, in the process, demonstrate his own competence or lack thereof. Considering the way everyone had just 'graduated' from the Academy, this was, perhaps, a 'final exam' for his tactical prowess.

He was quite glad to have Weber at the helm for her second shift, although he would have preferred Schubert for the simple reason that they had known each other that much longer. He also had another effective specialist for his bridge crew: Once working as a dispatch officer for the Army, Corporal Deborah Culp (who had, like Beccera, been given a 'temporary' Naval rank of Petty Officer first class) was probably more qualified to operate communications than anyone but Emily Mumford. At least she knew the equipment, even if she did have trouble translating the Army vernacular she was used to into Navy vernacular.

Chris had been dreading this first watch, so he was rather surprised – and quite a bit relieved – to see Burkhard waiting for him when he and his watch crew arrived. "Are you coming to take the watch off my hands, after all, sir?" Chris asked, only half jokingly.

"It's your first duty watch," Burkhard replied. "I figured you might need a little orientation."

Chris winced slightly. "Well, I have to admit I'm not entirely clear on my job, here. From the description, it mostly my job to ensure that the people who need to stay awake are still awake."

A slight lip twitch told Chris that Burkhard had similar thoughts, sometimes. "Yes, that's pretty much the job of the watch lead. There are a few... details, however, which that description leaves out."

"Such as?" Chris prompted.

"There are always minor decisions that need to be made, usually routine stuff. Your job will be to decide if it's something that requires alerting me, or if it's something you can handle on your own. For example, the flagship calls and says we're out of formation – we've been running too fast, for one reason or another, and need to reposition ourselves. Do you need to call me to the bridge, or can you make that judgment yourself?"

Chris frowned. "Well, I know I could handle it, regardless... but depending on the severity of the course or speed correction we need to make, you might need to be informed. At least, that's what the textbooks say."

"The textbooks are a bit paranoid about things like that," Burkhard replied, grinning slightly. "As long as there's little chance we will drift into the path of another ship, I'm pretty sure you can make the correction yourself and simply report to me when I take over. Okay, next scenario: A fight has broken out between two crewmen. They are pulled apart, and it turns out both were drunk. What do you do?"

"Hold both in the brig and make a report for you to deal with at the next captain's mast," Chris replied confidently.

"Right. Now, an enemy ship appears suddenly. What do you do?" Burkhard asked.

Chris' eyes narrowed. "Class of ship? Distance?"

"Within extreme firing range," Burkhard replied, lips twitching again. "Indeterminate configuration, although it may be in the size range of a frigate or light cruiser."

"Speed and course?"

"They're trying to intercept you, coming from the bow. Speed is approximately that of an average frigate traveling at top speed."

Chris nodded. "Okay. I should raise shields and call all hands to battle stations, change course to present our shields to the enemy and prepare the particle cannon, but hold off on engaging as long as possible. At the same time, I need to call you to the bridge while still trying to identify the ship. Until you arrive, it will also be my judgment call as to whether we should open fire or not."

Burkhard grinned slightly. "Yeah, that'll do. Speaking of unidentified ships, what is the progress on your little analysis project?"

"No results, yet," Chris huffed in frustration. "The problem is we still need to narrow down the search. We have limited it to the four foreign powers that intelligence suspects are capable of producing such a fleet, but there are still thousands of different classes of warships to go through; remember, we're talking about every warship produced in a two hundred year span. We've brought most of the Marines into the project, since they were getting a bit antsy and we needed more pairs of eyes. Mr. Orff insisted on joining the project when we tried going through him to get the extra personnel, and has since started taking over." He grimaced. "Rachel, Emily, and I didn't exactly appreciate that, but the others have started reporting to him. He'd have more recent results than I would."

"Hm," Burkhard mused. "What are the chances that this isn't a force from one of those four powers, but instead – say – a lost colony?"

Chris gave the matter some thought. There were quite a few expeditions which had left Earth to colonize another planet that were never heard from again – the so-called 'lost colonies.' The Virgin Planets originally fell into this category, after their initial generation ship had gone off course a hundred years into the colonists' journey and landed them much further away than anyone had anticipated, but they had been rediscovered about four hundred years later. By the time they had re-encountered human society, they were the fourth largest power in the universe, and would have been the largest by now if not for the fact that their internal political structure had been so unstable. There was always the chance that more lost colonies were out there, building their own empires which could eventually grow back into contact with the rest of humanity. And there was always the chance they would not be friendly when they did show up.

"It's possible, I suppose. I don't think it's very likely, though – outside of the new electronic warfare packages grafted onto the hulls, the technology is very much in line with the ships in most major fleets about a century or so ago. I'm no anthropologist, but I've never heard of parallel development of isolated societies quite that exact, before."

"Neither have I," Burkhard admitted.

"At any rate, we're continuing the comparisons. So far we've pretty much eliminated the Dragons as our attackers, but only because they had a lot fewer ship classes to compare with. The Cygni and Pleiades are both very... prolific, in terms of ship designs, and the Virgin Planets have more than everyone else put together. Worst case scenario, it'll be a week before we're done going through the records," Chris admitted.

"Well, keep it up. The con is yours." He paused, then glanced over to where Jonathan Rosebaugh was fumbling with his console. "You can kill time working with any station on the bridge, as long as you're here to be on call at a moment's notice. You might want to start by seeing to him."

One of the larger screens in front of Rosebaugh started flashing error warnings. Chris winced. "That might be a good idea."

Chapter XXV

"Captain to the bridge," came Chris Desaix's call echoing through the *Chihuahua's* hallways. "Ms. Mumford to the bridge. Flag to the bridge." Beccera's squadron had arrived at the rendezvous point earlier that day, but there was no telling when Vice Admiral Breslau's fleet would show up. The data packet accompanying the written confirmation of Beccera's commission and orders indicated that it could be anywhere from one day to one week before anyone arrived, even if nothing was wrong. They were off most space lanes, however, and therefore were pretty safe from encounters with hostile forces.

"This is Burkhard," the captain replied from the intercom by his bed, blinking himself awake. "Is it the fleet?"

"No, sir," Chris replied. "But it is *apparently* a friendly."

The subtle emphasis on 'apparently' was rather disturbing. Now that he was looking for it, Burkhard could feel the slight vibration in the hull that was caused by the particle cannons charging, even if the distinctive hum of the quantum wheels that powered the shields was missing. "Who is it?"

"The ship has been identified as the *Athena,* a Valkyrie class heavy cruiser attached to Breslau's fleet. It claims, however, to actually be the ambassadorial yacht for our representative on Cygni. And it is accompanied by a frigate identified as belonging to Cygni, itself."

Burkhard was instantly alert. Giving out the location of a secret rendezvous like this in time of war was tantamount to treason. The *Athena*'s captain had better have a good excuse. "Order all hands to battle stations, but don't raise the shields just yet. I'll be right there."

Beccera was the first one to make it to the bridge, but he wasn't quite sure what to do when he got there. "Report." he ordered.

"Switch to tactical display," Chris ordered, speaking over his shoulder towards Jonathan Rosebaugh.

"Certainly... but, uh, how?" the weapons tech asked hesitantly.

"Move," Chris said, clapping the man's shoulder (perhaps a little rougher than he intended). When Jonathan stood up and stepped aside, he took the tactical position and gestured to the keyboard. "And watch. You'll need to know this in the future."

"Yes, sir," Rosebaugh replied.

"This bank of controls lets you pull up and configure the tactical display. See? Ship sizes, strengths, identification when available, and relative positions all can be included, or not, as you select. Now, just press this button, and you'll put the display up on the main screen. Got it?"

"I'm not sure. I... that was very fast. I may have missed something." Rosebaugh admitted.

Chris sighed. "Well, assuming we get through this situation, I'll make sure you practice until you know how to use this station by heart. In the meantime, sit back down here; I've got another job to do."

Several more bridge crew arrived as the call to battle stations was answered, while Chris went over and briefly told Beccera about the *Athena*. Rachel was one of the first – dressed in nightclothes and a robe, but there nonetheless – and quickly relieved Rosebaugh. Emily Mumford came by and relieved Culp at communications, Schubert came to take the helm seat alongside Weber, and so on. Commander Burkhard was the last to arrive, and he didn't look pleased.

"Where's Mr. Orff?" he asked, glancing around the bridge.

"I contacted his stateroom just a second ago, captain," Emily said. "He's still getting dressed, but he'll be up momentarily. Uh, he was caught in the bathroom."

Burkhard rolled his eyes. "Well, I suppose we all have to go sometime. All right. Let's hear what these new guys are up to, shall we?"

"Hailing the *Athena*, Captain," Emily replied, grinning slightly. There was a brief delay as the query traveled through space, was received, interpreted, and responded to. "Transponders check out as friendly, and codes are proper. Due to the extended range, however, expect a nine second lag time between transmission and reception, sir."

"Understood. On screen."

The tactical display was replaced with the face of Captain George Tager, a man Burkhard vaguely knew from his Academy days. What he remembered of the man lead him to believe that this was, indeed, the right person, and that he didn't seem to be under duress at all. Assuming, of course, that there was no visual manipulation going on to mislead them.

Tager began without preamble. "I assume you just came from the Wargame?"

"Yes, sir," Burkhard replied – it wasn't like he could keep a secret of the fact that this squadron was run by Academy crews, after all. "Acting-Commodore Beccera, here, is our temporary flag officer. Is something going on?"

"Yes, something very bad is going on," Tager sighed. "Since you're here, I assume Earth has already been hit?"

Burkhard raising an eyebrow. "And just how did you happen to know about it?"

"We received intel it was going to happen, but too late to act on it. There's something more, but I can't talk about it here," Tager replied, grimacing.

Orff finally showed up at the bridge, looking immaculate. He glanced at Rachel and sniffed in disgust. "You're out of uniform, Ms. Katz."

"Quiet!" Burkhard snapped at him before returning his attention to the screen. "Mr. Tager, I am not entirely comfortable with your presence, to say the least. Our records still show another ship as the Ambassadorial Yacht in Cygni. Our suspicions are that Cygni might have been our attacker, and yet you led a corvette from the Cygni to a secret rendezvous point. And now, you have suspicious knowledge of the attack without explaining where you got it. I'm sure you can see my... concerns."

Orff hesitated. "Um, sir... we—"

"I said shut up!"

"But—"

"Mute!" Burkhard ordered, and Emily quickly cut the sound on the transmission to *Athena*. "Okay, now that we aren't being overheard, what is so damned important?"

"I don't think that Cygni is the attacker, sir," Orff stammered.

Burkhard glared at him in disbelief. "Oh? And just why is that?"

"We identified the attacking ships, sir," Orff explained. "Only a couple of hours ago. They're old Pleiades Confederation warships, sir, heavily modified."

There was a long pause. Beccera opened his mouth to say something, but couldn't get any words out. Burkhard, however, didn't have that problem. "You found this out *hours* ago, and I'm just finding out about it now. Why?"

"Um... we felt it wasn't a high enough priority to wake you, sir," Orff replied, paling. "While useful information, there was no actionable intelligence gained. We felt it could wait until your shift began."

Chris's eye twitched from his place by the engineering station. "Excuse me, Rob, but who is 'we'? I was the project manager, last I heard, and I certainly didn't know about this."

"Neither did I," Rachel added.

"You were on duty when the decision had to be made!" Orff protested to Chris. "And you were asleep," he added to Rachel.

"Then why wasn't I informed?" Emily asked, smirking at him.

"To hell with that!" shouted Beccera, finally unable to contain himself. "I ordered this project personally, and any report of this nature should have been made to me. I was off duty, but most certainly awake, yet you didn't even think to contact me. Explain yourself!"

"You ordered this project?" Orff replied hoarsely. "I didn't know. I thought—"

"All right," Burkhard intervened, glaring at his exec. "Mr. Orff, I am sorely disappointed in you. I had reservations about your actions that had I intended to discuss with you privately, but at this point it's a little hard to address them quietly. Not only did you take over a project that was not assigned to you, taking the ability to make decisions away from those who were supposed to be in charge, you also made the *wrong* decisions when the time came to make them. We'll discuss this later. For now, just get off my bridge."

"I... yes, sir." Orff hesitated, then stiffened to attention and left the bridge.

"Damn," Burkhard sighed. He looked at Beccera. "Maybe I should transfer him to another ship. I don't think I can keep him here after that, do you?"

"I didn't think you should have kept him as first officer at all," Beccera replied. "I'll certainly sign any transfer papers you put in front of me."

"Captain, Mr. Tager is wondering what's going on," Emily called.

"He's asking if we require assistance. He thinks we just had a mutiny or something...."

Burkhard flushed. "Please, begin transmitting again."

"You're on now, sir."

"Conrad? Is everything okay over there?" Tager said, his voice showing genuine concern.

Burkhard winced. "As you're aware, sir, we don't exactly have the most experienced crew on board. I had an extremely poor case of mismanaged protocol and had to discipline one of my officers. It will not happen again."

"I... see," Tager said, his tone clearly showing he didn't. "At any rate, I'm afraid there's not much I can tell you over a comm transmission. Is there any way to convince you of my trustworthiness without revealing everything in an open channel like this?"

"Perhaps," Burkhard sighed. "I still would like to know what you're doing leading a Cygni warship to a classified rendezvous location, before I make any sort of decision."

"I do have a reason, but that too should not be discussed over an open channel. If possible, I would like to shuttle over – with the Cygni captain – and talk about it with... uh, acting-Commodore Beccera, was it?"

Burkhard looked at Beccera, who nodded. "Very well. But we don't exactly have a decent meeting facility on board this ship. In two hours, we'll rendezvous on board the *Superb* – she's got the largest and most complete wardroom of all ships present."

"I'll see you then."

The connection closed. Burkhard sighed, closing his eyes. "Mr. Schubert."

"Sir?"

"Prepare a shuttle for transport to the *Superb*. Ms. Katz, Drew, I hope you'll accompany me. Mr. Desaix, you still have the con. Ms. Mumford, please inform the other ships of the impending meeting, and then ask Mr. Orff to meet us at the shuttle bay." He paused. "Ms. Katz, congratulations. Until further notice, you are my new first officer."

EAS Superb

It was the first time Rachel had ever seen the formal uniform of a Cygni Naval Officer outside of pictures. It wasn't nearly as silly looking up close as she had expected – in fact, it was rather intimidating.

The latest trend in military fashion took ancient designs retooled with modern materials. The fad had started with the Army of the Federal Republic of Iota Draconis, whose ceremonial dress uniform echoed the garb worn by ancient Imperial Roman soldiers, complete with intricate helmets, but in shades of green rather than red. The Dragons' naval officers soon followed suit, introducing uniforms that resembled a more lightweight version of ancient Japanese samurai armor, likewise in shades of green, but *sans* helmet. Rachel's own dress uniform was pieced together from several eras, consisting of a pair of comfortable black khakis, such as what was fashionable in the twentieth and twenty-first century, and an undecorated black dress shirt from the same era. Her accompanying vest resembled a Renaissance-era archer's jerkin, but was closed with modern magna-seal fastenings in a pattern reminiscent of the traditional tied lacing. And there were the deerstalker caps – Rachel sometimes wondered if the uniform designer included them because he read too much Sherlock Holmes as a child, or if he simply added them as a joke.

Cygni's uniform designers, however, had sought to surpass all others in their flamboyant historical extravagance. Cygni had nine distinct uniforms in their Navy alone, and nearly all mirrored something from the era of sailing ships, pirates, and buccaneers. 'Winter Dress,' for example, resembled the uniform Blackbeard the Pirate supposedly wore, right down to the tapers he'd light to wreath his face in smoke whenever he fought (represented by fiber-optic 'candles' and miniature fog machines). Rachel shuddered to think how an officer in the Cygni Navy was supposed to don a space suit over such bizarre accoutrements. Cygni 'Winter Undress' resembled the buckskin shirts and pants the original buccaneers wore in the early days of that people. They did have a particular set of khaki uniforms used only in diplomatic missions, but that was the only uniform that didn't fit the "ancient sailors" theme.

The two Cygni officers who had accompanied Captain Tager were not dressed in khakis, but in the complicated Winter Dress uniforms. It did little to alleviate the feeling of unease Rachel experienced meeting with representatives from a country with the reputation that Cygni had, to say the least.

Captain Tager stood in front of the room, clearing his throat to end the conversations that were going on so he could start the meeting. "Ladies and gentlemen, good to see you all alive and safe. It's been a pretty hard few days for all of us from Earth Alliance, hasn't it?"

There were some definite murmurs of agreement, but Beccera, sitting at the end of the conference table, didn't like the small talk Tager was opening with. Knowing that Pleiades was the likely aggressor had twisted something inside him, and now he was more desperate than ever for information.

"Please, Mr. Tager," he said. "Let's just get on to business, shall we?"

"Yes, of course, sir." Tager replied. "Let me start by introducing our guests from the Cygni Confederation, Commander Jared Aebischer, and the civilian intelligence representative he has been escorting to this meeting, Ms. Sophia Saprykin. Ms. Saprykin is the reason I'm here right now, fully informed, and not still hanging about around a Cygni dockyard without even knowing about the strike on Earth. Ms. Saprykin, if you would?"

"Thank you, George," the woman replied gracefully. She was middle-aged, quite a bit overweight, and looked like someone's kindly old stay-at-home mom. Most of those in the room, however, recognized her by name as one of the best 'declared' intelligence analysts Cygni could boast. She was known for an intuitive grasp of events that was unheard of, and frequently was requested by name by foreign powers whenever a joint intelligence operation was being enacted. Her presence showed just how important this meeting was to the Cygni, and she immediately had the attention of everyone in the room. "Ladies and gentlemen, over the past year, the Pleiades Republic has been systematically killing the intelligence officers and assets of every foreign power they could reach. The only nation which seemed capable of infiltrating even the lower echelon ranks of their government was the Larkin Triumvirate, whose information – from what we can tell – is spotty, at best.

"Recently, however, we acquired a new source we believe to be quite reliable. His report is, to say the least, astonishing. He is a project manager for the archaeology division of the Pleiades Science Directorate, and when Director Ian Karlsson gave him inexplicable orders regarding his recent archaeological discovery he decided to investigate his superior. At great risk to his own life, he made contact with the only foreign power he had reliable access to – us – and sent information he uncovered suggesting a secret alliance between Pleiades and an unknown power.

"It was this unknown power that convinced Pleiades to start a war with the Earth Alliance, hoping to prevent an expected delegation of foreign experts to come and investigate a certain archaeological discovery. From that, together with information we... obtained... from the Larkin Triumvirate, we correctly assessed Pleiades intention to assault Earth itself. The whole invasion is supposed to cover the destruction of a scientific fleet en route to the Pleiades home system; conquering Earth itself would merely have been a bonus to them, from what we can tell."

Beccera stiffened. "Destruction? Are they to accept no quarter, then?"

"None," Saprykin confirmed.

"Wait. You're saying they conducted a massive strike on our homeworld – sacrificed tens of thousands of military personnel and dozens of capital ships – just to cover an attack against a minor *archeological* expedition?" Burkhard interjected incredulously. "What is this discovery? Are they insane?"

Saprykin sighed. "I can only speculate that something about that particular expedition must have severely threatened them or their secret allies in some way.

"This behavior is... troublesome. I doubt it would come as any surprise for you to learn that we in Cygni have been preparing a possible action of our own against Earth Alliance, although not on so grand a scale as what just happened. After this intelligence assessment, however, we feel that Pleiades is too great a threat for us to stay on the sidelines. With that in mind, I'm here as Cygni's representative to offer you our assistance in this war."

The tension in the room suddenly went up. Cygni had been known to blame others for wars they started, just to get two enemies to fight each other. The thought on everyone's mind was that this could be just such a case... especially given the flimsy explanation for Pleiades motives and their admission of hostility.

Tager stepped in at that point. "Our embassy's analysts confirmed their data," he said. "While we do have trust issues with Cygni itself, all of the evidence points to their telling us the truth this time. Furthermore, we need to work together on this, because we have a window of opportunity to launch a counterstrike that we will lose without the support of their ships."

Beccera frowned. "Explain."

"In order to hide their massive military upgrade," Saprykin replied, taking over once again for Captain Tager, "Pleiades has been basing their new war fleet outside of their home system. When they officially admit they were the ones who attacked Earth – and we believe they will when they hear back about the success or failure of the mission to destroy the science fleet – the need for secrecy will be over, and they will redeploy the new ships defensively. Until this happens, however, a quick strike force could do significant damage to their home system's infrastructure.

Their current home fleet is relatively small, and is filled with older model ships that haven't had the new technologies integrated, yet. Cygni wants to strike, but the plan requires two separate major battle forces. We only have one assembled and ready to go at this time. Your command is moderately small – just a single squadron of outdated warships – but your one squadron should be all we need for the plan to work."

"What plan?" Beccera asked, narrowing his eyes dangerously.

"Well... I'd like to ask Commander Aebischer to explain that for me, as the military liaison," Saprykin replied, bowing to her Navy escort.

"Thank you, Milady." Aebischer stood, giving his seat to the intelligence officer as he took her place in front of the assembly. "Current estimates show that we have a sufficient force assembled to engage the current Pleiades Home Fleet effectively in battle, although the result of such a battle would likely be a mere prolonged stalemate. However, we feel we have sufficient force to draw the enemy out of position, pulling them from their home world and leaving their orbital infrastructure almost defenseless. These orbital stations are not entirely unarmed, but a single squadron of warships should be able to disable and hopefully destroy them with minimal losses in a short space of time.

"Pulling a squadron out of our own fleet, however, would likely not leave us sufficient force to pull the enemy fleet out of position and keep them there. We know of exactly two squadrons we could possibly call upon to aid us in this battle before our window of time opens up, and one of them still might not show up in time: Yours, and the other Earth Alliance squadron which you were supposed to rendezvous with at this location. If we don't move today, however, we may be too late."

Beccera nodded. "I see. So you think it will take, what, six more days for their attack force to return to Pleiades with their report?"

"I think it will take significantly longer, given that they are limping home and must tend to damaged ships the whole way," Aebischer replied. "Ten days, I'm thinking. However, in four days, the science fleet from Earth to Pleiades will meet with a task force intending to destroy them and likely be wiped out, and once that is done any other forces they've been able to assemble in their military build-up will be free to join the defense of their homeworld.

"As I alluded to earlier, it is imperative that we protect this archeological expedition and discover why it is of such extreme significance to the Pleiades Confederation. Unfortunately, we have nothing that can arrive in time to intercept the attack. We were hoping your forces... Commodore

Beccera, is something wrong?"

Beccera suddenly went so pale he looked like the white was painted on his face, and he looked like he was about to fall out of his chair. His wife was alive, yes... but in four days, she wouldn't be. And there was nothing he could do about it.

"Commodore Beccera's wife is on that archaeological expedition," Burkhard explained. "Perhaps we should take a moment and have some coffee brought in while we consider our tactical options?"

As the meeting paused for the wardroom stewards to attend to the refreshments (and Beccera to compose himself), Rachel started a hushed conversation with someone over her wrist comm. "Mr. Aebischer," she called, so loudly that everyone stopped to stare at her. "Precisely how long do you estimate it will be until that science fleet can be attacked by Pleiades forces? To the minute, that is?"

Aebischer hesitated, then checked the data in his notes. "Four days, three hours, twenty two minutes, milady."

"Four days, three hours, and twenty-two minutes," she relayed into the comm device. No-one heard the reply, but her relieved smile said that the answer was a good one. "Mr. Aebischer, you may not have a ship which can make it there in time, but we have one very special corvette which might."

"You've got two hours to leave, and yet you're spending that valuable time trying to transfer one of your officers?" Tager asked in disbelief. He was having a last-minute conversation with Commander Burkhard on the Sirius while both men were waiting for their shuttles. A couple of the other officers waiting to depart were also in the room, making it very obvious they weren't paying any attention. "I'm not even sure why you're bothering with this mission – what can a single corvette do against a fleet, anyway?"

"This is the last thing I need to do before leaving," Burkhard replied, ignoring the slight on the Chihuahua. He didn't want to have to brief Tager or any of the Cygni forces on the ship's upgraded capabilities. "It's a disciplinary issue. Orff is a good kid, really – he can take a watch, he's very organized, and he loves paperwork. His theoretical knowledge of tactics is impressive, although he has proven to be poor at applying that knowledge. He'd be a capable back-up tactical officer, or even an ideal logistics officer, but he needs a bit of humbling, first. He forced me to publicly admonish him in such a way that he can't serve in my ship's chain of command, so he's been taken off the watch rotation. With a fresh start he can still be a competent officer, and I need someone who can keep a watch to replace him. I've already appointed a new first officer to replace him, but I need either another navigator or another communications officer desperately."

Tager shook his head. "I don't have a navigator to spare, and none of my communications officers could take a watch. I do have a logistics officer who has experience keeping a watch, and might be able to sub in as a communications officer in a pinch – Lieutenant Jari Koivu. Would he do?"

Burkhard sighed. "At this point, a paperweight would do if it could handle a watch. I'll take him."

"I'll signal *Athena* to send him on over to your ship on the double," Tager replied.

"Good," Beccera said, stepping into the waiting room. "Then we can get going. Our shuttle is ready, Conrad."

"And just where do you think you're going?" Captain Barbara Meier of the *Natsugumo* protested.

Beccera glanced at her. "To my ship, of course."

Meier shook her head. "I'm afraid not. Mr. Beccera, you are the only flag officer we have, and because of that there are two reasons you should not go back to that ship."

"And those are?" the Army officer asked, turning a glare on her.

"W-well, sir," Meier began, stuttering a little under that glare. "A corvette – or 'pocket frigate,' if you insist on calling it such – doesn't have the command and control abilities that a flag officer needs to command a fleet. It was okay for you to stay on board the *Chihuahua* when your commission as acting-commodore was little more then a formality that would be terminated the moment we met up with the rest of the fleet. Now that you're leading us into battle, however, things are changing. You have now assumed genuine authority, and your rank of Acting Commodore, once a mere formality, is now much more than that... and the *Chihuahua* is not equipped for the reality of being a squadron's flagship."

Burkhard glared at the *Natsugumo's* captain. "Ma'am, if command and control is the problem, I am certain our engineering team could build a command and control center in a matter of hours."

"I'm sure you could," Meier replied knowingly. "After all, your ship was favored above all others when it came to picking your crew."

Rachel opened her mouth to protest, but found she couldn't. The facts just weren't on her side – they were allowed to hand-pick the ideal crew from the Academy, after all, and she knew it. It was entirely possible that nepotism was the reason they had been granted that particular privilege, and she certainly couldn't prove otherwise, or even come up with a plausible alternative explanation. Regardless, it seemed rather petty to bring it up now that there was a war on.

"However," Meier continued. "Even if that is the case, there is another matter you really should consider. As the only flag officer representing Earth Alliance, it is your responsibility to remain with the bulk of the fleet, especially when we are about to engage in joint maneuvers with a foreign power of dubious reliability."

"But my wife..." Beccera sputtered. "I need to be part of the rescue! I can't just—"

"Drew," Burkhard sighed, gently grabbing his right arm and turning the man to face him. "As reluctant as I am to admit it, Barb's right. You have to remain with the fleet. And you're emotionally compromised – we'll rescue your wife, and you'll be able to see her for yourself when you catch up. Trust us with her, all right?"

Beccera hesitated, taking Burkhard aside for a private conversation. "Conrad... I was very reluctant to accept this job. I only did because I expected to have your advice and council while I was in charge of the fleet. I'm not sure I can deal with this job without someone I trust nearby."

Burkhard smiled gently. "You are perfectly capable of handling this fleet, Drew. You know how to lead, how to make decisions, and how to command. All you need is a guide to Navy life... and I'm not the only one who can be that." He paused, then bent over to whisper in his ear. "I'd normally recommend the *Superb*, but Barbara's angling for her ship to be your new flag. Let's use that. Her ship's one of the newest in the squadron, and it came with modern command and control facilities, but that's not why you want to be aboard her."

"Then why?"

"While she has some of the things needed to be a good Naval officer, and her tactics are sound, I don't trust her as a leader. You can provide that leadership... and I have suspicions about certain members of her crew who I'll comm you privately about before we leave. Keep an eye on them while you're there, and let me know if you agree."

"But how am I supposed to provide that leadership?" Beccera asked, talking just as softly. "I can't command a fleet. Hell, I can't even command a *single* ship."

Burkhard smiled. "Just keep a level head, and that's all you'll need.

There are plenty of people who understand naval tactics, but not everyone can command men. You do."

Beccera paused for a long time, then finally nodded. "Very well," he said aloud. "But we'll be right behind you, so you'd better make sure my wife's in one piece when I see you again, got it?"

Burkhard grinned and saluted. "Yes, sir."

Part IV

Endgame

Chapter XXVI

EAS Keppler, in Hyperspace Transit

Dr. Kimiko Beccera was, to put it bluntly, bored. She had reviewed the briefing materials seven times already, and could recite everything included in the report from memory. She tried talking to the other scientists, but found dallying with the internal politics of their scientific cliques both tiresome and irritating, with Frank Orwell and Mara Sommers always taking opposite positions whenever even a hint of room for debate was given. The Navy did provide various recreational facilities throughout its ships, but none of what was available really interested her.

Which was why she had accepted the long-standing invitation to tour the bridge by Lieutenant Christian Shay, the captain of the science ship *Keppler*. She wasn't sure why she got an invitation and none of the other science team members did, but she wasn't going to question her luck.

Shay guided her around the bridge, explaining what each person did and how their station worked. While the *Keppler* was run by the Earth Alliance Navy, there were no weapons beyond a few basic side-arms on board. Instead, a large number of scientific instruments requiring expert specialists filled its hull. Despite the sizeable knowledge base required to operate them, however, the Lieutenant was able to demonstrate each of them to her skillfully.

"*Keppler* was initially designed specifically for the study of stellar radiation," Shay explained. "She holds the record for the closest approach to any known star – specifically Earth's Sun – when we actually went inside the chromosphere at a distance of twenty-five hundred kilometers. We had to apply some special ablative shielding for that mission, so it seems unlikely we will ever get that close again unless we want to start investigating significantly cooler stars."

"Amazing," Kimiko marveled, genuinely impressed both with the ship and with the young man. "Thank you, Lieutenant. This has all been quite fascinating."

Shay grinned at the woman. "It's a real honor just to have you here, ma'am," he said.

Dr. Beccera studied the young man in amusement. "I was unaware I had any admirers on this ship."

"Oh... I, um, it's not quite like that," Shay admitted. "While I certainly respect the fascinating discoveries you have made and your remarkable archaeological finds, I'm actually very glad to meet you for an entirely different reason."

"Oh?" she asked, curious.

"Yes, ma'am," Shay replied. "About thirty years ago, my father – a Marine – was involved in a joint training operation with an Army unit around Procyon A. As you are probably aware, there's not much at Procyon A beyond an asteroid belt. In that asteroid belt, however, were a number of Army and Marine training facilities... and at the time, it also housed the largest ammo depot in the Earth Alliance. It just so happens there was an organization that knew about the ammo depot, and believed that a few teams of Marines and Army soldiers engaged in training exercises would never be able to defend it. During the attempted raid, the Army commander saved the life of a certain Marine officer who survived long enough to become my father. That Army officer was your husband." He paused to grin. "I'm here today because of him, ma'am, and so I am very glad to be around to show you my ship."

Kimiko smiled gently at the lieutenant. "Thank you, Mr. Shay. I'll be certain to mention you to my husband when I see him next."

"Thank you, ma'am," Shay replied, bowing his head slightly. "I—"

"Emergency transmission from Flag!" the *Keppler's* Communications Officer called. "All ships stop."

"All stop, now!" Shay ordered. "All hands, to your stations."

"Initiating maneuvers," came the reply from the helmsman. Kimiko heard the gentle whirring sound caused by the vibrations of the quantum wheel coming to life and spinning the ship around. They were in hyperspace, so it took even longer to turn and decelerate than usual, but they finally came to a halt and spun back around.

"What is going on?" Shay asked.

"Apparently, the *Pascal* has detected something on its sensors, but I'm not sure what, sir."

"Well, take a look. Sensors?"

"Passive sensors do detect an anomaly. However, active sensors show that the 'anomaly' is actually a collection of warships. Readings are indistinct, but I think I'm reading a battleship, four frigates, and a dozen corvettes."

Shay's eyes narrowed. "We've got the best sensors in the fleet, and all we're getting are indistinct readings? We—"

"Particle cannon fire!" the communications officer cried. "And rail guns – headed our way! Sir, orders from Flag. Scatter and head fo—"

"Evasive maneuvers!" Shay snapped. "Get us the hell out of here! Mr. Toms, r—"

Suddenly, the bridge exploded around them. Kimiko felt something hit her hard, and then all she saw was blackness.

EAS Chihuahua

"Captain, ships sighted at extreme range on active sensors," Rachel called. "It looks like we're a little late – I'm detecting weapons fire."

"Are all hands at battle stations?" Burkhard replied.

"Yes, sir," Emily answered him.

"We'll save the shields for the last moment, then, to maximize maneuverability," Burkhard replied. "Clear for action, and ready the particle cannons."

"Rail guns?" Rachel asked.

"Not possible with the shields up," Chris reminded from his engineering station.

"So? We should have them manned in case the shields go down," Rachel replied.

"Rache... how many ships do the enemies have?"

"Approximately twenty," Rachel replied after checking her scans. "One battleship and an undeterminable number of smaller vessels – at least a dozen, probably more."

"Twenty," Chris replied. "If our shields go down... do you really think the outdated rail guns of a hundred year old corvette will help against twenty warships?"

Rachel grimaced. "I suppose not." She paused, then went back to work. "Captain, update on the situation. All seven science ships and the tender *Violet* are attempting to retreat, but the situation doesn't look good for several of them. The corvette *Yellowjacket* and light cruiser *Camel* are all they have for defense, but they are proving to be an ineffective rear-guard. I'm detecting serious damage on three of the science ships – the *Keppler, Pascal,* and *Discovery.*"

"Get us between the science ships and the enemy fleet," Burkhard said. "Mr. DiMarco, prepare as wide a spread of particle cannon fire as you can."

"I think I know what you want, sir," DiMarco replied. "Firing plan already laid in and sent to the helm."

"*Yellowjacket* has been destroyed, sir," Rachel called, her voice breaking slightly. "No life pods detected."

Burkhard swallowed. "And the science ships?"

"They're not moving very fast," Rachel sighed. "And the *Keppler* is at a dead stop. Her engines are out."

"I think the Colonel's wife was on board the *Keppler*, sir," Emily noted hesitantly.

Burkhard's lips pressed together in a thin line. "Time to intercept?"

"Thirty seconds," Rachel replied. "Twenty... nineteen... eighteen..."

"I think we'd better aim to stop right in front of the *Keppler,*" Burkhard said, watching the main screen's display. "Looks like the bulk of the enemy fleet are closing in on her."

"Twelve, eleven, ten..."

"Beginning deceleration," Wolf called.

"Seven, six, five..."

"*Camel* is launching life pods," Jeff Cohen snapped from the backup tactical station. "She's done for, sir."

"Two... one..."

"Shields!" Burkhard snapped. "Come about! Brace for impact!"

The hum of the quantum wheels was louder than before as they strained to maintain the shields under the direct, full-powered fire of one of the six frigates closing on the *Keppler*. The *Chihuahua* was a little rattled, but she survived intact... and so did the shields.

"They really work!" Cohen gasped. "Thank God, they work!"

"We're not out of the woods yet, boys and girls," Burkhard growled, staring at the screen. "We still have to return fire... and we'll have to expose ourselves to do it. Mr. Wolf, let's see if we can't do just that, shall we?"

"Turning to outflank them, sir," Wolf replied, grinning cockily. "Firing... now."

Were an observer looking from space they would have seen nothing, but the 'visual' presentation on the screen rendered the particle cannon fire as two fans of white flame jutting from the turrets with three additional steady streams of pure energy emanated from the chase guns. It was, perhaps, the strongest barrage of fire launched from a single starship in recorded human history. The fire was spread so widely that there were quite a few missed shots, but many more hit. In one brief moment, six frigates flared into six tiny stars and then were nothing.

"My God... we can actually do that?" Rachel whispered.

Even Burkhard was moderately startled at the amount of destruction his ship was able to deal out. A glance at the tactical screen, however, snapped him out of it. "We can't let them escape if we want our counterstrike to be effective. And one of them is a battleship... I can guarantee you that one will be a lot tougher to kill. Don't get overconfident."

"Plus, they can still harm us," Chris added. "Computer analysis of our shield performance is complete. Concentrated fire of several ships could conceivably penetrate our defenses down to our armor. Not to mention we've still got an unshielded band all around the ship they could get lucky shot into, and it's pretty hard to target them without revealing our biggest vulnerability."

"And there are the science ships to consider," Rachel pointed out. A quick check of the tactical display had her adding, "Though the enemy seems to have broken off pursuit of them to concentrate on us."

"*Keppler* is still unable to move," Cohen reminded everyone. "She's completely disabled. I doubt she could even leave hyperspace."

"Then we'll keep the enemies on us and off the *Keppler*," Burkhard snapped. "Mr. Schubert, let's go after that battleship, shall we?"

"Yes, sir!" Schubert replied. The *Chihuahua* danced under his fingertips, performing a fancy variant of an Immelman Turn to keep the shields towards the most likely angles of incoming fire. "Rache... that battleship. Quantum wheel or fusion drive?"

Rachel frowned at the data readout. "Scans are still scrambled. From the heat signatures, I'd guess she's a fusion drive. Why?"

Schubert grinned. "Just what I was hoping. Captain, preparing to strafe the battleship from the fusion drive blind spot."

"Fire as you bear, then," Burkhard agreed.

"Firing," Wolf said. The Chihuahua nimbly spun around once more, maneuvering faster than any of the Pleiades' warships despite the need to maintain their shields. She slipped through presenting only shields to the battleship until they were covered by the wake of its own engine exhaust, before turning to present its particle cannons once more.

Again, white lances of energy flared out from her bow, but the results weren't quite as spectacular. Terrible gouges seemed to tear through the battleship's hull, but its much thicker armor absorbed most of the damage. The Chihuahua zigzagged its way through the strafing run before once again turning their shield to face their enemy. "Well, it didn't kill 'em."

"No, it didn't," Rachel agreed, studying the sensors. "But I believe we've knocked out their main turret... and we definitely killed their electronic warfare package, because I can see them clearly enough to determine that."

"Come about for another pass!" Burkhard ordered. "Let's finish her off before—"

He couldn't finish his sentence as the ship rocked around him, sparks flying, as the concentrated fire of the battleship and seven of the remaining frigates slammed into – and partially through – the shields.

"Damage report!" he called instead.

"That penetrated, but the shields diffused the worst of it," Carol Verne said from the damage control station. "Reports are still coming in, however. Most of the damage appears to be superficial... although the shields were heavily strained. I don't know if we can deal with another shot like that before we conduct repairs."

"Well, then, we'd better kill that battleship before they can do it again, hadn't we?" Burkhard snapped. "Mr. Schubert?"

"Coming about," Schubert said. As the Chihuahua turned, he fired a few potshots at the frigates and corvettes now swarming around them.

"Receiving rail gun fire," Rachel piped in. "No effect. It seems they don't quite understand how our shields work, yet."

"We don't even understand exactly how they work, yet," Chris piped in. "Until this moment, it was only a theory they could stop a rail gun hit."

"Positioning for another strafing run," Schubert said. "Weber, prepare evasive maneuvers for me, will you? I'm not going to be able to concentrate on piloting when I'm firing, and there's some threat this time from their chase armaments."

"Will do," Weber said from the other helm station.

The particle cannons went to work again, once more tearing into the battleship. Weber carried the ship in, rotating in a spiral pattern to avoid return fire. The *Chihuahua* shuddered as one shot got through, but she was easily able to dodge most of them.

"Damage?" Burkhard asked.

"Structural only," Carol said. "A support beam for the hyperspace sensors was hit. There's a slim chance we could lose them if we take too stressful a turn."

"Noted," Weber snapped. "But I'd rather lose the sensors than the ship, thank you very much."

"I wasn't complaining," Carol replied. "No further damage reports. Sick bay mentions some bumps and bruises, but no casualties."

"Looks like we'll need a third pass to kill that beast," Schubert said. "Guns coming to bea—"

Chris's panicked voice suddenly called. "Wait! Cease fire!"

The particle cannon silenced. "Done. What's the problem?" Schubert asked, startled.

"The overheating problems for the particle cannons were effectively solved by the new design," Chris said. "But they seem to need a little fine tuning. The sustained fire overwhelmed the energy backwash absorbers' ability to keep the weapons from overheating. I can fix the problem, but not in the middle of a battle – we need a minute or two for the cannons to cool down, or we won't be able to fire them again at all."

"Don't let the enemy know that," Burkhard snapped. "Schubert, I want you to make it look like you're just repositioning us for a better run, got it?"

"Yes, sir," he replied. "Beginning maneuvers."

The *Chihuahua* began a complicated spiraling maneuver... but, just as it started making a high stress maneuver, everyone could tell something was wrong.

"What the hell?" Cohen snapped, nearly falling out of his chair.

"Oh, God, I think I'm going to be sick," Emily complained, then preceded to vomit all over the floor.

"Engineering! What's wrong with the ship?" Burkhard asked, trying to maintain a stoic demeanor while trying to keep his lunch in. "I've never experienced enough wrenching to induce... motion sickness."

Chris' voice wavered as well when he responded. "I'm pretty sure there's something wrong with the artificial gravity systems. Not my specialty, I'm afraid."

"Ensign Evans reports that he's personally going to lead the team to fix the problem," Verne reported from her station in damage control.

"Wayne?" Chris spat. "He's no good in a crisis!"

"We've better... ulp... hope he is," Burkhard replied. "In the meantime... Mr. Schubert? Would you please keep the maneuvering smooth enough to compensate, if at all possible?"

"I'm already maneuvering as smoothly as possible," Schubert complained.

"Wolfie," Weber, looking rather green from her own station supporting him at the helm, said. "I know how hard it is to make evasive maneuvers of the sort we're doing... but I also know you can keep things a little more gentle on those of us who don't have your cast iron stomach. If you don't smooth things out, I'm going to puke all over you."

"Hm, yes, dear," he replied. The spirals started widening as he reduced the rate of turn, and the corresponding feeling of the ship in motion lessened to a bearable level. The bridge crew could still feel it, however.

"Evans reporting, sir," Carol called. Usually, she didn't give status reports unless asked, but she figured this was one time everyone would want this one whether they asked her or not. "The repairs were simple – a circuit board that was apparently damaged when we were hit, and it can be easily replaced – but he needs to recalibrate the system that compensates for the artificial gravity generated by the centrifugal motion of the ship when turning. He says it will take him twenty minutes."

"That's bullshit," Chris replied. "Send Yannis Langer down to help him – what he needs is a computer tech who knows all the shortcuts. And Petty Officer Linda Flint, as well – just in case something else goes wrong, I want someone who can fix it fast... and he can't."

"Is that an order, sir?" Carol asked, amused. The Captain was the only person officially authorized to make such a request, but obviously Chris didn't care. Burkhard didn't look like he cared, either.

"No. It's an 'if you don't want to be puking your guts out for the next twenty minutes, you'll do as I say,' situation." Chris snapped.

"Yes, sir," the damage control officer replied, laughter in her voice.

At least someone's enjoying themselves, Rachel thought. *I suppose this whole gravity control problem is helping us forget how bad this situation really is... which might just be a good thing.* She squinted at the screen. "Captain, the enemy is halting their pursuit. I think they're turning to head back for the* Keppler, *sir."

"Damn," Burkhard growled. "Mr. Desaix, are the guns cooled off enough?"

"Particle cannon ambient temperature still reads higher than ideal," Chris replied. "But they should be able to manage another strafing run without overheating. Luke, reduce firing rate by three hundredths of a second per shot – that should keep them from getting too hot."

"Will do," Luke DiMarco replied from his station at weapons control.

Burkhard grimaced, although he kept the distaste out of his voice as he gave an order he wasn't sure he actually wanted to give. "Good. Mr. Schubert, if you would be so kind as to bring us back into an attack vector as quickly as possible, I will pardon you from Ms. Weber's wrath."

A slight chuckle arose from the bridge, although there was a grim undertone to it as they realized what they would have to endure. Schubert, however, just grinned.

"Yes, sir. Engaging the enemy."

"Hold on for five seconds," Chris called.

Burkhard groaned. "What now?"

"Since the battleship's electronic warfare package went down, the engineering computer has been able to analyze them for weak points. It's just coming through now. Feeding you a new firing pattern."

"That's my job!" DiMarco protested.

"No time," Chris said. "Sending to you now, Wolf."

"Firing pattern loaded and locked in."

Burkhard snorted. "Finally. Fire as you bear!"

This time, instead of ripping through random points of the thick armor hide and doing largely superficial damage, the particle cannons started making pinpoint hits in areas where the armor was weakest. Rachel, watching the tactical screen and not the rendered image on the main screen, gasped.

"My God..."

"What—" Burkhard started to ask, and then the 'visual' image caught up with her tactical readouts. It was immediately apparent that they had tunneled through into the battleship's fusion plant, as the hull was ballooning out. It rarely happened, but the phenomenon of exploding fusion plants was fairly well understood. Most of the time, surrounding ships were safe when another ship was destroyed... but, when a heavily armored ship's fusion plant exploded, the armor itself would shatter and be sent flying at speeds comparable to a rail gun. That many 'rail gun hits' could easily destroy a small ship like *Chihuahua*. "Mr. Wolf, get us the hell out of here!"

"Too late for that!" Schubert snapped. "Let's just hope the shields hold!"

Several people were tossed out of their chairs as he threw the ship into a hard right turn, putting the shield between the ship and the explosion. Almost as an afterthought, Schubert also managed to position *Chihuahua* between the explosion and the immobile *Keppler*.

The ship shuddered, but little more happened as the debris washed around them. Burkhard, who Rachel had last seen flying into the ceiling, was the first to notice that the imminent danger had passed. "Report!" he called, pulling himself to his feet. One of his legs looked a little off-kilter, however – probably a break.

Rachel had nearly flown into a neighboring station's monitor before Chris somehow caught her arm and eased her to the floor safely. She stood up and dusted herself off. "Um, stand by," she said, taking her seat again. She hoped Chris was all right – he paid for his act of heroism by cartwheeling out of his own chair and hitting his head against the ground – but she couldn't afford the distraction of checking on him herself when there was the chance that an enemy ship could come in and destroy them.

"Minimal damage," Carol called. "We were fairly well protected from the explosion, but some systems weren't prepared for the strain of the turn. Um, wait... the hyperspace sensor package is now detached from the support beams. We are still getting data from it, but if we move too quickly the line will likely break and we'll be flying blind."

"Fortunately it is still working, sir," Rachel added. "The explosion destroyed four of the smaller enemy ships, and I believe caused severe damage to all of them. I can't tell which ones, however, thanks to interference from the explosion."

"Sick bay calling, sir," Emily reported. "More casualties are being reported, though no fatalities yet. Mr. Rappaport is listed as one of the casualties."

Chris, still sitting on the floor and looking a little gray, sighed. "I'd better get down to engineering."

"Stay there," Burkhard ordered. "Ms. Mumford, tell Dr. Ehrlich to send a medic to the bridge. We've got at least two injuries – Mr. Desaix's and my own."

Carol suddenly winced, pulling out her ear bud. "Um, sir? I have a direct request for Mr. Desaix's intervention in the artificial gravity situation." She paused. "Mr. Evans refuses to allow Mr. Langer to use backup data to speed up the calibration."

"Tell him Mr. Langer knows how to make that computer calibration software work better than anyone else on this ship," Chris snapped from his place on the floor. "And he should defer to Yannis' judgment. Make it a direct order."

Verne nodded. "Yes, sir."

Chris took a deep breath, then coughed up a little blood. "Damn. Looks like I'm hurt worse then I realized. Someone has to take charge in engineering, though."

"Not your concern, Mr. Desaix," Burkhard ordered. "Just sit there and wait for the doc to send someone up here. Ms. Katz, what's the enemy doing out there while we're busy gabbing around out here?"

"I don't know, sir," Rachel replied, glancing over at Chris with concern. "They appear to be assessing the situation, themselves."

"I'm not going to abandon my engineers," Chris replied vehemently before coughing again. "But I obviously can't go down there at the moment. Jeff, could you take over tactical?"

Cohen, who had been relatively unfazed by the sudden upheaval on the bridge, nodded. "I could, but in a battle it's a good idea to have two people at tactical at all times."

Chris nodded. "I don't think I should move far, but I think I could limp over to the tactical station, and I'd be a lot more comfortable on a chair then here on this floor. Rache, I want you to go down to engineering and take over as chief. I'll take your station, but switch jobs with Jeff so that I only have to keep an eye on the monitors."

"You want me to take charge of *your* engineering staff?" Rachel gasped, incredulous. "I mean, I was able to handle the job on the *Ishmael*, but that's only because I knew more than the others there. You've got this whole crew better than me, even the ones who were just first-years yet to pick a major."

"Maybe," Chris replied. "But you've got enough knowledge now that I'd welcome you on my engineering team, and you know enough about command to make it work. You'll have team members who may know more than you, but none of them could run the place. I taught you how to run the shop while I was teaching you to be an engineer, so you should be able to handle it. Plus, you're the only person left with any real experience in the job. Go!"

"Excuse me," Burkhard intervened. "But I'd rather not have you making personnel decisions on my own bridge."

Chris scowled. "With Rappaport incapacitated I'm chief engineer, and we have an engineering crisis. I can't get down there, myself, but I can handle the tactical position. Rache, on the other hand, can do the job, and technically falls under my chain of command since you authorized my adding her to the engineering roster. You can relieve me if you prefer, but as your chief engineer I'm telling you this is the only option."

The Captain and the Engineer stared at each other defiantly for several moments before an unlikely source provided them both an out.

"Sir, I think we don't need to worry about it," Emily replied. "They just signaled their surrender. We don't need two tactical officers at the moment."

Burkhard smiled thinly. "Very well. Mr. Desaix, you can take Ms. Katz's station until the medic gets here. Ms. Katz, you are at the disposal of Engineering until further notice." He paused. "And I'll just forget what just happened here, since I'd rather not charge one of my best officers with insubordination. You get the pardon this *one* time because it's your first real combat situation, and I know what sort of stress that can cause. Just don't do it again."

Chris stiffened. "Yes... sir. I won't, sir. And thank you, sir."

Chapter XXVII

EAS Chihuahua, in Hyperspace Transit

"You know, until those ships surrendered and we had a chance to look at them, I still wasn't sure I trusted the information we got from Cygni," Burkhard sighed. "I'm not looking forward to working with them, to be honest."

Beccera, fresh from the debriefing they had just concluded after his squadron – and the Cygni fleet – reunited with the *Chihuahua*, brushed that aside. He knew that the *Keppler*, his wife's ship, had been abandoned... and that she was now on board the *Chihuahua* for medical treatment. "How's my wife?"

"Alive," Burkhard replied gravely. "Whole, and healthy. A bit bruised up, and she was nursing a concussion last I saw her, but she'll be okay. The officer who saved her life, Lieutenant Christian Shay, might not be able to say the same. He's still in surgery."

"I knew that before the meeting," Beccera snapped. "I mean, how *is* she? She was just very nearly killed by her home world for no apparent reason. That has to have come as a big shock to her."

"You'll have to go see for yourself," Burkhard suggested. "I've been too busy trying to get my ship repaired under a third string chief engineer to actually visit any of the wounded."

"Third string?" Beccera balked, momentarily startled out of his single-minded concern for his wife. "What happened to Jacques and Chris?"

"Mr. Rappaport's leg snapped when he was thrown into a table during the battle," Burkhard reported. "He'll be all right, but he's not supposed to walk on it any time soon. I've temporarily switched him onto the bridge, to take over the engineering station's bridge duties, since he can just sit in a chair most of the time he's on station."

"And Lt. Desaix?" Colonel Beccera asked.

"He had multiple injuries," Burkhard spat, looking rather annoyed suddenly. "I'm not entirely sure when or what all happened, but between a nasty fall and a rather heroic effort to save Ms. Katz, he tore his abdominal muscles, cracked a rib, and... well, I'm pretty sure something happened to him to cause internal bleeding, since he literally was spitting blood last I saw him. Possible concussion, too. The sad thing is, he'll be able to move around a lot sooner than Mr. Rappaport with his broken leg, and he's been bugging Dr. Ehrlich to release him to go back to work early. He intends to take the acting chief engineer's job on as soon as he gets out."

Beccera shook his head. "He's going to work himself to death if he isn't careful."

"In this case, I think it's more that he wants to give the *current* acting-Chief Engineer a bit of a break," Burkhard said. He gave the other man a rather deadpan look. "He actually convinced Ms. Katz to take the job for a bit. She's actually doing rather well – managed to get the hyperspace sensors reattached without the tender to help us, and settled a dispute which was threatening to halt repairs to the artificial gravity systems. She is rather overwhelmed with some of the more subtle aspects of the job, though, and Chris knows it."

"Good enough motivation for trying to escape the hospital," Beccera mused. "Speaking of which... what room is Kimiko in?"

"She's scheduled to be transferred over to the tender *Violet* for the evacuation pretty soon," Burkhard said. "So she's probably on board the shuttle already. It's not leaving for a few minutes, though, so you can catch her before she goes."

"Will do," Beccera replied. "If you'll excuse me..."

He took off at a sprint. He might be able to get to the shuttle bay in time just by walking but he wasn't going to lose any time with her, or take any chances he might miss the shuttle. He would see his wife before she left if it killed him.

He very nearly collided with three people on the run, but he paid no attention until he heard a very familiar voice call him. "Drew? Is that you?"

Col. Andrew Beccera, known to many as one of the most stable rocks in military service for over thirty years, very nearly fell stumbling to a stop as if he were a raw recruit being surprised by his drill sergeant when he heard that voice. He spun around, and almost couldn't believe his eyes... even though he had known he would be seeing her shortly. "Kimiko!"

She limped over to him as quickly as she could, almost leaping up into his arms with her last couple of steps. "I thought I heard something about you being in charge around here," she said softly, holding him. "I couldn't believe it, though. I was rescued by the Navy, not the Army, wasn't I?"

"Yeah, I'm sort of in charge here," Beccera replied, grinning happily. It didn't matter the circumstances – he was just glad to have her in his arms, alive and largely unhurt. "And yes, it was the Navy that rescued you."

"But how can that be?" she asked, perplexed. "You're an Army officer!"

Beccera laughed softly, smiling at her. "I said the same thing. It's a long story, but the short version is that I was loaned to the Navy and the Marines for the Wargame. It turns out I was the senior-most officer in the fleet, thanks to that, so they gave me the temporary rank of commodore when they split the fleet up into four different squadrons. I suppose that's a good thing – otherwise, I might not have been able to authorize your rescue mission."

Kimiko smiled, but her smile was very troubled. "And I'm very glad about that, but how did you even know we were going to be attacked? And who attacked us? We weren't at war seven days ago, and that was no pirate force."

Beccera flinched. "You haven't heard?"

"Heard?" she asked. "Heard what?"

"There was a massive surprise attack in Sol system," he explained hesitantly. "We didn't know who it was, but as we investigated we began to get tip-offs and clues. The captured ships just proved it, however."

Kimiko looked at him inquiringly. He didn't seem to want to tell her what they had found... and, unfortunately, she could only think of one reason why. "It was Pleiades, wasn't it?"

Beccera couldn't meet her eyes as he nodded. "I'm afraid so, love. And I'm very sorry."

She took a deep breath and sighed. "I see." She paused. "And you're probably going to play a major role in this war, aren't you?"

"I don't see how I can avoid it," he admitted. "And before you say anything, I know I might be coming up against your family if I do. I...

don't know what to do about that, but considering Earth itself was struck... I don't see how I can not fight in this war."

Kimiko shook her head. "I wasn't worried about that. My family won't get involved in a war on Earth, I will promise you that. You, however... I'm very worried about you. A Navy command is out of your element, and it doesn't sound like you'll be re-joining the Army any time soon. Can you handle it?"

Beccera nodded slowly. "Command is much the same, regardless of who you're working for. When it comes to tactics and strategy... well, I have good people working for me."

She smiled confidently. "Then I'll see you when you return. My fellow scientists and I are being taken to the orbital hospital at Barnard's Star to be checked out. I'll wait there until you can contact me again... and you will. You've never failed at anything you've ever tried to do, and so as long as you really try, here. I believe you'll make it work." *And,* she didn't say aloud, *I'll be praying for you.*

Beccera nodded, offering her his arm to escort her the rest of the way to the shuttle bay. *I wish I had your confidence, Kimiko...*

Chris sighed, looking over Rachel's analysis from his bed in sickbay. He wasn't able to leave just yet, but he'd managed to beg and plead for an update on the investigation into the enemy ships so he wouldn't go crazy from boredom. "Yeah, I agree. There just isn't enough left of their ECM systems to figure out how they work or how to counter them. They sabotaged them quite effectively before they surrendered. We should have taken some of that time arguing on the bridge to at least try a few things on the passive scans to penetrate their stealth. I didn't even think of that until just now. Damn."

"I think you can be forgiven for being a little distracted," Rachel mused dryly. "When I last saw you on the bridge, you were coughing up blood. I'd say that's a pretty good excuse for not thinking up something no-one else considered, either."

"I understand the *Keppler* and *Pascal* were able to detect something on their more advanced passive sensors, though," he said, deciding not to argue the point. At least, not when he was still nursing several broken ribs and just-repaired internal injuries. The dull pain he still felt was enough to kill much of his taste for debate with his favorite verbal sparring partner. "Do we at least know what those sensors can detect that ours can't, exactly?"

"Solar flare activity," Rachel replied. "Most ships are designed to filter out sensor disruption from sunspots and solar flares. The *Keppler* and the *Pascal,* however, were designed to study stars – their sensors are tuned specifically to pick them up."

Chris considered that for a moment. "So they mimic solar flares to make our sensors ignore them?"

Rachel cocked her head as she considered how to answer that. "Well, thanks to a certain science expedition we rescued, we've had a lot more scientists on board than usual to ask that question to, and their analysis suggests that it's more complicated than that. After all, *Keppler* and *Pascal* weren't detecting the ships themselves, only the 'solar flare activity' their stealth technology was mimicking. The scientists seem to think that the 'sunspot detection' was merely detection of their communications between each other rather than the ships themselves; if they were running silent, we wouldn't have gotten that much. It's something, but not much."

Chris ran his fingers through his hair, shaking his head. "Hm... an uncrackable technology that we've cracked, but the moment they know we've cracked it we've lost the advantage."

"The Second World War on Earth had several stories like that," Rachel sighed. "It's not much of a 'crack,' though. The supposed 'solar flare activity' wouldn't have even been noticed in real space; ambient solar energy would have masked it. In the starless void of hyperspace, though, it stood out."

"So it's useless at the moment," Chris said. "But it's our best lead. Maybe we can follow that thread through those stealth systems, in time."

"Perhaps," Rachel admitted. They lapsed into a bit of a silence after that. Rachel bit her lip nervously – she wanted Chris to be able to get out of sickbay and back to his job, letting her return to the tactical slot – not just because she was finding the job of Chief Engineer a little overwhelming, but because she knew he was bored and going stir crazy. The silence wasn't helping. "So... what does the doctor say about when you'll be allowed out of here?"

"She hasn't been by to see me in hours," Chris sighed. "She's not only taking care of *our* wounded, but also helping care for the crew and passengers of all of the science ships. Sick bay on the *Keppler* was destroyed, and its entire staff was killed, so she's been overwhelmed."

"Well, that was the case," Dr. Ehrlich said, coming into the room. "But now that Commodore Beccera and his ships are here, there are other doctors who can take over. Captain Burkhard wanted me to try and clear you and a few of the other wounded, now that I'm free. He wants you up available first, if possible, so you've just become my top priority. Rappaport was just cleared for desk duty, so he'll take your job on the bridge, and he wants Ms. Katz freed up for her spot on tactical, so he needs you to take over as Chief Engineer."

"Why does he need me so soon?" Rachel asked. "I was under the impression we were still waiting for some stragglers from Cygni to catch up before we began the attack."

"Commodore Beccera just returned to his new flagship, the *Natsugumo,* after giving the final briefing to Burkhard. I think he wants *both* of you available for a tactical conference prior to the assault. I told him I'd make sure you could attend." She paused. "Ms. Katz, it's possible Mr. Desaix may want some privacy while I remove his hospital gown."

Chris smirked cheekily, his eyes twinkling with humor as he glanced up at Rachel. "Oh, she can stay if she wants to. I have no problem with that."

Rachel flushed, but kept her cool nonetheless. Returning fire with a teasing wrinkle of her nose, she replied coquettishly, "I'd love to, Mr. Desaix, but I'm afraid I'm just a bit too busy for ogling at the moment."

Chris laughed, then winced as his laughter pulled on one of the temporary surgical seals holding him together. Ignoring the pain to get the last word in, he sent out a parting shot. "Another time, then?"

Ehrlich rolled her eyes. "Okay, you two, flirt later. We've all got a lot of work to do, and I'd really like to get it done in time to rest up before our next crisis."

Two hours later, Chris had been cleared to attend the tactical meeting. Stiff, temporary surgical patches had been replaced with more flexible ones that supposedly allowed him to move as if he hadn't been injured, but he still wasn't feeling well. He was having trouble focusing on the briefing, but he had already guessed the gist of it.

"Just like you," Burkhard said, wrapping things up. "The Commodore and I remain skeptical of our Cygni 'ally's' intentions, but the plan is solid enough. We are concerned about the reliance on silent running for stealth, but we don't have the same technology they used in the assault on Earth, so it's the best we can do. We did come up with a contingency plan... of sorts. You can read the briefing materials for the specifics, but it mostly consists of running away at top speed and maybe throwing a few potshots at the enemy along the way. If we get to that point, it's mission failure, so let's do our best to make the silent running work. Any other questions? No? Good. Dismissed, everyone, and head to your posts. Mr. Desaix, could I see you for a moment before you leave?"

" I'm extremely busy with the repairs, so..." Chris winced. Rachel, who had stood up, was holding her leg a little oddly... possibly because she was standing on his foot. She shot him a pointed glare. "...so I'd be grateful we can keep it brief." Another wince as Rachel shifted her weight. "Sir."

Rachel smiled prettily for him, patting him approvingly on the shoulder, and turned to follow the other officers leaving the room. Chris watched her leave until the door closed behind her, and then turned his attention to his captain.

"This won't take long," the Captain said, moving to sit closer to the younger man. "Mostly, I want to talk with you about that incident on the bridge earlier."

Chris frowned. "I knew what I was doing, there. I wasn't in the wrong. And I was within my authority as acting Chief Engineer."

Burkhard grimaced a little. "Perhaps, perhaps not. The rules that govern what constitutes an 'engineering crisis' are a lot more vague then the rules for a 'medical crisis.' It is also rare that such an incident would normally be overlooked by the courts, even if you really did have that authority." He paused. "You're a good officer, Chris. In many ways, one of the best on the ship. However, you simply *must* learn enough about the formalities of Navy life that you don't get yourself thrown in a prison ship for insubordination. I'm known as a maverick because I usually think I know better than my bosses... and I usually do. It's held me back from promotion for years. The thing is, though, I never let my 'maverick' tendencies go so far as to constitute criminal insubordination. I won't always be your Captain, and your next commanding officer may not be as understanding about the fact that you didn't have more than a semester and a half at the Academy."

"I—"

"No, let me finish," Burkhard replied. "You aren't ready to be an officer in this Navy. With another three years or so of schooling, you probably would have been, but you aren't now. The problem is, whether you're ready or not, you are one... and you're going to have to act like it. A good officer *never* contradicts his captain the way you did on the bridge. As an officer and as Chief Engineer, acting or otherwise, you can argue with him... up to a point. You have to go about it a certain way, though, at the very least."

The younger man shook his head. "In a crisis, I need to be able to think and act quickly."

Burkhard nodded. "I agree, but you also need to avoid those arguments so that you *can* act quickly. If we had been attacked while we were bickering, you and I might have gotten our ship killed. Naval discipline is sometimes a bit strict, but it also prevents situations like that from happening. Unfortunately, while otherwise a very fine officer, it is clear that you still need to learn that discipline, and imperative you do so." He paused. "Fortunately, I've come up with a solution."

"You have?" Chris' curiosity was peaked.

"I know you have been tutoring Ms. Katz in engineering for quite some time during your off hours and during your engineering work together," Burkhard said. "Well, she'll now be returning the favor. I'm assigning Ms. Katz to teach you proper Navy protocol."

"I—"

"So, get going," he gestured to the door. "You've got a lesson with her in ten minutes... which will be spent on the engineering deck while you resume your duties as our Acting-Chief Engineer."

"I... I..."

"The response you're supposed to give, by the way," Burkhard mentioned, "Is 'yes, sir.'"

There was a very, very long pause. Finally, Chris grinned, saluted and said, "Yes, sir."

"Now, that wasn't so hard, was it?" the Captain laughed. "Dismissed."

———

The captured enemy ships were being sent, with prize crews, to act as the escort fleet taking the science ships back home by way of the Barnard's Star System hospital. Barnard's Star was, technically, no longer part of the Earth Alliance, having long since severed political ties. However, its neutrality was mostly theoretical, providing just enough political protection to keep unarmed ships such as the science ships from immediate danger... although perhaps the King of Barnard's Star would be reluctant to release the captured warships once he got a hold of them.

The Earth Alliance was a particularly complex political structure. It was, in principle, a collection of hundreds of independent political systems which shared a unified military defense and guaranteed free trade between systems, but had little or no common civilian authority. In practice, however, the structure of the treaty dictated much of the political structure each member state must use, and the council heading the alliance had complete control over "new" colonies (meaning most of them).

Initially, the terms of the treaty that solidified the interstellar superpower known as the Earth Alliance were quite limited. Every nation which signed the treaty would agree to unrestricted free trade between the signers, to provide council members to serve on a governing body known as the 'Alliance Council,' and to subordinate all interstellar-capable military forces to said council (although planetary defense forces, such as civilian-run militias, sublight warships, orbital guard, and the like could be developed locally). The Alliance Council was given control of the power to issue currency, develop a military, devise a system for the induction of new members, and launch new colonial expeditions. In return, each member planet would be required to turn over thirty percent of all tax income to fund the Alliance. This arrangement, for most planets, worked out to be cheaper than building and running their own independent military force. In theory, any member state could leave the Alliance for any reason, at least during peacetime. In wartime, it was another story, but the Alliance had not intended itself to be an interstellar government when it was originally formed. It was instead formed to be a commonwealth of mutual defense and free trade.

The Alliance Council, however, had gradually expanded its powers. The original six systems – Sol, Epsilon Eridani, Epsilon Indi, Barnard's Star, Tau Ceti, and Vega – hadn't initially cared about such things as what style of government the member systems used, nor did they care about bills of rights or any other such things. The Council started expanding, however – initially by founding colonies in Castor and Pi Mensei. The Council had decided it needed colonies on which it could conduct Alliance Council work such as the construction of naval bases and shipyards, and so debate began as to how best to establish those colonies. Two opposing factions arose, and the debate nearly tore the fledgling alliance apart.

One faction, lead by the Kingdom on Barnard's Star, felt each member system should receive responsibility for one colony, each, with the rights to govern and tax said colonies falling squarely on the member system. Another, led by Earth itself, said each colony should be regarded as an equally 'independent' system as the member colonies, with an interim constitution and economic structure for each system set up by the Alliance Council for later revision once the colony was well established. Barnard's Star left the Alliance in protest when Earth's plan won. Many years after that incident, they tried to rejoin, but in the intervening years the Alliance had established new membership requirements that, it was claimed, Barnard's Star failed to meet. Barnard's Star and Earth found themselves at odds for decades until a separate treaty between the Alliance Council and Barnard's Star was settled upon, which only opened the borders for free trade purposes but left them independent from the standpoint of defense, colonization, and every other aspect of Alliance membership.

The Alliance and Barnard's Star were now strong economic partners, but on other fronts the relationship remained rather tense. Sending them the prize ships almost certainly meant losing them. But at least, since it was an independent power, it wasn't likely that the unarmed science ships were being sent into a war zone. Which meant Kimiko Beccera was safe.

And that was the only comfort Acting Commodore Andrew Beccera could take as he led the remaining fleet of warships into the first Naval battle of his life.

Chapter XXVIII

EAS Chihuahua

"They don't seem to have noticed us yet, sir," Emily Mumford whispered from her station. "The plan's holding up so far."

Burkhard chuckled. "'Running silently' means to deactivate anything that can produce detectable emissions, including the engines, and to reduce our power generators to minimum. It may even require some ships to take parts of life support off line, like the artificial gravity systems. It does not, however, require actual silence. Sound doesn't usually travel through the vacuum of space, so you don't have to whisper, Ms. Mumford."

She flushed slightly. "Yes sir."

Burkhard turned to his tactical officers. "Time to the launch of Phase II?"

"Twenty three minutes, sir," Cohen answered from the backup tactical station. "It's too late to do much about it now, sir, but the squadron will be a few hundred kilometers out of position at the start of Phase II, and about three thousand kilometers when the third phase begins. We have no way of correcting course before Phase III begins without giving away our position."

Burkhard took in a deep breath, and then let it out slowly. "Well, I've never been on a mission where everything went according to plan. If that's the worst issue we have to deal with, today, we'll be in luck. Ms. Katz, how is it going with the passive sensors?"

"Too many false positives to be sure of anything. Alcyone has multiple stars that are heavily active with sunspots, solar flares, and the like. It's causing a lot of interference," Rachel replied. She glanced over at the Engineering station before remembering that Chris and Lt. Rappaport had switched places. "Mr. Desaix made the suggestion that we attempt some sort of visual identification through still snapshot images of the system upon entry, but there will be significant delays before any ship sightings are confirmed until we can start using active sensors."

"Keep me informed," Burkhard said. "How about the rest of our forces?"

"Despite the course correction problem, which appears to have originated with the navigational data provided by the *Natsugumo*, approach should be relatively safe. No danger of collision from anyone during our transit under inertia. We aren't going to maintain a perfect formation, however, due to poorly charted gravity effects from smaller local planetoids."

Burkhard nodded slowly, merely grunting an acknowledgement. He had considered double-checking Captain Meier's tactical navigation plot during the briefing with Commodore Beccera, but decided he was just being paranoid. Surely, even if Meier were to have made a mistake, the Cygni flag officers would have noticed and made their own corrections. Now, it seemed, he should have had one of his tactical officers (likely Cohen, since both Rachel and Chris had been busy with repairing the ship) confirm the plan's details after all.

I should have known better, he thought self-reproachfully. *Didn't I just say I've never been on a mission where everything went according to plan?*

"New data coming in!" Rachel announced. "I've completed the optical scan analysis. Total of three blips not accounted for as legitimate sunspots. Two of them can be visually identified. The third item, however... well, I'll put it on the main screen."

The ship that appeared on the screen looked sleek, slender, and deadly. It was small – maybe even smaller than the *Chihuahua* – but it was large enough to be considered a corvette, and it looked as if it might be atmosphere-capable. For a ship of its size, being atmosphere-capable was a shocker.

And it was decidedly unlike any ship anyone in the Earth Alliance had ever seen.

"What the hell kind of a ship is that?" Schubert snapped from his position at the helm. Silence was his only answer.

Alcyone Star System, Pleiades Alpha, Hexagon Park

Doctor Whitlow Foley couldn't help but feel like he was marching to his death as he walked through the cavernous hallways of the Pleiades Science Directorate. He had been summoned by Director Karlsson, for reasons that had yet to be explained, but there were a lot of things that were going unexplained right now. The last time he saw the man, Foley had been threatened for having innocently invited foreign scientists to help him investigate an archeological dig as protocol usually demanded. Foley's latest transgressions were not so innocent.

Anger and curiosity combined had driven Foley to secretly start a private investigation – stretching all of his resources – to determine the real reason why the Director and the ever present WISPR officers were so intent on preventing exploration and analysis of the alien ruins, artifacts, and fossils.

What he had found so shocked him that it left him few choices. Elements of the Pleiades government were making plans not just to keep out those scientists he needed, but to kill them outright, and perhaps even start a war just to cover it up! Through his contacts, Foley found a man he thought had a chance of getting the information off world, working for the 16 Cygni Confederation, and sent him off with a plea to take some action and save the millions of people who would die should such a war break out.

Foley still had no idea if what he had done saved anyone's life or not. However, he was now being summoned into the private – and isolated – office of the Director of Science, and it seemed likely that said Director of Science was the man behind it all. To refuse the invitation was to give himself away, which would be a disastrous mistake should the Director not already know about Foley's betrayal. To go, however, was to risk being 'disappeared,' which would almost certainly mean he had failed... and millions still might die.

Foley pulled together every scrap of courage he could muster and knocked on the door of Director Karlsson's office. There was no turning back, now. If he had been found out, he was dead.

"Ah, Whit," Ian called from his chair. As had become habitual, Skorrjh the WISPR agent was standing at his right, wearing the fully masked power armor of his profession. Foley took note of the fact that on this occasion, he was also wearing a formal-looking but presumably functional sword. This didn't look good for Foley, if he was any judge of situations, but he had to play it through to the end, and pray for a miracle. "Come in and sit down. We have a lot to talk about."

"Yes, sir," Foley replied hesitantly. There was no hiding his nervousness, but hopefully that could be explained away.

"So, how have you been since we last talked?" Ian asked casually. "I understand we pulled you away from some sort of family event."

"I've been doing well," Foley replied as calmly as he could. His voice, at least, wasn't betraying his nervousness overmuch, although inside he was trembling. "I was having a meeting with some local scientists and their families, hoping to find skilled replacements for the foreign anthropologists and archaeologists I originally planned for on my dig."

That wasn't entirely true. He was having a meeting with certain archaeologists and anthropologists, yes, but it had nothing to do with the dig. Rather, it had to do with the fact that those archaeologists and their families were all in danger from the government. They were the close friends and family of Dr. Kimiko Beccera, and he was fairly certain they would be targeted for assassination once Kimiko's death was confirmed.

"Yes, your dig. That's what I called you here to talk about." The Director tapped a few things on a screen in front of him. "I recently received the lab analysis of the fossils discovered on your dig site," he said.

The dig site? Does this actually have something to do with the dig? "I haven't received that analysis, myself, yet, sir," Foley replied, relaxing slightly. "What does it say that I don't already know?"

"Quit a bit, I'm afraid. According to the radiological analysis, the fossils are a hoax," Ian replied, turning the screen so that Whit could see it. "Under the circumstances, I feel I have no choice but to pull the funding from your dig."

Foley read the information on the screen, frowning. The report stated that the fossils were dated to different ages, and that some were 'fresh' bones that hadn't been fossilized. He knew this was a false report – he'd checked for that himself during the preliminary analysis – but it left him even more puzzled. Just why was his dig so important, anyway? What was being covered up?

He couldn't ask that question, but maybe there were some he could ask. Foley suspected he would just be getting some sort of cover story, but at this point even the cover story could tell him something. "Where would someone get these fossils in the first place? This seems pretty elaborate for a hoax."

For the first time, Karlsson looked uncomfortable, glancing over at the WISPR agent. "Yes, well, it's possible that they really are human fossils that were altered and then transported to that location by someone else to discredit future finds."

Well, that was certainly interesting. "Then, maybe we should start looking into bringing in forensics specialists to find the people who did this?" Foley suggested, wondering how they would respond.

"We are the forensics team," Skorrjh growled throatily, and for the first time Foley realized he had always spoken through some sort of voice altering device in his mask. It was yet another layer to a puzzle that already had too many missing pieces. "And all of your scientists will need to leave the site *immediately* so we can do our job."

Foley paled. Just what was it he had uncovered, anyway, that would bring in WISPR? "I'll have my team start packing up their equipment, but it will take a little time. Besides, if you're doing an investigation, shouldn't someone stand guard until your team arrives to prevent—"

An alarm prevented Foley from finishing what he was saying. The communications system displayed an alert that a flash message was coming through, and such messages automatically took precedence over anything else they might have been talking about. Why the Science Directorate would be receiving flash messages, though, Foley couldn't fathom.

Karlsson pulled the screen back around so he could see it and pressed a button. "Karlsson here. Report."

A Naval officer, judging from his uniform, flickered onto the screen. "Sir, there's a fleet of hostile ships incoming – sensor signatures read as Cygni warships. We—"

The transmission was abruptly cut off. Karlsson immediately attempted to reconnect, but the system wasn't co-operating with him. After several failures he switched his station to show a system-wide tactical display, such as what might usually be found in a Naval headquarters.

"Well, well," Skorrjh muttered, examining the screen. "It looks like you have a bit of a fight on your hands."

EAS Chihuahua

"Phase II has begun," Emily Mumford announced. "And it looks as if Cygni is fighting a lot more effectively than we thought they would. They're tearing through the enemy fleet."

"Phase III begins in five minutes," Rachel called into her mouthpiece, addressing the crew throughout the ship. Technically, that was a breach of silent running, but a minor one, and planned for. With the Pleiades ships distracted by the Cygni forces, it was unlikely they would notice. "Prepare to break from silent running. Rail gun crews, begin loading your weapons."

Burkhard nodded slowly. "Is the enemy moving out as expected?"

"Detecting activity on board several ships," Cohen replied. "We'll need thirty seconds to determine exactly how many are pulled away, and whether any of those ships left behind are armed or not."

"Keep me informed," Burkhard sighed. "And I want someone to take optical stills every thirty seconds of the area in which that unknown ship was sighted – I want to know if it starts moving, and what it's capable of."

"Already in progress, sir," Rachel said.

"Passive sensors are detecting that all the overtly armed ships from around these orbital facilities have begun moving," Cohen called, highlighting several of their targets. "The stations themselves are supposed to be well armed with defensive satellites and the like, however, sir, and we don't seem to have located all of those, either through passive sensors or visual checks."

Rachel called. "No movement out of unidentified ship, yet, sir, nor any additional reaction which will show on our passive scans or visual reports. As far as we can tell, it's not reacting to us at all. It may not even be manned."

"Continue observation," Burkhard ordered. "I want to know as quickly as possible if it does something."

Alcyone Star System, Pleiades Alpha, Hexagon Park

"This is ridiculous," Director Karlsson said, shocked. "Our forces are equal in size and we have a technological advantage. We should at least be holding our own, but they're killing our battleships almost two to one!"

"These ships are not using the technology we gifted you, remember. You do appear to be slightly more advanced than these enemies, but being tied to a planet as a defensive force significantly limits the advantages many of your more advanced technologies provide," Skorrjh pointed out. "There's no opportunity for your forces to gain the element of surprise, and you're maneuverability is very limited if you wish to protect your stationary assets. A number of your commanders were acting a bit overconfident at first, as well, but that has been knocked out of them, so they should start performing better soon."

Foley just sunk into the background, trying not to draw attention to himself. Maybe he would be dismissed, thanks to the attack. Was this assault a direct result of his leaking information to Cygni? He'd been trying to prevent a war, not start one.

"Well, I certainly hope we *don't* lose. We might not be able to meet certain 'obligations' we are responsible for if our home fleet is destroyed."

Skorrjh stiffened. "Move. I'll contact our ship. "

At that point, Foley decided that both the agent and Karlsson were ignoring him completely. The archaeologist thought it best to leave, slowly and quietly, before they remembered he was there. Perhaps he needed to go into hiding. The confusion of the battle going on above their heads might present certain opportunities, and there was no point in staying around and waiting for them to find out what he had done.

As he left, he began hearing odd, guttural words in a language he had never heard before coming from the desk. Looking back, he caught sight of the monitor from an odd angle, and it took him a moment to grasp what he was seeing. *A face! A face to match the skull at the dig! A... a* Neanderthal's *face!* He quickly left the office. Now he knew he needed to get to his friends and family and move them to some kind of safety, and with haste.

This is big, and I can't afford to be caught before I manage to tell... someone, he thought absently. *What the hell was that creature they were talking to on the screen? It couldn't have been human... could it? And who should I share this with?*

EAS Chihuahua

"We're finally seeing some activity going on aboard the unknown ship," Rachel called. "And... wow, she's not bothering to disguise itself. Passive sensors are picking up huge power emissions from her. We still don't know what those power emissions are for, though, as they're much greater than needed for... oh, hell."

"What?" Burkhard snapped.

"I may be misreading this, because it's obviously operating on entirely different principles then our own, but... I think this unknown ship has an energy shield." She frowned. "The mass sensors just went haywire. I think their shield is manipulating *gravity*, not magnetism. And it's better than ours. I can't detect any holes."

Burkhard's heart almost froze at that pronouncement. "Keep me fully informed. We have a mission to complete, and we can't do anything about that ship until we're done."

EAS Natsugumo

"How are Admiral Hrudey's forces faring?" Beccera asked from his position on the bridge of the *Natsugumo,* trying to make sense of the tactical map he was seeing. Zdeno Hrudey was his counterpart in the Cygni force, and technically was in overall command of the mission, but it was Beccera's job to manage Earth's forces in it... and he felt totally inadequate to the task. He couldn't even fully understand the graphics on the display panels, much less such things as what tactics each side was employing or how well each side was performing.

"Better than expected," Captain Meier replied. "Mr. Farmburg, please explain it to him."

Farmburg was less than pleased to be in on this conversation. His people had managed to goad Meier into transferring Beccera from the *Chihuahua* to the *Natsugumo,* which he thought probably contained the worst tactical crew in the entire squadron. It would have been just what he wanted... if his people were still preparing to fight the Earth Alliance instead of joining them for an interstellar war. Now all the work he had done to undermine the Academy from within was backfiring on him. The 'Captain' of his ship was an obvious fraud – for one thing, if she were as great of a tactical genius as she claimed, they would not now be struggling to work around her course plotting error – and the Commodore was forced to rely on her and her staff for tactical advice.

And, while he might be a little egotistical for thinking so, Farmburg had arranged things so that he was the only person in the entire ship capable of giving anyone reasonable tactical advice. But he was only an 'acting-Lieutenant,' and it didn't exactly seem likely that he would be listened to very much. The only thing he could do, after almost begging Captain Meier to be put on the Commodore's staff as a 'technical advisor,' was to interpret the icons on a map. The Commodore knew Farmburg by reputation – apparently from his time with the crew of the *Chihuahua* – and clearly wouldn't trust him with anything more important.

"There are two points on any ship which you can attack without your enemy being able to launch a significant counterattack," Farmburg explained, bringing up the base external schematics of one of the enemy battleships. "Shipbuilders are always trying to make turrets which can target the enemy from any direction, but even the best have blind spots they can't cover along the spine, or rather the top of the ship. The other spot is at the bottom, or keel, of the ship. Again, turrets occasionally are added to provide some ability to return fire, but since the hydrogen collector and hyperspace sensors are most often mounted on a structural frame extending from a ship's keel, the blind spots that the turrets can't target are actually wider then what is usually found on the spine."

"In our case, by a stroke of uncanny fortune, the entire Cygni fleet exited from hyperspace inside firing range of the largest enemy concentration, facing their keel side. While the enemy fleet was able to return fire after making some quick maneuvers, the Cygni fleet took advantage of the opportunity to get off several devastating salvos first.

"But these opening moments are by no means decisive. These icons here illustrate where the Pleiades reserve ships, drawn off from our primary targets, are coming around to act as reinforcements against the Cygni fleet. It's entirely possible for Pleiades to recover and take the advantage, once the reserves join them, but as of this moment the Cygni forces are more than holding their own."

Beccera continued looking at the map, frowning. He had to grudgingly admit that Farmburg was a better officer than he'd been led to believe. "What's this blip, here?" he asked, pointing to something that was moving faster then anything else on the map.

Farmburg frowned and typed a few keys. "I'm afraid I don't know, sir. Configuration unknown, but it's obviously a ship, and it's putting out a lot of power. More then I would expect a ship that size to be capable of producing, by far."

That caught Meier's attention. "For what purpose?" she asked.

"Unknown, ma'am," Farmburg replied, although he had a rather uneasy feeling about the situation. "The data doesn't match any ship class we've ever seen before."

"Give me a visual of it," Meier ordered. "Let's see if we can puzzle it out."

The image on the screen was distorted, as if looking at the ship through a drop of water, and the resolution was a bit weak, but the unidentified ship was clearly something none of them had ever seen the likes of before. The visual representation was demonstrating it capable of a degree of maneuverability that was practically unheard of as it approached the Cygni fleet. Nothing they had could match it... well, except possibly for the

Chihuahua. Regardless, the unidentified vessel was clearly a remarkable craft.

"These visuals – the distortion looks similar to how the *Chihuahua* does when it has its shields up," Farmburg noted in amazement. "Except the *Chihuahua's* shields leave a band through which you can see the image undistorted. I don't see any gaps in that image."

"Did Pleiades develop their own shieldclad ship?" Beccera asked, unintentionally using the term he had picked up from Desaix and Rachel. He watched as several particle cannon blasts and rail gun charges either bounced off or dispersed around the unknown ship. "Or is this based on our own design from the Wargame?"

"I'd say that ship was purpose-built to handle whatever that shield system is," Farmburg replied. "And I don't see any quantum wheel emitters like the ones needed for the *Chihuahua's* shields, though these spots in the image may be something similar. Regardless, this is a different technology altogether. We are aware, though, that Pleiades has been getting unusual advanced technology from somewhere... it's possible that this ship is the source. It could be a salvaged alien craft."

Beccera looked at Farmburg closely; *he* didn't remember the intelligence reports on Pleiades mentioning anything about that, and he wasn't sure how a Cadet Lieutenant would have learned more than he did. Burkhard's suspicions seemed to have some basis.

"Are they moving it away to protect it for further study, then?" Beccera questioned. "She hasn't fired yet, and I don't see any turrets or other obvious weapons. Plus it shouldn't be possible to fire through a shield, so—"

He cut off as the image on the screen did, in fact, fire off a single brilliant stream of white energy. Meier gaped at it before saying, "Track that – what is she firing on?"

"Cygni Battleship *Calypso,* ma'am," Farmburg replied before her tactical officer could speak up. "Power output reads... " he paused, swallowing as the unidentified ship sent out another long burst. "*Calypso* is destroyed, ma'am. It took them twenty seconds to tear one of the largest battleships in the Cygni fleet in half."

"Analysis of the firing pattern suggests she only has the one weapon, ma'am," the *Natsugumo's* tactical officer piped in.

Even Beccera, whose Army training allowed him little more knowledge of naval tactics and abilities than the average civilian, knew how unimportant that was. "Son," he drawled. "If you can destroy a battleship in twenty seconds or less, and your enemy can't hurt you back, all you need is the one weapon. Anything more would be redundant. The *Chihuahua* would have been able to save the *Keppler* in half the time if she had a weapon like that."

Before that could sink in, the communications officer let out a call of his own. "Tight beam encoded transmission received from *Chihuahua,* ma'am, sir," he said, addressing both his Captain and the Commodore. "Reads as follows: '*Chihuahua* turning to confront unidentified ship. Initial maneuvers being conducted as silently as possible. Suggest you continue mission as designed. Unable to await confirmation.'" There was a pause. "There's a postscript, as well, but I don't understand it."

"What does it say?" Beccera asked.

"I don't get the reference. 'Time to see if we're the *Merrimack* or the *Monitor.*'"

Chapter XXIX

EAS Chihuahua

"We're now far enough from the squadron that we likely won't give away their position by engaging engines," Cohen reported.

"About time," Burkhard snapped. "The Cygni fleet is going to barely be able to regain a stalemate at this rate – the *Fortune* was the fourth battleship they've lost in three minutes! Mr. Schubert, full power to engines. Shields up. Begin battle plan Alpha."

"Commencing battle plan Alpha," Schubert replied.

"Sir, their vector is changing again," Rachel called. "They seem to be targeting the *Zephyr* this time."

Burkhard felt a slight twinge in his stomach hearing that. The *Zephyr* was the Cygni flagship – if she was lost, his past experience told him that the remaining Cygni fleet would turn tail and run. "Time to maximum firing range?" he asked cautiously.

"We're traveling at our top speed with shields activated, but may need to make maneuvers depending on what the remaining enemy fleet does," Rachel considered. "And they are moving in a somewhat unpredictable pattern. Given those variables, I'd say twenty five to thirty seconds."

"Concentrate all fire on a single spot," Burkhard ordered. "And fire as soon as that unidentified ship comes in range. Let's try to draw it off of the other ships as quickly as possible."

"Entering firing range in ten... nine... eight..." Cohen reported.

Gradually, his countdown ticked away to zero, and the powerfully destructive energy blasts generated by the particle cannons lanced out from the bow of the *Chihuahua*. At first, it appeared that the streaming fire was just as ineffective as the single blasts generated by the Cygni fleet, but then the glow of the weapons' energy started penetrating deeper into the field surrounding the unknown ship. The unknown ship continued to bear down on the *Zephyr* as long as it could, but soon *Chihuahua's* cannons forced it to turn away before it could open fire, itself.

"Well, it looks like we can scare them at least," Cohen said triumphantly as most of the bridge crew cheered.

"Not exactly," Burkhard sighed. "Quit your celebrating – we've done nothing. There's almost no way we can make them stand still long enough for our weapons to be effective. We can't hurt it, but maybe we can drive it away from our allies." He paused as the target turned course towards them. "And we have yet to see if our shields will hold."

EAS Natsugumo

Beccera, Farmburg, Meier, and several others on the tactical staff of the *Natsugumo* watched as the battle between the two shieldclads began in earnest. The *Chihuahua* had managed to pull the unknown ship away from the center of battle, freeing the Cygni fleet for its intended purpose of battling the bulk of the Pleiades fleet. However, the battle on both fronts wasn't going well. Thanks to the devastation the unidentified ship had caused, Cygni was barely holding on to their initial advantage. The battle between *Chihuahua* and its foe was even less promising – the enemy ship was the *Chihuahua's* equal in maneuverability, and apparently had stronger shields and a more powerful weapon.

The unknown shieldclad had managed to line up one shot since being driven off of the *Zephyr,* and while the *Chihuahua's* own shields were able to hold back the bulk of the blast they quickly had to dodge before their shield was completely overwhelmed. As it was, Beccera suspected they were being badly rocked by each glancing blow. Her return fire was entirely ineffective, as the enemy shields were quick to recover once the streams of energy from the particle cannons were halted. It would take prolonged fire in order to penetrate them.

Beccera shook his head. "This doesn't look good. We have to find some way to help them."

"How?" Meier blurted in frustration. "We don't have shields. The

Chihuahua's crew didn't share their discoveries with the rest of us until it was too late to do anything, so we're no better off than those Cygni ships it was mowing down earlier. Worse, actually, since we don't have any weapons which could match the caliber of what is on those Cygni ships."

Farmburg frowned, wondering how she had rated high enough in either tactics or leadership skills to qualify for command. Then he recalled that his own research indicated that she may have cheated her way through the Academy, taking advantage of at least a dozen other people... including the *Chihuahua's* current commander. She seemed quite happy to build a career on other people's work. At the time, Farmburg had been pleased to find that such an unqualified woman could make her way into the command structure of an enemy power. Now that Earth and Cygni were allied, and he had to depend on her command ability to keep him alive, the prospect seemed less appealing.

Still, someone had to point it out. "We do have certain resources that could help them, I think," he offered hesitantly.

Meier looked down at him furiously. "Who are you to tell—"

"No, please," Beccera said, interrupting. Farmburg was clearly more than just an Academy student, and this battle appeared to be drawing out his real expertise, so he would use it. "Tell me, young man. I'm not a naval tactician, but I imagine allowing your most valuable assets to speak when they know something makes good sense even in the Navy. If you can think of something, please, tell me."

Farmburg was a little surprised. Beccera hadn't liked him from the moment he stepped on board, and for good reason. They barely talked, even in an official capacity, and the Army officer seemed to ignore just about every suggestion the 'Academy officer' would offer, no matter how reasonable it was. Now, though, he was listening. He might have a chance to redeem himself, after all.

"Well, sir," he began. "The mass readings for the unknown ship keep fluctuating because of their shield, but we're starting to be able to compensate for that distortion. None of the readings we have suggest they're very heavily armored; the ship is just too small and light. If our forces can hit it with enough firepower to penetrate their shield, even a little, we should do some serious damage. *Chihuahua* keeps getting close, so all they need is a *little* help...."

Alcyone Star System, Pleiades Alpha, Hexagon Park

Director Karlsson watched the monitor display the results of the battle alongside the impassive Skorrjh. "It seems," he said slowly. "As if our trump card isn't going to be quite as helpful as I'd hoped. Somehow the Earth Alliance has already developed a ship to counter yours."

Skorrjh snorted. "In the fog of war, intellect and guile are even better trump cards than simple technology. I have full confidence in Captain Raknuh and the *Flynohr*. I'm sure he has spotted the vulnerabilities in their rather primitively shielded ship, even as I have, and is preparing to use them to full effect."

"Such as?"

Skorrjh gestured to the screen impatiently. "You're a scientist. The data is there. Draw your own conclusions."

EAS Chihuahua

"Tactical," Burkhard called to Rachel and Cohen. "Have we yet been able to pinpoint a weak spot in those shields?"

"Not yet," Rachel replied. "There are no obvious holes. They don't even bother to open a portal for that weapon of theirs when they fire. It seems that whatever that weapon is firing, their shield doesn't interfere with it. Furthermore, their shield is shaped roughly like an eggshell, with no obvious stress points to target. We even considered trying to see if the shield would allow solid objects like rail gun fire through, but the Cygni fleet tried that and even battleship-grade rail guns weren't able to penetrate their shields. I'm stumped."

"I think we need to return fire more often," Cohen suggested. "We need to study how their shields react to weapons fire, how quickly their shields recover from particle cannon fire, and anything else we might be able to find out about them."

Burkhard nodded decisively. "Mr. Schubert, can you maneuver us to get in a clean shot without opening up the unprotected portions of our hull to their fire?"

"I'm trying, sir," Schubert admitted. "It's pretty difficult. They're both faster than we are and a touch more maneuverable. I'm also still waiting for a firing pattern to figure out the best position."

"Concentrated firing pattern locked in," Lieutenant DiMarco said from his position at Weapons Control. "It'll provide the maximum amount of fire to a single concentrated spot. All you need to do is get him dead center in front of us, Mr. Schubert. Sorry for the delay."

"Sir," Emily called from her station. "I'm receiving a very odd transmission. I don't understand it at all, sir, but—"

"Put it through," Burkhard snapped, unwilling to wait for her explanation.

"Aye, sir," she replied, keying in the speakers.

"*...was old and foul and slow,*" a chorus of people were singing. "*But the French are gone to Martinique, and Nelson's on the trail, and where he goes the Ol' Superb must go!*"

"Target acquired!" Schubert reported over the singing. "Opening fire!"

Once again, *Chihuahua's* barrage of particle fire streamed outward into the enemy shielding. This time, however, it was joined by similar streams from two other sources.

"Sir, the *Superb* and the *Ishmael* are emerging from silent running," Cohen reported. "And they're both concentrating their own particle fire on the enemy ship."

As the concentrated fire finally pierced through the unknown ship's shields, the sound of the transmission continued echoing throughout the *Chihuahua's* bridge.

"*...Round the world if need be, and round the world again, with a lame duck lagging, lagging all the way....*"

Alcyone Star System, Pleiades Alpha, Hexagon Park

"I believe you were saying something about intellect and guile?" Karlsson echoed dryly.

"Our ship can handle it," Skorrjh replied, undaunted. "What concerns me more is where all these fresh ships are coming from. If they have another fleet in flanking position you'll need to re-vector...."

Just as he said that, the tactical display showed a large number of ships emerging from silent running just outside of firing range on the majority of Pleiades' orbital stations, their sensors suddenly active. There was nothing left to defend the stations outside of their own point defense mechanisms, and those wouldn't protect them long enough for reinforcements to arrive from the center of the battle.

All that Karlsson and the WISPR officer could do was watch as Pleiades' entire orbital industrial complex was systematically destroyed.

EAS Chihuahua

Burkhard was too busy focusing on the action with the unknown ship to pay much attention to the rest of the battle, although he noted with some satisfaction that Beccera's squadron was able to make the attack a success. Had it not been for the initial course error, *Superb* and *Ishmael* would never have been able to peel off from the rest of the attack force without drawing attention to the fleet. Making very slow adjustments as the *Chihuahua* had done, they had managed to keep their maneuvers below sensor background noise and evade detection. A whole fleet couldn't turn unnoticed like that... but two individual ships had no problem making such maneuvers.

"Press them," Burkhard ordered harshly. "We're the only ones on our side who have shields, so we need to keep their attention and draw their fire to us. We can't afford to allow them the time to turn their fire upon the others."

"Yes, sir," Schubert replied, although he sounded a little uncertain. "But I don't think that we're going to have a problem keeping their attention. They're coming about to an attack vector against us...."

"Enemy vessel opening fire!" Cohen called a few seconds later, confirming Schubert's assessment.

"Keep our shields to them!" Burkhard snapped. Schubert was already in the process of turning the ship as he spoke, and he was able to get the shields to take the brunt of the blow. However, the weapon used was significantly more powerful than anything their shields had absorbed before, and even the muffled blast through the shields nearly sent the *Chihuahua* reeling. It didn't last long – Schubert managed to outmaneuver them after a split second – but the hit was still powerful enough to cause significant damage... damage that hit squarely on the *Chihuahua's* bridge.

As with many ships, the exterior of the bridge was in one of the most heavily armored parts of the ship's hull. That extra armor was the only reason anyone on the bridge survived, but the damage was severe nonetheless. Instrument panels exploded, shards of glass went flying, chairs snapped off their spindles and flew across the bridge. The devastation was overwhelming, and it took a while before the survivors could move enough to see what they were doing.

Rachel was bleeding in several places – there was a cut across her forehead, a small piece of shrapnel imbedded but easily removable from one arm, and she could tell something happened to a spot on the back of her shoulder although she couldn't immediately tell what. Her wounds were all superficial, thankfully, but most of her friends couldn't say the same.

Luke DiMarco was dead... or at least she hoped he was dead, considering how much of his lower body had been severed from his upper by a large piece of bulkhead. Nothing would save him at this point, even if he wasn't.

The Navigation console had been ripped out of the floor, and was now lying on top of both Schubert and Weber. They were both breathing, and looked to be alive, but Weber was unconscious and Schubert's left leg was bent at a funny angle. Both were covered in blood, but most of it wasn't theirs.

Cohen was bleeding profusely as well, and he looked quite pale. He'd need immediate treatment, or he would die of blood loss. Even Rachel, with no medical training, could tell that without a second glance, and her eyes darted around, looking for a First Aid kit.

Rappaport and Emily had both escaped the worst of it, and neither of them looked especially wounded from the attack. Emily had burn marks on her hands, though, from a fire that had burst out of her communications console. Nothing serious, but they would blister.

None of those casualties, however, had as strong an impact on Rachel as the person lying at her feet, pale and clammy and barely breathing. Lying unconscious in front of her was Burkhard, their Captain... the only experienced officer in the chain of command.

EAS Natsugumo

"All secondary target defensive systems have been eliminated," a tactical officer reported on board the bridge of the *Natsugumo*. "The *Kilauea* and *Acadia* will concentrate on the remaining secondary targets, while the *Sherwood* and the *York* will join us in the assault on the primary."

"Good," Captain Meier replied, obviously pleased. "Very good. I'm glad we're having such an easy time of it, even with twenty percent of our forces occupied with that... unexpected surprise."

Beccera was not nearly as pleased. He was paying more attention to the rest of the battle, and it wasn't exactly looking good. Yes, he knew that the *Natsugumo* was involved in what some people would have called the *only* important part of the mission, but he was not one of those people. He'd tried to make the *Natsugumo's* captain understand that, but she wasn't exactly interested in the opinions of an Army officer masquerading as her Commodore, as she apparently thought of him. Not that she'd said as much in so many words, but it was pretty obvious considering how she reacted every time he made a suggestion or asked a question.

The Cygni fleet was starting to take a bit of a beating of its own. Despite the initial success, that unknown ship had managed to more than level the playing field, and the Cygni were finding that, without the element of surprise, their ships weren't quite a match for Pleiades' counterparts. The Cygni forces were still holding things to a stalemate, but that wouldn't last long.

The battle with the unknown ship, though, was much more distressing. Beccera had just seen *Chihuahua* take a powerful hit to her broadside, and while her shields held out most of the damage some of it had peaked through and slammed into several areas, including the bridge and several weapons ports. Beccera wondered if any of the friends he had made on that ship were killed, and if so whether he would survive to attend their funerals.

He frowned. "Is it just my imagination, or is the *Chihuahua* flying oddly?"

Farmburg stared at the display. "You're right, she is. I'm not sure what... oh, wait, she's starting to maneuver again. If I had to guess, I'd say that something happened to the pilot or the navigation system, and the new person isn't as experienced of a pilot. That's pure speculation, however."

Beccera clamped his teeth together grimly.

EAS Chihuahua

Rachel had just managed to reroute navigational control to her station, and was doing what she could to get the *Chihuahua* turned around safely. In principal she knew how to pilot a ship. She was a licensed civilian pilot, after all, and the only reason she wasn't allowed to take the helm in a Navy ship was that her eyes rendered her 'medically unqualified.' Navigating a warship with megatons of mass and armor was a lot more complicated than she expected, however, and she started to understand why two people really were needed during combat. It would take her full attention to fly the thing at all... and, right now, she was also the acting captain and only tactical officer.

A team of Marines – drafted into duty as emergency medical staff –

had been slowly carrying the wounded off of the bridge. Cohen was the first person they took out, and there still was no word on whether or not he would survive. Burkhard was second, and Weber and Schubert had gone down together. But now they needed replacement personnel, and fast.

Rachel was the only person available to pilot the ship. Personnel requirements labeled certain other individuals as 'navigators,' but they had been Academy freshmen who hadn't had a single lesson in how to fly a paper airplane, much less an interstellar warship, and were essentially being used as unskilled labor. Mumford, working as best as she could with her blistered hands, was calling people up to replace the wounded – Tarbell for Weapons Control and Langer to fill the second tactical slot. There was no-one to call to take either the pilot's or the navigator's slot, though... which left Rachel with a decision to make, and no time to make it in.

"I can't do this and command, too," she finally said, shaking her head. She put on her personal headphone and speaker set, not wanting to have this conversation public. "Ms. Mumford, put me through to Mr. Desaix. Make it a private channel – I don't want the whole engineering staff to hear all of this."

"Yes, ma'am," Emily said, although her voice cracked with pain as she worked. "He's on private with you now, ma'am."

"Whatever it is, Rache, we're rather busy down here," were the first words she heard him say. "So keep it short."

She glanced over, meeting the eyes of Rappaport and nodding to him. He slowly stood up and limped his way off of the bridge. "I'm sending Mr. Rappaport down to relieve you," she said. "You're needed on the bridge."

"I thought he didn't have medical clearance to work down here, yet," Chris protested, obviously resentful of her decision. Apparently, he was under the impression that they were unsatisfied with his work. "I'm handling things down here just fine, and you can tell the Captain that!"

Rachel swallowed. "Chris, you're doing as good a job down there as anyone could ask... but right now I need you up here more. And I'm not able to tell Captain Burkhard anything at the moment – he's unconscious, and I have no idea if he'll live."

There was a long pause at the other end. "So you need me at tactical?" he said, understanding that command had fallen to her.

"Not quite. The bridge was hit hard, really hard. Wolf and Weber were both injured along with the Captain. I'm the only one who understands enough about flying this thing to take over for them, but I can't do it, and run tactical, and be Captain at the same time. Just keeping this ship under control is going to take all my attention." She paused. "I'm hurt, too, and so is everyone else on the bridge, and half the stations are ruined so we've rerouted controls to the other half. There's no one left to replace us, and several of us are trying to run two stations at once. But we need a Captain and a tactical officer, and you can be both."

Chris paused. "I can't be Captain, Rache. I'm not fit for it. I'm sure you can, though. You have a talent for command, and you'd do a much bet—"

"Not right now I can't, damn it!" she snapped, her voice cracking. "But you can. I know how much stress command and tactics puts you through. You think I want to do this to you? You think I want to be the navigator, for that matter? But I don't have a choice. We need someone who can beat all of those damned no-win scenarios... and you're the closest thing we've got. I can't do it. Especially not and fly the ship, too. Please, Chris. Just... please."

She heard a very long, deep intake of breath on the other side of the microphone, and was bracing herself for him rejecting her plea again. Obviously, he couldn't do what she was demanding of him – his own internal doubts wouldn't let him, echoes of the one time in his past he had truly taken charge in a crisis. She was disappointed, and felt betrayed, but she had known he might refuse when she called him.

"Okay, Rache," Chris said softly. "I'm on my way to the bridge now." He paused. "Make sure there's a complete tactical evaluation waiting for me when I get up there. And let's just hope we don't all regret this."

Rachel closed her eyes, blinking back a tear that had been threatening to drop.

Thank you, Chris, she thought. *No matter what happens from here, I don't regret it at all.*

Chapter XXX

EAS Chihuahua

"Dear God," Chris gasped as he stepped out onto the bridge. "It's even worse then you said."

Then he saw her bloody face and was by her instantly. There had been some temporary liqui-stitches clumsily dabbed on her forehead gash by one of the Marines, and bandages across her arm and back where two pieces of shrapnel had been removed – without anesthetic. Her uniform was burnt and tattered. In short, she was still a mess.

"Are you okay?" he asked softly.

"I'm better than just about anyone else who was on the bridge," she sighed. "Now, quickly, find a working station and take the lead tactical position. Get your report, and take command."

He wiped a spot of dirt and blood off of her forehead and gave her a brief kiss there. "Thank God you're all right. I wouldn't have argued if I'd known how bad it was," he said softly into her ear before stepping away. "I guess we've both got jobs to do, now, don't we?"

She nodded. "Yeah. And enough of that. This is hard enough without distractions like that." She paused. "But when this is all over with, I think you and I need to have another talk."

EAS Superb

Captain Daniels of the *Superb* paced across his bridge apprehensively as he studied the tactical situation unfolding around his vessel. Shortly after their combined attack had actually managed to wound that beast of a ship that had been dogging their forces, Daniels had received a communication from the *Chihuahua* that she was temporarily out of the action. Her bridge had been hit, and while control was quickly being re-established it would take time. That left his ship and the *Ishmael* in something of a bind, given that they had attracted the attention of a ship they couldn't defend against.

The good news, though, was that the enemy seemed momentarily blind. Since hitting the *Chihuahua* in a counterattack, the enemy shieldclad had started making circles, emitting a band of signals much like their own active sensors. The band was too tight, however, to cover the entire solar system, and so the *Superb*, the *Ishmael,* and the *Chihuahua* were all able to escape its immediate attentions. It was getting harder and harder to avoid the search without leaving the fight, however, and the *Chihuahua* still wasn't fully back in action.

"Sir," Nathaniel Turk, now Daniels' lead tactical officer, began hesitantly. "I think they're going to catch sight of us shortly. Before they do, however... it is possible that both we and the *Ishmael* could get into a good firing position. In other words, we can get the first punch in."

"Maybe," Daniels admitted grudgingly. He continued to watch the tactical displays, keeping a close eye on the *Chihuahua*. It was looking a little hesitant, although at least it was starting to maneuver again... but it still wasn't returning to action. *Come on, Burkhard, what's going on over there,* he wondered.

"Encoded transmission from *Chihuahua!*" Lt. Eure relayed. He was doubling as the communications officer, having gained more experience with signal interception and interpretation then anyone present in a past job operating civilian comm traffic. The original communications officer had taken several of the basic Academy classes, but had no experience with such things as telemetry analysis, signal processing, or similarly specialized skills, and was instead working non-combat shifts. "They've asked us to clear out of the sensor sweep area, sir. They say they'll handle the enemy ship on their own."

The Captain's eyes narrowed. *What are you up to, Conrad?*

———————————

EAS Chihuahua

"Are you sure you don't want their help?" Rachel asked as Emily was relaying the request for *Superb* and *Ishmael* to leave. "I know you've been down in engineering this whole time, so you're probably not aware of this, but we can't get through her shields without—"

"I know that," Chris shot back, typing at his console... which just happened to be the station next to her own. "I went through all the data on the enemy shield systems. To be blunt, we can barely scratch them even coordinating our fire with both of the other ships. We might be able to do some damage with all three of us working together, but not enough. *Superb's* and *Ishmael's* streaming cannons aren't as well tuned as ours, so it's likely they'll burn their weapons out before we inflict any significant damage. I don't like it, but we have to handle this on our own."

Rachel nodded slowly. "Okay. In that case, what are we going to do?"

"We'll lead them as far away from the battle as we can," Chris replied slowly.

"And then?" Rachel prompted after a prolonged silence, expecting more.

"I don't know," Chris replied. "I don't have any answers after that. Don't expect miracles, here."

Rachel's lips tightened briefly, but she nodded briskly. "Okay, we'll lead them away. Where to?"

"Tight zigzag evasive pattern," Chris said after some thought. "We want to present a shield to them as much as possible, obviously. Course..." He sighed. "I'm not sure. If I knew better how that shield worked, maybe I'd know where to go. Electromagnetic shields like ours don't function well in certain environments, and while their shields aren't electromagnetic I expect the same would be true of their own, but without more data—"

"Excuse me, sir," Langer interrupted. "But I think I can help you with that. At least a little bit. I'm not sure if it'll do any good."

Chris looked over at him expectantly. "Well? What is it?"

"I've co-coordinating with Ms. Mumford on enhancing the sensor readings Ms. Katz collected early in the fight," Yannis explained. "I'm not sure what they did to make them work this way, but we've largely confirmed *how* they work."

"Let's hear it," Chris said. "I want to know everything I can."

Yannis hesitated. "Well, sir, it appears almost as if they've... reversed an artificial gravity field or something. Just as our shields produce so strong an electromagnetic field that energy and projectiles are distorted or deflected by, their gravity field is strong enough to deflect incoming weapons fire entirely."

Chris nodded slowly. "That would also explain why they don't need gaps in their shield for weapons or engines. Their field would actually accelerate any outgoing energy and matter." He paused. "But our weapons can penetrate their shields when concentrated over time, so how does that work?"

"The strain of maintaining it at that level, I'd wager," Yannis replied. "Any weapons fire hitting those shields shows a spike in their power consumption. The longer we maintain fire, the more power gets diverted from the rest of the shield to concentrate on the spot we're hitting. "

Chris nodded slowly. "So, you're saying that the longer we fire on them, the weaker their shields get where we're *not* hitting them?"

"It appears as if the strain first appears on the side opposite of the heaviest point of fire, sir," Langer answered. "It also seems as if the strain is heavier when deflecting solid matter rather than energy blasts, sir, so it's possible even rail guns could be effective. It would take something heavier than a battleship's rail guns to get through, though."

"Hm. Show me the numbers on when and where things happen," Chris ordered. "Both for energy weapons and for solid matter."

"We don't have enough data to be precise on the solid matter, but I can make it an estimate," Langer replied hesitantly.

"Well, you'd better make those good estimates," Chris snapped. "I think I need us to be accurate within a few hundredths of a second."

The entire bridge crew balked at that one. "Hundredths of a second?" Rachel sputtered. "What in the world are you planning which demands accuracy within hundredths of a second?"

Chris grinned a tired, lopsided grin at her. "When the *Monitor* and the *Virginia* fought in the first battle of ironclad warships, neither side could penetrate the other's armor effectively. The *Virginia* was destroyed to prevent capture – and we may not even last that long if we don't finish this thing off before he gets a good hit on us again. The *Monitor,* on the other hand... well, she sunk in storms trying to move along the coast."

The smug grin on his face told Rachel that he felt he had given her the answer, but she was too busy trying to keep the ship flying to puzzle out the clue. "What does that have to do with anything?"

"Well, if that thing's the *Monitor,*" Chris said, pointing to the tactical display of the unknown ship. "It seems to me the best way to beat her is to sink her in a storm." He then pointed at the readings of Alcyone B, which was displaying an unusual amount of solar storm activity. "And there's our storm – all we've got to do is make it sink her. And thanks to the fact that we've got yet one more piece of obsolete technology on this ship, I think it's possible we can do that."

EAS Natsugumo

"What are they doing?" Beccera mused softly to himself, bending over a tactical display showing the *Chihuahua's* maneuvers. The main screens were now taken up with readouts of the assault on the orbital stations, and this one small station was all that Barbara Meier could afford the Commodore as she directed her Marines to scuttle a certain orbital station that had just surrendered to them. If he'd known that she wouldn't be able to offer him the command and control facilities she'd promised, he never would have come aboard the *Natsugumo* regardless of what Captain Burkhard and everyone else suggested. Still, he had the one display center, and he supposed he should be grateful for it. Meier seemed to think he was an irrelevant passenger whose presence should only be tolerated – with the appropriate lip-service provided – because he made her ship the squadron's flagship. So far, he hadn't said anything... but he felt the time was about to come where he would have to remind her that he was in charge.

Farmburg managed to catch what he said, however... and did appear to be taking him seriously. "Who, sir?"

The former Army officer looked up. "Excuse me?"

"You said 'what are they doing,' sir. I asked who 'they' are."

"The *Chihuahua,*" Beccera answered. "She's changed course. And tactics, I think. She's no longer trying to shoot her way through the enemy's shields, but instead started using a hit and run tactic to get them to chase her. Now, she's on course directly for this system's star."

Farmburg hesitated. He could think of several reasons for a ship to be doing such a thing, but he doubted Beccera would like any of them. "Well, sir... there are a few possibilities. That could be, ah, retreating, sir, and hope to draw the enemy off as they go."

"Running away? That crew?" Beccera snorted. "Sorry, I don't see Burkhard allowing that."

"And if Burkhard is no longer in charge?" Farmburg shot back. "We know *Chihuahua* took a serious blow to the bridge, sir. Possibly the

Captain was hurt and someone else is in command."

"That would be Rachel Katz," Beccera mused, considering what he remembered of the crew. "You aren't seriously suggesting she ordered the retreat, are you?"

Well, no, Farmburg thought. *I suppose I wouldn't say that. My intelligence reports on her were fairly extensive, and she has always been one of those cadets I was supposed to 'watch out for.' She is just a rookie, though, and you can never be sure how rookies will act under pressure.*

"I don't know her, sir, except by reputation," he replied, which was true from a certain point of view. "But she isn't exactly the most veteran of officers."

Beccera snorted. "Son, I don't care if an officer serves in the Army, Navy, Marines, Orbital Guard, even the Planetary Militia. It's possible to meet and talk with someone in the service and just *know* they have what it takes to be in the military, to lead troops into the heat of battle, and to fight with courage regardless of the circumstances. Ms. Katz is one such officer. In fact, I've never seen such a crew of capable recruits and rookies as I saw on that ship. I could name for you a dozen men on board that ship who have what it takes to be the best the military has to offer, and I'd wager all but a handful of that crew will prove more than serviceable. About the only person I could see running from a fight on that crew is Lt. Commander June Ehrlich, and that's only because she's a doctor, sworn to do no harm. They aren't retreating, boy, and you'd better think twice before suggesting such a thing to me again."

Farmburg winced. *Well, there goes the goodwill I've been building since he came aboard,* he thought. "Sir... I didn't mean to offend you, sir. I was just making a tactical analysis of the situation, without consideration of who was on board that ship. If the enemy has been analyzing the *Chihuahua*'s tactics, that will be what they believe, also, sir."

Beccera grinned ruefully. "Yes, I suppose they would. But we aren't them, Mr. Farmburg. We know better. So what is the *Chihuahua* really doing, Mr. Farmburg?"

Once again, Farmburg hesitated before answering. The second possibility, he was sure, the Army colonel would like less than the first. "Well, sir... they might be considering a suicide mission."

Surprisingly, Beccera's grin widened at that answer. "Hm. I suppose it would look that way, wouldn't it?"

That unnerved the Cygni spy considerably. "Well... yes, sir. When we first learned of the *Chihuahua's* shields during the Wargame, I talked with our engineer about them. He didn't understand precisely how it worked without the blueprints, but he could interpret the theory well enough. He laid out for me the strengths and weaknesses of the design, and there are a few things which stood out. For example, when two shielded ships bring their shields together, the electromagnetic fields would push against each other, and whichever one had more mass and engine power could, in theory, move the other one wherever they wanted. If they can lead the enemy ship into an orbit of the star, they could use the stars gravity and this shield principle to push the enemy into the sun... although they likely would be caught by the gravitational pull and destroyed, themselves."

"I thought of that one, myself," Beccera chuckled grimly. "And I could see just about any one of the command line officers on that ship attempting it."

"You what? I mean, how did you figure that one out, sir?" Farmburg asked, astonished.

"Well, I played with magnets as a kid, too," the older Army officer explained. "I know two magnets will push against each other, and I can guess how easy it would be to push someone into a star if you didn't care about going in, yourself, using that principle. There's just one small problem with that."

"And that is, sir?" Farmburg asked.

"It won't work," Beccera sighed. "And I'm pretty sure they know it, too, given that one of them taught me the reason why."

"Taught you, sir?" Farmburg prompted. "Taught you what?"

"Lieutenant Commander Emily Mumford is not a great tactician, and there's a reason she's not in the command track, but she's good at her job," Beccera explained. "People think that she was put on the crew of the *Chihuahua* because she's related to Admiral Mumford, but I think she was one of the ones hand-picked for the crew *in spite* of that particular connection, rather than because of it. At any rate, she knows a few things about analyzing energy patterns." He typed a few commands on the keyboard, and suddenly the display of both the *Chihuahua* and the unknown warship changed. "Now, look at this and tell me what you see."

Farmburg's eyes narrowed at the screen, but then he stiffened. "They aren't the same. That other shield isn't using an electromagnetic field..."

Beccera nodded. "Exactly. Now, it seems pretty obvious that any attempt to use the two shields to 'push' the enemy into the star – or anywhere else, for that matter – would fail. And if the *Chihuahua*'s crew could teach a luddite like me why it wouldn't work, surely they could figure it out themselves. But I certainly agree with the assessment that they're trying to lead the enemy ship into close orbit around the star... which brings me back to the question: What are they planning?"

Farmburg started chewing his lip nervously. "Well, sir, I... I'm stumped. If they do go into close orbit of the sun, though, it might be difficult for them to get back out without something big, like a heavy cruiser or a battleship, to tow them."

Meier stepped up, interrupting the conversation. "Forgive me, Commodore, but we've completed the assault on the orbital facilities," she said. "Time for you to order our fleet into retreat."

"I'm not giving that order yet. We still have ships fighting," Beccera stated firmly.

Meier smiled placatingly. "Of course, Commodore. Naturally, as part of our retreat, we should try and help our Cygni allies break free of the enemy fleet. It'll take every ship we have available to achieve the necessary impact, but we should be able to force the enemy to scatter again and allow our allies and ourselves to make the run out of the system."

"That's not who I meant," Beccera said, tapping the monitor still displaying the *Chihuahua*.

Meier shook her head. "Now, Commodore. There's nothing our fleet can do to help them. Besides, which is more important, a squadron of our Allied ships, or a single broken-down old corvette?" She smiled patronizingly. "I'll just signal the other ships that we're beginning the retreat."

Beccera had reached his limit. "*As I just stated*, that is not the order I am giving. I do not appreciate having to repeat myself. Return to your post, *Captain,* and while you're at it, put this display here on the main monitor. We need a plan that doesn't leave the guys saving our butts out to die."

————————————

EAS Chihuahua

"Solar activity is within expected parameters, sir," Emily reported. "Sensors indicate no surprises... yet. Solar flares could erupt at any time without warning, though, and we're certainly going to get close enough for that to be a concern."

Chris shrugged. "Not much we can do about that now."

"Our squadron has completed their assault on the enemy orbital facilities, sir," Langer reported from his tactical station. "With great success." He paused. "Sir, it appears as if the squadron is now moving to assist the Cygni fleet."

Chris shook his head. "As expected. I asked them to stay away, remember? We're on our own for this one."

Rachel sighed. "I don't like it. In theory, I agree your plan could work, but when you factor in how precisely you have to time everything... I don't think we can do this, Chris. I don't think *I* can do this – not with this much precision."

He just smiled at her. "Rache, all you have to do is maintain a steady pace for one orbit around the sun and then rotate the ship so we can open fire. At this speed, it'll only be a few seconds, maybe a minute at most. The computers will figure the rest out, and the program's already set. I took into account your inexperience at the position. It will work."

She frowned. "But maintaining a steady pace when we have to worry about things like solar flares, enemy fire, maybe even sunspot activity blinding our sensors... Chris, we're going to have to make evasive maneuvers, and I'm not sure I can make them."

"If you can't make them, you can't make them. Don't worry about it."

"Don't worry about it?" Rachel repeated incredulously. "But the enemy's weapon is devastating – a solid blow will destroy us, and our shields can only hold it back for so long! Not to mention what happens if the damned star decides it's going to shoot fire and plasma at us. The ship won't survive it!"

"Rache," Chris answered, his voice sure and steady, but also quite depressingly final. "I know this is risky. I know we probably won't survive this mission. Do you think, for one moment, that I didn't realize how badly this could turn out? Hell, we're all just guessing that those shields work the way we think! But if we don't try something, our odds of keeping them from attacking our fleet are virtually zero, and our probability of survival is about the same. This guy won't let us escape. We're too dangerous to him, even if we aren't a match for him by ourselves. And he's too dangerous for us to let him live. We probably won't survive this plan... but I don't see any alternative."

Rachel paused, then sighed. "Okay, Chris. If this is our last chance to talk, I don't want to spend it fighting with you." She turned to Lt. Tarbell, who was making the final refinements to the fire control program at weapons control. "You ready?"

"Yeah," the new firing control officer said, grinning half-heartedly. "I'm pretty sure this won't work, and we're all going to die fiery deaths engulfed in the middle of an enemy system's star, but I'll give it my best."

"That's the spirit!" Chris cheered. "Let's get moving – a person shouldn't be late to his own funeral. Begin combat maneuver program Monitor Storm One!"

"Initiating!" Rachel called.

Langer started ticking down distances as the *Chihuahua* got closer to the sun. "Ten thousand kilometers distance. Six thousand kilometers. Four thousand. We are now inside the chromosphere, and closer to any star than any ship we know of. One Thousand. Five hundred kilometers. We're actually touching the photosphere, sir!"

"Now in orbit," Rachel reported.

"The enemy ship is matching our orbit... now!" Chris called. "Initiate firing pattern program."

"Initiating," Diana replied. "Well, we're committed now."

The enemy ship tried firing on the *Chihuahua*, but missed wildly. "Looks like the star's gravity is messing up their targeting," Langer commented, grinning.

"Let's hope it doesn't affect ours. Execute now!" Chris shouted, his ringing voice a match for any ancient war cry.

"Firing!" Rachel called. "Sixty seconds to impact. Fifty nine, fifty eight, fifty seven..."

The *Chihuahua* was an old ship, but many of her most obsolete systems had been removed as Chris and Jacques Rappaport had conducted her refit. Most of them were 'repurposed' in some way, such as the shock chair electronics packages being turned into the primary component of the streaming particle cannons. A few of them were abandoned altogether. One or two, however, they were unable to remove, thanks to the lack of any time in either a dry dock or a ship tender.

One such system was the *Chihuahua's* missile launchers. Missiles were a fine technology to use in the days when ships were still so slow that simple chemical fuel engines could actually hit enemy ships. They were more effective than just about anything else – a high yield thermonuclear warhead was more powerful than even a battleship's entire rail gun broadside or a cruiser's entire weight of fire with particle cannons. However, their inability to actually hit a target made them little more effective than mines... which were cheaper, even more powerful, and easier to conceal. They were still often used by Army forces for attacks on fixed position targets, but the era of ship to ship missile combat had long passed. Unless one was aboard a century old warship which just happened not to have had its missile tubes removed yet.

Space demands had left the *Chihuahua* with just two missiles, which were always loaded into the tubes because there was nowhere else to store them after all of the modifications. Both of which had just been launched.

"Three, two one..." Rachel spun the *Chihuahua* around, straining to keep their shield between the ship and the star. The enemy warship had no time to react before Chihuahua fired its particle cannons at point blank range, straight into its bow. Its own weapon charged up, and a spark of fire left it.

Using *Chihuahua* herself as bait, Rachel's careful flight plan and Tarbell's precision firing program, they had been able to predict exactly where the enemy would be at this moment. The two slow-moving missiles, fired a full minute in advance, now struck the enemy vessel from behind, a hundredth of a second apart. *Chihuahua's* particle cannon continued to dig into the enemy ship's shield from the bow, having no immediate effect but drawing strength away from the shields on the opposing side. The same opposing side where two nuclear warheads were detonating.

Amazingly, the weakened shield still deflected most of the blast from the missiles, but it then collapsed completely. Without the artificial gravity of the shields supporting them, the enemy ship's engines weren't powerful enough to resist the star's pull at such close range. And so, as Chris had planned, the unknown warship was, for all intents and purposes, sunk, spiraling into the burning hot plasma storm of Alcyone B.

The enemy's parting shot, however, managed to slip through *Chihuahua's* defenses.

Fires, debris, and electrical sparks shot across the bridge. This time, while the lights went out, and smoke filled the bridge, there was nothing like the devastation of the previous hit. The bridge had not been the target.

"Report!" Chris said, trying to see if everyone was unharmed by the dimmed light of various control panels. He could make out Rachel, still moving about, and was quite relieved, but he couldn't see anyone else in the darkness.

"I have confirmation that the enemy ship has been destroyed," Emily called from... somewhere hidden in the smoke. "We're pretty much blind outside of short range detail scans, however. Long-range sensors and hyperspace sensors are both gone."

"Damage reports coming in, sir," Tarbell said. "In addition to various shorts in the electrical system, that last blast severed the keel-mount tower from the ship."

Chris winced. "So, our hyperspace sensors, long range sensors, and hydrogen collection are completely gone?"

"Yes, sir," Koivu replied dutifully. "Worse still, we seem to be getting reports that the cold fusion plant is down. As are the fusion drives and the magnetic rudder."

That sent a chill down Chris' spine. "Time until repairs are complete?" he asked.

"The cold fusion plant can be repaired in a couple hours, if the hydrogen collection tower can be restored to any functionality. I'm told, however, that the fusion drive needs dry-dock time, sir."

Chris paused for a long time. "Well... it looks like we are the *Virginia,* after all," he sighed.

"Chris?" Rachel called. "What's wrong?"

"Rache... have you got any ideas for how to get our escape pods past the star's gravity well?" Chris asked softly. "Because I'm all out of ideas."

Her eyes narrowed at him. "What do you mean?" she asked – not angry, but worried. "What's this about escape pods?"

"Without the fusion drive," Chris explained, "we can't leave the star's orbit. The quantum wheel system will keep us alive in orbit, here, for some time... but we'll be stuck here. Until the power systems give out, that is."

"Well, then, we'll just have to figure out how to restore the fusion drive," Rachel snapped, although the finality with which Chris was speaking was starting to make her wonder if that was possible.

"Given enough time, we might manage that," Chris agreed, to her surprise. "After all, who would have thought we'd be able to get this old dog flying again in the first place? But I'm not sure we have that much time." He paused. "We're duty bound to keep the technologies and secrets we have on board this ship from slipping into enemy hands. She must not be captured... even if we have to destroy her with all hands to prevent that capture. So back to my earlier question, have you got any ideas how to get our escape pods away from the star? At least we might be able to avoid the 'with all hands' part of this mess...."

"But the rest of the fleet—"

"Who could rescue us?" Chris argued. "They'd need to devote a battleship, probably, or at least a heavy cruiser, and there's still an enemy fleet they have to contend with. The battle was just too even. The only way a ship would be available to rescue us is if there had been one prepositioned to save us outside of the main part of the battle zone. "

Rachel was now seeking a rebuttal somewhat frantically at this point, but she had none to give. She opened her mouth a few times to say something, but nothing came out... because she had nothing to say. Nothing, except, "Well... how long can we afford to wait out here to make sure?"

Chris considered that question for a moment. "Estimating the top speed of enemy battleships as 0.16c, I'd say we're about twenty minutes away from their nearest ship. It'll take them about ten minutes to detect what happened out here and arrange to come get us, and as I said – there's still a battle going on. So... perhaps an hour." He paused. "Like I said, not enough time to fix the engines."

Rachel sighed, sitting back in her chair and letting go of the controls for the first time since Captain Burkhard had gone down. She swallowed nervously. "So... we're going to die, aren't we?"

Chris paused for a while before answering. "Maybe not. There are alternatives."

Rachel and the rest of the bridge crew turned to stare at him hopefully. "What alternatives?"

"You might not think them much better than death," he began uncertainly. "Option one: We could boost the power to the shields, shut down all non-essential systems, and move in as close to the sun as possible. So close that we can't be towed out. The problem with that is we'll only survive for as long as our quantum wheel nodes are capable of producing a shield strong enough to protect us from that star – a few days, at most, before they start to fall out of tune under all the strain. It could give us time to repair the engines, but if we get close enough for that plan to work we'd almost certainly never be able to escape the star's gravity even at full thrust."

Rachel shook her head. "I'd rather die the quicker death of scuttling the ship now than that futility. What else?"

Chris looked even more hesitant as he laid out his next idea. "Well... I have a theory. One I could probably get working in just about an hour, but I'm not sure it would work."

"Spill it. I want to know all of our options, even the ones which might not work."

He took a deep breath. "It's kind of based on the Azumah Station Incident. I know a theory about how to take our artificial gravity generator and use it to make a miniature black hole. That black hole would last for a few seconds, at most, but in the process – if we timed it right – it would consume a large portion of the star we're now orbiting. It would reduce the mass of the star considerably before collapsing into itself and exploding. The end result would be a much weaker pull of gravity from this star, allowing us to potentially break orbit with the quantum wheels alone."

Rachel turned a little green. "Which would drastically alter the amount of heat and light it gives out, too. Slowly freezing to death all three worlds inhabiting this star system...."

"We *are* at war with them," Tarbell noted, listening in. "And they started it. That would bring a quick end to it."

"And we'd be responsible for the destruction of three inhabited planets and over ten billion people," Rachel reminded her. "Branding us war criminals. We'd live just long enough for our trial and execution. It wouldn't matter how innocent some of our crew members might be – we'd all be equally guilty in the court of public opinion, and politics would force any government to demand all our deaths in retribution for such an action."

"The final option," Chris intoned, hoping to keep the others on the bridge from thinking too hard on that choice. "Is to allow the Pleiades Navy to capture us. We'd all live, albeit as POWs. The worst part is I'm not even sure there are any real technical advantages we'll be protecting by scuttling the *Chihuahua*, if that ship we just 'sunk' is any indication." He paused. "I doubt the Navy would even blame us, considering we're just Academy students called up on an emergency basis. We're not expected to have to make these kinds of decisions at this point in our careers."

Rachel considered it for a long time. "No," she finally said. "I think protecting the secrets we built into this ship from an enemy is worth our lives."

Emily sighed, and then smiled tiredly. It didn't reach her eyes, and her voice shook slightly, but she tried to keep a tinge of humor into it. "I would hate to be the first member of the Mumford family tree to be involved in a surrender of any kind."

Tarbell coughed. "I, for one, think our lives wouldn't be spared even if we surrendered," she said. "I read the intelligence report provided by the Larkin Triumvirate. They have a lot of reports on Pleiades citizens being 'disappeared' when they become inconvenient to their government. The government appears to be trying to protect certain information. What, we don't know, but it's a good guess it has something to do with the technology in that ship we just fought. Our chances of staying alive after surrendering probably disappeared the moment we figured out enough about that ship's shields to destroy it."

Chris sighed. "That clinches it. No surrenders. Even if we could figure out a way to get the escape pods out of here, the Pleiades government will kill the survivors."

Rachel felt her heart drop. They were going to die, and she wasn't ready. There were so many things she hadn't done, that she had wanted to do, but now there wasn't the time for it. She had wanted to get married, have kids, make a name for herself in the Navy, retire into the Orbital Guard and maybe get placed on the same station as her parents... all those things that every person dreams of doing some day. And none of it was going to happen.

Well... maybe one of those things would happen. "We're going to die, right?" she asked, looking hard at Chris.

He looked back unflinchingly. "Yes," he said. "We are."

"Then, like all people sentenced to die, I have a last request," she said. "One only you can fulfill."

Chris checked a clock he'd set to time down the last few minutes they had before they would be forced to scuttle the ship. "Well, name it. We've got fifty minutes left."

Rachel stood up from her station, walking over to him. He stood up to face her. "There are a number of things I'm going to miss out on, being dead. A few of those things, though... well, I want to go into the afterlife knowing I managed to accomplish at least one of them." She paused, and then stared straight into his eyes. "I want you to—"

"Message coming in!" Emily cried. "From Commodore Beccera aboard the *Natsugumo*. Someone on board that ship must have figured we'd need a rescue before we did, because he says he was following us here and just caught up. He was wondering if we might want a bit of a tow?"

Part V

Resetting the Pieces

Epilog

Admiral Michael McCaffrey stood alongside Acting-Commodore Andrew Beccera as the two of them watched the *Chihuahua* limp into the space dock. Beccera stared in horror as he caught his first visual glimpse of just how crippled his old ship was.

"Where did you hide what remains of Home Fleet, anyway?" Beccera asked, astonished at how unusually empty the traffic lanes around Earth appeared to be, even to a novice spacer like himself.

"A Captain Mia Spirit had a wonderful idea involving some old jump gates," McCaffrey said. "I can't say where they are right now, you understand, but I will say that they can return to Sol at a moment's notice."

Beccera nodded. "I'll accept that. But what are we going to do now? They had shield technology, and it looked to be better than our own in terms of pure sophistication. They're going to crush us if they deploy that full scale."

"We'll be deploying our own shield systems full scale, as well," McCaffrey noted, amused. "There is a technology gap, perhaps, but I think we showed we had the edge in tactics and ingenuity. I must say," McCaffrey continued, "I was quite pleased with your own actions. You were a very effective flag officer, despite your inexperience."

Beccera shook his head slowly. "Thank you, sir, but it wasn't me. I didn't know what I was doing. I could only listen to my subordinates and make a decision based on their recommendations. Not all of those recommendations I took were sound, either. I'm afraid I let Captain Meier pull me around by my nose a bit too much before I started to catch on."

McCaffrey huffed under his breath. He was one of the few people who knew exactly how Barbara Meier got where she was, but he had no evidence to prove it. She'd been held in place by what could best be described as office politics, a game she played better than most. A recommendation by Admiral Michael 'The King of Maverick Officers' McCaffrey would do little to harm her in that regard without something more substantial to back up his allegations. Plus, they were now heavily understaffed, and the Navy would be unlikely to rid itself of any Captain that could possibly be considered capable.

"The key is that you figured her out, and took charge when needed," McCaffrey pointed out. "It's true even in the Army, is it not, that a flag officer must rely on his subordinates, but also must maintain discipline and know how to say 'no' when necessary?"

"Of course!" Beccera snapped. "That's why I'm so angry at myself over this. I should have picked up on it sooner and stopped her right out of the gate. We wound up making several mistakes during that mission because I didn't. Some were mistakes we were fortunate enough to turn into advantages, but they were mistakes nonetheless. I'm looking forward to going back to my little job leading a field battalion in the Army."

McCaffrey coughed nervously. "Yes, about that... I'm afraid you won't be going back to the unit you left."

Beccera paused. "And why is that? Are they finally forcing my promotion to General?"

"You are being promoted, but not to General," McCaffrey admitted. He pulled a small box out of his pocket, revealing two golden pins shaped like five pointed stars. "Congratulations... Rear Admiral Beccera."

"What the hell? I'm an Army officer!" he protested.

"Yes," McCaffrey agreed, grinning. "However, the Army has agreed to extend their loan of you to us indefinitely. Come on, take the box. We won't let you refuse, and you know it."

EAS Chihuahua

Most of their crewmates had departed, preparing for the major overhaul needed to salvage what was left of the *Chihuahua,* but Chris and Rachel remained. Somehow their small, battered quarters on that ship felt like the right place. It felt like home.

They had shed the rest of their doubts along with their clothes, settling easily into what they hoped would be a life long attachment. Now, however, it was morning, and Rachel sighed, listening to Chris sleep. She could tell he was wrestling with another nightmare as his tossing jostled them both. She pulled his arm around her more tightly. *Every night since the battle. Well, we'll fix that in time...*

She glanced at the old fashioned analog clock, still ticking despite all of the damage *Chihuahua* suffered. As soon as the work crews were briefed as to the modifications they made to the ship, she and Chris would have to leave as well... and that meeting was scheduled to take place in two hours time. "Chris?" she whispered gently, twisting round to look at him.

His eyes opened suddenly, in a panicked stare. Then his eyes settled on her, and he relaxed and smiled. "Morning, Rache."

"You need to get up and get dressed," she said. He nodded slightly, but didn't move the arm that was pinning her to the bed.

"You know we'll have to tell the Navy officials. That is, if you want us to be official."

Rachel stared into his eyes, giving him her most intimate smile. "If you want me to, I will. Somehow, though, I don't think the Navy would object if we keep things 'unofficial' for a little while. Until this war calms down a bit, I doubt they'll mind if we... fraternize." Her nose wrinkled in just the way Chris found so appealing, and she ran a hand over his chest. "I admit I'm being selfish. I *really* don't want one of us to be reassigned to a different chain of command right now."

Chris stared back, holding her gaze. "Well, 'unofficially' then, let me just add that I want to marry you some day. Wherever and whenever you want me to."

She squeezed his arm reassuringly. They still had a lot of issues to work out, she knew, but it could wait. Right now, she wanted to bask in the delight of having just 'gotten engaged...'

...Unofficially, of course.

Sol System, New Gosport Commercial Spaceport

"I heard about your, um, promotion," Burkhard said uncertainly, reaching from his wheelchair to offer his good hand to the newly-made Rear Admiral Beccera. "Are congratulations in order, or..."

Beccera grinned ruefully and took the hand. "Well, I don't seem to have much of a choice. I threatened to resign, but McCaffrey reminded me that there's a newly instituted draft, now, so if I tried resigning they'd just draft me into the Navy and I'd *never* make it back to my old Army unit. I suppose, if I've got the right leadership team around me, I'll be able to stay out of trouble as a flag officer. My superiors at Army Headquarters promise me that I can even take a field duty post when I return, whether I'm promoted to general or not, if I agree to stay on loan to the Navy for a while. And I suppose I could use the pay increase, so I guess that's a worthy enough cause to celebrate."

"So, what's going to happen to my ship?" Burkhard asked, gesturing out the window into the repair bay that housed the *Chihuahua*.

"They'll fix her up, even better than before... using Mr. Rappaport's and Mr. Desaix's plans, of course. They can't afford to waste salvageable hulls at this point. They'll even be able to make the changes Mr. Desaix wanted, but the lack of time in the tender prevented – things like pulling out her ancient single-barrel rail guns and replace them with higher caliber double-barreled versions. That will cut your gun crew requirements by about half. They'll also make some modifications to her to allow for greater ammo storage, a full sized sick bay, and a rather non-standard engineering lab." Beccera paused. "She'll be bought back into the service as an experimental pocket frigate attached to my flag, sort of a test bed for crazy ideas. Which, I suppose, will make you one part of that 'right leadership team' that I mentioned will be needed to keep me out of trouble, since they're going to keep together as many of the old crew as they can. That is, after your officers all undergo a three month crash course at the Academy to finish their training while the repairs are completed."

Burkhard smirked slightly. "Hm... I guess this means I get to keep my new rank?"

"Not exactly. You're being promoted straight to Captain. The personnel situation is so bad that almost every surviving officer in the fleet is getting some sort of promotion... a few of them pretty radical. The Academy students' acting ranks are all being confirmed. Ms. Katz is being promoted to Commander, and should still wind up your XO. Given your ship's experimental functions, you'll get a new, hybrid position on your bridge named 'tactical engineering.' Mr. Desaix will be a Lieutenant Commander and will assume that role, possibly sharing it with Ms. Katz if they decide to give you a more experienced second-in-command. You'll be given two new fully-trained navigators to work with Schubert and Weber, but not replace them. Rappaport also will be promoted and retain his position as chief engineer. Some of your other officers will remain as well... provided, of course, they all graduate from the Academy crash course they'll be starting next week."

"Of course," Burkhard laughed, and then nodded to a corner of the room. "But I think it's time I made my excuses. I believe you have some company of your own to meet with."

Beccera started, before noticing a well curved figure he was quite familiar with stepping into the room. "Kimiko! I thought you were still at Barnard's Star!"

"I'll leave you two to catch up. I need to go to the doctor to see if I can be released from this stupid chair," Burkhard replied, knowing he wasn't really being heard.

Kimiko rushed over to join her husband, pulling him into a tight embrace. "Thank God you're alive," was all she whispered in reply. "They say the casualties from that battle were horrible, and I was afraid you were one of them."

"Admiral Hrudey of the Cygni Confederation was wounded pretty seriously," he admitted sadly. He'd grown to like the pirate-like officer of their newly allied force, even if he'd barely met the guy. The words 'A peg leg will get me a ton of respect around here' were still ringing in his ears from the last conversation he had with the man. The last he saw of him, Hrudey was being taken away for surgery to amputate an irreparably damaged left foot. "But my own ship wasn't even fired upon outside of a token shot across our bow by an orbital platform. I think we should have been more active."

"I'm glad you weren't," she said, pointing to the wrecked hull of the *Chihuahua*. "I saw what that thing could do first-hand, and look at what happened to it. I know you wanted to be on board her in the heart of the battle, but what would have happened to you if you had?"

The scars of battle were quite visible, and indeed Beccera was shaken by the damage he saw. He'd helped bring *Chihuahua* back to life from her airless grave, and it was rather astonishing to realize he felt the same pride in his ship that many Navy men were famous for... and the same pain they felt at her crippling wounds. "I know. She's a tough old dog, though, and she'll come through it better than ever. So will her crew... at least those that survived." He paused. "Are you all right? You're straddling your loyalties between two powers at war, and that can't be easy for you, either."

Kimiko took a deep breath. "I've heard you're going to be stuck in the Navy for a while, right?" she said.

Beccera narrowed his eyes. "Yes, I am."

"Which means you'll probably be sent away for a while, right?"

"I'm told that I'll be given a permanent squadron in three months time," Beccera said. "Which, yes, will probably be far away from Earth."

"So... you won't mind if I leave for a while, since you won't be here either. Right?" she asked cautiously.

"Where are you going?" he asked, feeling his stomach drop.

She sighed. "I'm taking a round-about route through neutral shipping into Pleiades." Kimiko paused. "But not because I support them over Earth. *You* are my home, now, and that means Earth is my home. However, I have family in Pleiades which I need to contact, and if things are as bad over there as I've heard, they will need a rescue."

"You aren't trained for that," Beccera said, alarmed. "How do you expect to manage something like that? If you're so worried, I have friends who could arrange a covert mission to—"

"Shh," Kimiko said, putting a finger to his lips. "You know as well as I do that sending in a team from Earth will just get everyone killed. I have some protection, at least, with my Pleiades citizenship. And I can manage. I beat down your defenses to win your love, and you're a pretty tough cookie. Plus, I've learned a few things from you over the years which should help. I've even arranged for help – Lt. Christopher Shay is being discharged from the Navy for medical reasons after losing an arm and an eye. He says he'll come with me, though, and watch my back."

Beccera sighed. "I'm not going to be able to talk you out of this, am I?" he said.

"No," she replied. "But I love you for trying."

Earth Alliance Naval Academy, Earth Campus

Farmburg, ostensibly packing to move out of his old dorm room, studied the encoded communiqué from Admiral Hrudey (via his Cygni handler) intently. It seemed that despite their mutual interests with Earth, there were still some secrets from the battle with Pleiades that weren't to be shared, at least until Cygni intelligence could make sense of them first. Chief among those secrets was that during the fight, the Cygni forces had intercepted an encoded transmission from Dr. Whitlow Foley, a reliable informant now claiming to represent a group of anthropologists and archeologists whose lives were in danger from their own government.

In a rare moment of insight, the captain of the Cygni battleship

Peregrine had put two and two together and put a priority on interpreting the message, realizing that if an archeological expedition on its way to Pleiades was worth starting a war to stop, then scientists *from* Pleiades might be even more valuable. The full import was still unclear, but something Foley had to say clearly had Farmburg's superiors spooked. Farmburg's new instructions were to cease disrupting the Academy, which made sense, and instead to immediately report any information he learned in Earth Alliance circles concerning fossils, skeletons, or archaeologists, which quite honestly confused the hell out of him. His curiosity was piqued, but at least this had the flavor of a real intelligence assignment, and for that he was grateful.

Alcyone Star System, Pleiades Alpha, Hexagon Park

Director Karlsson glared at Skorrjh... who glared right back at Karlsson. Without his WISPR agent mask, the Neanderthal looked more intimidating than usual.

"I've read your reports," Skorrjh snapped. "And I can't see how you think you can paint the situation as anything but a complete failure. You failed to prevent Foley from unearthing the burial ground. You failed to prevent him from publishing his findings or alerting the Earth Alliance and others. You allowed much of your military infrastructure to be destroyed despite having what should have been superior forces. Finally, you failed to prevent Foley's escape, along with a number of accomplices and their families!"

"We might have stood a better chance if you had seen fit to assist us with more than a single corvette," Karlsson said angrily. "And in fact it was your own shock from seeing your one *supposedly* invincible corvette defeated that created an opportunity for Foley to escape. You talk of failures, but of all our mistakes *that* is the only one which might give us trouble in the long run. You realize that at this point he probably knows who you are, or rather *what* you are?"

"Then I suggest a two pronged strategy. On one end, we focus on recovering Dr. Foley and his colleagues, preventing them from revealing that information to others. On the other, we prepare for a renewed attack to weaken Earth Alliance enough for my people to act ahead of schedule."

"We can try that, but I suspect it's too late to stop Foley," Karlsson laughed bitterly. "You are trying to close the door after the target has fled. The Earth Alliance now has shield technology, too, and it looks like they can adapt it to their ships pretty quickly. Pleiades has no power to match that, unless you give us something more. Like, say, a handful of your 'invulnerable' ships. "

"That's out of the question. For one, I can't even get a message to my people right now," the Neanderthal said, although he was a little more subdued this time. "I don't have the authority to reveal my home fleet's position, and even if I did, the *Flynohr* was the only ship here that my people would not destroy on sight." He paused. "Without regular communications, however, it's likely someone will be sent to check on us in a few months."

"Earth will crush us before then, if they can adapt that shield technology and streaming particle cannon technology fast enough," Karlsson noted.

"Then I'll begin helping you with your technology now," the Neanderthal declared. "But not, perhaps, as directly as you expect."

Earth Alliance Naval Academy, Earth Campus

"Come on, Chris! Wake up! Rachel commed me, and she's on her way *here!* You've simply *got* to wake up!" Lieutenant Wolfgang Schubert, who had only needed a few days rest to recover from his injuries, whispered frantically, shaking his bunkmate. "You can't afford to get into trouble like last time!"

"God, Wolf, I feel like hell. Can't whatever it is wait for another hour or so?" Chris squinted at a nearby clock – an antique dial-face clock with laminated gold numbers. "I just got to sleep an hour ago!"

"Didn't you hear what I said? Rachel's already on her way, and she sounded royally pissed off. You've got to get up and get into uniform, pronto!"

The newly promoted Lieutenant Commander Christopher Desaix smiled in his sleep. "Oh, shut up and let her read the riot act to me," he sighed. "She loves it and I do, too. There's a war on, after all, and we should take such pleasures when we can get them."

The door opened suddenly – Chris had given Rachel the pass code to their bunks, of course, and she hadn't hesitated in abusing that privilege. "Chris!" she growled. "What are you doing still in bed? I told you I was coming today! We were going to study for that Engineering qualifications test you're insisting I take!"

Chris waved in acknowledgement from his bunk without waking up.

"Hi, Rache. What's up?" he drawled casually.

"'Hi, Rache?' You, Mr. Desaix, are to address me as 'Ma'am' when on duty, and 'Ms. Katz' when off. You are *never* to address me as 'Rache.'"

"Yes, ma'am, Ms. No-longer-a-Cadet-but-still-a-student-for-the-next-three-months-*Full*-Commander Rachel Katz, ma'am," Chris grinned slightly as he acknowledged her promotion. "Except it seems to me you don't mind so much when we're off duty any more, ma'am."

"Why, you little—"

There was a twinkle in her eye as she pounced on him, determined to forcibly get him out of bed and on to classes in time. And there was a twinkle in his, too, as he continued to tease her... at least until she employed her newest persuasive tactic of tickling him awake. Then, he was laughing too hard to keep his eyes open at all, and trying to retaliate without being able to see was proving something of a challenge.

Schubert left silently, doors swishing behind him. Some things were too private to interrupt. He grinned to himself as he walked toward class and thanked God they were all still alive.

Also from Fennec Fox Press and David A. Tatum

http://www.fennecfoxpress.com/

The Law of Swords
Genre: Heroic Fantasy, New Adult

A set of laws written to prevent infighting among Svieda's Royal Heirs if the King dies unexpectedly. One of these laws has never been needed... until now.

I. In Treachery Forged

When Svieda is betrayed and invaded by a former ally, Sword Prince Maelgyn must travel to the province of Sopan to take command of his armies and help repel the invaders. Along the way he rescues a Dwarven Caravan, forges a badly needed alliance, and accidentally gets married. And then he learns about the dragons...

Ebook: $5.99 retail
Print: $18.99 retail

II. In Forgery Divided

With the defeat of Paljor, Maelgyn proved himself the strongest Mage in the Human world. There are more powerful things than Mages he has to worry about, however. He returns home to find that his old enemies can still hurt him while new enemies threaten to tear his kingdom apart from the inside. The Law of Swords is supposed to protect them from this sort of thing, but it is actually helping his enemies. And then there's

the Elves to deal with....
Ebook: $5.99 retail
Print: $18.99 retail

III. In Division Imperiled

Still coming to grasp with his new status, Maelgyn finds himself fighting a war on two fronts.
Coming Soon

Inari's Children

Genre: Heroic Fantasy

Once magic was plentiful and the world was dominated by a singular empire whose name has long been lost to history. In its time, the great wizard Inari developed his greatest creation: The kitsune. His enemies were quick to copy him, and soon the world was populated with many different types of this remarkable creature. Two thousand years later and these different breeds of kitsune are fighting amongst themselves, and the rest of the human world joins them.

I. The Kitsune Stratagem

To avoid being used as a political pawn against her father, a young kitsune vixen named Kieras must leave her homeland. She soon gets caught up in the fortunes of Mathis, a vagabond hunter from Ekholm, a once sleepy little town on the verge of becoming a small city. To find a way to return home, Kieras must first help Mathis save Ekholm from threats both inside and out.
Ebook: $5.99 retail
Print: $18.99 retail

II. By Claw and Arrow

Mathis and Kieras return to Ekholm. They don't get to stay for long, however, before the Myobu Priesthood approach them with a mission that sends them to the ancient ruins of Eskesa. Yulaev takes Kobach to Erixonite lands, while Kazdri and Heshka resolve the issue of just who the

reigning King of Kassia is, anyway.
Coming Soon

Nine Tales of the Kitsune

An Anthology of nine stories focusing on the history of Norre, Inari, and the creation and evolution of this world's Kitsune.
Coming Soon

The Rink of War

Genre: Science Fiction, Space Opera

Former professional hockey star Alexander Zednik had a career-ending injury very early into his career. To rehab his injury, he went into space, to the "gold rush" in the Main Belt Asteroids. There, he attempted to set up a new sport: Microgravity Hockey.

Several years later, he and his plans have been largely forgotten. He is making a living running a small warehousing business for the local miners, which introduces him to Anita Condon. All she wants is warehouse space for her uncle's science lab, and a guide through this new world of the Main Belt Asteroids....

I. To the Rink of War

When Alexander Zednik accepts a warehousing client named Anita Condon, he finds himself fighting off a rogue mercenary intent on destroying her cargo. A short story.
Ebook: $0.99 retail

II. The Rink of War

A novel chronicling the adventures of Alexander Zednik, Anita Condon, and the Emperor Norton II. Includes and expands greatly upon the original short story.
Coming soon

Standalone Titles

This Book Cannot Possibly Make Any Money

Genre: Multi-genre Collection
A collection of experimental fiction, inside jokes, story fragments from the cutting room floor, and high school poetry, all of which conventional wisdom says cannot possibly make any money.
Coming Soon

From Other Publishers

Worlds Enough: Fantastic Defenders

Genre: Fantasy, Anthology
Published by Tannhauser Press
http://tannhauserpress.com/

Across astounding and magical worlds, five heroes step forward to defend against magical threats:

- A sorceress in a besieged city faces a malignant force even more dangerous than the city's would-be conquerors.

- An unassuming bureaucrat stumbles upon a threat to a vast empire and deals with it in his own inimitable fashion.

- A resourceful bodyguard for an infant princess, trapped and surrounded by merciless assassins, finds a unique way to hold them at bay.

- A mage press-ganged into the Royal Navy finds himself volunteered for a dangerous secret mission on foreign soil.

- A disgraced royal guardian who failed in protecting his king hunts down those who cost him his honor.

These are the... FANTASTIC DEFENDERS!

Ebook: $2.99 *(for a limited time!)*
Print: $15.99

www.ingramcontent.com/pod-product-compliance
Lightning Source LLC
Chambersburg PA
CBHW072259020726
47501CB00002B/318